A SISTER'S GIFT

Brought up on the peninsula of Gibraltar, Giselle Green moved to London to attend university. Giselle is now a full-time mum to six boys, including twins, and a part-time astrologer who specialises in medieval astrology. *A Sister's Gift* is her third novel.

To find out more about Giselle Green go to www.gisellegreen.com

By the same author:

Pandora's Box
Little Miracles

GISELLE GREEN

A Sister's Gift

Published by AVON
A Division of HarperCollins*Publishers* Ltd
1 London Bridge Street
London SE1 9GF

www.harpercollins.co.uk

This paperback edition 2018

First published by HarperCollins*Publishers* 2010

ISBN: 978-0-00-829626-1

18 19 20 21 22 LSC 10 9 8 7 6 5 4 3 2 1

This novel is entirely a work of fiction. The names, characters and incidents portrayed in it are the work of the author's imagination. Any resemblance to actual persons, living or dead, events or localities is entirely coincidental.

Typeset in Minion by Palimpsest Book Production Limited, Falkirk, Stirlingshire
Printed and bound in the United States of America by LSC Communications.

For more information visit: www.harpercollins.co.uk/green

Acknowledgements

The first person I'd like to say a big 'thanks' to is the artist who drew the picture of the Old Rochester Bridge which inspired the use of our rich local history in the setting for this novel. Deepest appreciation goes to Oliver Green – you're one talented guy!

Next, many thanks to Jane and also to Eric at the Bridgewarden's Trust, for being so generous with your time and showing me around the Bridge chambers and answering my many questions. The story is of course completely fictional, but I hope I've captured something of the 'feel' of the Bridge Trust's ancient building and also some of the romance of the surrounding city of historic Rochester.

To the bridge engineer Graham Madden who patiently answered my many emails on a 'theoretically' broken bridge, my grateful thanks also. Any errors of course are completely down to me.

On the editing front thanks once again to Maxine Hitchcock, who as always did a superb job and to the other girls at Avon editorial. Grateful thanks too, to my agent Dot for your time and encouragement – you know I always much appreciate our chats!

Special mention must go to some of my writing friends too, for their delightful company when we've been away together to write – Jan Sprenger and Kate Harrison in particular for their helpful thoughts when I got stuck.

And to my family as always, for allowing me the time and space to write, especially my husband Eliott who first made the observation which I had not, that 'this is your first romantic book'.

To my dearest Ollie, *weil Du, in meinen Augen, kostbar bist.*

Prologue

'Just make a wish,' he's urging. 'Wish for your heart's deepest desire. Write them down, ladies, on the tags.'

He winks at the small group of us gathered in front of him, tugging at the bunch of red helium balloons in his hand. 'All proceeds to charity.' The man's smile broadens as one of the American tourists fishes out her camera. 'All wishes are guaranteed so – as they say, ladies – be careful what you wish for!'

The women giggle as one of them utters a comment under her breath.

Click, and there he is, his pasty face immortalised forever against the steep backdrop of Rochester Castle, the blue-grey September sky behind him, the flaps of the white marquee to his left fluttering in the breeze.

Oh, there is something I wish for, all right. I have wished it for such a long time that I no longer remember a time when I didn't. When I was a kid, racing my doll's pram along the length of the Esplanade, I expected it. As a teenager, romantic and moody, wishing on the first 'star light, star bright', I was certain that one day what I hoped for would be mine – when I was ready.

But these days I'm not so sure.

I pull my jacket about my shoulders, feeling hope stiffen in a small rigid space inside me. Any time now I expect to be hearing and then I'll know . . .

1

'Hey you.' His eyes brighten for an instant, homing in on me. 'You're Scarlett's sister, aren't you?'

I nod, suddenly uncomfortable. I can't remember his name.

'Haven't seen Scarlett around here for a while.' He jumps down off his podium, rounding on me.

'No.' I shake my head, glancing behind me at the steps that will lead me out of here.

'It's funny.' He takes me in curiously now. 'You two aren't a bit alike, are you?'

'She's blonde,' I put in, but that's understating it. Scarlett has a mane of blonde curls that cascade about her heart-shaped face, giving her an appearance that is nothing short of angelic. I, however, have a dark, neat bob that stays put no matter how much the wind gusts. Scarlett always said it gives me the air of a woman who is in total control, organised and efficient.

'I didn't mean that,' he mutters darkly. 'I meant – you strike me as someone who takes life a bit more seriously.'

What if I am? What's it to him?

I need to be getting back to work . . .

'Not stopping to make a wish, Hollie?' And at the mention of my name, his own comes surging back on a floodtide of memories. I didn't realise at first that it was him. 'Come on. There must be something you want.'

'No thanks, *Duncan*.'

'You sure?' Duncan waves a tag at me enticingly. 'It's for charity.'

'I bought one earlier,' I put him off.

'What a coincidence.' His smile is thin, unconvinced. 'So did I.' He glances up at his bunch of ready-tagged balloons and they're straining in the breeze. '*My* wish relates to your sister, actually!'

'She finished with you, didn't she?' She *dumped* you, I think cruelly. 'Nearly two years ago.'

If he asks I'll say I don't know where she's gone. I thought he'd moved away. I thought we wouldn't be seeing him around here any more. That feeling of unease is working its way right through my belly.

'The thing is, Hollie.' He leans in closer for an instant. 'Your sister owes me, see? We had an agreement and she ducked out of her end of it. And you can't just *do* that.' He frowns. 'It isn't right, is it? That's why I need to speak to her.' His voice is slow and laboured now, almost imploring. 'If we can sort out our differences like grown-ups then I won't feel the need to talk to anyone else about what she did.'

'Oh, give over,' I mutter, annoyed. He's making the hairs stand up on the back of my neck but I'm not going to let him know that he's affecting me. 'She didn't do anything.'

His pale eyes look both piggy and sentimental at the same time.

'She did, Hollie. And she has to make reparation for it.'

Creep. I stick my hands in my pockets and turn away from him. Even if she did do something that's got him miffed, I think, what's he going to do?

'She's not around,' I throw at him as I back away. The wind chases the brown leaves along the square path round and round in circles. When I glance over at the old castle retaining wall there are no flowers to add vibrancy to the summer beds along the Esplanade and the river looks slow and grey. My little sister hasn't been around for an awfully long time. I'm not sure she'll ever come back. He's left it too late. A tall girl steps between us now, her baby bump clearly visible beneath her thin summer dress.

'I'll have one. I'm wishing for a boy.' She writes out her tag in large rounded lettering. 'It's guaranteed, you say?'

Duncan smirks back at her. That girl – she can't be more than seventeen, surely? A good fifteen years younger than me . . .

Maybe I've left it too late, as well?

Hollie

If you are thinking and hoping of becoming in the family way and matters not going according to plan, Dr Shandaree's 'Help for Ladies' is at hand. Where delicate matters of producing the desired child/children are concerned, Dr Shandaree has the expertise of twenty years in dealing with ladies of faded hope. Success rates using own eggs are in the hundreds and fees reasonable. Only ladies of the highest quality are used as 'surrogate mums' for the carrying of your precious child. Please phone or email Dr Shandaree for all discreet and confidential enquiries on number below or at www.BabyinIndia.com

No. I stare at the picture on Dr Shandaree's enclosed leaflet for a very long time but I can't bring myself to open her letter. Is it a good sign that she has included the leaflet for her services or not? I finger the leaflet for a while, with its picture of a brown lady in her beautiful orange sari holding a blue-eyed child.

Out there, somewhere on the outskirts of the small Indian city of Surat, there is a whitewashed building where babies can be produced for couples like Richard and me. Couples who are desperate. I picture it, this place, so very far from home; there, under a ferocious blue sky, there will be a gentle doe-eyed lady, attended by a doctor and a nurse in a crisp white uniform, who will carry the child that I long for.

My child. If I close my eyes I can see him, just as I always have, plump-fingered and red-cheeked. I will take him for walks every day – even when the wind is blowing – in his little bobbled hat. On sunny days we'll pause at the ice-cream van and buy cornets with chocolate flakes in them or we'll run along the Strand watching the paper boats we've made as they duck and bob in the water . . .

Dr Shandaree's letter feels very light in my hands and I can't keep my fingers from shaking as I open it. Attached, with one large paperclip, is the wad of medical records I sent Dr Shandaree last month. The results of all the tests I've had done over the years . . .

'Not looking good, is it?' Ben Spenlow makes me jump. He's walked right up the wooden stairs to the office in the Bridge Warden's chambers and I never even heard him come in.

'What isn't?' Guiltily, I shove Dr Shandaree's letter under a pile of engineer's drawings that need to be returned to archive. He *can't* be talking about BabyinIndia, can he? I straighten. No, of course he isn't. Ben isn't in the slightest bit interested in my private concerns. He's leaning over my desk, peering through the wide bay windows that look out over the Medway and the Old Rochester Bridge, his arms folded tightly over his chest. He indicates with his head and, when I follow the line of his gaze, I spy the desperately long line of traffic that's snarled up over the bridge.

'Not good at all,' he repeats.

'They haven't found out what's wrong with the bridge yet? I thought they said the investigations wouldn't take more than a couple of weeks?' My fingers inch the tell-tale edge of the BabyinIndia leaflet further under the pile.

'They've found evidence of an unusual amount of erosion on the riverbed which indicates there *might* be scouring under the piers and abutments.' He looks over his shoulder. 'It makes sense to limit the weight of traffic flow till we know if the bridge needs to be closed down altogether.'

I stare at him, jolted out of my own troubles for the moment. Could things really be that bad? I join him at the window. For a brief moment, the sun has come out again. It's not the deep, dry, burning sun shown on the leaflet but the winking, teasing, in-and-out, early autumn sun in England.

'That traffic is backed all the way up to Star Hill,' Ben admits miserably. 'And it won't help the situation one jot if we have to shut it all down.'

The faint honk-honk of impatient drivers is louder than it was a moment ago and my heart sinks. Am I going to have to put up with this for weeks yet?

Ben turns to me. 'Did you manage to get hold of the chief structural engineer at Crossings Constructions for me?'

Crap. I didn't. That's so *not like me*, to forget about something so important. I colour, brazening myself to find some excuse for not having done it but—

'Good grief! What in heaven's name is that?' Ben is peering over the top of his thin-framed round glasses. 'It looks like a . . . a . . .'

'A flock of red balloons?' I finish, relieved at the interruption. 'They must have just let them off. They were selling them at the castle; wish balloons, for charity.'

Which is when I met that guy, Duncan. And he made me feel so off-balance that I had to nip back to Florence Cottage to get some Rescue Remedy before I came back to the office after lunch. And while I was home, that's when I picked up Dr Shandaree's letter and *that's* why I forgot all about the chief engineer at Crossings Constructions . . .

'They're all flying together, look at that.' Ben's face softens. He's an old guy with a thin, stern face. I've barely ever seen him smile but he's enchanted now. We stand and watch for a few moments as the metallic balloons huddle together and shiver, a scarlet cloud, a swaggering cloak of shining festival red, almost totally obscuring our view from the window of the opposite bank.

A crowd gathers along the Esplanade to watch them now. A cheer goes up. We can hear laughing and clapping, a frisson of delight as a line of schoolchildren stop to point, and for a moment even the honking drivers on the bridge give it a rest.

'Wish balloons,' Ben marvels. 'Well, *I* wish this whole worry over our ancient bridge would get sorted. And cheaply,' he adds for good measure.

'You didn't buy a balloon,' I remind him. 'So it probably won't count.'

I want Ben to go now. I push my chair in under my desk as a sign that I mean to get on. I want to see what's in that letter. *I have to know.* Are my eggs still in good working order, and are Richard and I going to be asked to travel over to India for the making of our baby?

'I'll let you know as soon as I've got hold of the guy you want.' I leaf purposefully among the papers on my desk and Ben finally takes the hint.

'OK. ASAP, Hollie.' Ben shakes himself out of his reverie and scuttles back down the stairs. The people who had gathered for a moment along the river are beginning to disperse, too.

I ease out the letter from its hiding place, leaving the leaflet behind. I unfold it, fingers trembling so much I can barely hold it. Will I be going to India or not? I drag out my chair and sit down on it again with a bump.

Unfortunately, tests are showing low viability of eggs and the same of such poor quality it is my opinion that you have low chance of conceiving by this method. Therefore I have concluded that you are unlikely to be a good candi-date for this form of support and I will not be inviting you to come to clinic . . .

So that's it then? I bite my lip and a small, unhappy tear drips down onto the letterhead. I take out a tissue from my bag. I should

8

have known it. My head is suddenly pounding with a tension that has been building up for weeks.

I have to stop this, that is all. I have to stop it, now. All this dreaming and longing for a child of my own. I've spun too many daydreams out of it, that's the problem. I've made the expectation grow so big, there *is* nothing else that I want . . .

I need to think about . . . other things. Work. That's it. I pull a pale blue folder towards me. It's labelled 'Charity Applications – Ongoing' but my heart just sinks. Usually I love my job. Why is it that just now everything seems like such an onerous task?

I open up the letter again. My eyes skim over the words, skip through to the bottom which I didn't bother reading earlier. There Dr Shandaree has added in a handwritten scrawl at the bottom:

If, however, you have good quality eggs from a willing close relative that may be donated with partner's sperm, there is always the possibility that said child may be produced.

I ditch the tissue and wipe my eyes with the back of my hand to read it better.

A willing close relative, she says? A sister, does she mean, or a cousin?

I . . . I have one relative who would be genetically similar enough to me, I suppose. But Scarlett is not close. Currently, she is foraging for orchid seeds somewhere in the deepest jungles of Brazil. And I do not imagine in a month of Sundays that she would ever be *willing*.

Another cheer goes up now and one last red balloon is on its way, floating across the skyline. It's higher than the others were at this stage. I catch the weak September sunlight glinting off its shiny surface, the long string wriggling downwards, the little envelope containing the secret wish fluttering happily in the breeze.

9

And there is Duncan, standing by the line of parked cars along the opposite pavement, catching my eye. *I made a wish.* He points at the balloon and gestures to himself. I want to turn away, to get away from the sight of him, but I can't. He's mouthing my sister's name, and holding up his little finger and thumb in a 'phone me' gesture.

I shove Dr Shandaree's letter into my handbag, possibilities and thoughts tumbling through my head.

Scarlett. My sister. He wants her.

And I don't exactly know where she is but right now, I want her, too.

Red Balloon

Up, up and away flies the shining balloon. Over the Old Rochester Bridge it goes and the industrial estate by Strood Esplanade is left behind in a breath. A child at the top of Rochester Castle cries out, pointing upwards, but too late because the balloon is already on its way.

For a moment, following the trajectory of the river, it sails over Command House. And then, where the water swirls in thick grey waves round the steep bend in the bank it bears north-northeast and up past the imposing main gates of Chatham Dockyard, past Chatham Pontoon. For a heartbeat, the sun glints off its metallic red surface giving a stiff salute to the proud naval history of the town. The flags on HMS *Ocelot* and HMS *Cavalier* shiver and flutter their own salute in return but the balloon isn't hanging about. The higher up it goes, the smaller the lands spread out below are getting; cosy Frindsbury to the west, sprawling Gillingham to the northeast with the white dots of so many rooftops all in a cluster, opening out at the edges to the faded grassy greens of the farmers' fields beyond. And then, gathering speed over the grey-green river, the red balloon passes the ordered rows of houses at Wainscott to the east, the stark grey spectre of Upnor Castle to the left, the glint of a thousand panes of glass on St Mary's island to the right.

How far can it go, how high can it go? The river widens out. The air gets colder as the land drops away and still the blue sky winks, beckoning it on further. The long white string twirls and flutters beneath it. The message sealed inside the envelope, addressed to Scarlett L. Hudson, is still intact.

And it's on its way.

Scarlett

Shit. What was that?

Did José hear it? I just heard a low growl but I can't see anything.

I move my head backwards a fraction and my young guide's still close enough for me to see the whites of his eyes in among the shady foliage high above me. He blows a shock of black, ruler-straight hair away from his face but he doesn't move a muscle.

Quietly, as still as he is, I breathe in long and slow through my nostrils. What is it? Will I pick up the acrid scent of a big cat nearby? Is that what he was trying to warn me about? I've been out here eighteen months and I've only been really close to one once before. They stay away from people for the most part. And they move so silently you never hear them. If you see them, it's just for an instant, a dark shadow you could have imagined. Out here, the Yanomami say, you need to develop another way of knowing when danger's near; you have to develop a sixth sense.

Fuck. I glance down at my row of collecting pots. I can't afford to lose these seeds now. I need to hand these samples in as part of my Klausmann Award submission. I wish I could just push the sticky hair away from my face. What should I do now – try and save the seeds, or should I be more worried about saving my own skin?

To add to it, that tantalising itch that's developing on my left arm . . . Ugh, that's got to be some nasty bug that's just crawled in under my sleeve. I should be used to it by now but I still hate 'em. They'll eat you alive if they get half a chance . . .

Mind you, I shiver – so might a jaguar if its belly was empty and it came across me and José up here in the cloud forest. I'm definitely not imagining it. There's that low growling noise again, just like I heard before . . .

I pull in a breath, fighting the urge to breathe harder and faster as my heart begins to race. José did warn that they some-times hang out in the remote areas, that we'd have to be careful, but I wasn't really worried. All the way up here I was on the look-out, kinda hoping if I'm honest that we'd see something special 'cos none of the other graduates have, even the more adven-turous of the blokes. I wanted to be the first, make it a victory for the girls. I'd have enjoyed seeing the look on Emoto's face.

Now I'm not so sure.

I blink as a fat drop of condensation plops down from the canopy and into my eyes. Visibility in here is pretty much zero, except for wherever you happen to be shining your torch at any given moment. And, man, now I can't stop shivering.

It's the cold, I tell myself. We left the paved road behind hours ago, walking in the darkness of the misty forest for the best part of the day to get to this spot and – bizarrely – it's freezing because the jungle in here above the hills of São Paulo is so incredibly thick that no sunlight can penetrate. Even though it's got to be 45 degrees out. How weird is that? As silently as I can, I switch my torch off. It makes a quiet 'click' and then I'm in total darkness. Fool, I think immediately, the beast will probably smell its way to you if it wants you for dinner, it doesn't need to see you . . .

Where's José gone now? I'm only twenty-four . . . too young to . . .

I try and catch sight of him again as the breeze moves through

14

the shimmering foliage higher up. The trees at this altitude are shorter and thicker-stemmed than the ones lower down and at last I catch sight of him again. He's barely moved a muscle; he's so still, he could be a mushroom growing out of the pale twisted bark.

What is that stench? It is so black and bloody and rank you could just retch. It's an animal smell obviously, but where is it coming from? I see José's hand moving now. It's reaching very slowly towards his belt where he keeps his arrows, the ones he keeps tipped with curare and venom from the tiny poisonous frogs. What can he see that I can't?

José looks down at me. His brown eyes seem to flash out a smile of reassurance. He isn't afraid. He looks away again. I do not move and he lifts the tip of the blowpipe to his mouth and aims . . .

Over a day's hike from here the brown water of the Amazon trundles along, widening out a little way down. I think of the old canoe tethered to the battered vellozia tree by the bank. That canoe could take me home. Man, even though this is the adventure I was dreaming of, I'd love to take that ride home right now. I'd do anything to be back there.

The needle-thin arrow is in position in the blowpipe now. I can see José, shifting his body, ever so gently repositioning himself to take the shot. He's only going to get one chance to get this right, the thought flashes through my mind, he won't get another shot. And he's just twelve years old . . .

The roar from the creature's throat when it takes the hit turns my legs to water, reverberates in my stomach. It's coming from directly above me. It is somewhere up there among the branches and I can hear it now, a mixture of anguish and fury so primal I just know that if I'm in its path when it comes down I'm going to get torn limb from limb. And now there's the sound of branches breaking as it cracks every single bough on the way down, falling heavily. I see it for a split second only. It is a huge creature, black-coloured, its bristly fur sticking up in tufts over its head and on its back – an old dominant male howler monkey. And a wounded one at that. I catch a glimpse of the blood spurting darkly from a fresh wound to its neck.

Instinctively, I put my hands over my head as it crashes down right onto my seed pots and lies still, just a few feet away.

'Jesus Christ!' I cover my face, waiting for the monkey to spring up and attack but it just stays where it is. José shins down the banyan tree, his eyes still wide but shining now. He shoves the beast with his foot. Surprisingly strong, he manages to roll it over. I switch my torch back on. I can just spy the tip of the deadly arrow sticking out of its neck.

José gives out a whoop of triumph and I just let my backside slump down against the springy green forest floor in relief.

My pots, I'm thinking. I'm still alive but that *creature* has smashed all my sample pots to smithereens. All the seeds and spores will have been trampled and sucked into the boggy humus beneath the trees. I should be grateful, I know. A moment ago I was worried about not making it out of here intact but, hell, I worked *so* hard to get them.

Emoto's the better ethnobotanist, I can't deny it, but ever since Eve took us aside at the beginning of the year and said she'd put us *both* forward for the Klausmann Award for Services to Plant Sciences, I've allowed myself to dream. I've never won anything in my life before. To achieve an award would be so exciting. Especially this award. It'd be a recognition of everything that's come to mean so much to me. The Amazon is my life now. To get recognition of that fact would be so wonderful . . .

Now José is trampling all over everything, too. He's bending over the old male, his knife out of his belt, hacking away, sawing intently and after a while he stands up straight and comes over and plants his prize carefully at my feet. I look down at the half-curled bloodied monkey hand.

16

'I'm not going to pick that up, José,' I croak, and he laughs at me, the delighted giggle of a triumphant child.

'You take it,' he insists in his own language. 'Monkey paw mean you will always come back home to us, yes?'

'I'm not going anywhere, José.'

He grunts in reply, and I watch him scamper back to the prize, his short brown limbs clambering all over it to get better purchase. For a good few minutes, sitting among the succulent dark-green bromeliads, I can't bring myself to even move.

'Hey!' Emoto's expressionless face appears out of the darkness, his guide at his side. 'What are *you* doing here?'

Nice.

'What am I doing here?' I glance at the empty collecting pots attached to his backpack – he's obviously just arrived. 'We've been here all morning, Emoto – this is our patch.'

'Not likely. I heard this was a prime spot for collection. I'd have been here ahead of you if Eve hadn't waylaid me before I got out of camp this morning.' He grins amicably at me. 'She wants to talk to you too, Scarlett.'

'Me?'

'ASAP. But at least you get a ride in the posh boat back downriver. Your admirer is there. He told me to let you know he'd be waiting for you.'

'Guillermo?' I look up sharply.

'Friends in high places, eh?'

I ignore that. 'What does Eve want to talk to me about?'

He shrugs noncommittally, though I think he knows exactly what she wants me for.

'Say, is *that* what I think it is?' He shines his torchlight on a mossy tree trunk and the brilliant bright red flowers of Cattleya Alliance are visible, even in the forest haze, all the way up the stem. Damn him, I was hoping to come across that species myself. Now he's bagged it.

'And this?' He swivels the light beam around and, hey presto,

17

there's another treasure right in front of us – a pale green and yellow specimen of *Encyclia patens*, its petals splayed out like spiders' legs on a fallen tree trunk. 'It's a real Aladdin's cave up here, isn't it?'

And he's just spotted the dead monkey too. 'Had a bit of a mishap here, Scarlett? I thought I heard something falling . . .' Emoto's torch is flickering over the monkey's corpse now, taking in the smashed collecting pots, the broken branches, everything . . .

'Yep. We're going back to base camp empty-handed, I'm afraid.'

'Not *quite* empty-handed.' He can't stop the grin that springs to his face as he catches sight of José's offering. That half-curled monkey hand at my foot looks so human. I swallow down the bile that rises to my throat as Emoto picks it up and hands it to me. Shit, it's disgusting. And it's dripping blood all over me. I don't care if it's supposed to be a lucky charm that'll always bring me back to the tribe if I should leave. I'm not going to leave. I've made this my home now and it's where I intend to stay for a long time to come.

Scarlett

The steady phut-phut of the engine breaks its rhythm a little and Guillermo twists his head round slightly and gives me a wry grin as José nudges him to let him take over the wheel. He comes to join me under the shady part of the boat.

'You OK?' He leans in and touches my arm gently.

'I'm OK.' My sleeve is soaked, and I'm having difficulty pulling it up to examine my arm where it's started itching. Gui gives me a hand, rolling the material up purposefully to reveal a thin angry line where a bug has chomped its way across my forearm. He winces sympathetically.

'You'll get that seen to?'

'José already gave me some Andiroba oil for it. Everything we need is all here, all around us.'

'Sounds like something the Yanomami would say.' He smiles at me and I smile back. He's got nice eyes. Gentle and kind.

'You didn't have to come all this way out to fetch me, you know. José and I came up in the PlanetLove canoe, we could have got back to camp in it.'

'I know you could.' He leans back a little now, arms folded across his knees. 'Maybe I wanted to, though.'

'And waste two days punting up the Amazon when you could have been attending important meetings?' I tease gently. In his stylishly-cut crisp white shirt and cool chinos he does look more dressed for the board than the boat. 'Why are you here, really?'

'Maybe I find you pretty.' He watches me through half-closed lids. 'Maybe I wanted the chance to spend two days cooped up on this boat with you.'

'Ha ha.' I push back my hair which hasn't been washed since last Tuesday, and open out my dirty hands. 'Sorry to disappoint you then, because right now I don't look too tasty, do I?'

'Even like this – covered in mud – you look lovely enough to convince me you're the woman I could happily spend the rest of my life with . . .'

My eyes open wide at the unexpectedness of his comment. I laugh out loud. We've known each other for about a year and a half but only on and off. He's kidding. He's got to be. I give him a sideways look, searching for any signs that he might be pulling my leg but he's keeping a pretty straight face. I gulp. Shit. Did he just . . . ask me to marry him? He did. Just wait till I text Lucy Lundy later on and tell her this big-shot South American dude has asked me to marry him. Hilarious. I'm far too young to be thinking about getting hitched. Flattering, though.

'The mud,' I begin unsurely, 'is because I ended up falling onto the forest floor this morning.' He doesn't seem to find anything unusual in my response, so I continue: 'We lost all the seeds we just spent this entire trip collecting, I nearly got killed by a falling monkey and . . . and all my clothes have been completely and utterly soaking wet for the last three days. And I *hate* being wet.'

'Yet you love your job,' he reminds me. 'And you're very good at it. I heard you're even up for an award, is that right?'

I blush. 'You heard that?'

'A little bird told me,' he smiles. 'I heard Eve put forward the thesis you submitted for your original job application. She thinks you stand a good chance. Is the award worth much?'

'I really, really want it!' I lean forward, suddenly excited at the thought. 'Even though I can't imagine I'll get it. Emoto's done some brilliant work, it'll probably go to him. And no, it's not

20

worth anything monetarily. It's just a peer-recognition thing . . .'
As he pulls a face, I add: '. . . which is *important*.'

'They should give you a big trophy.' His dark eyes are dancing, playing with me. 'A great big trophy,' he spreads his arms wide, 'for you to put in pride of place on your mantelpiece.'

'I don't have a mantelpiece that big.'

'No, but I do,' he puts in significantly.

'I think you really need to get to know a woman better before you go round proposing marriage to her,' I put in cagily. 'I mightn't be all that you think I am, Gui.'

'The fact that you don't jump at my offer tells me a certain amount.'

I lift my eyebrows questioningly.

'It tells me you aren't over-concerned with riches, for one thing.'

'I've not been adverse to a little bling in my time . . . but no,' I laugh, 'money wouldn't tempt me.'

'What would?' he leans a little closer. So close, in fact, I have to catch my breath.

'The man I marry,' I tell him at last, 'will need to have proved to me that he knows me and loves me just as I am. That he'll be prepared to stick with me through thick and thin. It won't matter two figs to me how much money he's got.'

'Well said. I take it *you* will be prepared to prove likewise to him?'

'Naturally. But right now –' before we get too carried away with all this talk of marriage and before he gets a chance to see how confused he's making me feel – 'I've still got to make my mark in this field. I want my work to be recognised and used to some good purpose at the end of the day,' I run on. 'Getting an award – well, it makes it more likely people will sit up and take what I do seriously.'

'That's one route,' he says thoughtfully.

'You've got a better one?' I give him an arch look.

'Having friends in positions of power and influence. That can be the easiest route to getting your work noticed, don't you agree?'

I shrug. 'All I know is my mum slaved most of her adult life out here, doing exactly what I'm doing, collecting and categorising seeds, logging their tribal medicinal purposes . . . and in the end, it was all for nothing, because she died before she got any of her work published or put to any purposeful use. I don't intend to end up like that.'

'You won't,' he promises, and then laughs as I almost fall into his lap as José veers to avoid a line of harassed-looking water birds that are steaming straight towards us.

'I hope not. I really want what I do to make a difference, Gui.' I pull back from him a little as the boat straightens again. 'I hope I get the chance. We just came across Emoto up in the cloud forest and I'd swear he thinks Eve's going to tell me I'm to go back home.'

'I heard PlanetLove were cutting back. I could pull some strings for you, if you like.' Guillermo looks at me candidly. 'You know my dad owns Chiquitin-Almeira. And Chiquitin-Almeira pretty much funds PlanetLove . . .'

'I . . . I don't want you to do that, Gui.'

'You don't want me to do that for you?' He picks up my hands and I'm suddenly very aware that my nails are broken and dirty, my T-shirt is stained with monkey blood and I haven't had a proper wash for days. I must look a sight. I can see in his eyes that he doesn't think that, though. 'I remember when you first came out here. There were over five hundred people present at the conference meeting that day and you were the only one in the whole place I felt drawn to talk to, the only one I wanted to spend time with. I still feel that way.'

I turn away from him, confused. There's only one other person in the world who has this kind of effect on me and I haven't seen him for eighteen months . . .

'You made me feel special,' I admit. I look at him shyly. 'You still do.'

'But here?' He touches his hand to his heart. 'Do you feel anything here?'

'Oh, Gui, I haven't the time to fall in love.' I shrug off his question like I always do. We hang out together on my days off. I love being around him because he's always so sweet and so gallant in an old-fashioned kind of way. He takes me to nice places, all the exclusive nightspots in Manaus, expensive restaurants and so forth. Sometimes we go dancing. Guillermo dances better than any man I've ever been with. I've thought I could fall in love with him just for that – if I were up for falling in love right now, that is.

'No time?' He looks at me curiously. 'Or is it something else?'

'I have important work I need to do here, that's all.' I wrap my arms around my knees and watch the bright flicker and fade of the long white liana stems, the 'Tarzan ropes', that hang from every single tree as we skim past the bank. I don't want to go back to the UK right now. That would be the worst thing possible. 'It's taken me the best part of a year to gain the tribe's trust. And to get to grips with their language. Do you know, Eve said they've never had another worker learn the dialect as fast as I have?' I look at him proudly. 'The Yanomami are opening up and telling me secrets about forest plant lore that they've never told anyone before. There is so much that I'm learning from them right now. And if I don't write it down for them, then who will? It'll be lost forever.'

'And you?' Guillermo smiles softly. 'When will you tell me your secret, Scarlett?'

'I don't have one.' I open my eyes wide in denial.

'Ah, but you do,' he says assuredly. 'I have wondered what it is all this time. What was it that propelled you all this way from your faraway land to mine, two summers ago? Will you tell me what it is you ran away from? Or should that be – *who* you ran away from?'

'Gui, I'm devoted to my job. You know that. I love it here. I adore these people. What makes you think I was running away from anything – or anyone?' I laugh lowly. 'What, you think I'm not being totally honest?'

'I know you are totally honest.' He leans forward and touches the side of my face gently and I realise that I've just stuck my tongue in my cheek. 'You have to be honest, don't you, *querida*? Because you aren't in the slightest bit good at telling lies.'

Hollie

I'll be home in time for Christmas.

I blink, rereading for the third time the postcard that's just come in from Scarlett. My God, she's coming home. And it's . . . what, the fifteenth today, which means she must already be en route from the rainforest. It'll take her a good few days even to get to the nearest city, let alone an airport. She doesn't give any details about what flight she'll be arriving on or even what day. The girl doesn't change, I smile to myself. 'Expect me when you see me,' that's her motto; she's just like Mum in that respect.

I take my mug and the postcard and go sit at the table where I've been writing the last of my Christmas cards. Except I can't concentrate any more. I've got butterflies just like I used to get when I was a kid, every time I knew our mum was due back home. Scarlett was too young when Mum died to really be aware of her. In fact, I muse now, given that she scarcely knew her at all, it's incredible how similar in character to Helen Hudson she's turned out to be.

I stand up again, sidling over to the wide bay-window seat. The view from here, of the sprawling apple tree slap-bang in the middle of the front lawn with the little path doing a detour around it down to the gate hasn't changed much. My God, sitting here like this with the thrill of anticipation in my stomach about Scarlett's homecoming brings back so many memories . . .

The last time my mother came home for Christmas, she'd promised to arrive on the twenty-fourth 'with a wonderful surprise'. I remember I sat here all day, waiting. Sat still so long that my bum ached, my legs got pins and needles, my eyes grew tired and sore with the effort. She would keep her promise, I was sure of it. I wasn't having any of Flo's 'don't get your hopes up, girl' because it was far too late for that. We'd seen a lot less of Mum than usual that year. Her work kept her abroad, we all accepted that, but Christmas was a time to be home, wasn't it? A time to be with family. And Flo had let out a few hints that maybe – just maybe – this time Mum intended to come home for good.

I can recall every second of that day as vividly if it were scrolling away in front of me now. I remember Flo getting a call about four o'clock that afternoon saying there'd been a 'little delay' but Mum would be there within the hour. Why were the minutes ticking by so slowly? And what on earth was she bringing with her for my 'wonderful surprise'? It was already dark by then. I couldn't see a thing outside the window any more and I remember I went and put an old kerosene lamp down by the gate to light the way for when she came in.

We'd eaten our tea eventually, reluctantly, without her and when nine o'clock arrived and Mum hadn't, Flo had sent me packing off to bed. I'd had to go up, bitterly disappointed, hurt and worried as I was. You didn't argue with Flo, but what if something had happened to Mum? I couldn't understand why Flo didn't share my concern. She seemed more irritated than worried, but if she had more information than me about Mum's whereabouts she never shared it.

It must have been gone ten before Mum finally turned up at Florence Cottage. I was out of bed like a shot. I remember the anticipation of sitting on the top step in my nightie thinking, *any wonderful moment now she'll be up here to see me*. I still recall Flo's low, curt tones in the hallway, followed by a sound that

I only ever heard Flo utter the one time – a low, choking sound, like an exclamation of horror, that curdled my blood to hear it. Whatever could be the matter? What terrible thing could have happened on this day that should have been a joyous one? And then Mum, her voice as low as Flo's, and equally inaudible to me in reply.

I heard the taxi driver taking all Mum's things through to the parlour and the two women going through into the kitchen and closing the door. But what about *me*?

I stood up, the cold night air hitting my bare legs under my nightie as I crept down the stairs, fearing Flo's wrath if she found me up, and desperate to know what was going on in equal measure. I took one step at a time, holding my breath as I went, the better to hear the two women's voices, muted but nonetheless distinctly unfriendly behind the kitchen door.

They could at least have waited till Mum said hello to me before having their argument! Why did adults have to argue over such unimportant things anyway? And why did Auntie Flo have to give Mum a hard time when she'd only just got in? Didn't she realise that such a confrontation might make it less likely Mum would want to stay with us?

When I stole into the parlour the room was pitch black save for the kerosene lamp that someone must have brought in and placed on the sideboard. The air was so cold, the fire having died down about an hour before. I could see Mum's coat hanging on the back of the chair and the sight made me want to rush into the kitchen to her but they were still arguing and I didn't dare. Nor did I put the big light on. I could just about make out what they were saying.

'You take the biscuit, Helen Hudson, you really do.'

'What's done is done,' my mother countered. 'It's not how I planned things but it happened. I was hoping you'd be a bit more supportive, Florence, seeing as you adore Hollie so much.'

'How I feel about Hollie doesn't excuse you from your own responsibilities, Helen.'

'I need to get back to work. We're making such headway in the Amazon at the moment you can't imagine . . .'

My heart sank in my chest. Mum *hadn't* come home for good then. Oh, but she had to, she couldn't let me down now. Flo had hinted so strongly and it was what I'd been waiting all day to hear . . .

A small mewl, like from a kitten, drew my attention to the wicker basket in the middle of the parlour floor and I stole over to peer into it. A cat? Was this the surprise my mum had been promising, to make up for the fact that – yet again – she wasn't staying with us?

But it was no kitten.

That was the first time I ever laid eyes on my sister.

Hollie

'Is she *his*?' Flo's voice had come through again, cutting, disapproving.

'They both have the same father,' my mother admitted at last.

'And the same mother.' Flo's voice, thin and unsympathetic, seeped under the door. 'Who intends to look after neither of them.' There had been a long silence then as her words sank in for all of us.

As I stare out of the window even now, the apple tree in the half-darkness forms a shape that reminds me of my sister's little white face in the bassinet. Her eyes a tourmaline blue, wide as saucers, her little rosebud mouth paused in a half-pout. For a split second, a flash of anger at the betrayal that had taken place that night coursed through me.

Who was this? I remember leaning over, meanly prodding her with a fingertip as the unwelcome realisation had sunk in. This was it? Mum's . . . wonderful surprise? This wasn't what I wanted! I wanted Mum, not some useless baby. A sister.

'I'm not . . . mothering material, Flo.' Mum's dull voice came through from under the kitchen door again.

'She's been waiting a long time to see you, Helen. It's been months. You have another child now . . . surely you can stay a little while?'

I waited with bated breath to hear her answer. I wanted Mum. I missed her. I wanted to go back to the time when we'd lived in a bedsit, just the two of us together, a time before the settling and steadying influence of Flo had come into my life, a time almost passed now from my memory.

'I know, I know! Just stop laying a guilt trip on me, OK? I'm home for Christmas like I promised, just don't expect any more from me than that.'

When she said those words, the child in the basket let out a great cry, a noise that seemed to me far too loud to come from such a small being. It was as if the little thing knew what I was feeling and she felt the same way. As if it were this great big lament from inside her for something she'd lost and she couldn't get back.

Were we both in the same boat after all? When I relented and leaned over at last to pick her up, her little body, hiccupping and shuddering against my shoulder, felt warm as toast. Her head fell against mine and I realised she was so floppy she couldn't even hold it up. I had to help her with everything. Instinctively I folded my arm about her neck so she wouldn't fall forward and she became quiet. She moulded into my arms as easily as if she belonged there and in that instant she filled . . . she filled a space in my heart.

I turn from the bay window now, my eyes lighting on all the cards that still need to be written and hand-delivered, the Christmas decorations I bought yesterday that still need to be hung up on the tree. The room is somehow suddenly and inexplicably *not ready* for something as important as Scarlett coming home. Especially now that I have something I want to ask her.

Will she even be prepared to help me? I daren't begin to hope that it might be so. Oh, but she's coming home, though.

It's the first part of the puzzle.

Scarlett

'Scarlett, this is marvellous. Really.' Eve pats the sheaf of notes that she's just been flicking through and pulls up a chair on the opposite side of her worktable. 'Some of these plants are brand new to us. We're finding out exciting new stuff all the time and your work here has been incredibly useful . . .'

Has been. I lean forward on the canvas deck chair – standard issue at PlanetLove base camp – with my head in my hands and wait for the axe to fall.

'So, has Barry relayed anything to you about our current position with Chiquitin-Almeira?'

'I came back with Guillermo in the end, so Barry wasn't with us.'

'Guillermo Almeira?'

I nod and my boss brightens visibly. 'How are you two getting along, Scarlett?'

I laugh. 'I think he may have just asked me to marry him.'

'Well, well. Marvellous! Congratulations.'

'Actually, I don't think he . . .'

'Yes.' She taps her short fingernails on her knees, suddenly businesslike. 'As you know, Chiquitin-Almeira have had interests in our work from the outset, both financial and humanitarian. Without them, we as an operation would cease to exist.' She pauses. 'I imagine Guillermo has already told you they're now scheduled to pull out of the Amazon?'

31

My eyes open wide. Gui never said a word about *that*. Mind you, I reflect, I have only myself to blame because I always steer him away from business talk.

'They are?'

'Worldwide recession and all that. They've got to stick with the money spinners – stomach upset pills, sexual performance enhancers – it's what people want.' She pauses. 'Scarlett, I know you've been a little homesick recently. I was with you when you sent that postcard to your sister recently, remember? The thought of going home has been on your mind, I know.'

I stare at her, surprised. 'Oh.' It comes back to me suddenly, the monkey postcard with the Santa Claus hat on. I thought it was funny and I haven't been in contact with Hol all that much since I left. When I scribbled that message on it, I'd only meant it as a kind of half-joke. I had a vague idea I might spend some of my holidays doing some travelling in Europe, so why shouldn't I spend a day or so with Hol? When I said I'd be 'coming home for Christmas' I didn't mean the whole of it.

'When money's tight, research is always the first thing to go, and don't we know it!' Eve continues. 'The fact is, PlanetLove are having to cut back too.'

I look at her tensely. 'Cut back?' I swallow. 'Are you saying you're letting me go?' I can't keep the crushing disappointment out of my voice no matter how hard I try.

'No, that's not what I want to do.' She shakes her head. 'In fact, it's the *last* thing I want to do, which is why I'm sending you back first. I'll explain,' she says, seeing my confusion. 'You see this tract of the jungle that we've been exploring?' She turns and indicates the tattered map she's got pinned up on the tent wall behind her. 'Here's us. This part outlined in yellow is the acreage currently managed by Chiquitin-Almeira. We have governmental permission to study and work in all these areas: here, here and *here*.'

I look at her blankly. What's all this got to do with me?

32

'Chiquitin-Almeira are still interested in our projects. They want us to stay on in this area for as long as we can because they know that, given the rate of deforestation in other areas, in five years this whole ancient tract will be wiped out, clean. The whole of the Yellow Zone will be torn down by either loggers or other developers.'

The very thought makes my eyes water. I've already seen the huge tracts of forest that are being opened up like scars all around us but I thought our bit was safe. I suspect that this is a large part of why the shaman Tunga, José's father, has been so keen to open up with me – because I was working with the company who've vowed to protect his part of the jungle. What the hell am I going to tell him now?

'Look. There is an outside chance that Chiquitin-Almeira will be back on side with us in about a year to eighteen months from now, when the recession eases, but if our Yellow Zone which we've become familiar with and the special relationship which we've forged with the Yanomami is allowed to slip away in the meantime . . .' She doesn't need to finish.

'So you're saying, if we can hold on till then, it might still be OK? We have to find a way to fend off the developers till we can get some powerful business or governmental backing?'

'Exactly.' Eve pushes her short springy hair flat back on her head. 'We need to stall all logging or pipeline building or any other development in this area. One way to do it might be to buy out the area ourselves.'

'*Us?* You mean PlanetLove?' I look at her askance. 'We've got no money, have we?' Eve runs this operation on a shoestring as it is.

'I mean us – me, you, Barry, and the guys. Whoever we can get to donate funds. The figure we need to reach to buy out the Yellow Zone is one million sterling.'

I hold in my gasp – she might as well ask for the moon – but Eve's already continuing. 'Chiquitin-Almeira have promised us

33

a goodwill stake of £250,000. Barry and I and the guys have come up with ideas that'll net us maybe £350,000. All we need is the remaining £400,000 . . .'

'£400,000!' I breathe.

'That's right, and we've got to find it within the next three months because that's when Chiquitin-Almeira pull out.'

'O–K.' I let out a breath. I still haven't been told what any of this has got to do with me leaving but I'm getting the picture it's all much bigger than me.

'Until such time as they do pull out, we're still all officially appended as part of the company and in their employ. We're still entitled to apply for all work permits and visas and such, so I'm asking for everyone's papers to be renewed while we're still under their banner. You're the one with the least amount of time left on yours – so you're going home first. Renewal shouldn't take you much more than a month or so, I imagine. We'll ask Professor Klausmann to confirm all the details are still correct and applicable – he sponsored your place here, didn't he? It looks better coming from him than from us. Then we'll send it all off while we still have an employer to name on the form. Chiquitin-Almeira are keeping their plans pretty close to their chest at the moment so there's no reason for anyone outside to suspect we mightn't be working for them after the summer.'

'Who *will* we be working for?' I narrow my eyes now. 'Even assuming we get the funds together to buy out this tract of forest so we continue our research . . .'

'We're flying by the seat of our pants now, Scarlett, let's make no bones about that. I'm touting for backers. We need money. Lots of it. Don't know any rich men, do you?' She laughs nervously when I shake my head. 'We've had some initial interest from a lady called Defoe at the European Alliance Group. I'm sorry this has happened so unexpectedly for you – it's taken us all by surprise, believe me.'

'So I've got to go home to renew my papers and none of us might have a job here come the summer?'

'We've enough in the kitty to keep us going for maybe a month after Chiquitin-Almeira pull out but the situation is pretty bad, I won't lie to you.'

'We could still rescue it, though?' I look at her uncertainly. 'If we all pull together, I mean?'

'That's the spirit,' Eve nods. 'You don't mind going home first, do you? I'll be honest with you – you're the person who I feel has the best chance of all of us to persuade people to part with their cash. You persuaded Tunga to give up the tribal secrets, didn't you?'

I swallow down my first response to that because she won't want to hear it. I *do* mind going home.

But there are more important things at stake here than just my feelings.

'I understand you'll be disappointed, Scarlett, but at least you'll be coming back. And you haven't seen any of your family for a good year and a half, have you?' I get up and walk over to the tent flap because I need to take in some air. 'That's got to be one of the bright sides to going home for a bit,' Eve says encouragingly to my back.

'Sure, one of the bright sides, Eve.'

That's what she thinks.

Hollie

'I'm so sorry, Rich.' I sprint the last frozen metres up to the bench on Jackson's field where Richard is waiting for me. 'That meeting with the whole board at work went on for an age.'

I put my hand over my chest, my breath coming in short white puffs as he looks up, bemused.

That guy I've seen hanging around before – the one with the hoodie – he was just behind me, I'd swear it was the same guy. He started walking towards me like he wanted to talk so I just ran. I don't want to talk to him. I don't want to even think about him. Oh God. Rich is going to see something's up if I don't calm down . . .

'All the Bridge Wardens were there,' I puff. 'They wanted to get this business over with before we close for Christmas. I thought I'd never get away.'

'Don't worry about it, Hol.' He pats the bench beside him sympathetically. 'You didn't need to rush so much.'

'Of course I did.' I look for a place to put my bag down but the bench is frozen, wet. 'I didn't want to miss you.' I distract. I glance over my shoulder but the hoodie guy has gone. Automatically I feel myself relax. 'How long have we got before you catch the train to London?'

'About twenty-five minutes.'

'Damn it. This bridge-mending business is dragging on for an age.' Richard hands me one of the cups and I take a grateful sip.

It's lukewarm but still welcome. 'They haven't found any evidence of scouring on the piers yet, but it looks as if the riverbed has definitely been lowered . . .'

'Sounds good.' Richard grabs hold of my gloved hands and pulls me towards him for a kiss.

I don't think he's been listening to a single word I've just said.

'It's good?'

'Of course it is. They're getting to the bottom of it, aren't they? Maybe that means the next time I invite my wife to have lunch with me I won't be forced to sit beside a mile-long line of traffic crawling along the New Road,' he teases. 'Poor buggers have been stuck there for ages.'

'Ha! Maybe *next* time you'll treat me to the Italian,' I retort. 'Then we'll get to sit in the warm instead of out here on the freezing cold bench.'

'If we moved to Italy,' he says out of the blue, 'we could eat Italian all the time. We could eat it sitting on a sun-kissed patio with a blue sky over our heads.'

I laugh at his comment. 'I'm not planning on moving out of the country just to get a decent meal,' I shiver. He holds my gaze for a fraction of a second and then shakes his head, as if thinking better of whatever he was going to say.

'Sorry, darling. You're going to have to accept a raincheck on the restaurant. This is all we've got time for today.' He points to the brown paper bag with an assortment of sandwiches on the other side of him. I sigh. I suspected this was going to be a hurried rendezvous when he texted me earlier about needing to go to London, but with the delays at my end it's become even more of a rushed affair.

'Where's my other one?' I peer at the chicken and cucumber sandwich he's just handed me.

'I fed it to the pigeons. I thought you weren't coming.'

'You didn't!' I punch his arm jovially. 'Those were *your* crusts. What have you done with it?'

'Kiss first.' He tilts his head challengingly as I make a grab for the brown bag. 'Come on. Kiss – or no sandwich.'

'That's blackmail,' I murmur, but I give him what he asks for, gladly. Even though his nose and cheeks are cold, his lips are warm.

'You can't take the train up a little later, I suppose?' I look at him hopefully. 'Then we could be a bit more leisurely.'

He shakes his head. 'I'd love to, darling, but I just heard Dad's got to go in for his first set of tests this afternoon.'

'Oh, Rich! I thought this was a *work* trip. You didn't say . . .' We both watch the birds squabbling over the last piece of crust for a bit, lost in our own thoughts. I swallow, suddenly nervous. 'It's all been rather sudden, hasn't it? How's your mum taking it all?'

Richard shrugs. 'She's keeping upbeat. Chances are there's probably nothing wrong with him at all, apart from stress, which is what his doctor reckons. I thought I'd spare her going in with him, though. You don't mind, do you?'

'Of course not! Do you have any idea when you'll be home?'

'They want to keep him in overnight so I'll stay till tomorrow.'

'The family are still all planning on coming to ours for Christmas Eve, aren't they?'

He nods. 'They're all still keen to come. And Jay will drive Mum and Dad back up on Boxing Day. Hol, there's something else . . .' He turns to me, hesitant now. 'When I spoke to Jay on the phone earlier he hinted that . . . he and Sarah might have some "good news" to celebrate.'

The sandwich in my mouth suddenly tastes like cardboard.

'Oh. What *sort* of good news, did he say?' I'm trying to keep my voice breezy but he knows full well I don't feel it.

'No, but we could hazard a guess . . .' He looks apologetic. 'You're sure you're OK with me going up to London today?'

My mind is racing. How could Sarah be pregnant already? Rich's brother and Sarah only got married in the summer . . .

I make an effort to concentrate, get back to what Richard's just asked me.

'No, of course you must go. I'll be fine.'

'Did you manage to get hold of your sister this morning?' he reminds me. 'Find out if she's actually left Brazil yet?'

'Her mobile was switched off as usual and then it got so busy at work, I couldn't try again.'

'And . . . are you still planning on asking her if and when she does turn up?' he asks softly now.

I bite my lip. 'You don't think I should, Rich?'

'I can understand why you want to ask her,' he says carefully. 'She's your sister, the child would be related to you. It keeps it all in the family, and you don't have to rely on strangers who might let you down. I understand that. It's just . . .' He puts his hands around my shoulders as we get up to make our way down to the station. 'Face it, she doesn't even live in England any more. And she's already involved in a demanding and dangerous and – to her – irresistible job. Don't forget, we're talking about Scarlett here,' he reminds me. 'Not just anybody's sister. Scarlett's – well, she's got a lot of ideas about what she wants to get out of life. I can't see having someone else's baby being top of her agenda.'

'No. There wouldn't be anything in it for her at all, as you say. It could only be a gift.'

'A gift, indeed. The greatest act of charity a woman could do for another. Well, who knows?' he smiles. 'Until you ask we won't know what her answer will be.'

Scarlett

Home in time for Christmas, just like Eve said, but I've been travelling for so many days now, I barely know what date it is. I try and count the days in my head. Eleven days on the boat from base camp to the brown waters of the Solimoes river – I woke up just in time to see a flock of prawn-coloured flamingos rising up over the mangrove treeline – one more day to reach the port at Manaus then thirty-six more hours on the sleeper coach out of there to Caracas International airport – nearly two weeks.

It feels as if I had that conversation with Eve in her tent only a few days ago but . . . I rub my eyes, getting my bearings, I am back in Rochester. It is – I glance at my Mickey Mouse watch – quarter to four in the afternoon on the twentieth of December, and it's already starting to get dark.

I pull the rusty latch on the gate at the bottom of the garden and the familiar 'click' echoes into the early dusk. The sound of the latch has alerted Ruffles and I can hear him ambling expectantly down the garden path. The wooden gate sticks and even before I've got it open I can hear his laboured breathing on the other side.

'Hey, boy! It's me. How's my old boy, my lovely boy?'

And here I am again, my face buried in the familiar smell of wet Labrador fur. He's missed me like crazy, the silly old thing, and I've been too busy to even give him a second thought. One and a half years. Has it really been that long? But I see that the clump of Physalis, bright red berries swaying in their delicate paper cases by the herb beds, has almost doubled in size. It *has* been that long.

'Scarlett?'

I spin round at the familiar low sound of Richard's voice as he closes the garden gate behind him now.

'Is that really you?'

I laugh, running into his arms, at his surprise. Oh my God, I'm really home.

'Do I look so different?' I challenge. Though the sky is bright tonight, the garden where we stand is getting darker by the minute and he peers closer at my face.

'You've – grown up,' he professes. 'You always looked so young . . . but, Lettie . . .' He pushes his dark hair out of his face, laughing, and I remember that my brother-in-law is shy. 'We knew you were coming but we had no idea when. Why didn't you tell us you'd be arriving today? I'd have picked you up from the airport. And you know Hollie. She likes to be prepared for guests . . .'

Good, I think. I'm glad she hasn't had time to prepare for me. Let her learn to be spontaneous and go with the flow, for once.

'I'm twenty-four,' I remind him. About bloody time everyone stopped thinking of me as a kid. Just because Hollie's eight years older than me doesn't mean her little sister's going to remain a 'kid' forever. 'I don't need any special treatment,' I laugh at him. 'I didn't expect anyone to bake me a cake.'

Richard grins good-naturedly and Ruffles does an old dog impression of a young dog, rushing between us and nuzzling his hand and mine, not knowing which way to turn in his delight.

'Hollie's been so looking forward to seeing you.' Richard puts his arm about my neck companionably as we walk back towards the house. 'You're staying with us for Christmas, of course?'

'That's the plan.'

'She'll be over the moon,' Richard promises me. 'She's been talking about you a lot lately.' His voice changes almost imperceptibly. 'You're not so easy to get hold of, out there, are you?'

'No. We move about quite a bit. It's easier for me to contact her than the other way. *Sorry*,' I add, because I know I haven't kept in touch half as much as I should have. When I'm out there I have so much else to think about. So many things ... The mission I have come over to accomplish rushes momentarily to the front of my mind, all those funds that Eve hopes I'm magically going to be able to wheedle out of people. Will Rich and Hollie be able to help?

I push my fringe away impatiently from my eyes; I'm not going to go into that right now. I have so much to fill them in on, so much to share, but the comforting touch of Richard's hand on my neck makes me silent, calms me down, reminds me that I'm home.

When we step inside Florence Cottage, the flickering from the huge log fire glowing in the inglenook is the only movement. Where is my sister? I drop my damp rucksack on the rug.

'Hollie's out shopping getting some bits in for the holiday. It's Saturday,' Richard reminds me.

'Of course. Christmas Eve in a few days' time as well.' I glance around the familiar room. The plump red and gold cushions we once embroidered for Auntie Flo as part of a school project are still in place on the deep settee beside the fire. The original oak beams are still hung about with drying herbs, just like Flo used to have them. My sister has somehow managed to maintain the authentic Olde Worlde air of the place just as Florence would have wanted it. And trust Hollie to have added some mistletoe to the mix. Hoping Richard'll kiss her under it no doubt – always the romantic, my sister – not like me!

'Can I fix you a drink?' His question pulls me out of my reverie.

'Sure, I'd love one.' While Richard disappears into the kitchen I linger by the fire for a bit, pulling off my wet gloves, warming up my fingers and taking in my old home a little more closely.

I see Hollie's got that picture of the three of us taken on their wedding day still hanging on the wall. I must have been all of fourteen there. Hollie was just twenty-two. So young. I look about eleven, though. Ugh. It might be a good one of the two of them, but I wish she'd take it down.

'I'll have whatever you're having,' I call in the direction of the kitchen. I could do with a nice drink. Everyone drinks rum at the weekends in Manaus – not my favourite beverage, I'll admit. A Long Island Iced Tea now – that would go down a treat. I should change out of these damp clothes I suppose. I glance at the clock. I should, but I won't, because once Hollie gets back she'll want me all to herself and then I'll never get a chance to spend any time with Richard.

'Here you go,' Richard's back with a large mug of steaming cocoa. 'I've remembered your usual mug. The one with the baby chimps on,' he says, pleased with himself.

'Oh, that's sweet of you.' I deliberately keep my face straight and take a sip. 'At least it's not camomile.'

'Hollie's tea? No.' Richard sits down at the other end of my sofa. 'Yuck! You're more of a chocolate girl, aren't you?'

More of a Cabernet Sauvignon girl nowadays, I think but, hey, maybe cocoa is a better prospect in front of this lovely warm fire just at the moment.

'I still can't quite believe it,' Richard is shaking his head. 'You're back, and looking so well, and . . . all in one piece!' He laughs. 'Are you still staying with the Yanomami Indians?'

I nod. 'I've been living with a family unit of about fifty Indians.' I lean back into the sofa and regard him with half-closed eyes. His hair is dark, like Guillermo's, but that just about ends the resemblance between them. Richard is taller. He's slim but still muscular. Guillermo is more . . . wiry. His features are quicksilver, Latin, urgent and hard. More . . . dangerous. I give a secret smile. Should I tell Rich about Gui, or should I wait until Hollie is here too?

'Fifty of them?' Richard prompts. 'And your tribe – do they have much contact with the outside world?'

43

'My people prefer to keep to themselves. When the white men come – the *pelacaras* as they call them – they keep on the move. The truth is, they're scared witless of the illegal loggers that come with their tractors. The machines make such a noise when they chomp down the forest, clearing everything away. They think the machines are going to eat them up too.' I give a small shiver, remembering. 'So they run.'

'They run,' Richard's eyes narrow. 'And you?'

'I'm not scared of the loggers.'

He takes a sip from his mug, places it thoughtfully down on the coffee table in front of us. 'No. But you're working with them, aren't you? When they run away from the loggers – what do you do?'

I smile. 'Sometimes I run with them. *When* I can keep up with them. Once or twice I've woken up in the morning to find the camp broken up, everyone gone, just disappeared overnight. When they go, Rich, they don't leave any trace. No remains of the fires that were burning. No branches that were torn down as shelters, no footprints; *nothing*. You wake up and find it's just you there. Alone. It totally creeps you out, that.'

'I can imagine,' he says. His eyes are alive with interest and I shuffle a bit more upright on the sofa, trying to reconnect with some of the adrenaline that propelled me back home in the first place.

'It feels . . .' I stop to consider for a bit, recalling the gaping feeling of emptiness I felt the first time it happened. 'I can't really describe it. The first time it happened I thought they'd all been killed or something, I didn't *know* what had happened.'

He makes a sympathetic face. 'That must have been terrifying.'

It had been. I had felt . . . utterly abandoned.

'I got through it,' I tell him softly, 'by thinking of home. I've come to think of them as my second family,' I continue. 'You and Hollie are my first family and they are my second family. It took me three days to find them again that time, and I only managed it because our tracker guy Barry from PlanetLove came and helped me and it turned out my little guide José had left us a secret trail.'

Ruffles comes and pushes his nose right under my hand like he always did when he wanted to be stroked. The softness of his fur beneath my fingers feels so familiar but I see now there are little flecks of grey among the yellow; he's getting old. It makes me sad.

'Poor Lettie. That can't be easy for you, seeing your friends suffer like that.'

I shake my head, not wanting to say any more because the truth is I never expected to feel like this. I went out there to document the plants and seeds they use for medicinal purposes, I never meant to become as involved with the people as I have.

'There is so little I can do for them, Rich. A lot of the time I feel so helpless, so useless . . . and, oh, the destruction that's going on there! You read about it in the papers but when you actually see the acres upon acres being stripped bare of so much life . . .' I trail off, not knowing where to even begin at the injustice and the stupidity of it all. 'The Amazon has been called the pharmacy of the world. The shaman I'm working with there – Tunga, he's José's father – he has pharmacological knowledge that would put any Oxbridge chemist to shame and we will lose it – all of it . . .'

'You're doing what you can, Lettie,' he smiles sympathetically. 'But I'm glad you're back. You've been away from home a long time, you know.'

'I had to go, Rich.' My voice has gone suddenly quiet and I know he hears it.

Does he even realise why I left when I did, the way I did?

'But I'm glad to be back too,' I admit. 'The reason it's all happened so suddenly, well – I'm here on a mission, actually and if there's any way I can enlist your help I'd be really grateful . . .'

Richard leans back and regards me fondly and I know he's going to say, ask away because there's nothing you would ask us and we'd deny you, you know that, but I stop him even as

45

we both hear the key turn and the sound of footsteps at the front door.

'I'll tell you all about it when you're both together,' I explain. 'Because – to be honest – this is a biggie.'

I put down my mug of cocoa and uncurl from the sofa but before she's even come the length of the corridor Hollie has already spied me. Her shopping basket drops to the floor. One green and red apple rolls rapidly down the hallway and comes to a halt in the corner.

'Oh my God, you're here!' Her hands go to her mouth, her eyes bright with joy and surprise. 'I can't believe it! Why didn't you ring to say you were arriving today?'

I run to hug her, my sister who is all muffled up against the winter weather, her scarf and coat feel cold to my touch, her face pinched and frozen against my lips even though it is nowhere near cold enough to snow.

'Is everything all right? I mean, when you contacted me to say you'd be coming back you didn't say *why*. You haven't quit your job, have you?' My sister is looking at me, wide-eyed with concern.

'Everything's *fine*, Hollie. I came back because I missed you both and I wanted to see you again and . . .' I glance at Rich.

'She's on a mission,' Richard adds mysteriously, eyes twinkling as we both turn to look at him. He holds up his hands to her questioning gaze. 'I have no idea what it's about, Hol. You came home just in the nick of time . .'

'Hey, I really wanted to see you both too,' I protest. And that's true. They're just not the *only* reason why I'm back. 'Oh, it's nothing we need go into now,' I answer in response to their curious stares. 'I've only just got back! I need to touch base first. I want to see my room and I want to watch the telly and some local news and . . . I'm ravenous. Were those mince pies I just spotted in your bag, Hollie?' I pick up the bag while she hangs up her coat and carry it through to the kitchen.

'There were a couple of things that arrived for you among the post this morning – cards, I think,' Hollie calls through. 'That's a coincidence, isn't it?

I pick up the two envelopes that have been propped up beside the toaster. One's an official-looking letter in a brown envelope with the PlanetLove logo on the outside – that'll just be run-of-the-mill admin stuff no doubt. The other one's a card. I throw that one down on the surface impatiently. I'd recognise that handwriting anywhere. Duncan.

Bollocks to that. Without opening it, I rip the card in its envelope to shreds and pop it into the bin on top of some potato peelings. I warned him not to contact me and he shouldn't have.

'Who was the card from?' Hollie appears at the door, eyes still sparkling at my sudden arrival, Rich behind her, his hands on her shoulders.

'No one.'

'I still can't believe you're really, actually here!' She comes over and gives me a long sisterly hug. 'I missed you so much. And I want to know – oh, everything. Everything about everything. And all about your *mission*, of course,' she smiles encouragingly at me. 'It'll have something to do with seeds, let me guess?'

'Not seeds,' I correct her. 'It's about people this time. My friends in Manaus. I need to do as much fund-raising as I can while I'm here.'

'Whatever we can help you – or them – with, you know that we will,' Hollie wraps her arms comfortably around mine. 'I can't tell you what it means to me to have you back here with us this Christmas.' Her eyes are shining. She means it, I know that. About any help they can give me, too.

Except it isn't just a small amount of money I'm talking about here – a bring-and-buy sale in the village hall isn't going to do it. And they don't have any real money. The only thing they have that's worth anything is Florence Cottage. I look around at the medieval cottage that's been in Auntie Flo's family for generations.

This is probably worth a bob or two.

Hollie

There's a mist of fine rain pattering down on the leaves outside. I can hear it and a chilly damp morning air greets me as I walk into the lounge. That's because Scarlett is out already inspecting the winter shrubs and she's left the French doors open. I don't suppose they have to worry about central heating bills in the jungle . . .

Typical Scarlett. I always had to remind her about things like that when she lived here, but, instead of the irritation I used to feel, I get a shiver of happiness instead because *she's back*. Suddenly and unexpectedly and miraculously, Scarlett's back, summoned like some elemental out of the depths by my wish.

'Hey, sis!' She appears with a bunch of bright red berries in her hand. 'Just getting into the festive spirit here. I thought I'd make you a garland. Holly for Hollie.'

'Wonderful!' She's wearing Richard's dressing gown and a pair of my PJs and everything looks far too big on her. We're going to have to feed her up a bit while she's here. She's been eating some strange things in Brazil, she was telling us about it last night – howler monkeys and bright orange fruit with many pips and *insect larvae* . . .

Ruffles is out there with her. I can just about spy the plumy tip of his tail wagging happily from behind a clump of elder. *Sambuca nigra*, she'd call it. She was always a natural botanist, passionate about the garden at Florence Cottage. From the time she was old enough to follow Flo around with her little plastic watering can she could name the plants that covered every inch of it, but when she came back from horticultural college I remember fondly, it was suddenly all Latin names with her.

'Look at how well the *Lunaria biennis* has thrived in the peat patch over there.' She bends to pick up a bunch of Silver Pennies growing freely in the beds beside the hydrangeas. 'So pretty, they used to be my favourite winter harvest out of everything.'

I nod. 'Auntie Flo called that plant Honesty. She said it suited you.'

'Honesty?' my sister giggles.

'Yes, because you were always rubbish at lying to get yourself out of trouble . . .'

'Ha. I can *still* remember the day Auntie Flo told me I was wasting my time putting them in. But I didn't have anywhere else to put them,' her clear wide eyes look up at me earnestly now, 'and I've always thought – "Nothing ventured nothing gained", don't you agree?'

I nod, hugging my mug of tea closer to my chest as I join her on the lawn. I wonder if I'll get the chance to speak to her properly this morning? She hasn't gone into what her 'mission' is yet, but she's come back so full of all her new friends and exciting life. I can scarcely dare to hope there's any point in asking her about the baby thing, and yet, as she said, nothing ventured . . .

'Scarlett, it's really funny that you should turn up right now because . . .'

'Smell that.' She holds a sprig of festive yellow Winter Sweet under my nose, twisting it to release its spicy fragrance. 'I planted that against Flo's advice too. D'you remember?'

'It's lovely.' I curb what I was just about to say to her, feeling her excitement catch in my own belly. 'And you've always had a sound instinct about what to plant and where. The garden has always been your baby, hasn't it?'

49

'Talking of babies,' she nudges me gently, 'how about you and Rich? When I left I thought you two were really going for it – another round of IVF and all that?'

'No.' I look down and my thin slippers have begun to soak up the dew and rain on the grass, making my toes curl. 'I mean – we did, but nothing came of it.' I clear my throat. 'Actually, Scarlett, I . . .'

'It's funny how we change, isn't it, sis?' Scarlett turns to me, earnest-faced now. '*I've* changed. Have you noticed?' She twirls around and her laughter scatters like a circle of bright droplets of water out of the sky.

I stop and regard her. She's not been back a full day yet. In some ways, she feels like a stranger still. She's got the essence about her of somebody who's been to faraway places, an air of the exotic and the strange and unknown. At the moment she doesn't feel very much like my kid sister.

'Your hair – you've cut it shorter.' She seems to be waiting for a response so I have to come up with something. 'It's shoulder-length now,' I add.

Scarlett laughs. 'It was hardly practical in that heat! I had it all chopped off as soon as I could but it's grown back.'

I raise an eyebrow. 'You *have* changed then.' When I think of the hours she used to spend with those straightening tongs, hogging the bathroom mirror . . .

'Hollie, I meant that I've changed *here*.' She puts her hand over her heart, 'You know, inside. I've had my eyes opened to the world. I wish . . .' Her gaze flickers over her once-beloved garden, taking in everything proprietorially and yet at the same time dismissing it all. 'I wish I could even begin to describe to you what I've been through over the last year and a half, the people I've met.'

We were all up till two last night as she tried to describe it all, I remember now with a yawn. We heard all about the Yanomami, her second family as she described them, who've been looking after her during her time there. It was a huge relief to hear that she's got caring people looking out for her.

'It's just . . . changed my values, you know.' She looks at me earnestly. 'The way I feel about everything.'

I give a little laugh. 'You've just grown up,' I tell her. 'You've experienced a different culture so you can see the world from a different perspective, that's all.'

'Yes,' she enthuses. 'A totally new perspective. That's it. And I want to share that with you and Rich, Hollie. It's just . . .' She takes in a deep breath, unable to impart the magnitude of these new truths she seems to have stumbled upon.

'Well.' I pat Ruffles briskly. 'I guess there'll be time to debrief over the rest of your stay with us. You haven't told me yet how long you're planning on being here?'

It won't be nine months, though, I realise with a sudden pang. I must have been crazy to ever imagine there could be any hope in asking *Scarlett* to carry my baby for me. She won't. She can't. She's had her 'eyes opened to the world' now. What could I possibly offer her that would entice her to stay?

'How long I stay here will depend on . . .' She looks at me solemnly and stops. 'Your face has gone pale all of a sudden. Are you all right?'

'I'm just hunky dory.' I take a deliberate sip of my tea, shrug my shoulders. I'm all right. I have to be all right. I turn my face away so she won't see the foolish tears that have suddenly sprung into my eyes.

'You sure you don't want to go back in? You see, I've become . . . more aware of other people,' Scarlett says deliberately. 'Being with the Yanomami people, it's made me more aware of just how selfish I've always been. I have, haven't I?'

'I wouldn't have called you selfish,' I protest. A little self-centred maybe.

'No, I was. Selfish. And, well . . . I hope I'm not any more. Because my second family, they – well, they aren't so hung up on possessions, because for one thing, they're always on the move. The forest gives them everything they need, you see. It's their larder on tap. How can I explain it?' I wish she didn't feel quite so strongly that she had to. She's scanning the garden at Florence Cottage again as if she could draw some comparison between it and the Amazonian jungle.

'I think you've been living on overdrive these past few months,' I tell her kindly. 'Being home for a bit will do you some good. You can potter about in the garden for a bit and that'll help calm you down.'

Scarlett sighs then. It's a sound that I'm familiar with from the past. It means *you really don't understand anything, do you?*

And maybe I don't.

My sister makes a deliberate effort to shift the conversation back onto me now. 'So, um . . . what have *you* been up to, anyway? How's Beatrice Highland doing next door? How's . . . the bridge?'

'Great. Everyone's great, thank you . . .' I throw her what passes for a smile, glancing up at the grey sky. The misty rain has turned into bigger droplets and I can feel them running down my cheeks. 'In fact, you're right. Perhaps we should head back in now?'

What am I up to? Let me see. I struggle for anything to compare with her adventures.

'There's a new picture of Rochester Bridge that we've just acquired for the Trust's collection. It's by a local artist, Oliver something. I've got to organise the framing of that.'

Scarlett looks at me blankly. 'You've got to frame the picture?'

'It's going to be quite a challenge,' I bluster, realising that she's just travelled eleven days down the Amazon in a dug-out canoe surrounded by alligators so it probably doesn't sound like much of one to her.

'Is it any good?'

'What?'

'The picture,' she says levelly.

'Oh, the picture. Um. It won a competition with a whole panel of very distinguished judges including the Pro-Rector at the Royal College of Art, no less, who chose it to hang in our permanent collection so I guess it must be very good.' I don't care about the picture. I look at my sister openly now, wanting to share my real concerns with her, but Scarlett laughs.

'You don't "get" it, though? Too modern for you?'

'It's not very traditional,' I confess.

'And everyone knows how our Hol loves her traditions . . .' My sister pulls a face.

'Scarlett . . .' We've reached the French doors and I pause to pick up the old towel I keep to wipe the mud off Ruffles' paws before he's allowed back in the house. Scarlett smiles, watching me, and I remember she's been living in a round hut surrounded by mud, living, eating, breathing mud, and all this is going to seem a little pernickety to her now. I hold my peace.

'I think,' she says mildly once the warmth of the cottage has thawed us out a bit, 'you shouldn't give up so easily on your plans to start a family. It's what you've always wanted to do, isn't it, sis? And they're so clever with technology these days. There's all sorts of help for couples who are having difficulties . . .'

'Seeing as you've brought it up,' I swallow, pausing in my brisk rubdown of the shivering Ruffles, 'actually I . . .

'And I was thinking, when you do start a family,' she runs on, gesturing to the lounge, 'this place really isn't going to be big enough for you, is it?'

'That may be jumping the gun a bit.' I sit up on my knees and Ruffles slinks off to lie beside the log fire. 'I'd need to actually *have* a baby first.'

'And it isn't happening?' Scarlett gives me an unexpectedly sympathetic hug. 'I want you to be happy.' She takes my hands in hers and her fingers are as warm as toast while mine are icy. 'Look, tell me what I can get you for Christmas? What would make you happy, Hollie? Anything at all?'

I give a small, choked laugh. If only she would *listen,* I might

53

be able to get it out. I might be able to share with her the thing that's been on my mind for weeks now.

'I've got a pay packet now, don't forget,' she reminds me. 'I'm not a penniless student any more.'

'I don't need you to *buy* me anything, Lettie.'

'No, come on. You tell me.' My sister has taken on a businesslike air now. 'Something nice. Something lovely. Something to really cheer you up. What'll it be?'

'Nothing, really. Nothing at all.' But I know Scarlett, she'll never take no for an answer. She'll have her way if it kills her so I'll have to think of something. 'Um . . . bath oil?' I offer, but she shakes her head dismissively.

'No, no, no! Think big! Think *bold*. I'm thinking adventure days out here. I'll buy you and Rich a balloon ride, how about that? Or a day racing cars at Silverstone?'

'That . . . really isn't the kind of thing I'd appreciate, honestly.'

My sister sighs exaggeratedly. 'What about scuba diving then?'

'I don't swim,' I remind her. If there's one thing she can't have forgotten it's *that*, surely?

'You haven't learned yet?' She looks shocked. 'I really thought you would have learned to swim, Hol. After . . . you know . . .' She bends to pick up Ruffles' towel and examines it thoughtfully. 'I think you should. I'll book you in for a course of lessons, OK? I'll find a really sympathetic instructor and . . .'

'NO!' I tell her bluntly. 'Thanks for the offer, but absolutely not.'

'Why not, for Pete's sake? I just . . . I worry about you sometimes, Hol, you know.'

'Whatever for?'

'I get the feeling,' she says carefully, 'that maybe you just don't get out enough, you don't get to taste enough of life. There's more to the world than just Florence Cottage and your work with the Bridge Trust and your cosy life with Rich and his family and all your little hobbies like – like your *knitting*.'

'What's wrong with knitting?' I give her an injured look.

'Nothing, Hol! But don't you ever worry you might be becoming old before your time because you never try any new stuff?'

'No. And you can stop worrying too, please, because I'm perfectly content.'

She only raises her eyebrows in reply, as much to say 'oh, no, you aren't'.

'I am, you know. I don't need any adventures. I just want ordinary things. I'd hate to go up in a balloon. Or go sky diving.' I look at her. 'And I am never, ever going to go in the water, so you can forget all about that.'

This isn't what I want to talk to her about right now, though. Why won't she *listen*?

'You don't look happy.' She observes me critically now. 'You don't seem very content, that's all. I'm just suggesting that maybe you need to get out of your rut a little. Do something different that you never thought in your wildest dreams you would do. What have you got to lose?'

'Huh! A limb, maybe?' I stand up huffily. 'And I'm not ready to let go of one of those just yet.'

'Nor your fear of . . . of anything that might be in the remotest bit risky or exciting?' She throws Ruffles' towel back at me and I catch it before it hits my face.

'I don't have wild dreams,' I say quietly. 'Just ordinary ones.'

And even those don't look like they have the remotest chance of coming true.

55

Hollie

'What time are they all arriving this evening, did Rich say?'

'About six,' I call back to my sister. 'Chrissie and Bill are getting a lift down with Jay and Sarah, so they should be here in good time for dinner.'

With *their celebratory news,* I remember with a pang. 'At least the preliminary tests on Rich's dad came out OK.'

''Course they did! People worry far too much about stuff, that's what I think.' I hear her say now, 'All I'm worried about now is what I'm going to get you for your Christmas pressie.' Scarlett's standing by the grate stoking the fire I lit earlier. It's Christmas Eve and *now* she's worrying about getting presents? I can hear the crunch of the poker against the logs. 'I already got a little something for Rich,' she admits, 'but for *you*, it's going to be a book token, you know.' She calls into the kitchen: 'Unless you can suggest something else?'

'There isn't anything, Scarlett,' I try to say, but the words stick in my throat.

'Remember the year we planned to hijack Father Christmas on his way down the chimney?' she remembers suddenly. 'We set that booby trap with a bag of flour.'

'*You* set the booby trap,' I remind her. 'And I was the one who ended up poking around in the dark with a coat hanger trying to dislodge it before anyone found out . . .'

'I held the torch!' she protests. 'I kept thinking if Santa comes in and finds us we'll be doomed – we'll lose it all. I was terrified of getting caught.'

'I'm surprised you still remember that.' I come out of the kitchen with the mixing bowl still in my hand. Is she still going to give me a hand with tonight's dinner like she promised? 'You were always getting in scrapes when you were a kid. You've been addicted to danger all your life, haven't you?' I smile as she comes up and prods me in the ribs.

'It's not the danger I'm addicted to, believe me. I've just got this terrible . . .' her eyes roll upwards, searching for the words, 'This huge *urge* that always pushes me towards getting what I want. If something's on my mind, I find I can't stop thinking about it till it's mine. Whereas you, darling sister, are precisely the opposite. You never even *want* anything, do you? I've *got* to get you something for Christmas, there's only a couple of hours before the shops shut. If only there was something you really *wanted* . . .'

I look into my mixing bowl and give it a little stir but my heart isn't in it. I can't ask her. I can't.

'There *is* something, isn't there?' She's looking at me triumphantly now. 'I've sussed you out! There's something you want and you're not saying. Tell me.' She shakes my hands insistently. 'Spit it out! In fact, I promise you right now the answer's yes, so don't be coy.' She does her Jane Austen impression, shaking an imaginary fan in front of her face. 'Anything you want, dear sister . . .'

'It's not quite that simple,' I croak. I wish that it was. 'Look, there is something I want. I mean, something you could do for me, but it would involve a huge sacrifice on your part. And it wouldn't be fair to ask you because your own life is really cooking at the moment – you've got everything going on, haven't you?'

I bite my lower lip as my sister pressures me further. 'Ask, Hollie. Just ask. You never know your luck. How much does it cost?' she teases.

'It'll cost you not a penny,' I breathe at last. 'But maybe a hell of a lot more than that. What I want will cost you perhaps a whole year of your life . . .'

Scarlett

'So, let me get this clear . . . there are these surrogate women in India . . .' I look up from the BabyinIndia leaflet which she's just placed in my lap '. . . but you're telling me that this route isn't any good for you because . . . ?'

'Because of the low quality of my eggs.' Hollie's voice is subdued.

'Bummer,' I console. But where do I fit into any of this? My sister doesn't expand, even when I open up my hands in a gesture of *where are we going with this?* 'I don't understand,' I concede after a while, but a huge silence has opened up in the room. Right now Flo's old grandmother clock in the hallway is the only thing that's making any sound at all. Even the fire crackling in the grate seems to be burning lower. I skim over Dr Shandaree's letter again. Then the penny drops.

'You'd like me to donate my eggs?' I say at last. 'Is that it?'

Of course, that way the baby will be as genetically similar to her as possible.

I didn't see that coming. When I said I'd give her anything I never thought she'd be asking for anything quite as . . . personal as this.

'The timing is not the best,' I begin, wondering how on earth I'm going to be able to get out of it. The timing is the least of it as far as I'm concerned because there will never be a good time to ask me for something which I have so little inclination to do. But she's my sister and she's desperate . . .

59

'Hol, are you saying that if you got some good quality eggs you'd be able to have the baby yourself?'

'Unfortunately no. My body doesn't produce the right level of hormones any more – that's why the IVF failed. In the beginning, when I was producing the right hormones, the eggs didn't implant. Now I haven't got the eggs or the hormones . . .'

'OK,' I say gently. 'So you'll still need a surrogate. But if I donate the eggs for you, that should do it, right?'

So why does she need a year of my life?

Hollie shakes her head, almost imperceptibly. 'No,' she says decisively. 'Thank you but no. I can't do that because I can't risk using a surrogate mother who might just change her mind at the end.'

'Why would a surrogate change her mind?'

'She might. There have been cases documented where just such a thing has happened. I can't risk it.'

I frown at her stubbornness. 'Life's all about taking risks, surely? And . . . if someone volunteered to do it for you, they surely wouldn't just change their mind? There must be contracts and things.' I nudge her elbow when she doesn't respond. 'What do you mean by that anyway?'

'In this country, the law states the baby belongs to the birth mother,' she says slowly. 'People can and sometimes do change their minds. If that happened it would just about finish me off . . .'

'You've just said you're going to go to India, aren't you? Maybe the law is different there?'

'Scarlett, I'm not sure if I can explain this to you in a way that you'll understand it.' My sister looks up at me now and her dark eyes are hooded with pain. 'After all these years of trying I feel . . . battered. Sort of used up. I could go out to India and use your eggs with a surrogate, sure. Originally that's what I was going to ask you for. But the more time goes by, the more I realise that this has got the best chance of working if *you* agree to do

60

it for us. Not some stranger, out in some foreign place far from here. But you, my own sister who I can trust and here, in our own home without the need for medical fees and international air travel and all the huge expectation that goes along with it. Here we could do it quietly, privately, without all the risk and the fuss . . .'

'No!' My hands fly up to my mouth. 'Have a baby for you? Are you . . . *completely* mad, Hol?'

There's a silence again. A wide grey silence that bounces off the walls, gets stuck in the faded yellow hops she's got hanging from the oak ceiling beams. For a few minutes we both stand there looking at her pastry sitting in a bowl in the middle of the table.

'I can't.' It makes me feel queasy even thinking about it. I get up and bolt out of the kitchen door and Ruff follows me loyally out into the garden. How could she ask me that? She's out of her mind, she knows what I'm like, what my life is like right now and I *can't* give it to her. A year of my life. A life sentence more like . . .

The crisis in the Amazon – the work I'm doing there – it needs tending to now, it's not going to wait and I can't either.

'I'm sorry,' she calls out desperately after me but she doesn't get up to come after me and I don't want her to. I need her to leave me alone.

I need her to let me get on with my own life.

Hollie

When I look out into the silent garden, growing dark now with the early evening that's drawing in, there's still no hide nor hair of her. For an instant I feel the twinge of an old ache, the familiar worry of not knowing where my sister is, who she's with, if she's even all right . . .

How many nights would I go out and catch her sitting up on a wall by The Vines. The irony of it never escaped me then, either – that the garden where medieval monks from Rochester Priory once grew grapes for their wine should end up being the place where local kids hang out to drink their cider. And often enough that's where Scarlett would be, when she should have been in her bedroom, doing homework. But she's a grown woman now.

Still though, she's a runner, Scarlett. She always was. If she didn't like what was going on she'd scarper. I often never knew where it was she went, though, boy, did I search. She could be away for hours. A couple of times, almost a day went by before I saw her but never quite the twenty-four hours needed for the police to get involved. She was just happy to take it close enough to the wire.

I wonder if she even knew what she did to me on those occasions when, at fourteen, fifteen, she'd just disappear? I don't suppose she ever cared enough to consider. She'd be guided by her own moods. If I was upset or worried or concerned . . . well, why should she fret?

I straighten now at the sound of Jay's and Richard's cars pulling up at the front, feeling a small tensing in my stomach because they're all here – everyone except her – and any moment now I'm going to officially learn that Sarah is already pregnant.

I should be glad for the happy couple. I *am* glad for them. We're all going to have a new addition to the family, that's one way to look at it. Rich becomes an uncle. Christine and Bill become grandparents at last. Christmas next year will be even better, I tell myself firmly, because Christmas is a time for kids, I've always said so.

I'm getting jaded, that's all, and I don't want to be. I've always loved this time of year. All the anticipation and the preparations and the little rituals that surround the Christmas season, I've always been in my element.

So why has this year felt like a huge effort?

I didn't want to be bothered with making all my own mince pies or preparing that bowl of mulled wine for my guests. Or laying out the table settings so beautifully as I always do. Or dressing the tree, hanging the garlands.

I wanted to do . . . *nothing*.

I should never have asked Scarlett to be my surrogate. I should have known what her response would be. I did know it, I just didn't want to accept it because every so often in life a wave of change comes along and then – given the right tide – things can all work all right. I lean back, closing the curtains, hearing the family's excited voices approaching now down my drive and wanting to join in their Christmas cheer. But I sense that this year, it's really going to cost me.

Scarlett

Damn it.

I close my eyes, pull my legs up to my chest on the wooden bench in the gazebo, and Ruffles jumps up after me.

I *saw* Hollie's face when they all trooped in about half an hour ago, announcing the 'happy news' that Sarah and Jay were expecting in the autumn. She immediately broke open the champagne, good hostess that she is, but I thought that the effort of smiling was going to make her face crack. Christ, what kind of timing is that?

I can hear them from here, clinking glasses and laughing and moving about in the kitchen, but I don't make a move. When I peer through the glass, it isn't raining outside but there is so much water in the air that long rivulets are running down the windows. I hope they can't see me in here.

'I can't stay outside forever pretending to take you out for a walk, can I?' I lean forward to scratch Ruffles under the chin. 'They'll know something's up.'

Ruffles growls, as if in agreement. Hollie's been organising her dinner party all day as if everything is normal, as if we didn't have *that* conversation this morning.

But everything isn't normal. Ruffles is sitting stock-still, eyes locked devotedly on mine as if he really understands what I'm saying.

'I know she's upset about this whole baby thing, but I offered her what I could. I said I'd donate eggs for her. And even that is more than I want to do; I only offered because she is desperate and sad and I felt I somehow *should*.' I give Ruffles a rueful smile. 'Just to give her even *more* reason to be upset with me, I just remembered I already ate half the raspberries that she set aside for dessert earlier. Just you wait till she discovers that!'

There is a rap on the wet glass of the gazebo. I sit up guiltily.

'Just you wait till Hollie discovers what?' Richard enquires.

'I ate Hollie's raspberries,' I confess. 'But apart from that . . . look, if you've been sent out here to fetch me, I need to know she's not still upset about what happened earlier.'

'Sarah announcing that she's expecting, you mean?'

'No!' I give a small laugh. 'Though I don't imagine that went down too well. I mean . . . about what happened between Hollie and *me* earlier.'

'I don't know, Lettie.' He ducks under the doorframe, running his hands through his damp hair and I remember he hasn't been back home long. '*Was* she upset with you earlier?'

'I think so . . .' I tell him quietly. He sits down beside me and I shove over a bit. 'Yes, she was upset with me. She's been rushing around like a demon all morning . . .'

'Poor Hol. This dinner party has given her a lot of work, hasn't it?'

'She *loves* it,' I retort. 'She loves being the hostess with the mostest and having her family all around her . . .'

'She does,' he agrees softly, 'but she's under a bit of strain right now. Don't take it to heart if she snapped at you. Is that the reason you're hiding out here?'

I shake my head. He hasn't asked me what I've done to upset Hollie, I notice. Perhaps he already knows?

'Oh, I don't know! Sometimes families are so complicated, aren't they?' Ruffles is standing up on the bench now, nuzzling his face into Richard's neck. 'It's not so for dogs, is it?'

He smiles into Ruffles' fur.

'D'you suppose Ruff still remembers the day he and I first came into your life? Is that why he adores you as much as he does?'

'Do you remember that?' Rich glances at me for a second. 'I'd never seen such a forlorn sight. That hit-and-run driver just left you with the dog after he'd run over his legs.'

'And you were just on your way to some important meeting. I remember you had your suit on and a briefcase. It was a Tuesday and it was raining and it was dark and there was hardly anybody else about and you picked him up and you told me to come along with you and you said . . .'

'Whoa! A Tuesday?' he interjects. 'You've got some memory.'

'You said . . .' I shoot him a glance '. . . you would take him to the vet's for me and you did. You put him in your car and then you walked me to Hol's office because you said I shouldn't get in the car with a stranger.'

'You were only – what – ten?' He shrugs.

'I was thirteen. Nearly fourteen. I was a late developer, that's all.' My fingers accidentally brush against his as we both stroke the dog and I put my hand in my pocket instead, getting out my mobile phone. 'Look,' I tell him, clicking on the photos icon on my phone and changing the subject. 'These are the people who I need to get the money together for.'

'These are your friends?'

My friends. Yes. That's Guillermo standing there in the middle with his arms about my bare waist. I look pretty good in that one. Pretty fit. There's no mistaking the way he's looking at me while everyone else is busy posing for the camera. I glance up at Richard to see if he's noticed but if he has he isn't showing it.

'These people?' he frowns.

'No. Those are PlanetLove people and – other friends. I'll show you the Yanomami now.'

'Oh!' Richard laughs at the next one, leans in closer towards me so he can get a better look at the screen.

'That little guy brandishing the venom-tipped spear is José. He's my best buddy out there. Either him or his dad, the shaman Tunga, are always my guides when we're out scouting for plants. His mother Lalu is teaching me their dialect and I'm trying to teach her some English . . .' I trail off because seeing them makes me feel sad. They need me and I need to get back to them.

'Do you know,' I put my hand over Richard's now as the screen blanks out all by itself, 'what it is Hollie has asked me to do for her?'

Richard looks down and I see that he does indeed know.

'She wants me to have your child,' I continue and the robin redbreast who's been singing his heart out on the gate flutters down onto the lawn.

I flush. That's not what I meant. Hollie wants me to carry *her* child, of course. Well, using my eggs. And Richard's um . . . I clear my throat. His child, yes, that's it then, isn't it? She wants me to have *his* child *for her*.

'What do you think about that?' I murmur.

He looks up and his blue eyes hold mine for an instant. 'It would be the greatest act of charity,' he admits, and his answer throws me into even further confusion. I never thought of it like that. PlanetLove is charity. I consider the work I do for that organisation to be of a charitable nature because I'm doing it for the greater good. I'm doing it for a very small wage.

But this thing . . . *he wants me to do it, then?*

I cross my legs in front of me, wrapping my arms around them so as to half-hide my face.

'You want me to do it, Richard?'

'I'd be very happy if you would at least consider it, Scarlett.'

'You would?'

'We both would. It's not something I'd want you to rush into without considering all the implications first, though.'

'I owe you so much, Richard.' I jump up off the bench because I can't stay still any longer. 'I mean, both of you. You and Hollie.

Of course I'd love to give you – both – the chance to have this child. I thought maybe if I donated some eggs that might do it but . . .'

'I know.' He picks up my hands for a fleeting instant then drops them. 'She wants you because she trusts you. We wouldn't want you to do this thing because you feel that you owe us anything. You don't owe us a thing.'

'Of course I owe you! Hollie took me under her wing after Flo passed away, didn't she? I know she's my sister and all and she sort of had to, but I still owe her – pretty much everything.'

'She did everything she did for you because she loves you, sweetie. Not because she felt she had to. If you decided to go ahead with this for her – and given where you're at in your life right now, it would be a huge sacrifice, let's make no bones about that – then you must do it for love, too. Not because you want to please her or,' he lowers his eyes, 'me. But because it's an act of love.'

I am silent for a while, taking it all in.

My initial reaction might have been no, but I suppose I *could* do it. Why not? I glance at Richard and I'm aware that my heart has started hammering very fast again. People have babies all the time and it doesn't slow them down or get in the way of their life.

'Lettie, don't give us your answer now. Think long and hard about it before you agree. It won't be a small commitment. Once you make the decision you won't be able to back out of it easily.'

'Do you think that I would?' I lean back against the glass walls of the gazebo, challenging him. 'Do you think that I lack commitment?'

'Lettie, that isn't what I'm saying. It's you who I'm thinking of, right now. Thank you for being so . . . willing. But the more I think about it . . .'

'You sound a little bit conflicted over it,' I prompt. I let my hand come to rest on his knee. 'Are you?'

68

'If I'm honest, I have my reservations.'

'Because it's me?' I ask softly and he looks away. 'Because I have changed, Richard, I do think more about other people's interests now and not only my own. Do you believe me?'

He doesn't look convinced, but it's true. I smile as Richard – always so proper – takes my hand and places it gently back on my own knee. When I set out to make my way home via Venezuela just under a week ago I had the welfare of my second family in the forefront of my mind. I was absolutely clear about what I had come back to do.

Now everything has changed. I never expected that these two would want anything from me, especially anything so huge and so *intimate* as this, but . . .

Maybe that's all to the good. I glance at Richard but he's already taken pity on shivering Ruffles and is leading him back into the house. I have to hurry to catch up with them as he ducks through the low doorframe now and into the house, but my mind is in a spin, open suddenly to new possibilities, new ways forward out of the different dilemmas which we're *all* facing.

Hollie wants something that only I can do for her.

I want this cottage. I need it.

Besides, if they start a family, as I said to Hollie, they'll want something bigger, something more practical. If I have my sister's baby for her, then she won't mind moving. She'll *have* to move. And when they sell Florence Cottage, I'll get my share of the money due from the sale.

Maybe there's a way we could all win?

Hollie

I don't want to be like this. I don't want to *feel* like this, but I can't help it. I've been trying for a baby for so long and *she* only came off the pill two months ago . . .

I glance at Sarah's svelte figure in her dark coat walking up in front beside Jay and the others and a shudder of envy cuts right through me. I hang back, not wanting to join them, they'll see how I'm feeling . . .

'Hey, you there.' The young man in a hoodie looms out at me suddenly from the cathedral arch, startling me.

'I . . . haven't got any change,' I say automatically. 'I just put everything I had in the collection plate.' That was my pretext for hanging back and letting everyone else get ahead of me anyway.

'I don't want any change. I saw you go in. I've been waiting till the service finished.' His face . . . do I know him? It's that guy I saw out on Jackson's field, I'm almost positive, If only he would come out of the shadows . . . but I can feel a tightening in my chest, a panic rising standing here talking to him, suddenly regretting that I urged the others to go on, that I'm alone . . .

'I wanted to talk to you.'

'Well . . .?' I find my voice all of a sudden, 'I don't want to talk to you.' I veer away from him in a panic, my feet skidding on the wide pavement beneath me. We've just heard midnight mass and there are little patches of black ice here and there on the pavement.

'Rich.' I catch up with him and Chrissie who've hung back a bit for me. 'Wait up!'

'Are you all right, darling?' Chrissie pulls a concerned face at me now and I make an effort to shake myself out of it.

'It's nothing. That . . . that young man in the hoodie under the cathedral arch, just now – I thought he knew me. But I was mistaken,' I say to distract them. Rich and his mum look back, but the guy's already disappeared.

'Oh. Probably just a drunk. Still – while it's just the three of us together – I want to thank you both for the wonderful evening. The dinner was scrumptious, Hollie. And I really enjoyed the singing in the cathedral just now. We should make a tradition of this, don't you think?' Her glance shoots towards the couple up ahead of us. 'Do it every year?'

She's got Sarah's baby on her mind, I know. That guy was nobody, I decide. A drunk, like she said.

'*We* could, I suppose, though Jay and Sarah might be otherwise occupied.' I make an effort to get back to the here and now.

'Oh, the baby could come too. It's a family affair, isn't it? I saw several kiddies in there tonight, they seemed to be loving it.'

Rich and I saw them too. We couldn't take our eyes off them, they looked so cute in their Christmas togs . . .

But now Richard is very quiet, I notice. He seems thoughtful. At least Scarlett – walking on up ahead of everyone with Bill – is back in her usual high spirits. When she went out with Ruffles earlier she took so long coming back I thought maybe she wasn't ever going to. I was so relieved when she walked in at last on Richard's arm. Trust him to go out and find her. He knows how much it means to me to have her here for the festivities. I've missed her. Even though I was a bit mean to her this morning. God knows why. She hadn't done anything wrong. I couldn't resent her for saying no to my request. I don't *blame* her.

We stop at the top of Boley Hill so Chrissie can get her breath back. We've almost reached the entrance to the castle courtyard by the gates. In a moment we'll cut across the patch of lawn and down the steps back onto the Esplanade again but, for now, the night is so silent and still you can hear the crunch of everyone's shoes against the icy blades of grass. We pause for a moment, just taking in the sheer beauty of it. Richard nudges me and when I look towards where he's pointing there's a sprinkling of hoar frost on the ground, the street lamps picking it out, lighting it up like sugar frosting on a cake.

'Apparently, it's officially Christmas day already,' Bill calls out over his shoulder. 'The *kids* want to know if it's OK to go back and open up their presents now?'

I can see my sister doubled up with laughter at his request. This'll be her idea, no doubt.

'What – right now?' I work at keeping the disappointment from my voice. It's been a good evening; a success, I think. But I really would rather just go to bed when we get back.

'Maybe just a nightcap then?' Jay puts in, his arm tucked protectively around Sarah's shoulders. 'If that's all right?'

But it won't be just a nightcap, I know. They're all too awake and alert still, too excited. Like kids before Santa comes. They'll end up wanting to open up all the presents under the tree, too. I was hoping that would wait until tomorrow but it looks as if the evening's going to be dragged out a little longer now.

I shouldn't complain. At least it means they're all having a good time. I shoot a glance at my husband but his face is impassive. He'll go along with what everyone wants. With whatever *I* want, I know.

'Come on! If we *do* go back now, we could all find out what we've got each other, don't you think?' My sister's face is bright with excitement. Her blonde hair escaping from her bobbled hat frames her face just like an angel's. 'I already know what you and Rich have got me, Hollie. I had a feel of it earlier.' She's walking backwards beside Bill now, so she's facing us. 'It's that multi-coloured cashmere jumper I saw yesterday, isn't it?'

I shrug my shoulders, not telling. Trust her to have figured it out already!

'And yours.' She turns to Bill, teasing. 'I'm pretty sure Hol's got you some fetching bedsocks from the very same place . . .'

Bill laughs, rolling his eyes in mock delight. 'I've already had the very best Christmas present with the news we've had tonight.' He shoots an appreciative glance in Jay and Sarah's direction. 'A man of my age, well, I've already had pretty much everything a man could want in his life. There isn't much left that I'm hoping for . . .' He's seventy-eight, ten years older than Christine.

'It *is* the most wonderful news but that isn't the kind of present Scarlett was thinking of, I'm sure.' Christine looks at her husband pointedly. Then we all stand there awkwardly and no one speaks until Christine pipes up again.

'Oh, is that . . . is that the bridge being closed in *both* directions?' She's trying to divert the conversation, but she doesn't need to. I know Bill didn't mean to be tactless. He just expressed what was in his heart, and why shouldn't he talk about his joy at one of his boys finally presenting him with the news of a grandchild?

'It's . . . um, it looks like it,' Sarah murmurs. We all turn to watch as the cone-dropping lorry borders off all entry and exit points to the new bridge as well as the old one.

'Good grief, so it is.' Jay leans over the courtyard wall overlooking the bridge. 'Whatever are they doing that for?'

I don't know. I should know, but I've been far too preoccupied with domestic matters recently. I shall need to pull my socks up in the New Year.

'I *think*,' I rack my brains, trying to remember seeing any recent memos that could have come in, 'it *might* be something to do with the heavier flow of traffic that's anticipated during the Christmas period.'

'Except there won't be now, because they're closing the new bridge? That's going to be a darn nuisance surely?'

'I suppose it is.' My mother-in-law settles by the cold stone wall beside him. 'We're all just used to the convenience, aren't we? But you have to admit it's all rather lovely as it is. Quiet and peaceful. No traffic. Just a few people walking back home in the early hours of Christmas morning. Sometimes we appreciate things all the more if we can't so easily have them.'

She squeezes my hand gently behind her back. *You and Rich are going to be all right*, her eyes seem to say when she turns and smiles at me now. *I've got a strong feeling about this. Trust me.* I manage a small smile in response, but I know it doesn't quite reach my eyes.

Trust, I think. Surely to trust you have to have something to trust in? I can't just put faith in the notion that a magic solution will suddenly come winging its way out of the air. I need to know where the answer is going to come from.

'And expecting at least *one* of the bridges to be open is not too much to expect, surely? We *are* used to the convenience. It's the twenty-first century, Mum.' Jay's still chewing over her last comment. 'There's been a bridge on this site for nearly two thousand years, isn't that right, Hollie?'

I nod.

'There you go then.' He grins at his mother. 'That's a long time to get used to the convenience of the thing.'

'Two thousand years?' Sarah picks up the diversion. 'And this bridge is only such a very short distance across.'

'Five hundred metres,' I murmur. 'A long way for the medievals. Not much to us, I admit.'

'But if something's beyond your reach it might as well be a thousand miles, eh?' Jay shoots a sympathetic glance towards his brother and somehow, despite everyone trying their best to talk about something else, we're back onto the subject of the baby again. Scarlett sidles up to Rich and takes his arm protectively. She can probably imagine what he's feeling, and I feel grateful that she's noticed. I just wish that everybody wouldn't take every

74

random mention made as a reference to the fact that Richard and I have not been able to produce a child yet . . .

'Oh, come on! Nothing needs to be beyond anyone's reach these days.' Scarlett stamps her feet impatiently and the sound of cracking ice beneath her boots echoes around the still courtyard. 'It's cold! I want to be getting back. And I *wanted* to tell Hollie and Rich what I'm giving them for Christmas but if you're all going to be party-poopers then I'll tell you here and now before you all disappear off to bed.'

Everyone turns to look at my sister expectantly. Rich folds his arms, glances at me.

Whatever she's giving us for Christmas, *trust her* to have to make a song and dance about it. I love my sister to bits but why can't she just be understated and tactful and quiet and *normal* for once?

'I've thought long and hard about this so I don't want anyone telling me to think again,' Scarlett announces grandly. 'I've decided to give Hollie and Rich a baby; I'm going to be their surrogate for them.'

'Good God!' Bill's shocked voice is the first response to her revelation.

'Well?' Scarlett's face is expectant as she turns to me now. 'Are you pleased?'

I can't take it in. She's going to do it? Is she?

'I'm . . .' I look at Richard, feeling my heart suddenly going ten to the dozen. She was so adamant that she wouldn't, and understandably so.

Rich looks as shocked as I feel. He gives me a little shake of the head, denying any prior knowledge of this, but now Scarlett comes and puts her arms around both of us.

'Group hug, group hug!' she says. 'Take a picture, Christine.' And my mother-in-law, bemused and beaming, takes out her camera and obediently captures the moment.

'Are you really pleased? Neither of you is saying anything.'

Photo-shoot over, our little group is suddenly animated and buzzing again, everyone murmuring appreciatively in Scarlett's direction, hugging her and each other and commending her on her generosity and her lovely gesture. But I still can't take it in. She's got her work in the Amazon to go back to. How is she realistically going to do what she's promising me she'll do?

I push those nagging doubts away because . . . oh, because I've always got nagging doubts about everything.

'I'm only attaching one condition to it,' Scarlett adds, laughing, and everyone's eyes are back riveted on hers. I glance at Rich and his eyes seem to narrow a fraction. Does he know something about this after all? But the next instant his shoulders relax as Scarlett announces, 'I want Hollie to promise me she'll take some action to get over her morbid fearfulness and do something a little risky and daring.'

Sarah laughs nervously at this and Jay gives a small cheer, egging Scarlett on.

'It's something I've been nagging Hol to do for ages, but my sister's as stubborn as hell . . .' Gentle laughter again. 'However, I *really* think this is something that would help you, sis.'

'O–K.' I look at her, on tenterhooks while we all wait for her to come out with it. The silence stretches out like a piece of chewing gum, taut and unending, waiting for someone to come along and make it snap.

'I will have your baby for you but in return I want you to promise that you'll learn how to swim. Agreed?' Scarlett finishes and everyone heaves a collective sigh of relief.

Everyone except me, that is.

Christine gives a little clap and Bill actually says 'Bravo!'

No. No. *No*. She knows what she's asking of me. She of all people knows it.

'Sounds like a fair exchange!' Bill puts in jovially. 'Got off lightly, I'd say. She's just a little surprised, aren't you, dear?'

I hesitate, then I nod at her. My voice has temporarily deserted me. My God, she's going to have our baby! As for this 'condition' she's attaching to it, well, I'll worry about that later . . .

'You need to face your fear, Hollie.' She turns to the others and our little group starts to make its way back to Florence Cottage.

'When you start off learning to swim they only put you in two feet of water, anyway,' Sarah is reassuring me, but my head is buzzing. I can feel Richard's arms about my shoulders, hugging me as we walk along the crunchy pavement. The tiny granules of ice on the ground are like diamonds, a scattering of jewels before our feet just for the night.

'Two feet? You'll be able to stand in it,' Scarlett calls out over her shoulder. 'You'll be fine, Hollie, believe me. After all, in two feet, what's the worst that could happen?'

Hollie

What's the worst that could happen?

I don't know. I don't know how many feet of river water I went down in – was it more than two?

Sometimes I get a flash of it. The dark water envelops me, fills up my nose and my eyes and my mouth as I go down. I want to get back up and I'm fighting for that, my limbs scrabbling uselessly because there is nothing to hold onto.

All I can think of is I want to see the daylight again – one more blue sky shot through with gold, one more purple crocus on the grass verge. I want to stand at the top of Rochester Keep and smell the stiff salt wind as it blows in from the sea, see the ripe peaches on the market stall, hear the white pigeons cooing along the roof. I want to sit on the embankment and feel my fingers skim over the blades of grass on the warm earth on a new summer's morning, but the light disappears above, the cold thrusts like a sword through my innards, my hair is floating upwards.

I don't dream much now. I put the lid on that several years ago. And as for the question 'How bad could it be?', don't ask my head because the answer is stored somewhere else, deep in my body. I keep my memories locked like tigers in their cages and I never bring them out, I never see them, only sometimes I think I can hear them roar.

Scarlett

Dear Ms Hudson,

It has been brought to our attention that there may be a problem regarding the job application you put forward to us before taking up your current post. In order to help resolve any issues as speedily as possible, it would be appreciated if you could make an appointment with one of our directors at the PlanetLove Administration Centre, Berkeley Square, London, at your earliest convenience.

Yours, etc.,

William Barnoble.

I have no idea what this guy is going on about. William Barnoble. Never heard of him.

'Hey.' There's a quiet knock and then Rich peers around my bedroom door. I close down my laptop, flashing Rich a quick smile. There's no point worrying. It's probably just a stupid administrative mistake.

'I'm sorry,' I apologise as his gaze pans over the mess of papers on the floor. 'It's a bit, er . . . there's a teensy-weensy spot over here on the bed if you want to come in, though?'

'Busy girl.' Richard threads his way carefully through to join me. I move the files on the bed up a bit. He's got his dark blue skinny jeans and a black T-shirt on today: long-sleeved, I notice; it's still damp and foggy outside.

'Sorry to disturb you.' He sits down gingerly beside me. 'What are you up to?'

'Fund-raising,' I tell him decisively. 'I've still got to raise that £400,000 for Brazil that I told the family about. Christmas Eve, remember?'

'It's a lovely, caring thing that you're doing but . . .' He raises an eyebrow. 'You aren't worried it might all be something of a tall order, Lettie?'

'Not at all. Look, I've written to all these companies. I've had encouraging telephone contact with four of their CEOs already and I'm making a list of who it's worth really targeting and who I should use a scattergun approach with. It means stacks of paperwork, of course, and I'm planning on setting up as many meetings as I can just as soon as people are back from the Christmas break next week.' I pause to draw breath.

'I've already asked my dad, but to be honest I'm not sure if our firm are going to be able to help you.'

'Not even a little bit?' Oh. I thought they might give me some small amount. When I spoke to Bill last week at Christmas he seemed so encouraging of my efforts. Any little thing would be a start. I straighten my back and look Rich right in the eye, letting him see my disappointment.

'We've pretty much got our backs against the wall as it is. The firm's been scrabbling around for every penny for months now. Yours is a worthy cause, no doubt about it, but when the going gets tough, charity's got to begin at home, hasn't it?'

'I guess.' I purse my lips and let my gaze run over the twenty or so letters I've already printed out this morning. Let's hope they don't all feel the same way.

'I think you're going to find it difficult, Lettie.'

'That doesn't mean it can't be done, does it?'

'No.' He gives me the ghost of a smile. 'But be warned it's tough for businesses everywhere. I'm having to fly out to Trieste soon. Yes, we're needing to look that far afield for work,' he answers my surprised look.

'What, would you work out there? I mean, *permanently*?'

Hey-hey! Are they thinking of moving out of the cottage after all? My ears prick up.

'I don't know if Hol would be too thrilled about that.' He looks away suddenly.

'How about you though?'

'I wouldn't go anywhere without her . . .'

'Hey, you're allowed to have your own dreams, though? Your own hopes? Even if Hol doesn't agree with you. She can't have it all her own way, all the time, can she?' I press, aware that I'm positioning myself into the one tiny space there possibly exists between them, playing devil's advocate.

'Well, I guess I *have* long hankered after the dream of one day living and working abroad,' he confesses suddenly. 'I did a year's study in Italy when I was a student . . .' He smiles shyly at me.

'And there's a part of you that's always hoped to return there?' I finish.

'It's true. Now that Dad's needing to find a gentler way of occupying his time it would suit him and Mum down to the ground. I can't see as Hol would ever feel able to prise herself away from this place though . . .'

'Maybe *you* will have to prise her, then?' I laugh, grabbing his arm.

'Prise Hol?' He shakes his head disparagingly. 'Sometimes I wonder if she isn't more wedded to this place than to . . .' He leaves his sentence unfinished on what is clearly, if not a bone, then at least a splinter of contention between them.

'Come on, Rich. My sister can be stubborn. And she's wedded to this place, as you say. But maybe Florence Cottage just provides . . . roots for her, you know. Because we didn't have any parents. It's like this place has become a sort of anchor for her, standing for everything that's lasting and safe in her life.'

Richard falls silent and I can feel my words sinking in.

'An anchor? That makes sense,' he murmurs. I give him a slight nudge, lean my head in towards him affectionately. I want to help him, I do. And if Rich can get a grasp on what it is that ties my sister to this place then maybe he can help me untie her from it. I have to. It's probably the only viable fund-raising activity I have in the long run . . .

'But do you think,' he's examining his hands minutely, 'what with Hol having all the concerns about the baby on her mind right now, it would be unfair of me to push it?'

'When has she *not* had a baby on her mind, Richard?' I mutter lowly. He winces slightly at that, and for an instant his face looks so naked, so desperate, I want nothing more in the world than to give him a great big hug. But I don't.

Because suddenly, where we're sitting crushed so close up together, I can feel the warmth of his thigh against my thigh. Out of nowhere, I'm acutely aware of the proximity of him.

'Lettie . .' he begins.

'*Scarlett*,' I raise my chin a fraction. 'I want you to call me Scarlett.' Because that is the deep pulsing colour of flames dancing in the heat of the fire. It is the colour of blood, and so of life and death. It is the colour of danger and lust. Don't call me Lettie, which reminds me of a limp lettuce leaf that's been pushed round somebody's salad plate.

'Scarlett,' he says in surprise. 'OK. Well. I just want to say thank you. Talking to you just now has been really helpful. More than I can say.'

'Has it?' I allow myself to lean in towards him the slightest fraction. I know I shouldn't, but I'm only teasing really, toying, playing with my brother-in-law. 'How so?'

'You're just so . . . . understanding. So wise. What you said about why Hol finds it so hard to cut her ties to this place – I don't know why I didn't think of it before. Sometimes I think you must be an angel in disguise.'

I feel a warm glow in my stomach at his praise. An angel. He called me that once before when we danced together one time. Aeons ago. When I was fourteen. Does he remember that, I wonder?

I lower my eyes and look back up at him from under my lashes. Frustratingly, he's not even looking at me any more. He's looking at his hands, folded on his lap. He seems – quiet and peaceful. Not like he's going through any of the inner turmoil that I am experiencing at the moment.

'Oh, well.' I shrug abruptly, picking up a pile of letters that are about to slide off the bed and marshalling them. 'Now, this particular angel really needs to get her begging letters in while people are still feeling generous after the Christmas period, Rich.'

'Of course.' He stands up and I close my eyes as I feel his lips kiss the top of my head. 'Just . . . don't work yourself too hard, will you?'

I deliberately don't watch as he makes his way over the papers and out of my bedroom. OK, *think*. I blink back a tear that falls out of nowhere. What's all that about? Maybe I just wish I had a guy like Rich in my own life. Someone as loving and devoted as he is. Someone as caring and considerate. Does Hollie really even know how lucky she is to be so loved? I don't know that she does.

But that's none of my business. I have my own life to be concerned about right now. My friends waiting for me in the Amazon, my seed collection, all my plans for future projects. My work. My eyes fall on my open laptop again and I'm reminded what I was doing a few moments ago before my brother-in-law came in. This email from the PlanetLove guy – this is the kind of thing I need to be concentrating on right now, or I might not have any job to go back to even when I do get my papers renewed . . .

Hollie

'So. You are – uh – OK?' Mr Huang's little white consultation room is crammed with shelves full of tall glass jars promising magical-sounding solutions: *liver problems, backache, women's problems*, they announce. The jars are packed with exotic-looking dried herbs but in smaller tablet form you can buy a whole range of other herbal medications, these labelled in Chinese: *xiao ke ning wan*. I read the labels while he's getting out my notes: *suan zao ren tang wan*. I have no idea what any of those do.

'I'm perfectly fine, thank you.' I've still got my handbag on my knees, my fingers clasped around it. 'I mean, I'm in good – actual – health.' *I'm here because my pesky sister has forced me to make a promise I'm going to find it very hard to fulfill.* How do you explain something like that?

'You have no more problems here?' He indicates the area above his pelvis.

'The infected fallopian tubes? Oh, no.' I shake my head with a grateful smile. 'After you worked your magic, Mr Huang, I never had any more trouble with them again,' I assure him.

'Trouble for too long,' he sympathises. He's right. In my early twenties I had infections in my tubes for years that no doctor seemed able to cure or alleviate. I'd turned to Mr Huang's acupuncture in the end, more in desperation than hope but whatever he'd tried did the trick.

'And babies?' He looks at me curiously now. 'They come?'

I shake my head.

'Ah, big shame,' he says softly. Mr Huang's been paused with his pen hovering quietly over his writing pad for the last few minutes. Now he writes something down in Chinese letters.

'Yes,' I say shortly. 'It's a shame.'

The sounds of forest birds start up faintly in the background now as his tape suddenly kicks in. Mr Huang smiles softly. *Carry on*, he gestures.

'Actually I'm here about something else entirely today, Mr Huang.' I pause, knowing that what I'm going to say will probably sound silly to him. 'The thing is, I have a phobia. I want to know if acupuncture could help.'

'You have phobia?'

'It's very trivial,' I apologise again, feeling my throat constrict. 'I have this . . . thing . . . about water. I can't swim. Well . . .' I give a short laugh. 'It's more than that. I can't even *think* about going in the water or on a boat.' My fingers curl around the handles of my bag. 'I don't know if you can help a person with a problem like that?'

'You have fear of the water,' he says thoughtfully. 'You have it always?'

'Ever since I fell into the river one time. I thought I was going to drown. I *might* have drowned. My sister's been on at me to learn how to swim for years,' I add hurriedly. 'I *should* know how to swim. All the little kids know how to do it. I don't know how I ever missed out on that.'

He has put the pen down on the table thoughtfully. He takes my wrist now and places it on a little piece of sponge, holding it between middle finger and thumb. For a minute or two we are silent while he searches for my pulse.

'Ah. Could you tell me please . . .' He's softly spoken, polite. I can feel him searching for his words. 'What is your heart's desire?'

'I'm sorry?' I look at him, perplexed. He doesn't seem to have

85

understood. 'I want to learn to swim, Mr Huang. And I can't. I'm too scared of the water.'

'This is it? You want to learn to swim. Nothing else? To swim . . .' Mr Huang presses now, 'this is your deepest desire?'

Well, of course it isn't.

The sounds of the waterfall that come up now on his tape are supposed to be relaxing, I'm guessing. It's *meant* to conjure up visions of crystal clear water cascading over moss-covered rocks some place where the air is clear and sweet – but all that gurgling water, I hate it. It makes me feel sick. It puts me in mind of the stench of stagnant water at high tide, the water dark and flowing with seaweed . . .

'I don't actually *want* to swim, Mr Huang. I need to, that's all,' I confess. 'It's just . . . my um . . . New Year's resolution.'

'You do not want to learn how to swim?'

'To tell you the truth, I can't bear the thought of it. I just have to. Look, it isn't just a New Year's resolution – I made a promise to someone that I would conquer this.'

'Ah,' he nods sympathetically. 'Then – I still have not had the answer to my question.'

He waits patiently for a minute while I rack my brains to remember what exactly was his question. My heart's desire? I don't want to bring all that up again. It's got nothing to do with this at all. But he's still waiting for an answer and here I am in his consultation room, wanting his help, and it seems impolite not to reply.

'My heart's desire,' I tell him in a strangled voice, 'is what it always was – you know that I've long hoped to start a family – to have a child of my own. But I can't see why that's . . .'

He takes one of those wooden stick things – like lolly-sticks – and says 'Open, please', and places it on my tongue. Then he looks under my eyelids.

'Ah, so. And you have been trying *all* this time? For so long?'

Too long, I think, tight-lipped.

'Long enough to worry, ha?'

'Is this . . . relevant, actually?' I shift my bottom on my plastic chair. 'To . . . er . . . learning to swim?'

'It is most relevant.' He leans over and switches off the tape and I feel myself relax instantly.

'It's my sister,' I tell him at last. 'D'you remember I once told you about her, she works abroad? Well. She's back in the UK at the moment and she's agreed to act as a surrogate for me and Rich and have our baby . . .'

'This is most fortunate,' he says approvingly. 'In my country, each family only allowed one child per couple. If couple not fertile, big problems for whole family unit!' he grins wryly. 'Parents not happy. Grandparents not happy. But families can help each other out in this thing. This is good way, and this how we came to have our precious Daisy-Lou, too.'

'You did?' I crane my neck to look at him. 'You used a surrogate to have Daisy-Lou?'

He nods. 'A surrogate *father*,' he says. That's slightly different, but it's the same thing in principle.

'Oh! Who'd have thought it? Do you mind if I ask, Mr Huang, did it take very long?' I ask shyly. He might not want to talk about it, I realise, but it's the one thing that's been bothering me ever since Scarlett made her offer. Scarlett isn't known to be the most patient person in the world. If it's going to take more than one or two attempts she might reconsider . . . 'My sister needs to get back to her job, you see,' I offer by way of explanation.

'Ah, she must return to job. Sister *most* kind to do this for you. If sister is healthy, then it should not take too long. For Mrs Huang, it took only one attempt, which we considered a great good fortune. My wife not so young now,' he explains. 'And time was getting short. Like for you. We had to get conditions right.'

'I hope we can get the conditions right too, then. First attempt isn't too bad,' I say, heartened.

'Now, Miss Hollie. Tell me what you dream of.' He's picked

up his plastic skull with the little meridian lines drawn on it and he's considering it thoughtfully.

'I never dream, Mr Huang,' I tell him, surprised. 'I used to, when I was a kid. But not for years now. Not everybody does dream, do they?'

'Everybody does,' he asserts. 'That is the normal way.'

'Well,' I stop and consider, 'maybe I do, then. I just don't remember them.'

'Ah. Then you must try, Miss Hollie. It is important and – after first treatment, I think, you will become better at this. We say dreams are . . .' his eyes go to the ceiling, looking for the right words '. . . building blocks of future. Come from desire. *Very* important.'

I look at him, confused.

'Now. When you are awake, Miss Hollie. What do you dream of? The child . . .'

I swallow uncomfortably. Why is he asking me all this? He didn't quiz me last time. He just stuck a few needles into some acupuncture points. I imagined maybe he could do the same thing to release the phobia.

'Well.' I squirm. 'Silly little things, really. Daydreams.' You don't talk about daydreams to other people, do you? They're private. 'I imagine . . .' my eyes go up to the small white ceiling, trying to bring something down so I can tell him about it '. . . taking my son up the steps of Rochester Castle – one day when I have one, that is. When he's old enough. My Auntie Flo used to take my little sister and me up there when we were kids. The stone steps are very precarious – well, you live around here, you probably know that – so we'd have to climb very carefully. And it's dark in there. A bit scary, really. It smells all musty and old. But when you get to the top there's . . . this sudden release of light. You can walk along the edges of the battlements and look down over the river. The air is so fresh up there, Mr Huang. It smells of the salty sea wind. She used to say to us – Auntie Flo – that

that's where all the supply barges would come in. Auntie Flo was very big on history.' I realise suddenly I've been banging on a bit. 'Her ancestors had an important part to play in the history of the city so I guess that's why she was so proud of it.'

Mr Huang's eyes shine encouragingly. 'Your ancestors too?' he prompts.

I shake my head, embarrassed. 'She wasn't our auntie by blood. She was . . . she was my mum's best friend. And when my mum couldn't look after us any more she took over everything. Anyway . . .' He nods me on. 'I guess that's my deepest desire: to pass on everything she taught me to my own child. Not to just let it all slip away. Can you understand that?'

'It is sufficient that *you* understand it.'

'I came here because I need to learn how to swim,' I remind him.

'But in Chinese medicine, we say that all things are connected, Miss Hollie. You do not yet know this. Ah, excuse, please.' He stands up as the shop door bells sounds. 'Mrs Huang not here today.'

I'm left in the little white room all on my own. I don't know about all things being connected but I've got to learn to swim because it's the one condition Scarlett imposed on me, and she meant it, too.

'It's not about the swimming,' she told me this morning. 'It's about you facing your demons.'

But I know why she really needs me to do this. Perhaps it's time she faced some of her own demons too? I had an email at work from that guy Duncan this morning. I printed it out to show her but I'm in two minds now about whether that would be wise. I pull it out of my handbag and scan over it again while I'm waiting.

Dear Hollie,
She's back, isn't she? Please tell your sister I need her to make contact with me, Hollie. She should. Life has a way

of catching up with us when we don't fulfil our obligations. Remind her for me.

Regards,

Duncan.

Why Duncan doesn't just contact her himself, I have no idea. Still, I'm not acting as his messenger girl, I decide. Scarlett will only get jumpy if she knows he's after her. What if she changes her mind about sticking around here? The longer he remains out of the picture the better, as far as I'm concerned.

Mr Huang is back, beckoning me from the doorway. As we leave his little room and head down the tiny corridor on the way to his treatment area, the sun is beaming right through the dusty window that looks out over the river.

'Ah.' He pauses, entranced for a moment as some strange looking seagull type thing lands on the mast of a rickety sailing boat. 'Very rare. A Chatham albatross. Where I come from in China we do not have so many birds as you have here. Too many . . .' he searches for the right word '. . . buildings.' He turns to look at me then. 'Do not worry. You know many things. I will be your water teacher and I will help you connect everything up.'

'And you will help me with the – er – fear of water thing?'

'We will use acupuncture and herbs, Miss Hollie, to find the energy blockage.'

'And then,' I prompt, 'this "energy blockage" – you will release it?'

'Then,' he says firmly, 'it will be up to you to release it. Only you can choose to release your own fear.'

'I already choose that.' I grip the handles of my bag a little tighter. 'Then I will be able to swim?' I persist.

'When you release energy blockage, you will be able to *dream*.' He smiles, looking up at the very rare Chatham albatross that's soaring away from us even as we speak. 'Then you'll be able to do a lot more than swim, Miss Hollie. Wait and see.'

Hollie

'When I pop my clogs,' Scarlett nudges me as we drive through the ornate iron gates into St Margaret's cemetery, 'I want to be buried beneath a huge fuck-off angel just like that one.'

Trust you, I think.

'And I want a plot with a magnificent view of the whole place, just like that person has got. I don't want to be tucked away in a corner somewhere with just a view of a boring grey wall.'

Like our mum's got. I sigh, applying the handbrake and opening my car door to check I'm parked in a proper position before turning the engine off. It's cold this morning. It doesn't look it but it is.

'I think it's going to hail,' I tell her. 'We'll have to be quick.'

Scarlett spreads out her hands, palms up as we walk along the path. The sky is greying over but at the moment the air is quiet and still.

'And that person whose headstone you're looking at happened to be married to an extremely wealthy property tycoon,' I point out. 'She *would* get the valley view plot.'

We stop and examine the angel figure. Her eyes are mournfully downcast and her long slender hands are held together in prayer.

'Story goes that the man who erected this memorial was desperately in love with his wife. They say she had an affair which

91

broke his heart but in the end, when she got ill, he took her back and forgave her.' I pull my gloves out of my pocket as a solitary drop of ice falls out of the sky, darkening a spot on the ground in front of me.

'Imagine if *I* ever got to marry a hugely rich man who loved me that much.' Scarlett folds her arms primly. 'What would you think to *that*, Hollie?'

'I bet they're thin on the ground,' I venture. She nods thoughtfully.

'Mind you,' she laughs shortly, 'I suppose you've already got someone like that, haven't you? Apart from the hugely rich bit? Richard worships the very ground you walk on. I'm sure he'd give you anything you asked for.' She tosses her head.

'Within reason, I guess.'

'No, he would, I'm sure. He'd give you anything. I bet he'd even forgive you if you fell for someone else, too,' she adds mischievously.

'Neither of us is about to embark on an affair, Lettie!'

'*Faith.*' She flutters her hand over her heart. 'The very thought of it, child!' She can be a tease, my sister, so I just ignore her and we carry on walking down the path to Mum's plot.

'I just wonder, you know. I always wonder about married people. How can they be so trusting of one another? Is that what *love* is?'

'Do you love us like we were your own kids?' Scarlett had asked Flo once, wrapping her arms around Flo's floury apron, her hands full of sticky apricot jam.

'I love you like the very good kids that you are,' Flo had answered firmly.

'Like your very own?' Scarlett had insisted, her cherubic face looking up at her beloved Flo, holding onto the apron for dear life as Flo swung round from cooker to work surface.

'Who knows what that is, Scarlett? I haven't any of my own, have I? So how can I tell?' She'd rolled her eyes at me over the top of Scarlett's head then, as if I – as the older girl – must surely understand how she felt. But I hadn't understood. Not till that very moment had I ever fully understood the nature of the relationship Auntie Flo had with us girls. She looked after us. She cared for us, and very well too. But did she love us?

'Do you think that's what love is?' Scarlett spins round now to look at me suddenly. 'I think it must be. The tycoon guy forgave his wife. That's true love for you. I think that statue was made of pure marble. What money can buy, eh?' She's got a faraway look on her face, surveying the angel over her shoulder wistfully. 'And, let's face it really, what for? She's dead.'

'True.'

'I really believe if there's any money left over after people drop, it should be spent in improving conditions for the living,' she says piously. My eyebrows shoot up. Has she forgotten she was putting in for a huge angel headstone herself, moments ago? 'I mean, if people weren't so *selfish* with their money there is so much we could honestly do in the world that matters so much more than all this . . .' she waves her hands disparagingly '. . . memorial stonework stuff.'

'Like saving the Amazon forest,' I put in for her before she says it herself. At the moment all roads lead to Rome with her. She needs to raise £400,000 to put towards buying out a tract of forest, I know – she has told us this quite a few times already. There is no other topic of conversation. There is nothing on her mind apart from this one, all-consuming task which she appears to have no idea *at all* how she is going to accomplish.

Except she's warned me this fund-raising is going to take up a lot of her time and she won't have too much spare to be with me. I'm not even sure why she agreed to come up here with me this morning.

'The rainforest. Precisely.' Scarlett gives me a 'you've got it' glance. She takes a surreptitious look around and then, sussing that there's no one near, she sneaks her juggling balls out of her pocket. One, two, three, four balls, all harlequin-coloured, whizz up into the muted morning air as we walk along. 'To bring a bit of jollity to the proceedings,' she answers my raised eyebrow. 'Come on, this is a bit of a dull thing to be doing first thing in the new year, isn't it, Hol? Visiting graves. Do you think she even knows we're here?'

We come to a halt beside Mum's grave. It doesn't look like much. Very *ordinary*, now I look at it through Scarlett's eyes.

'Not much money wasted *here*, was there?' The balls thud down into her palm and stay there. '"Helen Hudson",' she intones. '"Born 1st April 1947. Died 3rd day of Jan 1990. Intrepid explorer, mother and friend." *Christ.*'

Is she looking at that chip in the gravestone that was always there from the first? The bit after 'friend'. As kids we always thought it looked like a question mark: friend?

My sister puts her fingernails to her mouth. 'Is that it? All her life amounted to, in five words? It all seems so . . . bald and . . . somehow sparse, don't you think?' My sister stares hard at the headstone for a few minutes. 'It all seems so unfair. After all the work she put in, to try and better this world. None of it ever got recognised, did it? Do you think sometimes her life was a total waste, Hollie?'

'Well – she had *us*,' I remind Scarlett. 'So whatever we do counts for her too, no?'

Scarlett shrugs.

'What if we don't do anything with our lives either?'

'Anything? Like what?' She doesn't answer. 'Hey,' I feel the need to fill in the sudden space that has opened up in the conversation, 'd'you remember Auntie Flo used to bring us up here every week? We used to bring her up chrysanthemums and place them in a jam jar.'

'Yeah, vaguely. After she died was the only time she was near enough that we could come up and visit her, wasn't it?' My sister kicks at the scruffy graveyard turf with her trainers which are pink and white and petite. 'I know you must have more memories than me . . .'

'Not all that many, Scarlett,' I put in. Lots of memories of waiting for her to come back, I think dully. Lots of memories of bright promises, so many plans made in the heat of lazy summer afternoons only to be forgotten and blown away like leaves in the crisp days of autumn.

'But *some*,' Scarlett insists. 'I can honestly tell you that I have not one memory of being with Helen Hudson. Zilch.' A bright breeze pushes back the blonde tendrils of hair that are hanging out of Scarlett's knitted hat, exposing her face so that for a moment she looks naked and vulnerable. A drop of water lands on her nose and she wipes if off. 'You'd think I'd remember something, wouldn't you? One little thing.' She gives me a crooked smile. 'Sometimes I think – maybe it was me, you know . . . maybe I was the reason she left the UK for good.'

I look at her, puzzled, and she gives a laugh. 'I've got this fantasy that the minute I was born she must have run, screaming, out of the country . . .'

'Why? That's not true. The last time we saw her you were just four years old,' I put in. 'She brought us both straw dolls with painted faces. She took us to London and bought you a huge lollipop in the shape of Big Ben. That was meant to be a keep-sake but you ate it.'

'I don't remember that.'

I shift my feet on the hard cemetery ground. My toes feel freezing. 'After that she went back to South America and stayed for two years before she passed away.'

'Did *I* do that to her?' Scarlett mutters.

'Oh, Scarlett! It was nothing to *do* with you, how could it have been?'

'Why did she leave us for such a long time then? Was I one of those babies that cried a lot? You know, unbearably puky and whiny and horrid?'

I put a hand on her arm. 'You were the most, placid, smiley, *beautiful* baby I have ever seen.' That happens to be the truth. She was gorgeous. I loved her as much as any other child on the planet has ever been loved. We spoiled her rotten too. 'Lettie, Mum left us because she was one of those women who would never have been content staying at home, doing all the domestic stuff. It was never anything in the *slightest* to do with you.'

'Auntie Flo always said that our mum had a vocation,' she says softly. 'Do you suppose that's what it was?'

'I guess you'd understand that one better than me, sis! Let's face it, in that regard you're far more similar to her than I am. I'm a homebody and I always have been. I *think* she wanted to make a difference in the world, and she had this . . . big plan . . . and it mattered more to her than anything. And it *was* something important. It was something that, had she finished it, would have mattered on a worldwide scale, but I suspect it didn't come without personal cost, Lettie.' My eyes flicker up warningly to my sister's face, because perhaps some of our mother's earnestness has rubbed off on her. 'It consumed her, in fact.'

'And then there's you . . .' Scarlett turns to look openly at me now, 'who wants nothing more in the world than to have a little family of her own to look after and that's so sad, isn't it, because . . . it just hasn't happened.'

'No,' I agree softly. 'It hasn't.'

'Which is one a hell of a shame,' my sister runs on, 'because you'd really make the most smashing mummy.' We both glance at the headstone at our feet. 'Whereas *I'd* probably make a goddamn awful one.'

I shiver, watching Scarlett as she pushes her hair in under her hat again.

'Funny the way things turn out, isn't it?' I turn away, pushing down the feeling of unease I feel when she says that. Oh, it's all this hanging about the graveyard – I must be imagining things!

'Hey, it's got darn cold out here all of a sudden, hasn't it? Shall we go?'

I check out my watch. The sky is getting more and more overcast by the minute. We've been here less than ten minutes, but who cares? We came and did the anniversary thing. It matters, somehow, even though I can't explain why it does. I nudge my sister in a comradely fashion as we start making our way back.

'Still want a huge angel guarding over your headstone?' I grin wryly at her as we come up to it again.

'Maybe not,' Scarlett accedes. 'I'd look a bit pompous, wouldn't I?'

'I don't think you'd look pompous.'

'So . . .' Scarlett reaches out her fingers and touches the cold white stone hem, 'he forgave her, even though he loved her so much and she broke his heart. That's kind of sweet, you will admit. I don't know if I would ever forgive a man who broke my heart. Do you think *you* would have forgiven her, Hol?'

'Hell, how do I know?'

My sister laughs, her maudlin mood suddenly lifted. 'If Richard broke your heart, would you forgive him?'

I shrug, laughing back at her then because she's such a funny old thing sometimes and she chuckles gaily, threading her arm through mine. 'Let's run, come on! The sun might have been out earlier but now I'm turning to ice in my boots, aren't you?'

So we run. The hailstorm begins before we even get to the car, pelting us with little balls of ice, making us breathless with laughter and I remember how as children, a huge group of us were playing on the green one moment and then the next thing we were running and screaming to get out of the rain and how I picked her up and tucked her under my coat and carried her because she was so fragile and so small and I loved her more than all the world and wanted to keep her safe.

I don't think she remembers that, either.

Scarlett

'Hey, Scarlett, is that you?' My sister's face appears, all earnest and expectant at the bottom of the stairs. 'Did you remember to take the temperature reading this morning like I told you?'

I roll my eyes, glancing at the calendar on the kitchen wall. How many days have we been doing this temperature-taking business now? It's the 5th January – only ten days? It feels like forever.

'Yup. I took my temperature.' I pick up the phone to make the call I came down to make.

'And what was it?' she breathes. 'You should be near the ovulation part of your cycle now. Did you write it down on the chart?'

Ah, no, I didn't. I was looking for Professor Klausmann's telephone number and I forgot. I've got other things on my mind apart from just Hollie's temperature chart – she doesn't seem to realise that.

'It's on a piece of paper somewhere. On the back of an envelope.' I call out. 'On the coffee table in the lounge, maybe?'

My sister disappears for a minute. She needs to chill out a bit more, let things take their course. I'm not *used* to having people fuss over every tiny little thing any more. It's beginning to get on my tits . . . I open up the fridge door, pondering while I wait to be put through to Professor Klausmann. I want something nice for breakfast, and there's that tiramisu left over from last night but it's got uncooked eggs in it so I'm not allowed that. Hollie would have a fit.

'Professor Klausmann is on the other line if you'd like to hold for just a moment,' a voice informs me in my ear.

'Sure I'll hold.' I'm not sure what to eat. Ever since I made the offer to be a surrogate for my sister on Christmas Eve, she's been flapping about me no end. She says she wants me to be in 'tiptop shape to ensure the chances of a successful pregnancy', in pursuit of which she's got me taking folic acid and vitamin tablets, eating healthily (not a drop of alcohol allowed either) and drinking water by the gallon. I've played along with her so far but the novelty is beginning to wear a bit thin.

I'm going to meet up with Lucy and some of the other girls tonight and I *will* have a glass of wine. Hell, I haven't even attempted to get pregnant yet, let alone got pregnant, so Hollie's going to have to stop being so controlling.

'I'm sorry, he won't be long, do you want to continue holding?'

'Sure.'

I mean, it's not as if it won't happen, is it? For most people I reckon it must be a pretty straightforward thing. I don't imagine all those teenage girls with their unplanned pregnancies ever take any folic acid or watch their alcohol intakes. They just have a shag and, hey presto, it's done!

I shut the fridge door. I'll pick up something to eat at the train station. She won't be able to see what I'm eating, then.

'Is this it?' Hollie's referring to something I cannot see and I don't bother answering.

'Hello, Eric Klausmann here.' The professor's clipped tones come down the line now.

'Ah, Professor . . .' Why am I getting this overwhelming urge to call him 'your eminence'? And where have all these butterflies in my stomach suddenly come from? 'It's me . . . Scarlett Hudson.' There's a pause as he figures out who I am. 'You were kind enough to take up my tutor's suggestion of sponsorship two years ago, for a job in the Amazon I went for.'

'Yes?' With a famous name like his, I realise suddenly, he must get asked to sponsor people all the time. Of course he doesn't remember me . . .

I'm one of the long-listed candidates for the Klausmann Award,' I offer helpfully. 'I just wanted to say, I'm so thrilled and honoured to have been considered . . .'

'Ah, yes, of course.' He's remembering where he's heard my name before, no doubt.

'I'm really honoured,' I repeat stupidly. Oh my God, I've forgotten what I wanted to say to him. Why I rung him up in the first place . . .

'We're holding a symposium on Mycorrhizal biodiversity in the spring,' he says now, randomly. 'I'm looking forward to presenting some of your observations.'

Mycorrhizal what? Oh well, I suppose he can't remember everybody's theses. I swallow down my disappointment. Maybe my work on medicinal orchids hasn't made such a huge impact on the board at King's College?

'Um, Professor, I don't know if you recall but I'm currently working for PlanetLove. With Eve Mitcham. I'm in the UK at the moment, renewing my work permit. I wondered if you'd be available some time today for me to bring up some admin forms that I need you to fill in, confirming that I'm working for Chiquitin-Almeira and all that . . .'

The pause this time is a longer one.

'I'm sure my secretary would be happy to fill in any forms for you if you'd like to post them down to her,' he says at last. 'She's off on holiday next week but any time after that . . .'

'Oh.' I can't exactly insist they rush it through, can I? But if she's away next week the delay might mean Chiquitin-Almeira announcing they're dropping PlanetLove in the meantime . . . 'Actually, if I could bring it up myself, maybe today . . . that'd really help me out, Professor.'

Again, that uncomfortable pause as if he's weighing things up in his mind.

'By all means, if you're in town, I'd enjoy the chance to learn where your views on Mycorrhizal biodiversity come from. Some of your insights were remarkable, I thought. But please don't come up specially. My work schedule is somewhat erratic at the moment.'

'Fine,' I breathe. Damn it. He doesn't know who I am at all, does he? Oh well. That just confirms where I am in the pecking order. I put the phone back in its cradle.

'Scarlett . . .'

I shoot up the stairs when I hear Hollie's voice. If I can get into the shower before she catches me I might still make my train . . .

'This paper?' She's back, waving the scrappy envelope at me, a huge smile all over her face. 'Your temperature's gone up,' she says. 'You're ovulating. Today's the day, honey!'

'Today?' The sudden sickly feeling in my stomach lurches right out of nowhere. Today what? Today is the day I'm due to get pregnant with Richard's baby. I look at her blankly. I wasn't expecting this so soon. I'm not ready, and I've got other things planned right now.

'You OK?' She starts coming up the stairs, a sympathetic look on her face and I back away before she gets to me.

'I'm fine, Hollie. It's just – can we do it later?'

'Later?' She looks surprised. 'Like – when?'

I look at her blankly. I've got other stuff to do – can't she see that?

'This – fertile period, when the temperature goes up – it lasts for a few days, doesn't it? Do we have to do this right now?'

'I'd like you to.' Hollie looks sad. She's waited so long for this now I feel bad about delaying her again.

'I need to have a shower now, that's all. I'm going up to London to see Professor Klausmann.'

'This morning?' Hol stops in her tracks. 'You're going to London *right now*?'

'Yep.'

'Why?'

'Why?' I repeat stupidly.

'What's so important about seeing him today? Can't it wait?'

No. It can't wait. Eve made it perfectly clear before I left Brazil that I needed to get the paperwork at this end sorted as a matter of priority. Because of the fact that new people might be coming in to take over and the whole PlanetLove infrastructure might be on the brink of major changes. Better if I'm already safely 'in place' as Eve put it, before that happens.

But now there's that PlanetLove email to add to my worries as well, I remember unhappily. I haven't even mentioned that to Hollie. That's because I didn't want her fussing. I can sort this out myself. I bolt into the bathroom and shut the door behind me. I can't do this pregnancy thing for her. Not today.

When that PlanetLove email suggests there may be a problem, what could they possibly be going on about?

The possibilities jostle together uncomfortably in my head. My exam results were all kosher. Apart from the maths, where I said I got an A when in fact I got a C. But would they really be worried about that kind of thing at this stage when I've been working for them all this time? It can't be . . . it can't be anything else, surely? I feel the slight sheen of sweat forming on my brow.

No, no no! Get a grip, girl! I am not going to become a worry-wart like my sister. I refuse to.

'Would you mind if I asked you to . . . make the pregnancy attempt first, before you go up to London?' Hollie puts in mildly through the door.

I switch the water on, so the sound of it running will make it seem as if I'm already out of earshot.

What did she say? Something about using a turkey baster and a little vial which holds the sperm – here's some we prepared earlier, sort of thing. Ugh! Poor Hol. How embarrassing is that? It's all so clinical. There's no magical 'making a baby' moment to this method. It's all about the science of temperature and timing.

102

Is this what it's become for *them*, after all this time of 'trying for a baby'? That's so sad. Does each month just become 'another attempt' at the right moment when she's ovulating?

I turn to the bathroom mirror which is beginning to get rapidly steamed up, and muss up my hair, trying to wake myself up, get myself into the mood. This is surreal. This whole morning has been surreal. I wonder if they're really going to use my work at that symposium the professor talked about in the spring? How exciting would that be? How unbelievably thrilling? Maybe I'm actually still in bed and dreaming?

'Scarlett, can you hear me?' Hol calls out louder.

I step in under the running water, feeling the soothing heat of it first against my legs and then down my back. I could write a paper on that thesis. I could have it published in *Nature* – my God, that would be something, wouldn't it? Who'd have thought it? I close my eyes and try to block her out because I need to *think*.

And because I'm feeling really, really nervous about what it is I've agreed to do for her. I never did read that article in the pregnancy mag on the 'possible complications of pregnancy' because I just didn't want to know. But I'm thinking now maybe I should have. Let myself know what I might be in for? It's not always so straightforward, is it? Having an actual baby. I'd opt for a Caesarean but Hol's dead against that and I don't like the idea of stitches down there at all. Oh, why did I ever agree to this in the first place?

I can feel my heart hammering ten to the dozen at the thought of it. I lean against the cool bathroom tiles and try and calm myself down and outside I can still hear Hollie hesitating by the door.

'Scarlett?' she persists.

'I'm having a shower,' I call out in what I hope sounds like a cheery voice. Just be matter-of-fact about this, I keep reminding myself. Just act like this is . . . normal.

You're doing this for *her*, for Hollie. And for José and Tunga and all the rest of them because once I've got my sister on board

103

I will be in a position to help them. It's the right thing to do. So why won't my pulse stop racing? And why won't she go away?

'Is everything OK? Why the sudden trip to see Professor Klausmann? I mean, is it urgent?'

'No!' I yell through the door. 'I just needed to see him, that's all.'

'I see. Well, Lettie, would you mind – if Professor Klausmann isn't really urgent – doing this thing for me first, please?'

'Sure. Whatever,' I sigh. I suppose I don't actually have an appointment to see Professor Klausmann.

I give my face a good rub with my flannel and the mandarin scent of my shower gel wakes me up and invigorates me. I can do this. I can do the turkey baster thing and then get dressed and get on the train and go up and see Professor Klausmann and sort out my own day just like I planned, sure. Why not?

'I'll just go and get everything ready for you,' Hollie is shouting through the door. 'OK?'

'OK,' I shout back. I step out of the shower. I can't believe how cool my sister sounds. She must be making a huge effort.

She must be, surely? Because, beyond all the on-the-surface gratitude to me, she must be feeling a little unease about the fact that she's got to get her sister to do it for her. That she can't do it herself.

Well, I hope she's not going to hold my fertility against me afterwards – feel resentment or jealousy or anything. I saw how she was when she heard about Sarah's pregnancy. She tried hard to hide it but she was dead gutted. Still, I frown, peering into the mirror again and rubbing it over to demist it, I'll not be hanging around here for too long once we've got the pregnancy confirmed.

Just as soon as I've sorted what I came over here to do, I'll be taking my bump back to sunny Brazil to finish off the job, far away from Hollie's prying eyes.

Hollie

That shower has been running for so long Scarlett must have drained the entire tank by now. I sit down on her bed and wait.

I've had a sense all week that today might be the day. I told Richard when we woke up, while we were still lying there in bed. When he looked at me I thought his eyes seemed happy – hopeful, even – but he didn't say anything. He has told me a thousand times that if I cannot have children he will be content. He has told me that he would be happy to adopt or to remain child-less, whatever I choose. But this morning he just hugged me close and kissed me. When I laid my head along his chest I could hear his heart beating hard. We lay there still for so long I thought, if I were quiet enough, I might be able to hear his thoughts and that he must surely be able to read mine.

I propped myself up on my elbows, needing to share the feeling of excitement that was coursing through me.

'I can't explain it, Rich. I know we've been through a long and weary battle to try and start a family but I just feel that this is *it*. It's going to happen for us this time.'

He laughed then, drawing my face closer to his for a kiss.

'I only want whatever makes you happy. But I'm already more than happy, you know that . . .'

Christ. I can't quite believe it. I clasp my hands in front of my face now and the jumbled mess of all Scarlett's clothes and her dog-eared map of the world that is peeling off the wall and all her odds and assortments that we've never quite got round to clearing out of her old room all disappear in a misty haze. This is going to be my lucky year, I know it.

The sound of the ancient water pipes gurgling brings me back to the moment and I open my eyes. How much longer?

But I am being impatient. I look around me, tempted to start clearing up the mess while I wait. This is a huge step Scarlett's about to take, and she's doing it all for me. I have to let her do it in her own way, in her own time, even if my stomach's all jangled up and I can't wait to get on with it. I can still scarcely believe it could really turn out to be this easy, after all we've been through.

No trip to India. No forking out masses of money to get some stranger to do it. No worrying about the health and the motives of the surrogate mother because Scarlett will surely want to spend the pregnancy here, under my own roof.

The shower has been turned off at last, but the bathroom door is still closed. Perhaps I should just lay everything out for her, on the bed? She'll know what to do with it I suppose – it's self-evident. On the other hand, no, I won't, because Richard's working far away from home today and if we have a mishap – if the vial gets spilled or something – then we may miss our chance. I'd better be on hand to make sure it all goes without a hitch, get it done, because, the truth is, I still don't know what it was that brought about Scarlett's sudden change of heart just over a week ago. And I don't know how easily she might change it back again. My butterfly sister is perfectly capable of changing her mind. *Just because*. That's how she always has been.

I get up and go over to the little window which Scarlett always insists on keeping open and I pull it to. She used to spend hours standing on her bed as a child, peering out of that very window. It looks out onto Strood Esplanade. I don't like it. I prefer to keep it locked shut.

I glance behind me; the bathroom door is still closed.

106

'Hey. How are you getting on, sis?'

'Good,' her muffled voice comes back. She must be drying her hair.

'Are you nervous?' I offer. My hands feel so clammy and sticky I don't know what to do with them. I sit there twisting my wedding ring round and round on my finger while I wait. I hear her laugh softly in the background. She doesn't sound nervous. She sounds pleased, excited even. As if she's really looking forward to this experience, and the realisation of that assuages my guilt a little.

I don't remember Scarlett *ever* being nervous, now I come to think of it. Well – only that one time a couple of years ago, when she was dead scared because she'd left the writing of her thesis for the PlanetLove foundation far too late. Ha! I haven't forgotten that look of terror on her face when she suddenly got scared that what she'd eventually written wouldn't be up to scratch, and she'd set her heart on going out to Brazil. She panicked then, all right!

It's the only time I remember seeing my sister looking truly vulnerable. She's always been so up for anything, so game, whereas I . . .

I bend to pick up a heap of her discarded clothes and carry them through to the laundry basket. I crane my neck down the hallway to the bathroom but it's all gone quiet and there's still no sign of her. I want to get this over and done with now, I really do. I hope she isn't bothering with putting on make-up or anything.

'OK?' My sister appears at last, a blue silk kimono robe (mine, unused till this moment, a present from Chrissie last birthday) wrapped about her. Her short blonde curls have all been primped into place, and I can recognise the almond scent of my most pricey hair lotion. She looks wide-eyed and innocent and far too young to be planning on getting pregnant. I feel another momentary jab of guilt. She is the perfect person to do this for me and at the same time probably the very worst.

107

For a moment we just stand there awkwardly. Then she goes and sits down on the bed. She picks up one of her old stuffed toys and holds it on her lap.

'Scarlett.' I sit down gingerly on the edge of the bed beside her, and somehow the words that come out next are more about reassuring me than they are her. 'Are you sure you want to go through with this?'

'I'm cool.' She smiles at me beatifically.

'No. I mean . . . I mean, have you really thought about how this decision is going to impact on the rest of your life? Your work . . .' I have to say all this, even though I don't want to. 'I have to make sure . . .'

When my sister smiles, a cherubic dimple appears on each of her cheeks. She's got that 'I know what I'm doing' look on her face right now. She strokes the bright blue tiger on her lap in front of her.

'It's OK,' she says.

'I was just thinking about Guillermo. The guy you told me about from Brazil,' I press. She only just mentioned him last night, and briefly at that. I have no idea how important he might be. 'Have you thought about how he might take it?'

She looks up, surprised. 'Why should he worry about it? I can't really see that it's any of his business.'

My God. She *hasn't* thought this through at all.

'Well, if he were someone you were planning on maybe having a serious relationship with . . . it might be significant, that's all.'

'This baby is something that I've decided to do for you, Hollie,' she tells me firmly. 'It's between us. You and me. No one else. I carry it, and eventually, when it's done, you get to keep it. So I guess there's no more to be said,' she attests. 'Let's go for it.'

'Well, OK,' I tell her at last. 'If you're really sure. Would you like me to stay with you while you do it?'

My sister looks up, shocked. She puts the blue tiger firmly down on the floor beside her.

'No,' she tells me crisply. 'I *really* don't think that would be such a good idea, do you?'

I flush. Of course. I didn't mean to embarrass her.

'How silly of me. I just wasn't sure if you knew what you had to . . .'

'I've pretty much got the idea, Hollie. I learned about the birds and the bees a long time ago.'

'Well, naturally.' I blush. 'I'll just go and sort out . . . the other side of it then, so to speak?'

'Fine.' She plumps her pillows up on the bed. She wants me to go away. I can see that. I go into the kitchen and stop by the sink for a few minutes to gather my wits. I need to calm down. If I pick up the vial of Richard's sperm in this state of mind then I'll drop it for sure and the day will be wasted.

I feel giddy now. I feel odd.

'So – do you still want to go ahead with this today or don't you?' Scarlett's voice behind me makes me jump. She's followed me out of the bedroom and she's leaning against the kitchen doorway now, arms folded.

'Of course. I'm just checking . . . we've got everything we need.' I fumble in the drawer, looking for the plastic syringe which I bought specially for the purpose. It's wrapped up in cellophane and I pull uselessly at it, all thumbs. 'I had a feeling that today would be the day,' I smile at her, 'so I woke Rich up early . . .' I pause, a little taken aback by the frown that crosses her face for an instant. 'Sorry. I didn't mean to make it awkward for you,' I bluster.

'Is that the um . . . ?' She's staring at the syringe in distaste.

'It's what you'll need to use. The . . . er . . . delivery system, so to speak. We've already got Richard's . . . contribution. It's in the fridge, don't worry.'

My sister's eyes widen and she moves to the counter where I've just put down the syringe.

'OK, so you need me to use this?' She picks it up curiously.

'And you'll also need . . . this.' I open the fridge and hand her the precious vial and she takes it in one hand, and holds it up to the light, peering at the very small amount of semi-opaque fluid in consternation. 'Well, obviously . . . it's . . .'

My sister makes a small choking noise in her throat which she turns into a cough. 'Of course,' she says.

'If you've changed your mind,' I begin, but she waves me away.

'I haven't changed my mind, Hollie.'

'It's just that you . . .' I open my hands, at a loss for words.

'I know what I'm doing, don't you worry.' She's got that look on her face again, the one she always used to get when she was younger and she was being brave about something but didn't want me to see it. I wish she would let me put my arms around her. I wish she would let me *see* how brave she's being in agreeing to go through with this because I know that she must be feeling all sorts of conflicting things right now.

'I've got very good reasons for doing this, Hollie.' In an effort to recover her composure she's gone quite cold and distant. She doesn't need to be like this with me though, she really doesn't. 'I've got the best reasons in the world for doing it so there's no need to look at me so apologetically.'

'I know you're doing it for the best reasons,' I begin but she doesn't let me finish.

'And anyway, there's a favour that I need to ask of you too. A big one. A *huge* one.' Her eyes are glinting. 'There's something you can do for me that's very important for me too,' she promises and then, before I get a chance to say anything else, she disappears into her bedroom with the syringe and the vial, and the door shuts firmly behind her with a resounding *click*.

Scarlett

'OMG. You're having your sister's husband's baby, you say? Omigod!' Lucy sounds scandalised. 'How? When? Does Hollie know about this?'

'Of course she knows. She was in the house with me when I . . .'

'Bloody hell, Scarlett.'

'What?' I ease the phone a bit nearer to my ear.

'This is a little bit risky, even for you,' she breathes down the phone. 'With Hol in the house! And . . . you've barely been back a few weeks. When did you do it?'

'We did it just now.' I've been sitting here with my pelvis leaning up against the headboard for the last five minutes to let gravity take its natural effect, but I'm not sure how long I'm meant to stay here for. I'm starting to feel a bit dizzy. 'Your sister's had three babies, hasn't she? I thought maybe you'd be able to give me a bit of advice.'

'Bloody Nora, the girl's so casual about it. Sorry – did you say you did it *just now*?' I can feel her almost frowning down the line. 'How on earth can you know if you're pregnant then? It takes a few weeks before you find that out.'

'I know that, you wally!'

'You mean you're . . . just hoping?'

'I certainly do.'

'I'm . . . I'm totally freaked out about how casual you're being

111

about it, that's all. Richard's a hunk, I grant you. I used to have a crush on him myself once upon a time . . .'

'On Richard? You did? Hang on a minute, I need to shift.'

'But being with him while Hollie's actually in the house . . .' she gasps. 'Never mind the actual ethical considerations of . . . Scarlett, I have understood you right, haven't I?' The penny is beginning to drop.

'*She* is the one who asked me to become a surrogate for her in the first place. Richard wasn't even here.'

'Oh. A surrogate . . .' There's a pause while Lucy realises her mistake. 'So you did it using a . . .'

'Well, naturally.' I gasp with laughter. 'What do you take me for?'

'Sorry, honey. My imagination ran away with me there for a bit.' God, this is uncomfortable. I hear her giggle before I put down the phone and shuffle my legs a bit higher up the headboard. I look at my watch. *How much longer . . . ?*

'Richard is a hunk, though, you've got to admit,' she says when I get back to her. 'He's just as good looking now as he was when we were fourteen, even better in fact.'

'A hunk who happens to be married to my sister,' I say quickly to shut her up.

'Come on. You used to have a thing for him too,' she remonstrates. 'We both did. We'd wait for him to come round the corner by the newsagents after work and then "bump into him by accident", remember?'

Man, this girl has a good memory. I had forgotten all about that.

'I never had a crush on him. And we only did that "bumping into Rich by accident" the one time. That was because you insisted. We came round the corner so fast you fell over and he had to help to pick you up.'

That's embarrassed her enough to put a lid on it. When she continues, she's changed tack. 'Anyway, surrogacy. Wow. Your boyfriend with the funny name in Brazil – what does he say about it?'

'It's not a funny name. It's South American for William, pronounced Gij-yer-mo.'

'*Gij-yer-mo* then. Is he cool with it? I thought some of these South American dudes could be a bit possessive about their women.'

'I'm not *his woman*!' I baulk. 'And Gui doesn't know anything about it yet. I've been debating how to put it to him.'

'So . . .' Lucy's voice has gone low and confidential again, 'how did you actually – er, I mean, what was it like?'

'Cold and plastic. Shaped like a turkey baster.'

'Yuck! Poor Scarlett. You get all the backaches and the stretch marks and your sister gets all the fun.' This was precisely what I rung Lucy up to have a moan about but as soon as I hear the words coming out of her mouth I just want to tell her to shut up.

'I don't intend to get any stretch marks,' I tell her airily, 'and, as for Guillermo, we're potentially an item – if he plays his cards right – but I'm not his property and he knows that.'

'I'm just saying . . .'

'Well, stop saying. It's annoying . . .'

My back is aching. Enough of this gravity lark. I swing my legs over the side of the bed and sit up.

'It may be annoying to you, but once you're in a committed relationship you have to learn to take the other person into account a little more. Can you imagine,' she runs on, 'what might happen if you didn't?'

Ever since Lucy got married a year ago she isn't so much fun, I realise. Lucy and I go way back – as far as primary school. She's the girl who used to laugh so hard she'd wet her pants then spend the rest of the day walking around without any on. But now she's all prim and proper I suppose she's forgotten about stuff like that.

'I don't worry too much about consequences,' I remind her. She knows me of old. She should know this. I'm lying here now, picking the fluff off my flannelette pillow and it suddenly occurs to me I still need to reply to Guillermo's text from this morning. Should I tell him about what I've just done? Maybe I should . . .

'If you're planning on getting pregnant I imagine all that'll change pretty quickly.'

'I can't see how,' I tell Lucy. 'I have no intention of letting this pregnancy get in the way of my normal life, honey.'

I hear Lucy give a snort at her end. She's an auntie three times over so she reckons she knows everything there is to know about babies but her knowledge is entirely second-hand.

'It does slow you up, Scarlett,' she insists. 'You'll get all sorts. Varicose veins, constipation, heartburn, exhaustion . . .' she tells me enthusiastically. 'You won't be able to carry on in the jungle just like it's nothing.'

'Of course I will!' I stand up on the bed so I can open that ruddy window that Hollie always closes. She's got this thing about heating and everything always being closed. It gets so stifling in here. There's a stiff snow-laden breeze blowing off the Medway this morning and a few icy particles land on my fingers. I put them in my mouth and let the flakes melt on my tongue.

'I shall carry on working right up till the end, just like . . . like all the actresses and other people you hear about do. I don't suppose I'll get too much heartburn and all that stuff – I'm pretty healthy, you know.'

'And morning sickness.' Clearly she's been thinking of other things that could go wrong while she was quiet. 'You'll get that for sure. My sister had three months of throwing up, *constantly*.'

'Your sister doesn't have to work,' I put in uncharitably. 'I do. I can't afford to languish. I'm going back to Brazil the minute the pregnancy's confirmed,' I carry on over her prophecies of doom. 'Then I'll come back once it's time to have the baby and hand it over. Mission accomplished.'

114

'In all that sweat and heat out there, are you sure? And you'll be heavy as an elephant, ankles swollen, hardly able to move . . .'

'People do have plenty of babies out there,' I tell her stiffly. I only phoned her because I didn't want to go straight out and face Hollie just yet. I thought she would be supportive. We used to have so much fun together. I thought she'd be well impressed at how much I've changed. It shows how much I've matured, doesn't it? 'Besides,' I tell her virtuously, 'I'm doing this for an unselfish reason, so don't try to put me off it. I'm doing this for Hollie and Rich. And I'm doing it for my tribespeople too.'

'Oh, yes?'

'Well . . .' I hesitate, wondering whether to fill her in on the most important part of my plan and then I go for it. In for a penny . . . 'As soon as Hollie's expecting she'll realise this place is too small so they'll sell up. The minute that happens, it unlocks my share of the funds from this place so I can use it for PlanetLove.'

'That's very decent of you.' Now Lucy does sound impressed. 'What you're doing is all so worthwhile, isn't it? I wish *I* could do something worthwhile,' she sighs.

'Well,' I console, 'I'm sure all the customers at Interbank Divisions appreciate the sterling job you do. I thought you loved it there anyway?'

'It's Interbank-Eurobank now,' she reminds me. 'And yes, it did used to be great – before all the consolidation measures and chopping and changing about of our roles. It's all a real bummer here. No time for fun any more.'

'Shame.' The thought suddenly inserts itself that I still need to get hold of Professor Klausmann; I need him to sign my papers for South America and I really should be making a move.

'My new boss is a *total* bitch,' she adds venomously. 'In fact I'm even thinking of . . .' She's been playing with something on her desk at work, like a penholder or somesuch, because it suddenly all comes crashing down and she gets all flustered. I

115

can hear her, picking it all up. 'Dave and I are trying for a baby too, as it happens.' Her voice has lowered a notch.

God, the whole world's at it, aren't they? She's kept that pretty quiet. That must be how she knew all about the side effects of pregnancy – she's been reading up on it.

'Hey! We can be pregnant together then.'

'Except you'll be in the jungle,' she reminds me. '*If* you actually get pregnant, of course.'

'Why ever wouldn't I?' My nose is getting cold, standing by the open window. 'Where has all this snow come from so suddenly? What's it like in Snodland? It's coming down thick and fast over here,' I tell her.

'They're expecting over six inches in the Medway later on,' she informs me. 'Trains back home from London tonight will be totally buggered as usual so Dave's called in sick.'

'Crap. I was planning on going up to town in a minute.'

'Don't bother,' she warns. 'I'd leave it till tomorrow if I were you.'

'Anyway,' I suddenly remember her previous comment. 'What d'you mean *if* I get pregnant? It's automatic, isn't it? The body does it all by itself.' From here I can spy the edge of a viburnum bush; I planted that eighteen years ago. It leads into the winter-flowering jasmine that climbs over the trelliswork on the fence. It has flourished and grown beautiful, just like everything I have planted. Just like the baby will. I really should end this conversation and go out and catch that train.

'It wasn't like that for your sister,' she reminds me.

'Well, it will be for me.' I'm certain of it. I've never failed at anything I've turned my hand to yet. I've never even had to try that hard, come to think of it. 'I've got to go, Luce. I bet you I get pregnant before you do,' I tease.

'At least I'm going to have a lot more fun trying,' she coos before she hangs up. Trust her to have the last word on it.

The snow is turning sleety now. Little puddles of melting ice are collecting on the window ledge. My fingers are red and frozen. If I get ready quickly I should still have time to go up to get my papers sorted. I *should* go, but I don't feel like it any more. Suddenly I feel . . . let down and disappointed. I feel as if my day has somehow been hijacked. I really wanted to get my papers signed today, not waste any more time.

'Who'd have thought it?' I freeze at the sound of Hollie's voice beneath my window ledge.

'Oh yes. The retaining wall this time. Front of building next time.'

What's she doing out there with the Bridge Trust's gardener in this weather? I never heard the front doorbell go.

'At least it's only the wall that's got cracks in it.'

'That's the problem with these listed buildings. Can't touch much, and when you do you wish you didn't have to. That's why a lot of folks sell up. Specially young folks. Got no choice, do they?'

He's right, I muse, she should listen to him.

'Come now, it's in the family, isn't it, Gaffer? Can't put a price on that.' That's our next-door neighbour Bea's voice I can hear now. What are they doing out there? Whatever it is, I hope they're not hanging about too long. I was about to go out there and fill Hollie in on her end of the deal and I don't mean learning how to swim. I might as well let her know what I'm expecting, it's only fair. She's far too attached to this place and she's going to need time to adjust to the idea of letting it go.

'Anyhow, I expect you'll be able to sort it before May without too much trouble?'

What's happening in May?

Enough eavesdropping. Time for me to go out and tell her that I've done the deed. That'll cheer Hollie up. With these latest test kits (she's got three in the bathroom) she won't have to wait too long to find out if it's worked, either.

'I'm so glad you agreed to do this, dear.' That's Beatrice's soft

117

voice now. 'Flo would have been delighted to know you're renewing one of the old Florence Cottage traditions. The garden parties she used to hold here every year were one of the highlights of our calendar.'

I hold my breath for a minute so I can hear a little better. What *are* this lot up to?

'The Bishop of Rochester has agreed to open it for us,' Beatrice's saying proudly. 'And the mayor's put it in his diary too. It's going to be quite a charity event. For the rainforest people of the Amazon, you say?'

Oh no; the penny drops. They're trying to raise funds, aren't they? For me. I feel a lump in my throat and sink down off my tiptoes where I've been standing so uncomfortably in order to hear what they've been saying a little better.

A charity event. Oh Hol. That's so thoughtful of you. But the amount of money you'd raise by doing this is titchy compared to the amount that's in my mind.

I flop down onto the bed. I just wish she hadn't gone quite so far with it before telling me what she was planning, that's all. Everybody's going to all this trouble and yet . . . it won't even begin to be enough. I lean over and pick up Hollie's 'delivery system' syringe and throw it in the bin in the corner.

I suppose now I'm going to have to make damn sure I *am* pregnant before I tell her about my plans for the cottage. Just to make sure she doesn't have any qualms about agreeing with me . . .

Scarlett

Dear Scarlett,
Just thought you might like to see your favourite little guy
again as you've been away for a while now . . .

Eve's letter contains a photograph – a 5x8 of José. I grin, noticing
he's got a missing front tooth. He's solemnly holding up a brace
of Paiche with his good hand. He'll have just speared those out
of the river. He's standing by a rock pool, half in the shade. A
smile spreads right through me at the sight of him. It's a nice
picture.

Behind him a stream of pure gold sunlight pours down
through a gap in the canopy. A profusion of bromeliads and
dense green ferns jostle in the foreground, the colours so crystal
clear I can almost hear the tinkle of water running at his feet; I
can almost *smell* it. And those fish: the flesh all pink and fat, the
scales on their heads shining like silver pennies where the light
catches them. The tribe will have cooked those over an open
wood fire later on that evening and everyone will have had a
share in them.

His eyes look strangely dull though. He looks less than happy.

The kettle clicks off and I fill up the pot, leaving it to brew
while I carry Eve's letter through to the better light in the lounge.
She continues:

119

. . . I hope you had a wonderful Christmas with your family.

The not-so-good news at our end is that we've had to move base camp. A whole load of rumours were circulating that gold had been discovered nearby and we had a lot of people coming in and sniffing around the camp, causing us a lot of trouble. They even started a fire which meant we were forced to evacuate camp and leave virtually everything behind. Sleeping bags, personal effects, our food stores and cooking equipment. All our clothes. It all went up so fast I don't know if they even had time to steal whatever they were after before everything was lost. We all ran out with nothing but the clothes on our back, but maybe the worst loss of all was the seeds which we had managed to collect . . .

No way. A huge black cloud descends on me as I read that. All my work, all the backbreaking labour, for the past God knows how many months. I flip the paper out sharply in front of me, as if I could shake off the words. Not my seeds!

I get up abruptly, pacing the lounge. I need to get onto the net and book my flight out of here *right now*. I need to be back there. I've got to go and get back to work to make up for all that's been lost . . . but I can't, I remember. My visa has run out and I can't go back till I get all the sponsorship papers signed. Oh, if only I'd gone up to London to see Professor Klausmann that day when I intended to . . .

. . . And I am afraid to tell you that even Mesopotamia is now completely vanished. The gold prospectors brought machines and hollowed it all out before a government agency that we called in managed to stop them going further. We must be grateful for small mercies, I suppose . . .

It can't be gone.

I sit down on the settee again with a bump, my legs gone all wobbly. Mesopotamia gone – and in such a short time? That's the place where I harvested all those seeds the day of the howler monkey, the day Eve called me to tell me I had to come back home. I found *dozens* of my most precious samples in that area alone. I don't know where else I can find them. I don't know if I'll ever find them again.

Oh, God, this can't be happening. I've only been away a few weeks . . .

'Are you all right, darling?' When Rich appears, all sleepy and rumpled and wearing nothing but his PJ bottoms, he could be an apparition from another planet.

'I didn't hear you come down,' I croak. I put the letter down on the coffee table, my hands trembling so hard he must notice.

'I just opened the garden door for *Monsieur* here. He's already been out once this morning but he's having a few problems at the moment . . .' Rich sits down beside me and Ruff flops down at his heels. 'You *aren't* all right, are you?'

I'm OK, I think. I'm over here, aren't I? It's the ones who I left behind who aren't OK. My people, my friends, my José . . .

'I've just had this note from Eve this morning,' I put the letter in his lap. 'It's becoming a total disaster zone out there, Rich. PlanetLove have just had to move base camp. I've lost *all* the seeds I've collected since last June . . .'

'Ouch.' He skims through it, spending more time on the picture of José than anything else.

'They really matter to you, don't they?' he says softly. 'You're not just worried about what's happening to the forest. It's the people.'

'Rich, you have no idea . . .' I wipe away the tears that have sprung into my eyes.

'Hey.' He puts his arm about my shoulders. 'I know. You told us. Your second family, right?'

'I can't explain it properly,' I tell him feelingly, 'but when I'm

121

with them, I feel more at home than when I'm *at* home. I feel . . . I feel really loved.'

He's stroking the hair at the back of my head, his fingers soothing everything away, making everything all right. Are we alone, I wonder? I want to talk to Rich, really *talk* to him in a way I just can't do with Hollie because she gets too emotional. The truth is, I can't see me raising those funds that Eve wants, not unless I can persuade these two to sell up here. I want to run that idea past him. See how he reacts first, see if I can get him on side with it. After all, he dropped that hint not long after I got here about how he'd like to move to Italy.

'You're loved here too, don't forget.'

I look up at him gratefully, my face shining. 'Oh, Hollie loves me in a sisterly way, of course. She loves me in a . . .' I search for the right word '. . . a *dutiful* way. What I mean is . . .' I rush on as his eyes widen '. . . there's still a part of her that hasn't forgotten, that hasn't let go of . . .' Does he see it? Can I speak of this with him or will he stonewall me? When it comes to Hol, Rich has a particularly wide blind spot. I sense I might be treading on thin ice here.

'It isn't your fault that your sister can't have babies,' he says after a while. 'And she does love you. More than dutifully. Very much.'

'Of course she's loved!' My sister comes in carrying a tray of tea and toast. She and Rich exchange a glance. Why did she have to walk in just now, I think irritably.

'Everything OK?' She puts the breakfast things down and goes over and murmurs something to her husband. He half-turns to look at me, smiling, gives me the thumbs-up and then kisses Hollie.

I look away. Can't they see it makes me cringe? After a moment Rich gets up and leaves the room and Hollie turns to me to pour out some tea.

'I do hope, darling, that you aren't having any regrets?' she puts in tentatively.

'Where did Rich just go?'

'Well, it's obvious that we two need a little bit of "girl time". You're feeling hormonal and . . . well, that's just natural under the circumstances. Men don't really understand these things . . . Would you like a bit of toast?'

Girl time? I let out a controlled breath. I don't want any more time with her. We're in each other's company enough as it is right now. And I'm not bloody hormonal. I shake my head.

'Are you sure? You've got to keep your strength up. You can't afford to skip breakfast, especially if you're planning on . . .'

'No. *No toast*, Hollie.' My sister fades into silence as I cut over her. 'I'm not hormonal. I'm . . . I'm gutted,' I tell her through gritted teeth, 'because I've just heard that the whole outfit I left behind in Brazil five weeks ago appears to be collapsing behind me.'

'Oh.' She looks mildly startled. 'I'm so sorry, darling. If there's anything we can do . . . Look, regarding the sponsorship money – we could really ramp up the idea of the open garden party we've been planning and rope in everyone we can think of to donate cakes and crafts and maybe even hold a little antiques stall. We could ask BBC South East to come along and advertise what we're doing and . . .' She stops, sensing that I'm not impressed.

'None of that is going to cut it, Hol.' I pour out some of the tea she's just brought through to soothe my aching throat. I want to cry.

But I'm not going to. The only thing that's going to do any good is if PlanetLove can buy that bit of land. Once it's officially ours then *nobody* will be able to get on it who shouldn't be there. I look at Hollie. I'm out of time. I didn't want to broach the subject of the house with her before I knew I was pregnant, but what the hell . . . she's got to know sometime.

'Hol . . .'

'Yes?' She freezes, toast in midair on the way to her mouth.

'I appreciate what you're trying to do. Really. It just . . . isn't going to be enough, nor fast enough. I need to get my hands on those funds quickly. And there is only one course of action I can think of to do that. Trouble is, you aren't going to like it one little bit.'

Hollie

'My mission – you know I need to make a lot of money, very fast, right?'

I nod dumbly.

'Well.' She takes in a breath, then comes out with it. 'I need us to sell Florence Cottage. And I need to take *my* half of the money out – as soon as possible.'

I don't answer her for a minute, she's totally thrown me.

'Your half?' I manage at last.

'Well, yes. I figure there's two ways you could do this,' Scarlett runs on. 'Either we sell up and split the money and you and Rich go and live in his Bluebell Hill property or else you sell Bluebell Hill and buy me out so you can stay here. Either way, I've got to get my hands on my share of the inheritance. Quickly.' She picks up a piece of her toast, seemingly feeling better now she's got that off her chest.

'Lettie.' I turn to look at her, confused. She's never mentioned anything like this to me before. 'I can't do that. I'm sorry.'

'I know it isn't what you want to do, sis. I know you love this place to bits. You buy out my half, why don't you, then you can stay?'

I'm still finding it hard to grasp where she's going with this. Surely she can't imagine I'm going to sell up Auntie Flo's beloved family home just to get some money to buy a bit of the Amazon?

'You're making too many assumptions, Scarlett,' I tell her slowly. 'You haven't thought this through. And you haven't taken us into account, either. For starters, Richard's flat doesn't just belong to Richard, remember – his grandparents left it to him and Jay. I doubt Jay would agree to sell up in this depressed market and even if he did it would take ages and besides . . .'

'Besides?' She looks at me challengingly.

'Look, the fact is, Florence Cottage wasn't left to you, Scarlett. Flo bequeathed it in my name alone. You don't *have* any half to sell.'

I didn't want to break it to her like this. I've known it for years, and admittedly I've never fully understood it myself. Why Florence named me as the sole beneficiary of her estate. Me and Rich were always going to be fair to Scarlett, though. We'd never turn her away if she needed a home and we'd always have helped her financially in whatever way we could when the time came for her to get her own place.

'What are you saying, Hollie?' Her face contorts in pained anger now. 'Flo would never have done that to me – just cut me out of her will. Why would she? And . . . and why for God's sake have you never said anything about it before?'

'Scarlett, I'm so sorry,' I appeal to her now. 'I guess the issue of selling the place has never cropped up. Remember that you were just a kid when Flo passed away – I guess that's why she left it in my name . . .'

'If you think that's really the case,' her voice catches in her throat though she's trying not to show how hurt she feels, 'then you shouldn't deny me my portion of it now. I'm not a kid any more. I'm an adult, and I know what I want to do with my life.'

'Lettie,' I stammer, 'you have to understand something. Flo *never intended* that this place should pass out of the family. Whoever's name it's in is irrelevant really.'

'Who are you kidding, Hol? We weren't her family, were we? She might have treated us like family but we never were. She took

126

us on after our mother abandoned us to go off saving the bloody world on her mission to conserve all the vanishing seeds . . .' She trails off because, after all, this is exactly what she's supposed to be doing in Brazil right now.

'Anyway,' she storms as I decline to answer her last point, 'I am planning on selling up so whose name the cottage is in becomes very relevant indeed. I'm not asking for this for myself, Hollie. I'm doing this for my other family. I have to. It's the whole reason why I came back here in the first place. If I'm being one hundred per cent honest,' she pauses for a mere fraction before plunging on, 'it's even a large part of the reason why I agreed to help *you*.'

'Oh.' I put my hand to my throat.

'I thought if I got pregnant that you'd want to move,' she's crying. 'And then I'd get my share of the money, don't you see?'

Confused thoughts whirl through my head. Half of me is secretly pleased Scarlett had an ulterior motive for helping us – it quells the guilt I've been feeling ever since I asked her. The other half is appalled.

'I wish I could help you, honestly I do. But I can't sell up, Lettie. I swore to Auntie Flo that I'd never let it pass out of our hands. I promised her . . .'

'You *promised* her!' She looks at me in disbelief now. 'Maybe that's why she left it all to you?'

'No! She didn't. She left it to me because she knew I'd respect the heritage behind it. Don't you see – she wanted it to be our *home*. She never intended for either of us to come into any money by it. Her wishes were that if either of us decided that we didn't want to live here any more then it would automatically pass into National Trust hands.'

'No.' She looks at me in disbelief. 'So this place is really nothing more than an albatross around our necks? How could you have known this all this time and never said anything to me?'

'I don't believe it's ever been an albatross, Lettie, and it's never been a potential pot of gold for us either. It's our *home*. Mine and Richard's . . .' I look at her remorsefully. 'I'm sorry I can't help you out with the money thing . . .'

'You're not sorry,' she fumes. 'Legally, we could sell it, right? We're talking about a deathbed promise, not a binding caveat to the will, I take it?'

'A promise, yes, but one that I intend to keep. I won't betray Flo's trust, Scarlett. I just won't.'

'She's dead, though. Whatever promise you made to her – it doesn't matter any more. There are other things that matter more. You must see that.'

'Lettie . . .'

'All this . . . all this heritage stuff,' she indicates the whole of our sitting room now with a dismissive sweep of her hand. 'It's all just bricks and mortar and ancient history. But people matter more. *Living people*, Hollie! You of all people should understand that. You want a child, don't you? That matters to you more than this mouldy old cottage, wouldn't you say?'

'Yes.' I can scarcely draw a breath.

'Well – that's good then,' Scarlett tells me. 'Because you know what matters most then. For me, my tribespeople matter more than this cottage. The rest is simple, wouldn't you say?'

'We don't even know if you're pregnant yet,' I remind her faintly.

'We'll know soon enough. And after that?' My sister scrutinises me carefully for a few moments before she turns away, but I don't answer her.

As for what happens after, we'll cross that bridge when we come to it.

Hollie

Inside Number Five the Esplanade, I head straight up to my office, unwinding my scarf from about my neck as I go. I stand at the top of the wide stairs thoughtfully and blow my nose. It's very quiet up here today. The pale light coming through the stained-glass windows at the bend of the stairwell is yellowed and closed in. It makes me feel like turning on every light in every room and I can already tell from the silence there won't be anybody in any of them. The way I'm feeling today, that's probably just as well.

I go and sit down at my desk, letting my head sink into my hands. Since we got back after Christmas, my desk has grown ever more crowded with papers and files. It's depressing. I don't want to even *look* at any of them. When I get up and go to the high arched windows the stone surround feels cool under my fingertips while the radiator underneath it belts out a huge amount of heat, warming up my legs. Medieval buildings weren't designed to be economically centrally heated, I remember Ben Spenlow telling me the first day I arrived here – ten years ago now, when I took over Auntie Flo's job here at the Trust after she passed away. It's mainly administrative, what I do – sorting our charity applications, taking minutes, greeting our visitors – not what I ever imagined I'd end up doing for a job though I have been happy here. When Flo died I should have been finishing off my final year at Canterbury University but I had to give that up – we needed the money.

I took over Flo's job of looking after my sister at the same time, I muse. Scarlett was only thirteen and Flo had been the only mum she'd ever known. After Flo died she'd gone through a really difficult teenage stage. That was really hard for me. I wasn't all that old myself, only twenty-one. We got through that though, didn't we? We'll get through this.

'Aha! Just the person I was hoping to see . . .' Beatrice Highland's plummy tones cut through my reverie; she's caught me staring out of the window when I should be tackling my paper mountain. I stifle a cough.

'Oh! Beatrice – sorry, I didn't realise anyone was in this morning. I'd have offered to make you a drink.' I make a quick show of sorting out some paperwork that has somehow found its way onto the window ledge. 'Such a lot to catch up on . . .' I mutter.

'Indeed, things have been moving apace here since Christmas.' Beatrice joins me at the window and I shuffle up a bit. With her long tweed skirt and her archaic way of speaking it's easy to imagine Beatrice travels here from next door every morning in a time tunnel from the fifties.

'Any sign of our new bridge picture being framed?'

'Soon.' I look away guiltily. Chrissie hadn't even *begun* framing it last time I asked her. My mother-in-law's had her hands so full with Rich's dad being unwell. I should have just taken it locally but I wanted to give her the work. 'I hear they're hanging it up by the front entrance, is that right?'

'That's correct.' Working with someone who's also my neighbour can have its disadvantages: she knows me too well, for one. 'You don't approve of our choice of location for it? I thought it would look marvellous there. That way everyone will see it.'

'Oh no, the location's fine. It's me. It's just me. I find the picture a little bit . . . scary, that's all.'

'My dear, it is a work of art.'

'I know,' I tell her miserably, because what do I know about art? 'Anyway, I'm . . . I'm really sorry about all this mess, Bea. I know that with the bridge being shut there's been even more paperwork to get through than usual. I'll get it sorted soon though, I promise.'

'Everything is all right, dear, isn't it?' She takes me in a little more closely. 'You don't seem quite yourself, that's all.'

'I'm fine, honestly. I just . . .' I look at my desk intently as if I'm really interested in the huge report from the bridge engineers that's appeared on my desk over the weekend. Oh, what the heck. Bea's known the family for decades. She's going to learn about the surrogacy soon enough.

'I'll let you in on something, Bea. Scarlett's offered to be my surrogate for me. She's going to have a baby for Rich and me.'

'Good grief.' Beatrice Highland looks shocked. 'That's . . . marvellous, my dear. What a hugely charitable offer. I can't think of anything greater a woman could give her sister . . .'

'Yep.' I'm not going to mention the small fact that Scarlett has just asked me to give up my home in return. Beatrice would be scandalised.

'And – if you pardon my making the observation – I wouldn't have put Scarlett down as a natural candidate for such an offer.' My boss picks up a discarded tea mug and holds it delicately by its handle. 'She's a lovely girl, your sister, so full of life and *joie de vivre*, but . . . I've never had her down as patient and persevering and just generally the self-sacrificing type, you know?'

'No, I know what you mean,' I give a small laugh. Beatrice has known Scarlett since she was a child so there's no point trying to pull the wool over her eyes. 'She's . . . she's always been a bit of a wild child.'

'A free spirit,' she rejoins. 'A butterfly . . .'

'Yes,' I concur. 'All those things. Not a natural earth mother sort, I agree. But she says she's changed.'

Scarlett's got an agenda of her own to fulfil too, I remember now, frowning. She's got her second family on her mind as much as anyone else. Scarlett's words come back to me now: 'It's a large part of the reason why I agreed to help you'.

I find another tea mug underneath a loose-leaf file and collect my boss' mug from her hands. I need to escape and go and get these washed.

'She says being in the Amazon has made her more aware of others and less selfish and she wanted to do this for us so . . . Well, we'll see.'

'If she really has grown up that much it'll be a marvel,' Bea mutters, almost to herself. 'Anyhow, with a bit of luck she'll conceive easily, and given that she does like her freedom, I don't suppose handing the child over will be too much of a wrench either. Goodness, that does sound dreadful, I didn't mean it like that . . .'

'No, that's perfectly all right . . .' I rush in. Nobody can say that Beatrice doesn't have the measure of my sister at any rate. 'To be honest,' I confide, 'the waiting around to find out if she's pregnant or not has been a bit of a strain on all of us. But never mind that, I'm here now and I need filling in on what's happened while I've been away . . .'

'Lots of engineering tests, mainly.' She rubs her hands together briskly. 'The mountain of paperwork stacking up on your desk is testimony to the fact that we have not been idle.' She gets up and goes to peer out of the window again where I join her. You can't see the bridge from here because my office is too far round the corner but you can see the river. We gaze out, silent for a bit, watching the eddies and the swirls in the river flow.

'It's going to take a little while to sort it all, isn't it?'

'Indeed. Sometimes, my dear, we know what the problem is but we don't always know straightaway what's going to be the best solution.' She gets up as the phone in her own office begins to trill. 'Sometimes, the first thing that springs to mind – the thing we want to go for – brings along a whole rack of problems of its own, do you see?'

She leaves me and I go to put on the kettle. When I return my own phone is going and I almost don't pick it up. I don't want to talk to anyone. I don't want to pretend I'm my usual efficient, helpful self. I leave it to ring seven times before I realise that they aren't going to go away.

'Hello?' I answer more sharply than I intend to, so it's a relief when it's just Scarlett at the other end.

'Hi. It's me.' Pause.

What, *what*? Is she going to apologise to me now? Is she going to say that she didn't really mean all those things she said to me before? My heart is thudding so loudly in my chest I put my hand over it. I need to hear her say that she didn't mean any of it. That she really did do this for me and Rich and not just to get her hands on that money. I pause, waiting for the words to come.

'Hollie, I'm not pregnant, OK?' She spills it all out in a rush like it will hurt less that way.

'OK.' I blink back a tear.

'Are you all right?' Her voice is anxious. 'I thought you'd want to know as soon as I did.'

'I'm fine.' Why, why couldn't it just have worked for once? Why couldn't it just be easy?

'I thought I was pregnant. I could have sworn that I was, I did one of those early tests, you know, you can find out just a few days after conception now, you don't have to wait . . .'

'You did?' I ask faintly.

'Yes. And the first one I did, it was positive, I'm sure I read it right. I knew you wanted to wait till things were more certain so I didn't say till now but then today . . .' she trails away, flat and disappointed. 'I tested it again after we spoke. I'm not pregnant. I don't understand.'

'These things happen, Scarlett.' I'm back into pretend mode. I'm so good at covering up my feelings, at telling everyone 'Oh, I wasn't really expecting anything', that I could almost fool myself.

'Yeah,' she says. She sounds almost disappointed

'So . . .' I hold my breath. 'Are you willing to stay and try once again?'

Can I really go through with this all over again, *another month?*

'Scarlett?'

'I'm sorry about earlier,' she says. 'Learning I wasn't in the will came on top of a whole lot of other bad news, that's all. I didn't mean to snap at you.' She stops and I don't know what to say because if I open my mouth she will hear that I'm crying.

There's a pause. While we both get it back together I randomly pick up the folder that Beatrice has just balanced on top of the pile on my desk: 'Suggested solutions for bridge repair. Long- and short-term strategies.' It looks like a lengthy document. Every potential solution seems to have a whole list of 'considerations' attached to it. No wonder they can't decide. The worst thing is, I feel so disconnected from it all at the moment. I really don't feel as if I even care. And I *should* care. I never wanted this desire to have a baby to turn into an obsession. I never thought that it could become so big it would crowd out each and every other thing in my life that holds some meaning for me but somehow it has, it is. The silence stretches out for so long I begin to think Scarlett must have got cut off or gone away and answered the door or something.

'Hello?'

'Yeah, yeah,' she says.

'Are you willing to stay?'

'I guess I have to really, don't I?'

'No, you don't have to.'

'I don't want to let Rich down, Hollie. Or you. I promised you I'll do it and I will, only . . .'

'Only what?' I tense.

'I really, really need to get together those funds we spoke about for PlanetLove,' she cajoles. 'If I'm going to carry on putting my energies into getting pregnant for you it makes it kind of difficult for me to spread myself so thinly.'

'Oh.'

'It would really help me to know – if I don't manage to pull together the funds any other way – I'll have your support?'

My sigh of relief is laced with trepidation. Who am I kidding? Having this child matters to me more than anything.

'If it comes to that, Scarlett . . .' I tell her at last.

OK, so she'll stay. I don't have the luxury of a load of potential solutions like the bridge engineers do. Scarlett *is* the solution to the problem which I've been facing for so long, and I don't want to let my last chance slip away.

I can't.

Hollie

'She's there, isn't she?'

Who wants my sister now? I feel myself bristle slightly at the caller's tone. Ten days to go before we find out if Scarlett's pregnant at her second attempt or not and who could this be, ringing up and demanding so abruptly to speak to her?

'I want to speak to your sister please, Hollie.' Then I recognise his voice.

Oh no, not *him* again! Why did I even pick up the phone?

I was already dreading this morning enough. I had no idea it was about to get much worse.

I'm not going to let this guy faze me. I pick up the towel which I have no intention of using and roll it into a cylinder to pack into my bag, along with the swimming cossie Scarlett's insisted on buying me. My sister's decided that my sessions with Mr Huang are taking too long and what I need to do is go down to the local pool 'even if you don't go in because it'll help you get used to the idea'.

'Look, Duncan – this really isn't the best time.'

'She's there right now. I just saw her walking in the garden.' I stiffen, edging slowly away from the window with the phone in my hand. Is it true, did he see her just now, looking for snowdrops under the dappled shade of the silver birch? And if Duncan can see her, then where must he be?

'This is beginning to sound like stalking, Duncan.' He knows we're both in the house; a shiver of discomfort works its way down my neck.

'I'm not threatening either of you, am I?' he says nastily. 'I'm making a phone call to an old friend. I was passing and I saw her. You never bothered replying to any of my emails and I've been waiting for her call and . . .'

'She doesn't want any contact with you, Duncan. That's why you haven't heard from us.' I'd forgotten all about his emails – he's sent a couple through after Christmas as well, but there's been so much else going on in the past few weeks I haven't had time to think about him.

The truth is, Scarlett's been really peed off with having to take her temperature and start up the regime all over again so I never even mentioned his emails to her. Should I put him onto her now? I always get such a creepy feeling about this guy . . .

'Look,' I try and keep my voice pleasant, 'she's moved on now, Duncan. You really need to let her go. My sister's got a boyfriend now too,' I add for good measure (not that she's made too much of that, herself). 'Someone she's serious about.'

'You think I'm not serious about her?'

'I think you're . . .' I want to say deluded, but I don't want to incite him. 'You're mistaken about things. She's moved on.'

'Moved on.' Duncan repeats slowly 'Maybe. But I'm only hearing all of this from you, aren't I? Look – I'm afraid I've done something a little bit foolish, Hollie.' His voice has turned sheepish now. 'And I need to speak to her. Give me her mobile number at least, I'll call her myself . . .'

'I'm afraid I can't do that.' *Stop being so stubborn*, a little voice in my head says now. *Give him her number and let them sort whatever it is out between them.*

'You aren't going to stand in the way of what I need to say to your sister, Hollie. Stop trying to protect her like you always did. She's not your little sister any more. In fact, you aren't protecting her, you know that?' His voice takes on a new energy. 'By standing between us you're only making things worse.'

'What do you mean, "like I always did"?' I retort. I've got a cold shiver running down my spine at the moment and my previous thoughts about putting him on the phone to her melts in the stream. He was her boyfriend for a short while. She might have told him things about us – personal, family things – that he thinks he can use against me now. I protected her, of course I did, what older sister wouldn't have done the same . . . ?

'She's still got her promise to fulfil to me, don't forget.'

'What promise?' I glance out of the window and I can spy Scarlett now, her cheeks ruddy and her hair windblown, her sketchbook under her arm, tramping back down the path. She's been sketching the February snowdrops, I can just about make them out from the delicate green and white colouring on her pad. 'Snowdrops for hope and consolation,' Auntie Flo would have said. But there's none of that here for this man. She made a promise to me too, I think. And mine's more important than yours.

'She knows what she owes me. She won't have forgotten, I promise you that.'

'Duncan,' I work at keeping my voice reasonable, 'even if she did promise you something, ages ago . . . she obviously hasn't kept in contact and clearly has no intention of fulfilling it, whatever it is. So what can you do about it?'

'I don't have to do anything.' His voice is blurry at the edges and I wonder if he's been drinking. 'But do you think . . . you think that we ever get away with anything in this life? We don't, you know. Not ever. She won't, either.'

'If you're threatening her . . .'

'I wouldn't harm a hair on her head, Hollie. Believe me. I wouldn't risk the bad karma. I believe in Uni . . .' he's slurring now '. . . in *Universal Law*, you see. I believe that the bad deeds we do come home to roost.'

'I'm sorry, I have no idea what you're talking about.' Bloody hell, this man really is some prize fruitcake. My sister knows how to pick them, that's for sure.

'Do you remember all those red balloons we sent up for charity in the autumn? The wish balloons?' he continues now. 'Well . . . I sent a special message for Scarlett in my one.'

'She'll never get that, Duncan!' I might be talking to a four-year-old. 'Only a fraction of those things ever reach their target recipient and, frankly, as far as I could see, none of those red balloons were ever meant to. Nobody was putting any addresses on the envelopes, were they? It was all more of a "sign of intent", a wish for somebody, that's all.'

'I didn't have to put her address on it,' he says confidently. 'The universe knows where she's at.'

The universe, right.

'That balloon will find her all right. And when it does, she'll bring herself to justice in the end. I won't have to do a thing.'

'What did you write?'

There's a long pause now. When he comes back, his voice sounds deflated, sapped of all its former determination. 'Five words, Hollie. Just five little words. But she'll know what they mean.'

'Listen, Duncan. Listen to me.' I lower my voice as the French doors open and I hear my sister pulling off her boots on the mat.

'*You* listen.' He suddenly changes gear again. 'I know what's important to your sister – her job, right? You think I don't know that? I went out with that girl for six months. I cared for her.' His voice wobbles. 'But you mark my words. I've got intel that could pull that job right out from under her. Just imagine. I could discredit her so as she'd never be able to go back to her precious seeds in the rainforest again. Everything she's worked so hard for – it'll come tumbling down about her ears like a pack of cards . . .'

'But you won't do that,' I remind him. 'All that bad karma, remember?'

'I told you. I won't have to.'

'Come on, you've got nothing on her, Duncan,' I mutter.

'She knows that I do. Ask her. Just you ask her.'

I hesitate, looking up briefly as Scarlett comes into the room now and makes a beeline for the magazine I was leafing through earlier. He's beyond odd, that's for sure – but he's right about one thing – he's *her* problem. When Scarlett sees the magazine's a pregnancy one, she drops it with a scowl and for some reason that makes up my mind for me in an instant. I'm sticking to my guns here. She's only still here in Kent because she's hoping to get the money from the house to carry on her work in the Amazon, isn't she? If she thought that Duncan really could pull the plug on all that – and that he has every intention of doing so – she wouldn't stay.

And she must stay.

'Tell her,' he says.

'OK,' I tell him calmly. 'I've got to find the right moment though.'

There's still ten days to go before we find out whether my sister's pregnant after her second attempt or not. I'm not risking driving her away before then by exposing her to this guy.

'Ready yet?' Scarlett points to the swimming bags. She's making a 'wrap it up' signal with her finger.

'She's there, isn't she?' His voice is suddenly wistful.

'No, no, she isn't.' I put the phone down too hard, too rapidly, and my sister looks at me, puzzled.

'For me?'

'Just a wrong number and, yes, I'm ready to go to the pool if you are?' I affect an air of nonchalance that I do not really feel.

Duncan is bluffing. He might think he's got something on her, but he hasn't. I rack my brains but he's using her devotion to her job as a means to try to get to her, I decide. She already had all that paperwork she was waiting for through from a Professor Klausmann, I remember, and everything seemed to be in order.

There is nothing, I decide, nothing for us to be worried about at all.

Scarlett

> Querida, when we spoke last night you were distant and I am
> left feeling confused. I do not understand. What secret are
> you keeping from me? Speak to me, I beg you. Gui xx

I put the phone with its text message back in my pocket and
fold my clothes away in the bag to place in the locker. Hollie's
still in the changing room, taking her sweet time. I could text
Gui back, I suppose. Better than speaking to him because he'll
worm it all out of me if I do and I still don't want to tell him
about the surrogacy. Silly I know, because it's my body, my life.
He isn't in control of me. I'm just not sure how he'll take it,
that's all.

'Are you nearly there?' I call to Hol through the closed changing
room door. I take her muffled reply as a yes.

Oh, fuck it. I pull my phone out again.

> I have no secret, Gui. My sister is ill like I told you and I'm
> staying on in the UK till she's well enough to be left alone.
> I hope to be back with you very soon. Within the month.

That should keep him happy for the time being. No good frightening him off. I'll make sure the pregnancy's a go-er first.

There are a couple of messages from the PlanetLove guys too.
Emoto's just sent me a pic of him holding up one of the rarest

orchids in the world – so rare it's only been documented once before – and I feel a real pang at not being there myself.

Eve's sent a message to say there's a new European group who might be about to offer us a lifeline. She didn't mention anything about my allegedly dodgy job application, which means either she's not heard of any problems or they don't merit a mention. Either way I feel really out of the loop right now.

I shut the phone down. Sometimes it can be really hard to do your bit, but I know I'm doing the right thing in being here at the moment. Now, where's Hol? The changing room door is open so I guess she's made her way down to the poolside already.

But she hasn't. When I get down there my sister's sitting hunched in the spectator area, still fully dressed and looking utterly miserable.

'Hey!' I'm on her case in an instant. 'Come on. Just a little paddle. Just dunk a toe in. Anything. You promised.'

'I can't.' Hol shakes her head.

'You can't, or you won't?'

'I wanted to try, Lettie, believe me. I know I promised you I would but . . . I physically can't bring myself to get into the water. I changed into that swimsuit and then I – I changed back again, because I knew I couldn't do it. You can't force me.'

'Hollie, darling,' I tell her patiently, like you would a little kid, 'if you'd only just try . . . Come on, try and go to the water's edge this one time. I don't ask anything more. You're scared of what you imagine will happen, that's all. And the more you let it go on, the bigger it gets.'

'I know.' She's closed her eyes now, she's not even looking at me. Her fists are clenched tight on her lap and her face has gone a strange shade of grey. 'I know all that. But it doesn't make any difference, I still can't do it, don't you see?'

'No. I don't see,' I tell her baldly. 'You won't try anything new, you're determined not to step out of your comfort zone even if it kills you . . .'

'I realise I must be wearying.' When my sister opens her eyes there's no mistaking the pained expression in them. 'And I want to go in, believe me I do. But trying to force me like this, it isn't the way.'

What does she think having this baby for her is going to do to me, though? Gui's text message right now has thrown it all into stark relief for me. After all, if he does get upset about it I'm potentially screwed, aren't I? I'm risking it all. What is *she* prepared to risk?

'Hollie, *Hollie* . . . you are a complete and utter . . . utter wimp!' I throw at her at last.

'I'm a wimp?' she repeats softly. She turns to look at me but for some reason I can't return her gaze. 'Maybe now, Scarlett. But it wasn't always so, was it?'

Hollie

'Hey,' Richard murmurs softly as the warm end of the quilt slips from him. He reaches out and pulls my snug body to him instead in sleepy protest. It feels as if we went to bed hardly any time ago and already the radiator is gurgling into life, warning me that it'll soon be time to be getting up again.

6.15 am? I stare blearily at the bedside clock. I turn in towards my husband, trying to lure myself back into sleep but it won't work. I kiss his face gently, not really wanting to disturb him but unable to stop myself nonetheless. I watch his face while he is sleeping. He's been away for just under a week this time. Rich and his dad have been negotiating some work with a building firm that belongs to an Italian guy who Bill used to know. Rich hasn't filled me in on all the details yet. But – I lift my face to look at him more closely – even asleep he looks preoccupied. Distant.

Was he distant last night? I cast my mind back to yesterday evening, our tenth wedding anniversary. Rich was massively contrite because he'd only remembered it at the very last minute, and had to buy a magnum of champagne from the duty-free, but I didn't mind. Last night he more than made up for it. I grin happily. Judging by the amount of time it took before we actually got to *sleep* last night, I'd hazard he was pretty happy to be back with me too.

'Penny for your thoughts,' Richard murmurs now, his mouth

on mine so sudden and warm and delicious that I'm loath to admit to having any thoughts at all. I want him to make love to me again. When we're in bed together that seems to be about the only time we have any privacy these days. We even shared our anniversary champagne with Scarlett last night. I didn't mind sharing the champagne, but it kind of ruined the intimacy.

'I'm not thinking about anything much.' *Only about how much I've missed you, and about how unsettled things are here at the moment what with Duncan ringing and there still being over a week to go before we find out if my sister's expecting our baby, and the fact that she nearly ended up having a massive argument with me in public yesterday when I couldn't bring myself to go into the pool . . .*

'No?' He opens one eye curiously now and looks at me. 'Nothing you want to share with me?'

I consider for a bit. He's preoccupied, I know. It's not just the family business he's trying to prop up on everyone's behalf, it's his dad's health that's always at the forefront of his mind, even though he doesn't go on about it.

'You go first,' I offer. 'You're the one who's been away for a week. Tell me all about Trieste.'

He'd been looking at me, but now he turns away, his face to the ceiling.

'It was . . . more than I expected,' he says thickly.

'What was?' I feel a pang. 'The place, do you mean?'

'Signor Bonomi put us up in a wonderful little cottage – a converted watermill, actually,' he smiles softly. 'You'd have loved it. It was only a little place, but so peaceful. We woke up every morning to the sounds of a babbling stream, and birds singing and cows calling – all very rural bliss. It didn't have a garden, but there was a huge overgrown field at the back where you could keep horses or that'd be just perfect for dogs to run around in . . .'

'I didn't realise you were going out there with a view to

145

buying a property,' I tease gently. 'I thought you were looking for *work*.'

'Yes, of course we were. And that side of it went well . . .' He opens his eyes fully now. 'In fact, you might say, rather too well.'

I give a small laugh. 'How so?'

'I got the impression Signor Bonomi would be happy to give us a *lot* of work,' he says carefully. 'And it would be the kind of work my dad loves the best – the actual, out-in-the-field measuring up and assessing and surveying actual buildings, as opposed to the stuck-in-the-office chasing invoices and customers side. It'd make his life one hell of a lot less stressful.'

It'd make it less stressful if he'd just retire, I think, but I know that's not going to happen.

'What's so bad about that?'

Richard doesn't answer immediately.

'The work wouldn't all be based in this country, love. It would entail me travelling more, being away more. And I wasn't sure how you'd feel about that. Especially now we're trying for a baby. I'm not sure how *I* feel about it. It'd mean sacrifices for both of us, no question about that.'

I consider his words for a moment or two. 'Are they sacrifices you feel happy making?' I ask at last.

'We'd have to talk about what exactly that would mean, wouldn't we?' He gives me a significant look. 'You know I don't like the idea of leaving you for too long.'

'I miss you so much when you're away,' I confess.

'Do you miss me?' His breath is hot and moist near my ear. He leans in and tickles my ribs suddenly, making me laugh, and I have to squirm backwards out of his reach. 'Tell me what you miss most.'

'Someone strong to put the rubbish out,' I gasp from the other end of the bed. 'Someone to fix the latch on the garden gate when it gets broken.'

'Ah, I thought as much.' His low voice reminds me of chocolate and for a second I get the strong urge to lean over and nibble his ear. 'And here was me thinking that I'd hooked myself an independent woman.'

'I still miss you like crazy when you're gone.' I lean into him again, kiss him softly on the lips. 'I don't know if I'd really be happy for you to be away so much of the time, darling.'

'I know that.' He pauses, measuring his words. 'It's just that at the moment I don't know how else I'm going to solve this. There really is a dearth of work in the UK at the moment. I've been racking my brains to come up with a solution.' He draws his face back a little now, comtemplating mine. 'Unless of course you would consider leaving England altogether?'

'Leaving?' I gasp, pulling myself up onto my elbows. 'Of course not! We can't . . . I can't leave. That'd mean leaving behind our home.'

'We could make a new home,' he suggests softly.

'I thought you understood how much this place means to me . . . I thought Florence Cottage meant the same to you too?' I stutter. 'I feel really hurt that you could even suggest we should leave it, Rich.'

'Darling, it is a *house*.'

'Our *home*,' I remind him. 'Flo's ancestral home. And I promised to keep it for her. You know that.'

He searches for my hand under the covers, gives my fingers a little squeeze. 'I know that,' he breathes. 'I know you mean to stay loyal to her. And to this place and to the promise you made, but . . . sometimes life throws things in our way, opportunities, that can melt away even the most cast-iron of our decisions. We *can* change our minds. It is permitted.'

'Except I don't want to . . .'

'Because this place has meant so much to you, I know.' He nods his head, understandingly. 'It's represented security, stability. Even . . . an ancestral line, of sorts, because it's been in Flo's family for so many generations. I can understand all that.

147

You didn't have your parents around, so I guess the cottage has come to symbolise your roots for you instead . . .'

'My parents have nothing to do with this,' I protest.

'Hollie, that might be just what the problem is. They didn't have anything to do with you. They should have. They left you two girls with Florence – well, OK, your *mum* left you both with Florence. But let's not pretend that's any substitute for the real thing.'

'Richard, the way I feel about Florence Cottage has nothing to do with the fact that my parents weren't around. It didn't affect me that they weren't, anyway. We coped perfectly well because we had Flossie . . .'

'Oh, Hol,' he says feelingly. 'How can you say that? How can you think that? I mean, being brought up your whole lives by a friend of the family, having to do without your mum and dad . . .?'

Outside the first threads of light are just beginning to filter in through the cracks in the curtains. I hear the downstairs door click which means that Scarlett is up, letting poor ageing Ruffles out for his morning pee.

'I never really think about it,' I say after a while. 'We had Auntie Flo and that was good enough.'

'You got used to it,' he says feelingly. 'But you must have wondered about your mother? When you were a kid, I mean? You must have wondered why she made the choices that she did. Maybe for you, even more than for Scarlett, that would have been a tough thing to accept?'

'Because Scarlett hardly knew her at all, you mean?' I can feel his fingers gently stroking the hair away from my face and the faint stab of an old sadness that I push away by putting my arms around him, pulling him towards me. 'Well, you talk of sacrifices, Rich. Doing something that we don't want to do because we believe that in the end it's all for the best. Mum had put a hell of a lot of work and years into her Amazon projects. She wanted to stay behind long enough to make something of them.

148

We all knew that. It was a sacrifice she made, leaving her children behind so she could fulfil her vocation.'

'How very noble of her.' There's an irony in Richard's voice that doesn't escape me. 'And how very understanding of you two kids.'

'What do you mean?' I give him a surprised look. 'What's brought all this on, anyway?'

'Oh, nothing. It's just . . . you defend her so staunchly and yet it's not something I could ever see you doing, is it?'

'Going to the Amazon?' I try and laugh it all off now, nibbling softly at his ear.

'No. Leaving your two little daughters with a family friend while you bugger off to the jungle.'

'Rich!' I admonish. 'She always meant to come back. She would have. Besides, it wasn't all that bad,' I say defensively. 'We did have good old Auntie Flo, and she was the best. She did everything for us, Rich. Everything that Mum would have if she'd been around.'

He lifts an eyebrow at that. 'It isn't the same though, Hol. Mums are . . . well, they're *mums*, aren't they?'

'Maybe. Not all mums are like your mum, Rich,' I remind him lowly. Christine has got to be one of the kindest, most selfless and loving people that I ever met. She's lucky to have you as a son too, I think, because not all sons appreciate their mums as much as he does, either. Richard adores Christine. If he weren't so attentive and sweet to me too I'd be almost jealous.

'Hey.' He tugs at my nightie as a sudden flood of tears swells in my eyes and rolls down my cheeks. 'I'm sorry. I didn't mean to make you sad. I love you. I love you more than anything, don't cry. It's just . . . I wish you could see, you don't need Florence Cottage to keep you safe any more, not while I'm here. You've got me. We could go anywhere in the world and I'll always be here for you.'

'It isn't . . . that,' I stammer. The thought has hit me like the flat edge of a sword: all this talk of mums, and what are the chances I'm ever going to be one?

'What if it doesn't work this time with Scarlett?' I whisper. 'She's not the most patient person in the world, is she? The month and half she's been here, hanging around – I think it's nearly killed her.'

'She's mercurial, I grant you,' Rich continues. 'That's just Scarlett, isn't it? But I think she really wants to help you, love. This was never going to be easy for her, was it?'

'When I first asked her, she said no.' I look at him carefully now. 'Did she ever say anything to you about why she changed her mind?'

'She changed her mind,' he gives a low laugh, 'because that's what Scarlett does. You've always said it yourself, she's like a weathercock, turning every which way according to how the wind blows.'

Though usually to suit her own devices, I restrain myself from adding.

'She could do with some of your steadiness now, though, that's for sure.' He kisses my nose. 'You've got to be the bedrock for her. Just like you've always been. She'll stick it out, never fear.'

'You think?'

'Sure. Take a few days off work. You two can go out to places together, keep her calm and happy. Do a bit of sisterly bonding – whatever it is that girls do. Keep her calm and happy.'

'Fine. I can do that.' Not the best time in the world for me to take leave, what with all the problems on the bridge, but I'll do what I can. I look at him suddenly, remembering how this conversation all began.

'Rich. Did you really mean what you said just now about wanting to move to Italy?'

He shrugs, lays his head gently back down on the pillow. And then, because even after ten years of marriage he's never quite got over his shyness enough to actually *say* when he wants us to make love, I slide back under the duvet gratefully. I know what he wants. It's what I want too.

I might not have had my mum around as a child and I may never get to hold my own baby in my arms either. But at least I've got Rich. He loves me and I love him and I need to appreciate that.

Because nobody's ever going to take him away from me, are they?

Hollie

'I haven't heard anything from Gui all week, do you know that?' Scarlett clicks off her phone crossly, hoisting her feet up onto my dashboard, and I look at her in surprise. It's the first time she's given any inkling she might actually be missing her boyfriend.

'You've been in fairly close contact up to now,' I remind her. Whenever she's not sitting there texting her friends, she seems to be on the phone to them. Him too, surely? 'Maybe work just got busy or something?'

She rolls her eyes. 'Maybe he's just got pissed off 'cos I keep putting off the date when I tell him I can come home?'

'Oh, Scarlett,' I say feelingly. 'Are you worried he might be . . . well, drifting away? Because you're not there?'

'He's a man, isn't he?' She looks at me sharply. 'I don't suppose he's going to wait forever.'

What does she mean?

'He does know, doesn't he?' The thought hits me suddenly. She must have told him by now. She shakes her head, her eyes suddenly watering and vulnerable.

'I didn't dare, Hollie. I know I said all that stuff about not being his property and all that, and I'm not of course, but I have been worried about how he'd take it. I thought I'd rather make sure it had happened first – before bringing it up.'

'Oh.'

'It's not been easy for me, being here either. Seeing the way you and Rich are with each other – especially after he came back from Trieste the other night. I know you two little lovebirds can't bear to be parted from each other. Just because I'm not in a steady relationship doesn't mean I don't wish that I was.'

'I'm sorry, Lettie,' I bluster. 'I never knew you felt that way. I assumed you had Gui in the wings and . . .'

'He mightn't stay in the wings too long if it turns out I am pregnant though. Don't you see?'

It looks as if she's backed herself into a Catch 22 situation. What can I say?

'How about Rich?' She looks at me suddenly. 'He's been a bit quiet recently, hasn't he? He's hardly spoken to me for days . . .'

'He's just preoccupied at the moment. Work and his dad and all. Honestly, I don't think he's given you a second thought . . .'

She shoots me a dark glance.

'I didn't mean it that way,' I placate. 'What I meant was, he's not available for anyone at the moment because he's got so much on his mind. He was even talking about us relocating to Italy the other day,' I share. 'That's how worried he is.'

'I got the impression he'd *love* to move abroad.' Scarlett winds down the window on her side and sticks her face out towards the cold breeze.

'You did? When? Have you two spoken about it before, then?'

'Not exactly spoken about it, but it was sort of intimated.' I watch her take her gum out of her mouth and roll it up into a little ball. 'He's not such a stick-in-the-mud as you are, Hol. I think he'd rather like a bit of adventure in his life.'

I feel my shoulders stiffen.

'The nearest you ever come to having an adventure is going for an acupuncture session with your Mr Huang,' she taunts now.

She didn't have to accompany me on my acupuncture visit this morning. She wanted to come. She *insisted*. Just because time is going so painfully slowly for both of us at the moment. Every hour on the clock takes an absolute eternity to tick by. And for the whole of the past week we've both been waking up so early, too, as if there aren't already enough hours in the day to have to get through. I keep expecting her to tell me, any minute, that her period has come and that my hopes are dashed again. I don't want to think that. I want to stay positive, but I have had this happen to me so many times. Part of me can't believe that it could ever be any different, that anything could ever change. So at the moment, because it is my day off and I have no work to distract me, we're just waiting, finding things to do to fill in the time.

After I'd driven Scarlett up to the two grammar schools along Maidstone Road like she wanted and she'd dropped off those recruitment cards for Eve ('Come and work in the wonderful Amazon rainforest during your gap year . . .'), Scarlett hadn't got a clue what else she was going to do with herself for the rest of the day, so she tagged along with me for my appointment at Mr Huang's.

'We could go back to the swimming pool after the acupuncture,' she suggests now. 'There shouldn't be too many people around at this hour. You could have another go at it.'

'Well, thanks for the offer, but . . .'

'You should take me up on it,' she urges. 'While I'm still here in England to help you.' There's a pause as we both absorb what she's just said. Her acknowledgement that she might well not be hanging around for much longer. 'Learning to swim is really easy, Hollie. To tell you the truth . . .' she reflects for a moment as our line of traffic moves forward an inch, 'I don't even *remember* ever learning how to swim. I just did it. That's how easy it is.'

'You were a water baby,' I grant her. 'I remember Bea's teenage nephew Tim used to come and take you to the pool every other weekend, didn't he?'

'You should have come with us. Why didn't you?' Scarlett looks at me pointedly now. 'Then you'd have learned at the same time. Then it wouldn't have become such a big deal.'

'Ha.' All very well for her to say, but by the time she was four or five and learning to swim, I was into early adolescence and the thought of going to the pool with her and Tim didn't appeal. Tim was always sullen and sulky towards me anyway.

'The thing is, Scarlett, I don't just need to learn how to swim. It's much more than that. I need to overcome my fear of water. It's a different thing entirely.'

'It's a circular argument, Hollie.' She shrugs. 'You're frightened of the water because you don't swim. You don't swim because you're frightened of the water. You need to just *do* it, OK?'

'I can't.'

'You won't,' she taunts. Scarlett folds her arms tightly in front of her, and looks out of the window again, the expression of a caged animal on her face. 'I don't know how you put up with all this, Hol.'

'With all . . . ?'

'All this.' She indicates with a hand out of the window. 'This – traffic. *This life.* Waiting in traffic jams. Waiting to find out if you're pregnant. Waiting to find out if *I'm* pregnant. Waiting for the guy to tell you your energy is right so you can take the first steps and actually learn how to swim.'

'I can't be you, Scarlett,' I tell her after I've recovered my composure. 'Scarlett . . .' Our line creeps forwards another three cars before the lights change again and the car in front of us slips through on full red.

'Go, just go!' She turns on me in frustration as I put my foot on the brakes. 'Whatever are you waiting for?'

'Well, the lights were—'

'Who cares what they were? You could have taken a risk and put your foot down. You'd have got through there. It's what

155

everyone else is doing. You can't faff around taking forever over things in your life.' She turns to me insistently. 'I mean, what's your fall-back plan if it turns out I'm not expecting after all?'

'My what?'

'Your Plan B. You know. If I'm not expecting a baby – what'll you do with the rest of your life?'

'I don't have a Plan B.' I look at her in consternation. 'Are you not . . . do you think you might not be . . . ?'

'We'll find out soon enough,' she shrugs, but I get the impression nothing can happen soon enough for her.

At Mr Huang's, Daisy-Lou opens the door to us, her mother laughing silently behind her as she gestures in a perfect imitation of her father. 'Please come in.'

'Oh, she's a *cutey*!' Scarlett warms to her immediately and the ice which has built up between the two of us on the journey down here starts to thaw. 'Sometimes,' my sister says disarmingly, bouncing Daisy-Lou on her knee as I go in for my treatment, 'I can actually see what it is you're making all the fuss about.'

Ha! My sister isn't actually getting a glimpse of what it's like to be broody, is she? That would be a turn-up. Maybe it's a good sign, I hardly dare to let myself hope, maybe she *is* pregnant and those are her hormones kicking in.

'Ah, so, stress levels very high.' Mr Huang nods sympathetically when I'm sitting there five minutes later explaining that we're currently waiting on results for Scarlett's second pregnancy attempt. When he takes my pulse today he emphasises it with a 'Yes, very high', as if he can feel my stress levels through the pulse in my wrist. 'And sister? Stress levels very high too?' he enquires in his soft voice. 'Needs to get back, yes?'

'Back to Brazil,' I nod. He gestures her over and she comes and sits down with little Daisy-Lou still clinging onto her arm, laughing, and Mr Huang takes her pulse too.

'Sister has good *chi*,' he tells me matter-of-factly when he's done. 'Good for having babies. Should happen most easily under the right conditions.'

'Well . . . that's good to hear.' Scarlett's grinning from ear to ear. 'I've got good *chi*,' she tells me proudly. 'Shall I take Daisy-Lou back out of here now?'

'Most kind of sister. I will place needles now please.' He indicates the couch and I jump up there, face down, pulling off my top as I go. After while I hear the faint tearing of paper and I know he's getting his hair-thin needles ready.

'So, sister works in jungle?' His voice has softened in interest. 'Many birds there. Different kinds of birds we don't see in the cold weather.'

I guess so. I lift my head and look at him blankly.

'She's a seed conservationist,' I tell him. 'She collects seeds for the PlanetLove foundation. Her work is very important to her,' I add, as he seems to be considering all this very thoroughly. Or maybe he's just concentrating on where he's placing those needles.

'Then sister most kind to do this work for you. To try two times,' he says after a while. 'This is good way. If jealousy not too high, ha?'

'Why on earth would I be . . . ?' I stop, realising that we're veering off into personal territory I'd rather not venture into.

'When man to sleep with wife's sister – can be big problems. Have to trust, ha?'

'Mr Huang . . . we're not doing *that*.' My eyes open wide with the realisation of what he's thinking. 'We used . . . artificial methods. My husband didn't actually sleep with my sister!' I give a little shake of my head, feeling myself colouring at the thought.

'Ah,' he says, pensive. 'Artificial methods not so good. Lose vital *chi*. Not so good conditions. If time short, better to use natural way.'

If time short . . .

He switches off the bright overhead light and I know he's

157

going to leave me for twenty minutes now to let the needles work. After what he's just told me, it's probably just as well because I'm not sure what I'd be able to say in response. I let my eyes close, my head against the pillow on the couch but my mind is racing.

So is that how they came to have Daisy-Lou? I wonder if they used a family member too? Good God, I'd have to really be in a state to do that. I lift my hand to stifle an embarrassed cough.

Damn. All my hopes that it might work out so easily using Scarlett are down the pan in an instant. If it hasn't worked this time she'll be back to the Amazon and her boyfriend in a flash. Even – I suspect – if I did agree to sell the cottage. And even then, it might still all be in vain. Mr Huang's revelation has left me feeling crushed. Ever since January I've been clinging onto the wonderful thought that Mrs Huang only needed one attempt, even though time was running out for her. I had no idea they'd used the 'natural way' as he put it.

I couldn't bring myself to ever do that. Have them sleep together, even assuming they could ever be persuaded to do it, which of course they wouldn't. No. Never. I'd never ask them anyway. I'd have to be *desperate*.

I turn my face to the wall, a strange stinging in my eyes as he leaves me alone for the acupuncture needles to take effect and in the darkness the realisation creeps in to haunt me.

I *am* desperate.

Scarlett

'I'm feeling pretty upbeat, to be honest.'

God, I am so relieved! I watch as Lucy slices an orange segment carefully then slots it over the edge of a lime-green cocktail. She slides it along her kitchen counter to me.

'You're *sure* you're not expecting?' she frowns.

'I'm ninety-nine per cent certain that I'm not.' I've been suffering with cramps all day. I know that feeling. Thank God. I'm three or four days late and every passing hour had brought me closer to the terrifying thought that I might be pregnant after all.

'Vodka?' I pull a face and then the heat of the alcohol hits the back of my throat in a none-too-unpleasant way. I haven't been allowed a drink since I made that first pregnancy attempt, I realise suddenly. 'How about you?'

My diminutive friend smiles mysteriously. 'We're still waiting to see. I bought a test kit yesterday . . .'

I let out an excited squeal. If she's pregnant, then that's cool. It's what she wants. If I'd been pregnant – well, I know it's what I set out to do but it was never something I wanted, was it? Right at this moment I feel as if I've made a lucky escape. I'm sad about the fact that I won't get any of the money Hollie would have made from the house but losing the terror I've felt over the past few days at the thought I might actually have a *baby* inside me more than compensates for it. I've tried my best. The vodka is also helping me to feel pretty chilled.

'So . . .' I try and size her up, but in that floaty chiffon top she's wearing there is no way I can spy any bump. 'When are you planning on actually using this test kit?'

Lucy tucks her short blonde hair behind her ears. 'That's what I was about to tell you. D'you remember Roma Kelly? She was in the year above us at Fort Pitt.'

Vaguely. I nod her on.

'Well . . . she's maybe pregnant too. I thought all three of us could check out our luck together when the girls came round tonight, what d'you think?'

I let out a snort of laughter. 'I wouldn't want to waste one of your precious test kits, Luce! I'm pretty sure I'm out of the running, so to speak . . .'

'Pity.' She sips at her banana smoothie, looking a bit disappointed.

'For Hollie, yes,' I admit. 'And I did want to do this for her. But – hey – it wasn't meant to be, obviously. It's more of a relief, to be frank. I'll be booking my flights back to South America tomorrow.' I take another vodka-and-orange-laden sip through my straw, relishing the taste. 'I got all my visa renewal papers and work permits through this morning.'

'That was quick.'

'Thanks to Professor Klausmann's efficient secretary, yes.' I had to phone her as soon as she got back from her break but once I'd explained the urgency of it she was straight onto it.

'But now it means you're going to leave us again all the sooner.' Lucy grimaces and comes round to give me a regretful hug. 'That means this'll probably be our last get-together with the girls for a while. Let's make it a good one. Hey – here they are now . . .'

We both look up as Toni and our old friend Jules and a couple more girls – including Roma, Luce nudges me – troop into the kitchen, laden with wine and snacks. Roma, it turns out, remembers everything we ever did at junior school, though I can barely

160

recognise her, so Lucy leaves us reminiscing while she wanders off to find some bowls for the dips and cashew nuts.

'Scarlett Hudson,' Roma drones. 'The original bad girl. D'you remember the time you climbed back into school over the locked gates because you'd left a packet of ciggies behind in your desk?'

'That wasn't me.' I shrug at the others. I never smoked at junior school. I did other stuff, but I wasn't that bad, surely? I get the feeling Roma will have probably have tagged everyone else's misdemeanours along with mine.

'You made up names for all the teachers though, didn't you?' she insists. 'You had us in stitches – Mrs Hogg became Miss Piggy, our French teacher became Kermit, of course, and . . .'

I roll my eyes at Toni. I'm going to need a few more of these green cocktails to help me loosen up, I decide. And why not? I haven't been plastered for a long time. I can't even remember how it feels. I glance at the intimate picture on display of Lucy and Dave snogging on their honeymoon and the thought occurs: I haven't been laid for rather a long time either. Even if I have been trying to get pregnant.

'You went abroad, didn't you?' Toni is back in the conversation. 'I heard you got some fantastic glam job saving the rainforest?'

Everyone turns to look at me and Luce pipes up, having returned with her dinky bowls.

'Scarlett's been living with an Amazonian tribe for the last eighteen months. She's working to save their ecosystem from destruction,' she announces proudly, licking chilli dip from her fingertips. 'Isn't that right, Scarlett?'

'Accounts for the tan,' somebody murmurs. 'I thought she'd been to a salon, to look like that.'

'It's not just their ecosystem that needs saving,' I begin patiently. 'What happens in Brazil affects everyone. It's going to affect all your children for generations to come. The Amazon jungle has been called "the lungs of the world".'

I can sense their interest waning almost immediately.

161

'I thought it might be spray-on,' Roma comments.

'Well, it isn't,' Luce glares at her. 'It's real. And Scarlett's been doing really great work out in the jungle, saving the planet, which is more than you can say serving up salami at the local deli, Roma.'

'Somebody's got to serve the salami,' Roma giggles loudly and I glance at her glass suspiciously. She's got more than just orange juice in there, I'd lay money on it.

Lucy's put Dave's band's demo tape on now so we can all hear it as we start making our way out of the kitchen.

'You're trying to have a baby for your sister, is that right?' Toni looks at me with interest. 'Cool beans. That's such an amazing thing to do . . .'

'I *was* trying for her.' We pause at the door to the living room where everyone's found a seat to listen to the music. 'But no luck, I'm afraid.' I pull a face at her. 'Now I've got to go back.'

'Oh, shame,' she says.

'We often go dancing at the weekends in Manaus,' I shout at Toni over the top of the band.

'You got a boyfriend out there?' Toni yells back. I do a 'so-so' motion with my hands. I could have if I wanted to. Last time I went dancing it was with Gui. He took me to an exclusive nightspot in Manaus where we danced till the early hours. It was a restaurant with live music, I remember now. They kept the place open long after closing time, with the entire band and all, just for us. I have no idea how much he tipped them to do that. That was October, now it's February. Christ. I got another text from him yesterday – thank goodness – and I texted him back this morning as soon as all my papers came through: *Looking forward to seeing you too. Be in touch as soon as I get to Manaus, all my love, Scarlett.*

I will not sleep until that time, he'd texted back. He's keen, there's no question about that.

'You used to go out with that weird guy – what was his

162

name – Duncan?' Roma is back, filling up her glass from the sideboard and yelling out her question just as Lucy decides she's had enough of the overloud music and turns it down several notches. Everyone laughs, looks in my direction again curiously.

'Tell us about Duncan, then,' Toni nudges me. 'What was so weird about him? Why did you dump him?'

'It was a long time ago,' I tell them all breezily. I hardly remember now why I went out with him in the first place. 'We were doing the same ethno-botanical course at uni. He knew a lot of stuff.'

'So why'd you two break up?' Toni's sister Kerris has arrived and hands me another drink as I've somehow finished mine. 'I love hearing break-up stories. Other people's break-ups are always so interesting and just – entertaining, don't you think?' She looks at me earnestly.

Well, why did I break it off with him? My head is starting to swim a little. I'm sure there was a good reason why I dumped Duncan. I know there was. A very good reason. Ah, yes.

'He promised he'd do me a favour and I promised him I'd marry him if he did.'

There's a short, shocked silence at that.

'You didn't think that might be taking it a bit far?' Kerris looks at me, then around at the others in bemusement.

'It was a *big* favour. I never thought he would do it, that's all.'

'And did he?' Toni asks for them all.

'Yep.'

'And instead of marrying him like you promised, you *dumped* him?' Kerris giggles.

'That's about the long and the short of it.'

'But you haven't told us the most interesting bit,' Roma puts in. 'What was the favour he did for you?'

I tap my nose and the girls all burst into laughter around her. Except Lucy. Someone puts the music on again and she pulls me over to one side where the others can't hear her.

'Duncan's been asking round after you, did you know?' She's frowning, a worried look on her face. She never did like him much. She didn't like Aaron, my first boyfriend either. I wish I'd listened to her on both accounts.

'So? I'm not contacting him.'

'No. Don't. He's got even weirder since you knew him. He's into all sorts of shit now. I saw him the other day when we were out and he told me he intended to either get you back or get his own back on you for dumping him, so watch out.'

'What can he do?' I shrug, laughing it off.

'I don't know, Scarlett. He was making out he had something on you, though. He said he sent a message in a balloon to you.' She looks worried.

'Looney!'

She shrugs, carefully scrutinising my face.

'I didn't do anything!' I tell her.

'I'm just saying – watch your back with him.'

'Sure. Will do. Now, when are you going to go and pee on that stick?'

'Ah, that.' She blushes. 'Actually, girls . . .' She turns and motions for the music to be lowered. 'I've got some news for everyone.' I'm suddenly aware from her flushed face and sparkling eyes, there's no question dear old Luce has just had a positive result.

'Oh my Gawd!' I dive towards her for a hug. 'I'm going to be a godmother. Awesome.' Amid shrieks and exclamations of congratulations and felicitations, Roma gets up and self-consciously announces she too is going to use Lucy's bathroom. I can't help but feel a little sorry for her as she goes out with Lucy, who's explaining to her how to use the test kit.

'Okay – your test kit is a bit different to the one I just used. Mine just had a line to indicate pregnancy. With yours we're looking for a single word in the little window of the stick,' she's saying. 'Pregnant. If you get two words – "not pregnant", tough luck!'

As if it isn't perfectly obvious! If the poor sod isn't pregnant there's going to be a very public display of commiserations in here in a minute. She might end up raining on Lucy's parade, too, I think. Let's hope she gets what she wants.

Ten minutes later, she's out of the bathroom and all eyes are on hers expectantly as she walks over, head held high and hardly able to contain her excitement.

'I did it,' she utters and an almighty roar of approval echoes through the room. There's such camaraderie between Lucy and Roma just now, I could almost wish I was one of them. Damn shame, the thought runs through me, that it's this easy for some people and yet my poor sis just can't manage it.

'Your turn.' Luce turns to me with another little box in her hand.

'Oh, come on!' I laugh her off. 'No point wasting your test kit is there? Save it for the next one. I already told you I've had cramps all day. I know the signs, Luce . . .'

'Try it anyway,' she presses. 'Just humour me, come on. If you're going to book your flights tomorrow you might as well be certain.'

Everybody's looking at me now, so I take the packet from her with a grin. 'Whatever you say, honey.'

I down the remains of my vodka and orange – somehow it's my third – and go to her bathroom with the kit, waving Lucy away as she tries to follow me in. I know how to read simple instructions. My eyes are just squinting a bit at the moment because I'm not used to drinking. I take the wand out of its packaging and pee on the end of it. That's what the others just did. Then I wait for a bit. After what feels like ages, I look at the results blearily.

That'll show Lucy. I *told* her I wasn't pregnant. I feel a pang of sudden sadness at the harsh black and white reality of the fact. I am not pregnant. I will not be able to give my sister the baby she so desperately wants. I will not be able to ask her to sell her house for me. I won't be taking back any funds to help my friends. I blow my nose on some tissue paper.

It must be the drink that's making me maudlin, because I have no other reason in the world to feel sad. I'm going back to the rainforest and that's all that matters.

I'm going to go back and maybe start paying more attention to Guillermo, because clearly he still wants me. I've been doing some serious thinking while I've been stuck here over the past few weeks and one thing I *have* realised is how much I want him too. Damn it, now the wand has fallen on the floor. Just the act of leaning down to pick it up is making my head pound. I'm going to have to take it out to them though, they'll be waiting.

'Here she comes! Tell us, is it a hat-trick?' Kerris raises her glass in joyful expectation.

'Afraid not,' I wave the little tell-tale wand at them with a wry grin. 'I did tell you girls . . .'

'Oh, bugger.' Lucy snatches the wand off me, clearly disappointed. 'There was just something about you that reminded me of my sister when she was first expecting and I thought you might be . . . oh, lordy!' She looks at me suddenly, her eyes widening in shock. 'According to this, you *are* pregnant.'

I give out a little laugh. 'No, I'm not.'

The girls all crowd round to look at the wand, and they all concur with her. I can feel my face growing hotter by the minute.

'But I am not!' I look at her helplessly. 'I just did the test and I know that I am not.'

'Did you read the instructions on the leaflet?' Luce asks.

I didn't. But it's as simple as hell to use. The others just described what they did, didn't they? I am not pregnant.

'I think I know what I just did,' I tell the happy group. 'I just picked up the stick you left on the bathroom sink, Luce.'

'You did?' Her excitement disappears in a flash.

'Yes. They were lying by the sink and I knocked one over – it must have been yours. Mine didn't have that line on it, I swear it didn't. I've had too much to drink, obviously. In fact, my cramps are really bad right now, Luce. I'm really sorry, I'm going to have to be a party pooper and go home.'

'You're looking as white as a sheet,' she observes. 'I'll get Dave to drive you round to your sister's.'

'I'd really appreciate that.' I'm confused, I'm feeling really unwell all of a sudden. My stomach is killing me and my head is feeling giddy as hell.

I am not pregnant. I know my stick didn't have that line through it like hers did. I'm sure of that. It's just that something doesn't feel right. In fact, something feels very wrong.

And that feeling of foreboding that I was feeling earlier when I thought I *was* up the duff has returned.

Red Balloon

It is icy this morning. When the roadsweeper brushes past the curb, turning into the cul-de-sac it normally bypasses on its route down the road, the old crisp and chocolate packets wedged under the soggy leaves that it disturbs are ones that have been there for months. The dog-rose bush in the corner, devoid of its leaves, looks bare and cold. Only the shiny metallic red of the deflated balloon still hanging from its twigs is left to catch the morning sun; the little envelope it once carried so proudly and so high up into the sky is still attached.

'What's this?' The student wheeling his bike on his way to college pauses to pick up the envelope, pulls at the balloon and the whole thing comes free.

'"Scarlett L. Hudson",' he reads in wonder. The name rings a faint bell. Someone who was at school with his sister, perhaps? He can't be sure. And who might be sending this girl Scarlett a card like this; a message on a balloon?

Should he find out who, or what the message is about? He hesitates, torn between curiosity and propriety. Curiosity wins and he fumbles with the glued-down envelope, his fingers encumbered by thick gloves, it's cold out this morning.

If it's important she'll be glad to have it. Maybe he can find out where she lives and deliver it sometime soon? He's a romantic at heart, it's true. It could be his good deed for the day. Though in which case, he reconsiders, perhaps it would be best to leave the thing unopened.

The student shoves it – string, balloon and all – into the zip pocket of his laptop, attached securely to his bike.

'Scarlett L. Hudson,' he mutters, as he pushes off on his bike once more, 'your message will shortly be on its way to you again, never fear . . .'

Hollie

The frozen mid-February wind whips into my face as I pull Ruffles to heel. It's not yet 5.20 a.m. We've just walked up along The Vines, past the cathedral and into the top end of the high street where the icy air that sweeps in off the Medway is laced this morning with the salty tang of the sea. I should just keep on walking, that's what I should do. I don't want to go home to where Rich is still sleeping because as soon as he's awake I'm going to have to tell him what Scarlett told me as soon as I got up. That it's over. She's not pregnant and my sister has wasted two months of her time hanging around here for nothing. And I've wasted two more months of mine in futile, hopeless longing and wishing for something that is never going to happen, wanting something that will never be mine.

When I left the house with Ruffles, Scarlett was sitting on the bed, already packing. She's been on the internet since the crack of dawn this morning, looking for the best deal out of here. She's texted her people at PlanetLove already and told them that she's coming home.

How could it end like this? Why give me so many signs that things are going so well only to dash my hopes again like this? That's just cruel.

I'm even overcoming my fear of the water. Yesterday I went – all by myself – and stood in the shallow end of the toddlers' pool, the water right up to my ankles, and I stayed there a whole fifteen minutes without any trouble at all. All the time I had Scarlett's words ringing in my head, egging me on: *You can't faff around taking forever over things in your life* . . . I kept thinking, Scarlett's right. She doesn't 'faff around', does she? She takes what she wants from life, jumps in with both feet; she takes risks.

So I did it. I went in yesterday and I faced my fear and for the first time in my life I began to see the possibility that, yes, I might actually do this. I could learn to swim.

I didn't go in any further than just dipping my feet in. I didn't want to push it. But it felt as if . . . oh, I don't know . . . some invisible barrier had been broken through. As if I had crossed some line where things that had previously been beyond my reach were suddenly very reachable. And the baby was one of those things.

I want to run along this pavement as fast as I can, as far as I can away from here because the discomfort inside of me is eating me up; but I know that no matter how far away I go, there is nowhere I can go to get away from myself. It cannot end like this. It can't. It mustn't. Should I ask her to try again? There is no hope in that, I know, because she's clearly dying to get away. Her heart is already back in the Amazon, that much was obvious the way she looked at me when she told me the news this morning. There is nothing I can do, nothing I can offer that would entice her to stay.

'Hey! Wait up, Hol!'

I turn, aware that I'm being called and of Ruffles' laboured panting beside me, and we slow down our pace a fraction. When I sneak a look at the man who's just caught up with me, his nose and cheeks red with the biting wind, but his kind and lovely eyes bright with anticipation, I almost cannot bear it. I know what Rich is thinking. It's obvious, isn't it?

'Scarlett isn't pregnant, Rich. The second attempt didn't work.'

He stops, rubbing his hands together; evidently he's left the house so quickly he didn't have time to put on any gloves.

'She isn't?' I catch a fleeting glimpse of sadness in the compassion that fills his face now. 'I heard you two talking – I was half asleep. Then I heard the door go and I knew you'd taken Ruff out but when you didn't come back . . . I was worried maybe something had upset you . . .' He takes in a deep breath. 'I'm so sorry, darling.'

'Have you spoken to her?'

He shakes his head.

'I came straight out to find you, hon.' He hugs me close to him and a sob catches in my throat.

'I only found out this morning – she'd just got in from Lucy's party – they all took pregnancy tests there, apparently, and that's when she found out.' My words are all gushing out in a tangled rush. 'I don't understand how it didn't work, Rich. It *should* have worked. I never thought that would be an issue for us because Scarlett is so young and he says she's healthy and we've done everything right and she's got good vital *chi* . . .'

'Vital *chi*,' he repeats softly, though I can't imagine it means very much to him. 'Will she stay on for a third month? Can we try again?'

'Oh!' I give a high-pitched laugh. 'She's going stir-crazy, Rich. She doesn't want to stay. She keeps getting all these phone calls from Brazil. She feels she has a responsibility to the people she left out there, she's dying to get back . . .'

'Let her go, then.'

Let her go? I stare at him, wide-eyed. He's stating the obvious, of course, and it's what I already know but when I hear him saying it, the reality of it sounds very different. Scarlett's going away. She's packing even as we speak.

My sister *is* leaving. And she's taking my dream with me. But what if . . . 'If you think outside of the box,' Scarlett's fond of saying, 'there's usually a way through.' I'm used to thinking *in* boxes, that's my trouble.

172

But what if . . . what if we could persuade her to stay on like Rich has just said, for just one more month? It might happen. Should I be prepared to give up now?

What if we were to look at the whole thing again, but differently? I feel my breath coming in quick gasps, but my thoughts are running even faster than my heartbeat at the moment. What if the fact that Scarlett wants to go back to South America just means that the whole situation has become a lot more urgent than it was, but not impossible?

Perhaps it just means we have to move faster; take decisive action. Perhaps it means – like Mr Huang – that we have to be prepared to make sacrifices?

'Just imagine; this must be what it's like when people have a toddler in tow,' Rich says after a bit, bending down to cajole Ruffles who has just caught up with us. Ruffles is standing there panting, as if he's just run a marathon, though he's been taking his own sweet time. 'You have to take things at the pace of the slowest one.'

'I guess.'

'Honey, if your sister needs to go back to the Amazon we should let her. You can't keep her here. You shouldn't. She'll be glad to be gone and I think maybe . . . so might you be.'

'Why on earth do you say that?'

'What you were saying recently about us never having any private space to ourselves any more,' he reminds me. 'It's true, isn't it?'

'Oh, that,' I give a nonchalant laugh. 'I only said it because the cottage does seem a little overcrowded at the moment.'

'Just imagine how much more overcrowded it will be with a baby and all the paraphernalia that goes along with it . . .'

'That would be entirely different,' I say fiercely. 'Look, Scarlett's here because we asked her to stay, I know. I'm not being ungrateful, I just . . .'

I just almost wish now she had never come back. I wish I

hadn't asked her to get involved. I wish Mr Huang hadn't made the suggestion that he did, and make it all seem so perfectly innocuous and innocent and *natural*. I wish I had not fallen in love with adorable little Daisy-Lou and been so envious of her happy parents before I realised what means they used to come by her.

It's not as if they would be *making love* or anything like that. Mrs Huang did it, after all, and she's a perfectly lovely, ordinary lady.

I don't want to do this. I bite my lip, turning my face away from Rich even though he can't read my thoughts. I've said in the past that I'd do anything, haven't I? Why not this? I have to look at it logically, objectively and impartially. It would be . . . it would be intercourse for the purpose of having a child. A means to an end. That's all.

It's not as if they feel anything for one another. She looks on him like an older brother, I know. They would both be doing it as a favour to me and only me. So what am I so worried about? Am I really so petty and unsure of my own marriage that I'd be jealous of my own sister . . . ? I look at Richard helplessly.

'You just . . . ?' Richard has stopped and pulls me by my arm to one side so we're leaning up against the stone balustrades opposite the narrow pier. We've walked nearly the entire length of the Esplanade now and in a moment we're going to have to turn round and walk back to Florence Cottage. We should, because my fingers are frozen right through to my bones out here, my teeth are chattering. It's barely dawn yet. The dog has done what he came out here to do and Rich and I have both got to get on and get ready for work this morning. But I don't want to go back home.

'Oh, Rich! I just . . .' I hang my head and he pulls me to him. His dark coat is wet with melting snowflakes. When he leans his head closer to mine he smells familiar and sweet and warm. Underneath that smart coat I know he is wearing only a pair of scruffy old jeans and a pyjama top that he hastily threw on so he could join me because I'd bolted through the door. Oh Rich, I can't bear it. I feel his kisses on the top of my head, reassuring and loving.

I know that he loves me. He wants me to be happy. He would do anything I ask of him. But dare I ask him this?

'Let her go, sweetheart. We'll find another way.'

My breathing is coming very shallowly now, my eyes closed tight, my nose buried into his coat.

'We *cannot* find another way,' I wail. There is no other way. I have been waiting for so long, too long . . . I have tried too many ways and now here for the first time, I feel I've come the closest that I ever really have. It must be Scarlett. I feel it in my bones. There is no one else that will do. The baby that she'll have will have our ancestors' blood in its veins, and so it will be truly mine. He's got to be made to understand this.

'There might be another way,' I start. 'But it would still involve using Scarlett.' I rub my face now, lifting myself away from his shoulder to look into his eyes. I suddenly feel so hot and flushed. I lift my face to the sky to feel the ice dropping onto my skin.

'She's going to leave us, Hollie. She's got to go back. She won't agree to stay on any longer, we've already established that.'

'She might be persuaded,' I croak. 'There's something she wants, and if I . . . if I agree to give it to her, then I know she'll agree to stay on. It's *you* who won't agree to it.' I start to cough as the phlegm builds up in my throat.

'You look a very strange colour, love.' He's frowning at me, concern building in his eyes, and he takes the edge of my scarf and gently wipes at my face now, my eyes streaming. 'Perhaps it's the cold that's getting to you? The upset. Will you let me take you home?'

'No!' I look at him desperately. My chance is slipping away, can't he see it? Receding like a paper boat tossed out on a fast spring tide, faster than I can ever hope to retrieve it. 'I don't want to go home before I've asked you what I've got to. And I know . . .' I lower my eyes from the grey snow-laden sky to look at him miserably '. . . I already know that you will never agree.'

'Why won't I agree?'

'You won't.'

He laughs. It's a short, puzzled laugh. He takes hold of my hands in my wet gloves and he gives them a little shake, as much to say – this is me here, Hollie. When have you ever asked me for anything and I've denied you?

'OK. Just tell me.'

I wish I could but my voice seems to have abandoned me right now.

'It's to do with the mysterious Mr Huang, am I right?'

Hollie

Mr Huang. How does he know? A shock goes right through me when Richard mentions his name. I give a little nod.

'Something to do with me needing acupuncture?' he ventures.

'No.'

'Ah. You want me to drink some Chinese herbal concoction then? What is it? Powdered scorpion legs in an ampoule of rice wine?'

'No! Stop making a joke of it, Richard! This isn't funny. It's not in the slightest bit funny. It's how Mr Huang and his wife managed to get their baby and he swears it will work for us . . .' I trail off, because I hate, hate, *hate* the idea and if he catches a whiff of my reluctance that'll only compound his own. I've got to make out like there is nothing I want more in the world than for this to happen.

'Richard. I really want you to agree.'

'To what?'

'To . . . you making my sister . . .' I cannot say her name '. . . pregnant. The natural way.'

Richard takes a step back, frowns. 'I don't think I've understood you right, Hol.'

'You have. I want you to sleep with her.'

'No.' He shakes his head, decisively, but his eyes are hooded now. 'I won't do that. You were right. I find it hard to believe you're seriously suggesting this, Hollie.' He sounds hurt, horrified even.

'It's the only way.'

'Then it's the *wrong* way.'

'How can that be true?' I reason now. 'If it gets us what we want . . .'

'But at what cost? You do realise the implications of doing that would be horrendous. It's wrong. *No.*'

'There needn't be any implications, Rich. It would just be a one-off act done for the purpose and never mentioned again. We're all adults, aren't we?' I can't believe I'm saying this. Devil's advocate, that's me. Because how will I feel if he turns around at last and agrees with me?

I don't want to have to ask him to do this. I don't. But I can't let go of my dream right now – all the signs are there, that if we just persevere, if we just hang on a little longer, this will all come right.

He winces, turns his face away from me to hide his anger and his disappointment. For the first time I feel the discomfort of someone who has crossed an invisible line.

For a moment we both stare out over the freezing river. It is fast-moving and choppy this morning. It is still barely light and the orange glow from the streetlamps skims and jumps off the surface.

'You don't need to worry that this might harm *us*. We'll last forever, won't we, Rich? No matter what.'

'I always thought we would. I loved you the moment I saw you, Hollie. Cheesy though I realise that sounds, it happens to be true. I've never wanted any other woman. I've never desired anyone else. What you're asking me to do now goes against every . . .'

'Only so we can have a family of our own, Rich! So I can have your baby. It would be a functional thing. A purposeful thing, that's all.'

'A purposeful thing.' Richard turns to take me in now. 'You think that? You think it would have no knock-on effect between you and your sister, let alone between you and me if I did this? Like some sort of stud, for you?'

I swallow hard.

'I love you, Hollie. I love you more than anything or anyone else but don't push it. There is nothing made in this world that can't be broken, don't you know that?'

'That isn't what you told me before,' I challenge.

'What do you mean?'

'Last month – when you forgot our anniversary – when you came back from Trieste, remember? You told me then that you'd love me forever. And . . . and you've also had to consider taking steps that you never thought you'd take, just to protect the interests of your father's business, haven't you?'

'*My* business too,' he says quietly. 'And that's different.'

'I'm just saying, Rich, sometimes when things are precious to us, we consider doing anything we have to, even things outside of our comfort zone – like you taking your father's business abroad, for instance. You were prepared to go that extra mile to try and salvage what you could.'

'My father has worked for forty years to build that business up. It's been his whole life,' Rich retorts. 'Any son would have done the same, tried to help out if his parent's business was going to the wall . . .'

'Except I didn't see Jay going out there with you, did I?'

Rich frowns. 'He didn't need to, Hollie. Because I went.'

'And because Jay has no interest whatsoever in running the company abroad, right? But you'll do whatever you have to – whatever it takes – to keep that dream alive for your dad.' I grab hold of his arm now, trying to persuade him. 'I want you to do this thing for me, Richard. I want to keep my dream alive too and this is the only way I can think how.' My dream which is rapidly turning into a nightmare. I put my hand up to brush away the strands of hair that keep whipping across my face and I can barely feel my fingers inside my cold wet gloves any more.

'Why, Hol?' My husband grabs hold of both my shoulders now. He leans his head in towards mine until our foreheads touch. 'I know that you've dreamed of this baby ever since we were first married. But why do you want it so much? Why so much that . . .' his voice breaks '. . . that you're blinded to anything and everything that may come as a consequence? *Why so much?*'

I look at him, dumbfounded for a moment, because the answer is, I really do not know. All I know is that it does matter. It's as if I began digging for treasure once, a very long time ago, and I've spent all these years digging the same hole and I've not found my treasure yet. But the conviction that there must be treasure at the bottom has never faded. There's still a part of me that believes that if I keep on going long enough, I will find what I'm looking for.

'I don't think this is healthy. I know how much you want this baby but it's got to the stage where . . .'

'Please . . .' I pull his face closer to mine for a moment, whispering desperately in his ear. 'Don't say no. Just please don't say no.'

'We could put in for adoption. We could try for another surrogate – one who lives in this country. BabyInIndia isn't the only place where surrogates can be found.'

I shake my head.

'You won't,' he says. 'Because it's got to be *her*, hasn't it? You've got it into your head that it's got to be your sister. And if it fails?' he says after a while. Have you ever stopped to consider that you will have risked your relationship with your sister – *with me* – all for nothing. Are you prepared to do that?'

'You say that we're strong together,' I challenge him now. 'And I think so too. But it's easy to believe that if there's never anything testing you, isn't it? If we really are as strong as you say then surely we have nothing to fear?'

He closes his eyes then. He lowers his head. 'Why?' he asks again. 'Just tell me why it's so important.'

'Because I don't feel complete without a child!' How can I

make him understand? 'Becoming a mum has always been part of my vision of . . . who I am. Without that, how can I be who I was meant to be? How can I give you the family I know you want too? I know you always tell me you're content but I saw your reaction when Jay and Sarah announced they were expecting at Christmas. You want a child too. I want . . . I want it for *us,* as well as just for me. And because – after all these years I've spent trying – if I give up at the last hurdle I will never forgive myself. I have to know I did everything I could, that's all. And I still think Scarlett is our best option.'

'Because . . . ?'

'Because she is my sister and we share the same genes. And because she has no maternal instinct whatsoever and she will never in a month of Sundays want to keep the baby for herself. And if you sleep with her at the right time – when all the conditions are right – then we don't run the risks of all the things that could go wrong along the way, just like when we tried IVF and because . . .'

Rich looks up at me now, looking heartsore and weary. 'And?'

'And because she owes me,' I finish, surprising even myself with that one. 'No, I don't mean that. I don't know why I even said it.'

I rub at my eyes, because it's as if the world's all gone dim for a moment and I feel so cold, so very cold. The wide river is rushing noisily past the banks this morning, wild and dark and headstrong, set on its course and there's nobody, nowhere, who's ever going to stop it. And if you can't swim, if you're a person who can't swim like me, you'll go down with it – I feel a dull slow ache in my chest at the thought – and the water will rise in you and all life will be squeezed out.

'She owes you.' Richard's warm voice reaches my ears and I look up, startled. 'Does she owe you a baby, my love?' He takes hold of my fingertips gently now.

No, of course she doesn't. I shake my head.

He shudders, then. He sticks his hands inside his pockets and makes a move with his head to suggest we should start heading back.

'So, you're prepared to risk everything. Would it be fair to say, Hollie, that you want this baby even more than you want me?'

'Damn it, Rich!' *Don't say that.* 'I need this baby.' I need it because . . . it will be like planting sunshine in the coldest, saddest place in my heart; because when I have my baby, that place will have life breathed into it again. And I have waited so patiently and for so long. And it has to be Scarlett. I know it has to be her because that is the only way to make things right again. Richard doesn't understand that. I look at him tearfully, but when he meets my gaze he is distant, perturbed, preoccupied.

'If this is what you truly want, and if she agrees, I will do it for you, Hollie. But make no mistake, it *will* affect us. There is no way that it won't come between us, or between you and her. It will.' The words are thrown over his hunched shoulders as we walk back together now. When he says them, I feel triumphant because I know I have achieved the impossible in getting him to agree.

But that feeling does not last very long.

We've been out just over half an hour. That's all it has taken for us to come to a decision that may change the rest of our lives.

It has already changed something. Walking down a moment ago he'd held carefully onto my arm, kept nudging me out of the way of the puddles I seemed to want to fall straight into. Now he's walking so fast I have to struggle to keep up with him. Something deep inside of him has shifted away from the centre of that place that is *us*. I can feel it.

It will pass, I tell myself. He's upset because he's going to have to perform an act that goes against his nature. When we have our child, he'll understand why I asked him. Things will go back to normal. Once she's pregnant, well – we'll be moving on into

182

the spring, the weather will be kinder, the days brighter. Things will start looking better again.

But for now, the puddles of slushy water that we passed on our way up have already turned to ice.

Scarlett

I've got to get my packing done. I want to sort out my stuff – if there's nothing left of the original PlanetLove camp I'll need to take over more than just the one little backpack I brought home with me. I need to concentrate. Why can't I find anything this morning?

I sit down on the edge of the bed, rubbing my eyes and trying to wake myself up properly. Right. I look at the list I've just begun to make myself on the bedside table; cheapest flights out are in a few days' time which gives me the opportunity to stock up on T-shirts and the like. Man, I wish I hadn't had so much to drink at Lucy's place last night. I wish I hadn't stayed up as late as I did – I've barely had two hours' kip. And I wish I didn't feel as sick as a dog with this hangover so I could get on and do what I need to. The worst part of that – telling Hollie that the dream is over – is already done. That wasn't too much fun. She took it just like I expected she would.

'Are you sure you waited long enough?' she asked.

'I waited as long as they say you should.'

'What tests were Lucy and the other girl using?' my sister quizzed then. 'If they were the cheaper versions off the internet you mightn't have had enough pregnancy hormones in there for it to show up yet. Some tests pick up ten microunits of hormone and some won't pick up anything till you've got at least twenty-five miu in there . . .'

'The tests worked well enough for the other two girls,' I'd pointed out. 'And I can't imagine Lucy picking up any cheapo internet test kits. I can't remember what make they were.'

'I want you to do it again for me,' Hollie had begged. Five o'clock this morning it was, still dark, and she wanted me to pee on a stick. 'Your hormones will be more concentrated in the morning,' she'd insisted. 'Even at this low level, the kit I want you to use should pick it up.'

And I'd felt so goddamn awful, what was wrong with her? Couldn't she tell that I wasn't even seeing straight this morning? So I'd gone into the bathroom and opened up one of her test kits and run some tap water over it, just to please her. 'Not pregnant' it announced to both of us ten minutes later. And she'd sat down on one of the dining room chairs and just looked at it in silence for a very long time.

Then she took Ruffles out in the freezing cold and she's been out for ages. Too long really, but I haven't got any more time to worry about her; I have to get away.

She'll be fine, anyway. I just heard Rich go out after her. I popped my head round the door and one moment he was standing in the hallway in nothing but his PJ bottoms and the next he was gone. I barely had time to come out and speak to him and I would have liked to. I know how much he wanted that baby too.

But anyway. That's over. And I'm glad it's over. I've been feeling such relief since yesterday when I found out. I don't know how I would have gotten through it, if I'm honest. Listening to Lucy and Roma and all of them banging on about pregnancy last night, well, it put me off the whole idea even more.

I spoke to Barry earlier and he filled me in on the changes that are happening over there. I've got it all scribbled down on my writing pad. European . . . what were they called? I crane my head to see what it was I wrote earlier: 'European Alliance Group have temporarily taken over our patch of the forest and are defending it against all-comers.' I smile, imagining a band of well-fortified and well-meaning Belgians and Germans wearing headbands and khaki trousers and wielding sticks. I'm not sure how long they'll be able to help us out for but they mean well.

I grimace as a sharp pain jabs my temple. My head feels like someone's tried to stave it in with a hammer. I need to rehydrate, I need some water. I need some coffee. Maybe some Alka-Seltzer? I drag myself into the bathroom.

At least Barry sounded as if he was pleased that I'm coming back. Two of their part-timers have left and they're really short on the ground right now. He admitted they are barely keeping track of the Yanomami. And some of the tribe – including José's dad, Tunga – look like they're about ready to leave the forest, which would be a complete disaster. It happened once before with the tribe Eve and Barry were working with before I came along. Once the men start to leave, the tribe gets dissipated and disbanded and their knowledge gets lost forever.

Hollie's bathroom cabinet is so jam-packed full of stuff for all eventualities that I just know she's got to have some Alka-Seltzer in here. It'll be all in some kind of order no doubt but I don't know her system. All I can see in here is a load of pregnancy testing kits! I reach my hand in to see what might be lurking at the back and no less than three test kits fall into the sink.

Man, that was weird what happened at Lucy's house yesterday. Me picking up her pregnancy wand by mistake – that nearly gave me a heart attack. Thank God it wasn't mine. I know mine didn't have any line or any message on it. I was pretty sozzled, but I know what result I got, and it wasn't a positive one. I didn't want any of them jumping to the wrong conclusion.

I don't know if I want that Alka-Seltzer after all. Maybe I should just have some coffee? Or maybe I should go back to bed right now, I'm sick as a dog and my stomach's still in a whole load of pain. I perch on the edge of the closed loo seat and just sit there, holding onto my stomach. I don't normally get sicky crampy pains like this. That'll teach me to try and get pregnant. Never again. And thank God it didn't happen. What the hell was I thinking of, anyway?

If I'd been in my right mind I would never have offered to do it. But that's what being here around Hollie and Rich does to me. It takes me away from who I am and who I want to be; I get caught up in stuff that's . . . well, it's not mine.

The front door goes and I lock the bathroom door. I don't want to talk to either of them right now. It sounds as if only one of them has come back in – only one set of footsteps. Maybe he never caught up with her after all?

I close my eyes, wishing that I felt better. I wish I could fast-forward the next few hours to the point where my head was back to normal again. After a while I lift my fingers away from my face and stare at Hollie's three test kits that are still sitting in the sink, the cardboard getting all damp. I should fish them out. Do these things even work? How reliable are they anyway?

I can't honestly remember what I did yesterday. I should do it again, like Hollie asked, I suppose. Just for thoroughness. I pull out the leaflet with shaking fingers and skim through the instructions. That's all exactly what I did yesterday. Right. That's simple enough. Pregnancy hormones human chorionic gonadotropin . . . blah blah . . . only present during pregnancy, so if it's picked up you get the word 'pregnant' and if not you get the words 'not pregnant'. Pee on the stick, put the wand in during mid-flow, etc. etc. – all what I did yesterday. Easy as pie.

So I do it again. I wait for mid-stream flow and then I pee liberally all over the bit where you're supposed to and put it down in the sink. I have to wait ten minutes. Thought I might as well check it just to be doubly *doubly* sure.

I want to go home, back to Brazil.

My phone beeps and I fish it out of my pocket. It's Guillermo again. He's sent me a big love heart text and a picture of a bunch of flowers. *I cannot wait* . . . he's written underneath. Neither can I. I'm dying to go home.

The front door goes again and someone else comes in. I should get out of here, really. Somebody might need to use the bathroom. I haul myself up and remember to pick up the wand and its packaging with me. I'll dispose of all of that in my room. No point in getting Hollie's heart racing again, is there?

Back in my room with a large glass of water and a cup of steaming coffee, I'm aware that the cottage is extraordinarily quiet this morning. No loving endearments being called out from Rich to Hol and vice versa, none of the cheerful banter that usually goes on between them. I shrug, picking up my mobile which is beeping again. They could have argued or they might just be so disappointed they don't want to talk. I glance at the little screen at the front of my phone but I don't recognise the number calling.

'Scarlett Hudson?' The curt, clipped tones of the woman at the other end takes me by surprise.

'Speaking.' From my bed, sick as a dog, so if this is some kind of 'courtesy call' you'd better hang up . . .

'This is Gillian Defoe from the European Alliance Group. You might have heard we've just taken over the day-to-day running of PlanetLove activities in Yellow Zone from Chiquitin-Almeira?'

'Oh. Hello.'

'I understand you're on leave in the UK at the moment but you're expecting to return to work shortly, is that right?'

'I . . . yes, it is.' I thought the European what-not were just holding the fort in our patch – I imagined in some sort of voluntary capacity. What does she means they've taken over from Chiquitin-Almeira? I sit up a bit straighter, take a sip of my water. I need to pay attention. It's all happening this morning. 'I've been checking up on the flights back to Brazil this morning,' I add when she seems to go quiet for a bit.

'That's fine. We're hoping that as many of the original staff as possible will stay on. You know the ropes and you've got the contacts, so that's useful to us. I'm just reading up on your file here. I see you were sent a letter from PlanetLove just before Christmas in which they ask you to contact them. Is that right?'

Crap, not that again.

'Yes, and I have contacted them, several times, about it. But everything in Berkeley Square is at sixes and sevens and nobody seems to know anything about it.' I've phoned half a dozen times, it's true. 'My project sponsor Professor Klausmann had no idea what it was about either.' I pause significantly here, just so she knows I have friends in high places.

'He wouldn't, Ms Hudson. He sponsors your place but he doesn't have anything to do with the running of PlanetLove.'

'But . . . he's already signed all my forms for me,' I run on. 'We think it was some sort of mistake.'

'I hope so. That's what we're looking into at the moment.' She goes quiet again and I imagine she must be reading my file.

'Hello?' I say after I've been hanging on in silence for a while. 'Was there anything else?'

'I'm just looking at the notes that have been written down here, Ms Hudson. I see Eve Mitcham has marked you down as an exemplary employee, showing enthusiasm and dedication to your job.'

'Thanks.'

'But I'm sure you understand that we'll need to look into these mysterious question marks that have appeared over your profile. It's probably nothing to worry about, but we have to check it out before your employment with our outfit can be confirmed.'

'Oh. Can you tell me what the problem is at all?'

'I'm afraid at this stage I actually have no idea. I've only just taken up this post so I can't help you there. But I'm sure it'll all be sorted soon. You might want to delay booking your flight over till it's resolved, though. Naturally we can't offer you back your old post till we've put this thing to bed.'

'That hardly seems fair,' I start. 'I have tried to contact the PlanetLove offices to get to the bottom of it and now you won't even tell me why . . .'

'Is that all right with you?' She carries on over me as if I hadn't spoken.

'It'll have to be, won't it?' I tell her through gritted teeth. 'So, what do you want me to do?'

'Nothing at all, for now. I'll conduct my investigations and then get back to you if I need to or if I have any questions for you. It's probably, as you say, just an administrative error. But we need to make sure everything's correct, you understand?'

'Fine.' I take a long glug of coffee. Then I take some more water for good measure. I can still fly out to Brazil. I can go and catch up with Guillermo. If these people have taken over the 'outfit' as she calls it, do we still even need those funds I've been working so hard to acquire? Maybe we don't. And as I'm not pregnant, maybe that's just as well. I don't think I like the sound of this European Alliance Group. Something tells me there are going to be big changes in my job when I get back and I'm not going to like them.

'I'll speak to you soon, then?'

'As soon as I can, Ms Hudson. Good to talk to you, and have a good weekend.'

'Yeah, you too.' Even though you've just pretty much ruined mine, I think crossly. What am I supposed to do now? I was about to book my flights for early next week. I suppose I should carry on and do that. They'll soon figure out that they need me over there. They won't bother with carrying out any investigations for too long, I shouldn't imagine.

'Hello?' Hollie's knocking so softly on my door I can barely hear her.

'Hi. Won't be a second.' I stand up, still feeling groggy, and the pregnancy wand falls off the edge of the bed where I'd dropped it. Just as well, too, because I'd forgotten all about it and she would have seen it when she came in and then there would have been all sorts of explanations needed.

I bend to pick it up, bloody thing.

That's when I catch sight of the unmistakable single word running through the little window of the wand.

Pregnant.

Hollie

'Can I come in?' I open the door a fraction but it won't go very far because Scarlett has her belongings scattered all over the floor. I push a bit harder, stooping to pull out a pair of socks that have got wedged under the door.

I'm going to ask her if she will do this. I'm going to ask my sister if she will sleep with my husband before she disappears out of my life for another two years and before anything that Richard's just said to me has a chance to filter down to the common-sense part of my brain.

It is madness. I know it. Even if she agrees, it's going to lead to the most uncomfortable dynamic imaginable between us all. If she does not agree I will only have succeeded in angering and disappointing Richard, because he'll see this as evidence that my desire for a child is greater than my desire for him or for us. Even though that isn't true – he's wrong and the fact that I'm willing to try this route is testimony to how much I trust them both.

I trust Rich because he loves me. I trust Scarlett because – well, because she has no interest in Rich. He's my husband and he's ten years older than her and she's got her own, very full life. I know she isn't interested in having any part of mine. I've got to stand fast now and remember that.

'I see you've managed to get quite a lot of packing done?' I stand on the small patch of carpet by the door which hasn't yet

192

been covered with books and papers and underwear and rub at my arms because I'm still feeling frozen from my walk earlier. Numbed, more like. What I have had to request this morning has somehow left me numbed, right to the very core. And now I'm going to have to do it all over again.

What have I got to offer her when Brazil is beckoning – judging by the state of her packing – in a few short days' time?

'Have you booked your flights yet?' I press when she doesn't answer. Scarlett turns from where she's just thrown some rubbish into the bin. Christ, she looks rough. If this is her hangover from last night then she's already more than made up for the alcohol-free Christmas I made her have. She looks as pale as the grey sky outside, and just as washed out. She shakes her head a fraction.

'Are you OK, Scarlett?' Rich hasn't been in here and told her already, has he? Surely not? A cold fear runs through me at the thought. My sister grimaces and sits down on the edge of the bed, scattering a pile of papers as she does. She holds her hands over her stomach.

'Are you going to be sick?'

'I was already sick,' she admits.

I fold my arms, feeling far from sympathetic.

'I just heard from the people who are taking over PlanetLove,' my sister croaks. 'They sound like a right bunch of tossers . . .'

'Do they?' I sit on the little chair at the bottom of her bed and the cold breeze from the open window blows onto the top of my head. The flash of irritation passes in an instant. It doesn't matter today. Not today. Today only one thing matters.

Scarlett grimaces. 'I was looking for some Alka-Seltzer and a whole load of your stuff fell out of the bathroom cabinet,' she gets out.

'That's OK. Would you like me to find you some?'

She shakes her head. 'I got some water and some coffee. I think maybe I'm going to need an aspirin. I don't know.'

'Headache? I'll get you a painkiller,' I offer, standing up. 'So, what's up with the new people?' I look at her curiously without making a move towards the door. Scarlett waves her hand dismissively, but, boy, does she look ill . . .

'It's all changing,' she gets out at last. 'Everything I left behind. By the time I get back it's going to be gone, all of it.'

'You've only been away for a few weeks.'

'And in that time the PlanetLove base camp has been raided and changed location, our unit has been taken over by some kind of European alliance, the woman running it has decided she needs to investigate something to do with the job application I made to them over two years ago . . .'

'Oh, how ridiculous!' There's a faint alarm bell ringing somewhere in my head but I am too taken up by my own concerns this morning to take heed. 'It's probably all just red tape and administrative hold-ups. Somebody forgot to sign and date a form somewhere along the line . . .'

'Probably, yeah. But they don't want me back there till they've checked it all out.'

'They don't?' I sit back down on the chair, the thought of getting her an aspirin instantly slipping from my head. 'What did your boss Eve say about it all?'

'She sent me a text recently but she was a bit vague, if I'm honest. I get the impression it's the other lot who are running the show now.'

'So . . . you'll be staying on here for a bit longer, then?'

'Ha!' she says in response, lifting her hands to her head.

'Scarlett – I've been thinking about what you told me this morning. Are you one hundred per cent certain that you did that pregnancy test properly?'

She nods at me, her face ashen. 'I know what you want to hear, Hollie,' she says at last. 'But it's no use . . .'

I hang my head for a minute, taking in the finality of her words and dredging up the courage I need to ask her the next thing.

'Then I have to run something past you. I've . . . I've had another idea.' My sister gazes up at me through bleary eyes. 'I don't know if this is something you'd ever consider doing for me.' I look at her helplessly. 'Under the circumstances, I know that your answer is more than likely to be no. But I'm going to ask you anyway.'

Scarlett picks up the large tumbler of water by her bed and drains it. She glances at me for an instant, her cheeks bulging with water before she can manage to get it all down.

'I'm going to ask you to consider staying on for a bit and trying out . . . what Mr Huang suggested.'

Her eyes widen.

'I'm saying I think we should try the "natural method" of conception.'

Scarlett chokes and splutters then and the water splatters all over the bedclothes, all over her papers.

'You're saying *what*?'

'I know, I know.' I pick up a little flannel that's sticking out of her washbag and hand it to her. 'It sounds outrageous. It sounds . . . desperate,' I trail off. 'But it worked for Mr Huang. He says you have very good *chi*. You're young and you're healthy and under the right conditions you should conceive naturally and easily, just like Mrs Huang . . .'

'Oh, no, Hollie. No!' My sister wipes up the spilt water, frowning furiously. 'Don't. Please. Just don't, OK? Let's not go there.'

'I have to go there. There is no other place for me to go.'

'Oh, yes, there is.' Scarlett's eyes suddenly take on a glint. 'There's adoption, for starters.'

'Then it wouldn't be Richard's child. It wouldn't be . . . it wouldn't be mine.'

'Yes, it would!'

She doesn't know, she doesn't remember all the things that I remember though . . .

195

For a moment, I can only stare at her dumbly.

'I used to think of you as being mine, once upon a time,' I tell her eventually. A child of my heart, if not of my body, but at the time I was too young to know the difference.

Does she remember the time me and Flo took her, aged four, for her pre-school booster injection at the clinic? She wanted to hold my hand on the way in. It was always me she looked to, for comfort and for succour, not Flo. It was me she wanted. But the nurse wouldn't let me go in the room with her for the injection, she insisted Flo take her through. That didn't go down too well. I don't remember all the details but I remember Lettie kicking up an almightly fuss. Several nurses were drafted in to hold her down for the doctor in the end, and I wound up yelling at them all to stop, just stop, because they were hurting my Lettie and everyone turned to look at me in astonished embarrassment.

'She's not *yours*, Hollie Hudson,' I remember Flo remonstrating with me afterwards, embarrassed by my noisy protestations. 'You may think of her as yours but she isn't. She never was and she never will be. I've given you too much of a free rein with her, that's the trouble, but all that's going to have to end.'

True to her word, Flo had taken Lettie's little bed out of my room and put it in her own after that. She took to walking Scarlett to school herself, reading her bedtime stories and doing all the things that I liked to do for her. At the time I saw it as her stepping between us, driving a physical wedge between me and my sister, but the truth was she'd done more than that. She made me long for a time when I'd have a child of my own. Someone who nobody else could ever come and lay a claim to. Someone I could say 'I love you' to, in a way no one had ever been able to say it to us as kids.

'There are other people in the world who could do this for you, for Christ's sake, Hollie!' Scarlett's shocked voice brings me back to the present. She stands up and a whole pile of socks that she'd been balancing on her lap fall now to the floor. 'Why the hell would you ask me to sleep with your husband you . . . you stupid fool!' She looks directly at me for an instant. 'If he were my man I'd never let *you* anywhere near him, know that?' She's only half-joking, I can tell.

'I know Richard is an attractive man. I'd like to think you wouldn't take my suggestion any less seriously if he were ugly as a dog.'

'Look, I'm packing to go now, Hol. Just let me go. I'm planning to take out a tourist visa if I can't get my work permit from the European wot-not group. I'm planning . . . I'm planning on making a go of it with Gui. I need to get back!'

'Please.' I do not know where the strength of my desire comes from; I know that it's foolhardy to be so persistent in the face of all this opposition, not to mention the opposition in my heart. 'Please, reconsider, Scarlett.'

'The thing is . . .' she looks at me pityingly '. . . I have already reconsidered, Hol.'

We look at each other for a long minute and the wind flutters in through the little open window and ruffles her papers so that they waft down off the chest of drawers and onto the floor. We both just stare at them. I don't make a move to shut the window as I normally would.

'You need to find something else to fill that void, Hollie,' she says slowly. 'Whatever space you think that baby's going to fill for you – find something else to fill it. Look – see what I found this morning.' She leans forward suddenly and picks up an old familiar tapestry bag. I'd forgotten all about that!

'I found it stuffed into the back of the wardrobe,' she says in answer to my puzzled expression. 'Look.' She opens the bag and tips out the contents. A pile of unfinished toddler cardigans and jumpers fall onto the bed. She shakes the bag a bit and the clatter of a dozen knitting needles follows. 'All these beautiful things that you used to make. Why did you ever stop?'

'Only a few weeks ago you were telling me I needed more in my life than knitting,' I accuse her.

'Well, I was wrong. Because . . . they're gorgeous. They're so creative. Why did you ever give up doing what you're so good at?' My sister's voice is coming in short puffs, as if she's been running.

'Because I wasn't so good at making the babies to put in them, was I?' I stare at the jumble of wool and tiny items for a moment. What's this got to do with anything? She's just trying to distract me. 'I still need you to do that for me.'

'Not that way. You've still got Richard, don't forget. Would it really be worth it if you gained a baby and you lost your husband into the bargain?'

'I won't lose Rich.'

'If this is how far you're prepared to go to get the baby then maybe you deserve to,' she throws at me. 'Look, I just told you, I've reconsidered. All this was one big mistake, Hollie. I should never have agreed to do this for you. I'm *so* the wrong person. I'm . . . I'm not consistent and persevering like you are. I don't stick at things when the going gets tough, I'm not made that way – I just get out. I know now that I'm not cut out for pregnancy. To tell you the truth . . .' she stares at the ground '. . . if I found I'd made a mistake last night and I'd read the pregnancy stick wrong, I'd still be telling you the same thing. I wouldn't be prepared to go ahead with it.'

'I don't believe you. Of course you would! You've never run away from a single challenge in your life, Scarlett.'

'I ran away from here, didn't I? I ran halfway round the world . . .'

'You never *ran away*. You went to Brazil to fulfil your dream. You love your work.'

Scarlett stares at me, dumbfounded, then throws up her arms in frustration. 'I can't explain this to you, if you can't already see it. But you're right, I did find some meaning in

Brazil. Some peace too. There are people there I can actually be useful to.'

'You could be useful here too if you stayed. *Please* do this for me.' I don't want to break down in front of her but my body does it all by itself.

'Jeez – you make me so mad, really you do! Richard would never agree anyway. He's as loyal to you as the day is long. He'd never agree to sleep with anyone else.'

'Maybe not just anyone. But I've asked him if he'd agree to sleep with you.'

Scarlett suddenly becomes very still.

'And?' Her stark gaze meets mine. 'He told you to get real, right?'

I shake my head. 'He agreed to do it, Lettie. He said if I could persuade you, then he'd do it.'

'Jesus wept!' My sister rubs her eyes so hard now I think she's going to poke them out. 'You've asked him. You've already persuaded him?'

I nod. I get up and go to squeeze her hand but Scarlett shudders. 'For God's sake, Hol. Don't ask me this. Just don't ask me . . .'

But something, somehow, has got through to her at last. I can feel it.

Scarlett

We hadn't had any music that day, Richard and I. But when he put his arms about my waist to dance with me in the cow-barn, our surroundings felt as grand to me as any glitzy ballroom in the movies. The musty smell of the bales of straw in the corner vanished in an instant, the damp patches on the sandy floor where the rain leaked through were shining Italian marble beneath our flying feet. We'd hummed along as we went, trying to be serious, as military as the music in our minds, but I hadn't been able to stop giggling.

Maybe it was the nerves. The fact that, at fourteen, I was way too short for him. He had to bend down as you would for a child, but he was so patient and attentive. *Here, you place your feet here; you must look this way. Keep your expression serious. No, don't look at me. In this dance the man has to woo the woman; she is proud and haughty, unattainable. Once you've mastered the steps you have to pay attention to the eyes. Think about what is going on between the couple in this dance. He wants her, but she will not let him know he is winning her over . . .*

But how could I stop myself from looking at him? He was the most beautiful man I had ever seen. All I wanted to do was look at him. When I danced with Richard I didn't have to worry about the fact that a new term at school was just around the corner, that my grades had plummeted the previous term after Auntie Flo had passed away and I couldn't see for the life of me

200

how I was ever going to get the energy to make them good again.

I didn't have to think about anything else: about my sister who had become so short-tempered and worn down with all the sudden responsibility; about the limp poor Ruffles still had on his left hind leg after the accident, or even about the garden that felt like it was sinking with the weight of rain bearing down on it that summer . . .

Does Richard ever think about the summer we first met? Does he remember it as I do? How my sister had come in and stood so quietly by the door where we wouldn't see her? How she had watched us right up until the end and how afterwards the sound of her pleased laughter and clapping had sent a shock right through me, because *damn her,* what was she doing there, where she shouldn't have been? Richard had looked up and – seeing her – let go of me in an instant. His face lit up the first time he laid eyes on her.

And I was forgotten. I don't believe either of them ever noticed how much I resented her in that moment. How I wished with all my heart she had never turned up that day and spotted us, never met him, never stolen my budding first love away from me.

No. My sister has not the first idea how I feel – how I have always felt – about her husband. I've pushed it away for so long I have almost forgotten myself. I would never have made a play for Richard. I would never have done anything to deliberately hurt her. Not in a thousand years.

But then yesterday she asked me.

And the moment she did that, everything changed.

Scarlett

My first reaction was: *Christ, no!* I was on my way out of here, wasn't I? I was packing my things even as Hollie came in to me. I'd provisionally booked my tickets to go back to Brazil.

I booked them and then that stupid test kit stick came out positive. I was trapped. All I could think of yesterday morning was that I had to get away. How could Hollie have ever understood that? Something's got into me over these past twenty-four hours – my wanderlust, Hollie would call it – though it is a great deal more than that. The truth is, from the moment I found out I was pregnant, all I have been able to feel is complete and utter panic.

Why? I have no idea. If this had been Hollie she would have felt joy. I feel panic. Oh, maybe it's because I cannot bear to feel tied down. Because I cannot bear to be constrained. Or maybe it's because I'm just like our mother.

I never knew this would happen if I found myself pregnant. How could I ever have predicted that? I'm good at handling most things; in the jungle I've dealt with stuff most people would run a mile from – snakes, poisonous plants, spiders, horrible insects, big cats. How could I have guessed a simple pregnancy would put me in this kind of spin? I would have given anything to have been able to open up and talk to Hollie about it this morning; to tell her how scared I felt; to make her understand that I wanted to fulfil my promise to her but I just couldn't. I know Hollie.

She wouldn't have heard a single word of it beyond learning that I was expecting.

And she would have never let me get away.

I wasn't going to tell her, I could have got away clean, and then – without having the first inkling of what she was doing – my sister brought out her ace card. Richard.

And with that ace card she has brought down the whole pack of my carefully laid plans, because she has offered me on a plate the one thing I have always wanted: a night with Richard.

I should have declined her request, I know that. I should have carried on packing and in a few days' time I would have been in the safety of that plane to Brazil and out of the way of temptation. I could have got to Manaus and gone to Tunga, explained I was in a bit of a pickle, and he'd have given me some herbs that would have sorted out my problem.

I could have walked away from here scot-free. Away from Hollie and all her expectations. Away from this pregnancy and all the demands it will bring. Away from this town with its traffic jams and sprawling urban population and away back into the wilderness where I know I'll be able to breathe.

I yearn to be back there, doing something useful and meaningful, collecting my seeds again; I long to see my second family again, to get in a boat and be back on that river, to wake in the morning to the constant calling of the birds and the monkeys through the trees, to be able to carry on with my exploring. It's what I was put on this earth to do – not this. I should have caught that plane and flown far away across the world, far away from the temptation that my sister was about to put in front of me.

But she sat down on my old narrow bed and she caught me. I watched as all the T-shirts I'd painstakingly sorted into a neat pile to take with me fell higgledy-piggledy onto the floor.

'You can't go, Lettie,' she begged me. 'Not while there is the slightest chance left for me. You promised me that you'd have this baby for me and there's still a chance you could do it.'

I froze mid-way in between putting some socks away into my backpack.

'What do you want me to do?' I must have sounded odd, my voice stifled. 'What else is there?' But her next words shocked me to the core.

'Sleep with him,' she said without missing a heartbeat. 'Mr Huang says that's the thing most likely to work for us now. He says you have good *chi*, remember? If we do it the natural way that's the most likely route to getting the result that we want.'

I'd stood up straight then and the backpack I'd been loading up had fallen onto the floor. Neither of us bothered to pick it up.

'Let me get this straight. You are actually asking me to sleep with your husband?'

'For the purpose of conceiving a child. Oh, Lettie, I know it sounds crazy . . .' She'd grabbed hold of my arm.

'You're bloody well right it sounds crazy.' I'd shaken her off. 'You can't ask me to go to bed with him. That's just crackpot!'

'Why ever not? He's an attractive guy, isn't he?' She'd looked hurt. Oh, you fool, Hollie. You bloody stupid fool.

'He *is* an attractive guy,' I agreed slowly. 'Far too attractive for you to be offering him out on loan to other women.'

'That's hardly what I'm doing here. Look. You are the two people who I love and trust most in the world, don't you see? If I can't trust you two . . . Of course I *trust* you. It's more a question of whether or not you can bear to stick around that little bit longer, that's all. You've probably forgotten, but if it hadn't been for you, darling, me and Richard would never even have got together in the first place.'

Oh, I remember all right. And the truth is I want him still. Just as I have always have done.

Now she's asking me to take something that I have longed to take for a very long time. Does my innocent older sister have any notion of how risky an enterprise that might be?

I suspect not.

Scarlett

When Hollie gave me the key to Bluebell Hill this morning, she didn't say a word. No more apologies 'for putting me through this' and no utterances of 'good luck'. Her face as pale as wax, she offered to drive me up to the flat but I refused. I didn't want her hanging around. I have already decided that somehow I am going to pull myself together and find a way through this pregnancy for her. I don't know how I am going to manage it but I am going to try.

I've thought and thought about this. Other than admitting the awful truth – that I knew I was already expecting and lied about it – how else can I get out of this? If I say I lied she'll know immediately that I thought of terminating – which she'll never forgive. Yet if I turn out to be suddenly pregnant without going through this with Rich first, she'll realise it anyway. I have to do this now, to spare her.

It is also something I want to do, for me. This once, because I will never get this opportunity again. Just because she has asked me and because he has agreed to it. And now I am going to put Hollie right out of my head. I am going to forget my sister's dull eyes as I walked away from her this morning, her pursed lips. I've asked the taxi driver to leave me at the entrance to Bluebell Hill village so I can walk the rest of the way. I want to stretch my legs, shake out all my nerves about what Richard and I are going to do today.

By the time I've walked up to the Viewpoint, the morning has opened up; cold, but mostly bright, and part of me wants to just keep on walking. I know Richard will be arriving soon though, so I can't. I just stand by the monument for a while instead, drawing in deep lungfuls of cold and sweetly-scented air.

I look about me in wonder. Am I really standing up here waiting for Richard to join me so we can go to his flat to make love?

I block out the fact that it will not be a secret assignation; that my sister knows about it, indeed, she has set this all up, because I want to think only about Richard, about how it might be between us. The breeze rustles through the grass, and it is so quiet and so beautifully still all about, I can hear a cricket chirupping. I can hear the high tinny call of a blackbird somewhere among the thickets. Wouldn't it be gorgeous, I muse, if we could do it just here, lying in the long wild grass? And the thought puts a shiver up my spine and a smile on my face too, because I know *that* would never, could never, happen.

With Gui, maybe. With Richard . . . no. How will he be with me today, I wonder? I sit by the monument and for a moment I feel a huge rush of nerves, of complete and utter dread as if I'm about to sit the most important test of my life, or take the most crucial interview. Because what if it all goes horribly wrong and he can't actually see me as anyone other than her little sister?

I don't want him to see me like that. I never have.

I still remember the day she barged in on us in the shed behind the vet's. Ruff had been so ill that summer. I hadn't known how to cope. I'd put my name down for some dance show just to get my mind off him and then spent weeks panicking, unable to learn my dance steps, unable to concentrate. Until the day Rich offered to help me out. He'd stopped by to check on Ruff's progress and found me bawling my eyes out. That's when he'd offered to show me the steps, help me out. And it had all gone so beautifully till the day she turned up.

207

Who knows how things might have turned out? If they'd never laid eyes on each other, maybe Richard's friendship with me would have blossomed in time? Who can really say how things might have turned out, how they would have turned out if Hollie hadn't appeared just at that moment?

Oh, screw her! Think about Rich. Today is about us two. She's going to get the baby after all, isn't she? It's all she cares about anyway. Breathe in the lovely air and calm down and be like you are with Gui – never any nerves there, are there? Maybe it could be like that with Richard too. But I can't imagine it. I can't imagine the sex just being sex, simple and uncomplicated, even though that is what Richard will be here for today. He won't want anything else, no hint of emotion, and how will I hide it, after all this time? How will I manage to keep up the pretence?

I glance at my watch. He'll be here soon and I need to make myself ready. I need to make the flat ready. I thought if I came up here early I'd at least get the chance to stake the place out – they've had no tenants in there for at least three months from what I understand, and Hollie mentioned that I might find the place a bit musty. I thought I should at least make the bedroom – well, *usable*.

But I've kept putting the moment off. I've been standing out here just waiting because to do anything else feels so odd. To actually go *into* the flat, to put the new sheets on the bed as I'd planned, to open up the windows and light some sweet-scented candles so the air would not feel so stale when at last he arrived – I've put it off for at least half an hour. But now I've probably left it all too late.

When I open the door into the narrow hallway, however, my first thought is, it's not *too* bad.

I don't look too bad either, judging by my reflection in the slightly smeary mirror in the hallway. I spent an age on my hair this morning and it's paid off because the wind hasn't blown it too much out of place. OK, it looks windswept but in a romantic, sexy kind of way. My skin is glowing from the walk and it's pleasing to think this will be the first sight he catches of me this morning – looking alive.

I walk around the flat touching all the surfaces with my fingertips, imagining a time when Richard lived here himself. It was ages ago now, granted, but he did once. He would have been living here when we first met him.

When *I* first met him.

He would have come to make his coffee in the morning and paused by this sink and looked out of this very window and the panoramic view that greeted his eyes every morning would have been the selfsame one that I'm looking at now. I wonder when he first brought *her* here?

I shake my head, putting that vision out of my mind because it ruins the fantasy.

In the bedroom – when I pluck up the courage to go in there at last – I see that the double bed is disappointingly small. We'll have to snuggle in a bit closer then, I decide. That's a good thing. When I inspect it all more minutely, I see the sheets are perfectly clean and laundered and the bed has been made to military precision – all my sister's work, no doubt. I decide to leave it all as it is, cursing my decision to go along with her suggestion that we come here for the event 'because if anyone we knew saw you booking into a hotel that might look a bit suspicious . . .'

Maybe so, but the problem with being here is that there is evidence of my sister at work everywhere. I remember when she bought that wicker bedside lamp at a New Year's sale one time. The off-white colour of the walls and the floral prints all have her stamp on them too.

I stomp back into the kitchen and have a nose around. There's nothing in here really. When I open the kitchen cupboards I find only one used washing-up sponge and a small amount of Fairy Liquid. Oh, and there's a brush and dustpan under the kitchen sink.

'You don't have to do any cleaning up in here, Scarlett. It really isn't necessary.'

When I hear Richard's voice I jump, nearly hitting my head on the sink. He looks smart, clean-shaved, tired. He puts his car keys down on the kitchen table and I remember that he was in Lincolnshire when Hollie phoned him. He would have stayed on longer but she asked him to come back because we'd found out I was ovulating. He had to take the train back down especially this morning to be here with me. I feel a rush of pleasure at that thought.

'Hollie told me you took a taxi here.' His voice sounds strange and strangled somehow. 'I'd have given you a lift if you'd waited.'

'No.' I give a little laugh, shake my head. We could hardly have left the house together, could we? 'I wanted to go for a walk anyway. It's so lovely out there this morning.' We both turn simultaneously to survey the view from Richard's kitchen window. Huge swathes of shadow that weren't there before are darkening the fields and landscape below. 'Well . . . it *was* lovely earlier,' I breathe. 'How did things go at your dad's place? Did you have a good journey back?' I turn to look at him and he shrugs noncommittally.

'Well, I'm . . . I'm glad you're here at last, Rich.' I want him to greet me like he normally would do, to take me in his arms and give me a loving hug, but he doesn't. 'God, this is so awkward, isn't it?' I can barely hide my disappointment.

'More than awkward.' He says it so quietly I can hardly make out his words. 'Perhaps even madness?' he suggests.

He still hasn't made a move to take off his coat. He's just standing there, stiff as a board, like an uncomfortable stranger would.

'You should know, your sister and I fought over this, Scarlett.'

I don't reply. What am I supposed to say to that? He sits down deliberately. He folds his hands on the little wooden tabletop, looks up directly at me now. 'I told her that . . . I felt what she

210

was asking of us all wasn't fair. Not on you, not on me – not even on her, because if we go through with this it's going to change the way we *all* are with each other. Forever.'

I sit down opposite him, eyes lowered. Maybe I *want* to change the balance between us, though? I don't dare look up yet because if I do he will see the truth in my eyes. He's no fool.

'It will, you know.' His voice is so soft and low. It mesmerises me. 'Hollie has wanted this baby for so long though,' I remind him. 'We're only doing what she wants us to do, to help her get it.' *He's not going to change his mind now, is he?* I feel a stab of disappointment running painfully through my chest.

'Scarlett, I want to be honest with you.' I lift my eyes now, meeting his. His gaze is penetratingly direct, and his hands play lightly with the car keys resting on the table. 'I've been feeling so conflicted about this whole thing. It's not . . . it's not been easy for me. I can imagine you're feeling the same way too?'

'I don't take it seriously,' I breathe, trying to keep my voice light.

'Am I wrong then, in thinking that us . . . *being together* – it's going to mess with your head?'

'Totally wrong,' I murmur. 'Completely and totally wrong.' His relief is almost palpable and I hurry on before he realises how badly I'm lying. 'But I'm curious. What was it made you change your mind and agree to go along with Hollie if you're so dead set against the idea?'

He sighs now, and I catch a glimmer of the weariness beneath the mask that he came in wearing. I slide softly into the chair beside him and my knee brushes against his. He covers his face with his hands for a second. 'Hollie is desperate and she believes this will work. You know that.'

'Do you believe it?'

He smiles softly. 'We can only hope, Scarlett.'

'She seemed so utterly convinced – about the Mr Huang

method, I mean. It worked for him and his wife, I guess.' God, I'm a bitch. Why am I doing this? I stare at the red polish on my fingernails now, giving it my complete and utter attention. I only put it on last night but already the edges of it are beginning to chip. I could come clean with him now, not put him through this. Except . . . I swore to Hollie that I'd done that test five times. I swore it was negative.

I remember that I didn't want to talk about my sister. I'd planned on steering the conversation away from her if she came up.

'I thought it would be – an act of love, Richard. Remember you told me that, soon after I first arrived? We were sitting in the gazebo in the misty rain and you told me you *wanted* me to help you both out. It would be the greatest act of charity, you said. An act of love.'

'I did,' he remembers slowly. He never meant quite like this, though, and we both know that. He's too nice, too gentle. He wants to get into bed with me for all the wrong reasons as far as I'm concerned. Because he loves my sister so much. Because he wants to wipe away all the sadness and despair that resides in her depths. Not because he wants me.

I might still change that, though. I stand uncertainly, remembering the overnight bag that I've brought with me. It's still in the hallway.

'Would you like me to go and get changed now?' Why is my voice coming out so hesitantly like this? I'm never this way with Gui. Not shy and red-faced and stumbling. It's not as if it's my first time for God's sake. I wait for him to reply before I make a move but he doesn't answer.

I remember the set of lingerie that I bought for Guillermo's Christmas present that's still sitting in the hallway in my overnight bag. I stand up to go and fetch the lingerie and then I bring it back and place it down shyly on the table. His eyes widen when he sees the lacy knickers, the teasing, pretty open-cupped bra

I've put in front of him. Would he like me to put it on? How does he want to play this?

'Oh, Scarlett! There's no need for that, really. You don't have to . . .'

Is his voice really trembling, or am I imagining it? He makes it sound as if the task ahead of him is the most onerous duty he's ever had to perform, so much so that I feel quite taken aback. Does he want me so little, then?

'It's all right, really,' he says at last. 'I don't expect you to undress any more than you need to. It won't be necessary.' He stands up and I follow him into the bedroom. I notice when he opens the door he recoils a little. Perhaps he doesn't like the scent of the jasmine and ylang ylang candles that I lit earlier?

'I know it's not strictly necessary, but I thought it might help with the . . . atmosphere . . .' I trail off, putting the lacy under-wear down on the chair as he goes in and pinches out the candles. He goes to draw the curtains and I can *feel* his reluctance.

'If it's all the same with you, we'll keep the lights off,' he suggests. 'If that's all right?'

'If you like.' I sit down on the edge of the bed gingerly. I notice he hasn't so much as touched me yet. He doesn't want me to bother to get fully undressed and he wants us to do it in the dark. He doesn't want to see me at all, in point of fact. I feel my face flush. This isn't what I expected. It's as if he wants me to be a nameless, faceless receptacle and he just a nameless, face-less donor so that a sperm and an egg can come together to make Hollie's baby. I should have expected that really.

I take off my T-shirt first and lay it on the bed, waiting for him to turn round. Instead, he hovers by the window, looking out through a gap in the curtains.

'Someone's outside,' he says after a while.

'Who? Oh. Well. Are they coming *here*?'

'No. He's just . . . looking. He's probably checking out next door. They're up for sale at the moment, I see.'

'Are they?' I come up behind Richard, so close that I'm standing right at his elbow. So close that I can hear his breathing. So near that I can almost feel his heart beating and he turns round and that's when he sees that I'm already half-undressed. He swallows, hard.

'I'll leave the room if you like. While you get undressed,' he offers but I just laugh.

'No need.' I bend and wriggle my jeans down over my thighs and I feel him tense. 'Might as well just get on with it, right?' Would it help if I kissed him right now or would he think I was stepping out of line? I don't think I want to do it at all if he's going to be as reluctant as this. I feel the sting of disappointment in my throat.

'Oh, Scarlett.' He turns and pulls me tenderly in towards him suddenly. 'I know you're being so brave about this and so sensible and lovely but I just can't help but feel . . .' he holds me in close for an instant '. . . so *wrong* about this. As if we're . . . using you in some way that we shouldn't. And I don't want to do that to you. Can you understand that?'

I lower my eyes, and my gaze comes to rest upon his lips. I've never been properly close to him like this before. I bring up my arms to curl softly around his neck.

'I can understand it,' I tell him gently. 'But I don't feel as if I'm being used. It's OK. I want to do this. For you both, I mean.'

'I love her, you know that, don't you?'

'Yes,' I sigh. I kiss him on the cheek. A featherlight kiss, but in that moment I get to inhale the scent of him and with a shudder I remember – oh, I remember – how very long it's been since he last held me as close as this.

'Do you remember when we used to dance?' I whisper into his ear and he turns his face towards me. Oh God. I have always loved him. My fingers go up and tangle in his beautiful dark hair, trembling.

'The summer I taught you to dance?' He gives a little laugh.

It is the first time I've seen him smile today. He hasn't forgotten, either. I take his hand now and I place it carefully just in the small of my back; the other I place around my waist.

'We used to dance like this,' I say. 'All summer long in that leaky cow-barn. We had that old tape recorder on the floor, d'you remember?' He laughs again and I kiss his cheek, his chin. His mouth.

He pulls away, his eyes shining, for one moment happy.

Gently, without him hardly noticing it, I've moved us backwards towards the bed.

'I'm going to finish getting undressed now, OK?' He nods, suddenly tense again. But I carry on and undo my bra anyway. I slip off my knickers and let them drop on the floor. Then I get in between the sheets which are cold and starchy and I wait for him to do the same

After a while he follows my lead. I watch him as he takes off his shirt first, his hands fumbling for an age over the buttons. His stomach is washboard flat and I admire it while he unbuttons his trousers and unzips and then he turns away from me to sit on the bed while he pulls off his socks. And then his boxers. At that point I turn away because it doesn't feel right to watch him doing that; it's Richard.

And then I feel him sliding in beside me at last. At last.

Hollie

'This is a stunning picture of Rochester Bridge, Hollie. I can easily see why it won that competition.'

'I'm sorry?' I glance at the clock and it's half past two already. How long are those two going to be gone? My sister left here at half past ten this morning. Richard phoned to let me know he was on his way up to Bluebell Hill at eleven. So that makes it . . . over three hours they've been there together.

'I was just commenting on what a good piece this was,' my mother-in-law says. 'I'd have it hanging in my hallway any day.'

The bridge picture. Right. I put my hand up to my head to ease the dull, slow throbbing that's started up over my right eye.

'It's a great piece,' I say dully. We're sitting at my dining room table which is absolutely stuffed to the gills with ongoing projects this afternoon. Normally I can't stand this amount of disarray but I hoped having lots of things on the go would help take my mind off what's happening up at Bluebell Hill today. Only it isn't working. My eyes graze over the jumbled mess: at one end are all the notes and jottings that Beatrice brought in earlier with her plans for the garden party; at the other, there's all the brightly-coloured second-hand jumpers Christine wants me to help salvage for their knitting wool. And now my mother-in-law's also brought her canvas bag out from the car with all her picture frame samples so I can choose the one I'd like to use for the bridge picture.

216

Oh, God. I don't want to choose a picture frame today. I don't want to look at Beatrice's plans for the garden party, either. I bite my lip. The only thing I want in the world right now is for my husband to come back home.

'What?' Christine's just put aside a thick black corner frame in favour of a thinner, more elegant silver-edged one. 'You don't think so? It's a powerful piece.'

'It is powerful.' I make a real effort to concentrate on what she's saying. 'This picture just makes me feel uneasy. I don't know why. It has done from the first time I saw it. I guess . . . I guess this is just not how I see Rochester Bridge.'

Christine places the silver frame alongside one of the corners of the picture. It matches the grey and black lead pencil drawing beautifully. 'Ah. This one would do the job to perfection. So.' She shoots me a sideways glance. 'How *do* you see it?'

'Oh, I don't know . . .' I shrug. I wish I could just tell her what's eating at me but I can't. What would I say? Right now your son is having sex with my sister so he can get her pregnant for me? I feel my stomach churn at the thought. But I don't want to think about that. Don't think about it because you've got to stay positive; see the good that's going to come as a result. Think about the outcome.

Christine is still waiting for a reply. 'I see the bridge as something positive and beautiful,' I finally get out. 'I've always thought of it as a way for people to reach . . . things on the other side that would otherwise have been beyond their reach. I see it as something . . . worthy and noble.'

'And you don't feel this picture represents all that?'

Why can't she just drop it? Usually I'd enjoy this kind of conversation with Christine. I love her to bits and we always talk about all sorts of things but today I just can't.

'It does, I suppose,' I say impatiently. 'But there's something in that drawing that seems to imply there's a danger and an instability about the bridge, too.'

'Entry number 12.' Christine peers at the little scrap of paper still attached with a paperclip to the top right-hand corner of the piece.

> . . . *I wanted there to be nothing fully consistent about this piece*, the artist has written, *to reflect the turbulent and powerful history of the bridges which have been on this site . . .*

Turbulent! That's a good word. That word describes perfectly how I'm feeling at this moment. I've had the sense that Christine's been pretty much on edge too, ever since she arrived from Lincolnshire last night. She can't *know*, can she? I know Rich and his mum are close, but he wouldn't have confided a thing like this, surely? I glance at her uneasily.

> *To make the work as dynamic as the crossing has been for nearly two thousand years, it had to contain several movements at once: the bridge thrusts forward past the viewer; the rippling light on the water snakes towards the foreground; the platform juts out from the left . . .*

'You see what I mean?' I interrupt her. 'Even the language the artist is using, it's . . . it's disconcerting. Topsy, get off the table.' I pull at next door's huge cat who's all set to have the time of her life with Christine's half-unravelled jumpers.

'Actually I'd say that what the artist has just described is precisely *why* this picture works so well. Because it shows both sides of the equation. Because it's real. Maybe . . .' Christine angles her head a bit to get a better look at the piece '. . . maybe reaching "things on the other side", as you just put it, can be a hazardous occupation as well as a rewarding one, wouldn't you agree? This picture shows that admirably. Perhaps that's what impressed the judges.'

'Both sides of the equation?' We both stand and look at it quietly for a while but I can barely take it in. I'm thinking how there might also be another side to what those two are doing up on Bluebell Hill right now. I mean, they're both young, attractive people, aren't they? What if they're taking so long because they're actually – God forbid! – enjoying it?

Shit!

I've got to stop thinking like this or I'll go mad. She's such a flirt, my sister, that's the trouble. What man could resist the little coquette when she gets going? I never really dwelled on it before, but all that instinctive batting of eyelashes she does and that throaty laugh of hers . . . We're so used to it here, but it might turn a man on, if that were her intention.

And Richard . . . I can hardly bear to think his name, to imagine him with her – if I ask him later, will he swear that she was rubbish in bed, that it was a torture to lie with her and that he thought only of me; that he closed his eyes and filled his head with images of me as he caressed her, kissed her – oh, God, is he kissing her now?

I feel a shot of pain at the thought. There is no need for kissing. Nor . . . tenderness, nor love. But they are both tender, loving people. I know this. All the things that I dread most, the things that I have not let myself even know that I feared – it is only what would come most naturally to them both, for they are neither of them robots.

Dear God, what have I asked them both to do? I feel a horrible pain in my chest as I realise that there are so many things I have not allowed myself to dwell on. So many things I have cast into the waves of chance, and trusted in without consideration, and any moment now they're all going to come back in on the tide.

Could I possibly make some excuse and get in the car and go up to them now? If it's not too late, can I still call it all off? It's so awkward that Chrissie's here. I'd have to make some excuse to go out and she's so damn perceptive she'd know something was up . . .

'Darling, everything *is* all right, isn't it?' Chrissie shocks me now by holding my gaze for that little bit longer than usual. I nod wordlessly but she continues slowly. 'Hollie, it isn't, is it?' Oh, my lord, she knows, she must know . . . her voice is so dull, so guilty now. Have we both been skirting around each other avoiding saying the one thing that's been on both our minds all day? 'You look so unhappy. I wasn't going to say anything but . . .' She leans forward and touches me on the shoulder lightly. 'Richard *told* me, darling.'

I catch my breath as she turns those sympathetic eyes on me now. 'He did?'

'I asked, forgive me. He's been so miserable recently and you know he and I have always been close. It's never been my intention to interfere in what goes on between you two, you know that.'

I watch her in silence as she struggles to get her reservations out. His mum knows! Oh, my word. What must she be thinking, what must she be feeling? I sense the colour creeping into my face, I feel so ashamed . . .

'I wasn't supposed to say anything. But how am I supposed to stand by and watch two of the people I love most in the world making themselves so unhappy?'

How long has she known? How *much* does she know, exactly? Does she know where they are, what they're doing right now? Does she wonder, like me, why it's taking so long?

I sit down at the table, feeling suddenly weak at the knees. If she knows, in one way it will be such a relief to share it with someone. Even if she doesn't approve, even if she thinks we've made a terrible mistake.

I stare at her wordlessly as she scoops up a pile of jumpers and sweeps them into her knitting bag, unable to maintain eye contact with me any longer and for the first time I catch a glimpse of something else; of how this must look to someone seeing it from the outside, of how obsessed I must seem to anyone looking in, to be prepared to go to such lengths. *Am* I obsessed? Anyone who ever achieves anything against all odds has to be, surely? Who dares wins and all that. But I know it isn't quite as simple as all that.

'I wish, Chrissie, that there had been some easier way around it.' I bury my head deep in my hands and my voice comes out muffled and squashed. I wish I could have felt satisfied – my thoughts are ringing in my ears so loud she must surely hear them – I wish I'd been satisfied, happy even, to try for an adoption. It would have been better. It would have helped some other little human being. It would have given me the chance I so long for, to *mother*, but it wouldn't have given me . . . It wouldn't have given me the child of my own blood that I long for. Oh, I don't know what the difference is, in truth, or why I feel it so keenly. All I know is that I never felt that bond of kin with Flo, who was so good to me, who did everything a mother could and should have done for me. I never felt for her what I felt for my own, itinerant and unavailable mother; that unseen bond that connects two people joined by blood. I never wanted to become another Auntie Flo. I wanted to become the person my own mother should have been to me. I've wanted to fill that void with the goodness of all the things Auntie Flo taught me, but for a child who would be with its *own* parent, not like I was. Oh, does it sound too crazy for anyone else to understand who hasn't been through it?

'Over the last couple of weeks I've felt so conflicted about it all, not sure if this was the right action to take or not,' I get out at last, my eyes locked on Chrissie's. 'I'm so frightened that this thing is going to come between Richard and me,' I add, my voice breaking. 'And I love him so very much. That would be the last thing in the word that I want. Do you think,' I watch the little tired lines around her eyes that are etched that much deeper than usual, 'we're doing the right thing?'

'I think so.'

'You do?' I breathe out in an agony of relief that is mixed with regret, because now that this huge tangled web is done, created and irreversible, I am having serious doubts about it myself.

'Oh, yes, I do. In fact, Hollie, I encouraged him,' she says softly.

Scarlett

'I am so sorry, Scarlett.'

He lies there naked alongside me, propped up on his elbows at first, his breath coming hard and short. Rich looks so remorseful that for one horrible moment I think he's about to say he can't go through with it. Poor, poor Richard. He's riddled with guilt and also at this moment – I know because I saw him before he got in beside me – inflamed with desire.

'Don't be sorry.' When I lean in to kiss him softly on the shoulder I can feel him ever so slightly pull back, so I stop. I'm going to have to let him take the lead in this. I lay my head down on the pillow beside him instead and just look at him.

God, he is beautiful. And I have wanted him so much for so long that it hurts to even be here in this position, unable to express my true feelings, having to pretend that it's all an altruistic act on my part when I know full well it is not. I know that by letting him take me now, I betray not only my sister's trust – and that is bad enough – but I betray his trust too. A sob catches in my throat at that thought. I do not want to betray him. I see his eyes widen in compassion at my distress, his tender and protective instincts drawing him to me and I know that he mistakes my tears for a sign of reluctance. He thinks I'm crying because of the sacrifice I'm about to make. He doesn't know it's because of the frustration I feel, because I cannot be honest with him.

'Oh, Rich.' I put up my hand to wipe away my tears and I can feel all his tension and his hesitation melt away in an instant.

'I'm the one who should be apologising.' If only you knew, I think. I haven't been completely honest with you. It's on the tip of my tongue to say it. *I can't sleep with you because I'm in love with you. And I don't need to sleep with you to get pregnant because I'm already expecting your baby.*

'There's something I need to say to you. I just don't know . . . how to say it.' Without making you hate me forever, that is. 'I don't want you to hate me,' I whisper.

'Lettie, that's . . .' He moves in a little closer to me, his face tender, compassionate. 'Don't you know that's impossible? Don't you know that will never happen, no matter what?'

'Richard, the thing is . . .' I sniff, but he stops me.

'I already know what you're going to say.'

I catch my breath. 'You do?'

'It's pretty obvious and I don't blame you.'

'Really?'

'You're about to say that you feel . . . strange and unnatural doing this. That you're only doing it for Hollie and I know that. I respect that.'

'Rich . . .' I arch my back, about to sit up and face him, but he puts a finger to my lips so I cannot say a word.

'We've both promised her to do this, Scarlett. Whether we were right or wrong, God knows. I haven't been able to talk to her about it. Or talk her out of it. I couldn't bring myself to explain to her how truly hard this is for me . . . because I can't hurt her, I don't want to let her down. But I've been feeling so conflicted these past two weeks, I can't begin to tell you. I've even thought . . . I felt . . . that I might just have to leave her over it, you know that?'

'You did?'

He tenderly wipes away the tear that rolls out of the corner of one eye and down my cheek. 'I never thought I would ever feel this way about her, Lettie.' He gives a short sad laugh now. 'I guess what I'm asking you to do is change my mind for me. Tell me I'm wrong.' He sighs heavily. 'Tell me that I shouldn't feel like this.'

'We none of us can help how we feel,' I say faintly.

'I do want to give her what she wants, Lettie. I want her to be happy. I've always wanted that, all these years. I knew the moment I saw her that I'd met the woman I wanted for life. Don't ask me how. But once you'd brought me to her I knew I would love her forever . . .'

Once I'd brought him to her. That was my one role, it seems. 'And now?'

He swallows. 'She's pushing me away, Scarlett. With this obsession of hers, this desperate, all-consuming need to have a baby.'

We've been talking for too long, I worry. About her. It's always all about her, isn't it? When he got into the bed with me a while back he was hard, hot for it, I saw that, but all this talk of Hollie, always bloody Hollie . . .

'Do you think, when we fall in love like that, so quickly – that it can ever truly be real?' I whisper now. 'I ask because . . .' Because I have never let myself fall in love with anyone other than you, have I? All these years, and all the men I have known and kept at a distance because of the flame that still burned in there somewhere, dampened and low but still burning, for you. 'I used to think so, Lettie. Now I . . .' he puts up his hand to brush the hair gently away from my face '. . . I really don't know any more.'

'Richard, I know this is something a brother and sister-in-law wouldn't normally be doing. And I know these are really very extraordinary circumstances, but . . .'

He lifts up one finger, putting it to his lips, silencing me. For a few long moments his eyes seem to melt into mine and while he does not speak I can imagine a whole host of things he might be thinking; a whole conversation goes on between us. In the silence behind the sadness in his eyes he tells me how much he's always loved me too . . . that it has always been nothing but a mistake that he ended up with her, but he respects her and he cares for her and he's a person of integrity so . . .

'I can't do this, Lettie.' He looks at me apologetically. 'I'm sorry.'

'You mean you don't want to do this?' My voice is thick with disappointment.

'I mean I . . . I can't. Because you aren't her. Because this all feels wrong.'

'Stop thinking about your wife, then. Think about me. No – don't think about me. *Look at me.*'

I push away the duvet to reveal my naked body and I see him gulp, taking me in. I lean forward then, letting the tips of my breasts lie lightly over his chest. I don't think I'm imagining that my boobs are larger than usual at the moment – it's the one single advantage of the pregnancy that I've discovered. I hope he likes that, I think, I feel him shudder at my touch but he doesn't back off. And I kiss him. He responds, at first, too. He returns my kiss. He pushes back my hair from my face and I think for one glorious moment that he's going to pull me to him but then something else kicks in. His protective, caring nature.

'I can't do this to you, Lettie. You're her little sister, for God's sake. Christ, how could I have ever imagined that I could?'

'I'm a woman, Richard. That's all you need to worry about.' I cling on to his chest but he's already pushing me away, gently but firmly.

'It's . . . it's wrong,' he says with a sudden air of finality. 'That's all.'

But he's agreed to do it. He *wants* to do it. Why can't he just . . . I pull the duvet back over me, swallowing down my disappointment, watching him swing his legs over the side of the bed, making his escape.

Why? When he kissed me just now I thought we were getting somewhere, despite his protests. Maybe we were, that's the trouble? Maybe he found me too arousing? I can't see if that's the case or not but the sight of his naked backside certainly arouses me. For all the good it does.

'Please don't . . . Rich . . . Don't leave me.' I grasp hold of his arm, making him turn to face me. 'You've been the most important person in my life since as long as I can remember.'

'Me?' He looks bemused.

'You. Everything I've done and everything I have in my life that means anything to me – it's been because of you. You were always the one who accepted me just the way I was. You've no idea how much that meant to me. You're even the reason I took up the study of botany in the first place. Because you suggested I should.'

'No, Scarlett.' He shakes his head. I can see that he is confused, perplexed, a whole host of conflicting emotions are battling inside him right now. 'You were passionate about the garden – about plants – long before I ever knew you . . .'

'But you're the one who suggested I should study them.' I sit up straight and the bedsheets drop off me. I see him gulp, turn his head away again. 'Listen to me! You said I'd be good at it and I could be like my mum and really make a difference in the world.' I lean in and put my hand on his shoulder. When he turns to me I kiss him softly just under his lips. 'So I did it. Because you said I could.'

He frowns, puzzled. He looks at the floor, avoiding my gaze.

'I did it for *you*, Richard. Because I wanted you to be proud of me. Because I wanted to show you that I could achieve so much more . . .' I hiccup '. . . than all those people in school and at college ever thought I would. Nobody but you ever really thought I was going to amount to all that much, did they?'

'Hollie always believed in you . . .' He says quietly. He half-turns to look at me but I can see he's taken aback.

'Everyone always said "Oh, Scarlett's got green fingers, everything that Scarlett plants will grow", but . . . but no one ever

227

believed I was really all that bright, did they? Nobody except you.'

'You were always bright, Scarlett. They'd never have given you that job of yours if you weren't incredibly bright.'

'Yes, but if only you knew what I had to do in order to . . .'

'Bright and beautiful.' He picks up one of my hands and kisses my fingers, slowly, one by one, and he steals away my voice and all my words. 'And we all knew it and were always proud of you.'

'Richard, I . . .' I look at him desperately, not wanting to say them, those words I can feel about to slip out so easily, after I've been holding onto them for, oh, so many years . . .

'I love you, Richard. I have always loved you.'

Hollie

'You – encouraged him?' I draw in a shocked breath. No, that cannot be right. Whatever Chrissie's feelings on the matter, it can't be right that she took such an active part in what's going on today. I look at my mother-in-law through horrified eyes.

'He had real reservations about it all but I could see how the family might gain in the long term. How he might gain. Can you understand that?'

I stare at her wordlessly for a second.

'What about Sarah and Jay's baby?' I mutter stupidly. 'Surely once you have a grandchild through them, you . . .'

'I'll want to be around them, naturally. I know. In so many ways it's the worst possible time for any of us to be thinking of moving abroad, isn't it?'

'Who's thinking of moving abroad?'

'Us!' She grabs hold of my wrist, shaking it earnestly. 'Isn't that what we were just talking about? You two and me and Bill. I've just told you, I know about Richard's hopes and dreams. I've just admitted that I've been the one to encourage him in them and I hope you'll forgive me for it. I know all about your opposition to moving to Italy, how it's pulling you apart.'

I stare at her, open-mouthed. So that's it. She's been talking about the move to Italy all along. Not Richard and Scarlett after all.

229

'Hah! You don't know the half of it,' I tell her, shaking. I'm not sure whether to laugh or cry. 'What did Rich tell you?'

'That he loves you to bits and doesn't want to do anything to hurt you. That the business here is withering away to nothing; that he's got the chance to make this move now and it might not come again.'

'Ah.' I don't know what I feel more keenly at this moment – relief, that she doesn't know the terrible secret, or disappointment, because I am on my own with it again.

'Help me?' she says after a bit. She picks up one of the half-unravelled jumpers and positions my hands so she can wind the wool around them more neatly. Once it's all sorted into skeins I know she'll wash them and knit them back up into something new. I used to do that with her, too. I cling to the memory because it's part of what first endeared me to her, I know, what bonded us. She used to laugh, this is an old-fashioned mother–daughter sort of activity, she used to say. You're the daughter I never had, Hollie. I know that's how she's always thought of me too, more than Sarah. Perhaps because I had no mum of my own? So many surrogate mums . . .

It's hard to recall that this was once my passion – making up designer garments and selling them on to boutiques. All a long time ago now. Where did all that go?

'Sometimes I worry that he cares too much,' she's saying now. 'He's always so keen to please, not to let anyone down. I worry that he's running the danger of sacrificing something very precious in favour of the more pragmatic.'

'Sacrificing what?' my hands tauten around the wool.

'His . . .' Christine shrugs, struggling with words again. 'His joy. My older boy has always been the quiet one, the dutiful one, the son who worries too much about looking after his parents when he should be looking forward to his own . . .'

'His own family?' I look directly at her as she winds the wool round and round my hands.

230

'His own life. Hollie, can't you see it? They're having to go to such extremes to get the new contracts in this country, whereas abroad he'd have a far better quality of life. I'm not just saying this for my husband's sake, believe me. I believe it's what would be best for Richard, and maybe for you, too.'

The wool she's winding up right now is bright daisy-yellow; it's thick and luxurious and soft all at the same time and I close my eyes enjoying the sensuous feel of it around my fingers. It's been such a long time since I've done anything creative. For an instant, a collection of images tumbles through my mind; patterns of flowers weaving in and out of trelliswork on the front panel of a jacket or cardigan. Little bright oxeye daisies, if I could use that deep blue I spotted earlier on; I imagine them dancing round the edge of a toddler's jumper.

'Darling, won't you even think about it?' she implores me now. 'Come and have a look at the place you'd be living in, in Italy before you close it all down. Didn't Rich tell me you once had plans to go over there yourself? You must have thought the idea of living in the sun attractive once upon a time?'

'Once,' I admit. Once upon a time I had an idea that there could be some life beyond the garden gates of Florence Cottage. I'd studied classical art and design at college and it had opened up new worlds. The idea of going abroad had beckoned to me then. I'd started night classes to learn the language. I'd scoured the libraries for books on all the world's ancient and beautiful cities, trying to decide which one beckoned me the most. Should I spend a year in sprawling Athens or in Venice maybe, surrounded by the knolling of ancient church bells, sketching out my ideas to the wheeling of a thousand pigeons in St Mark's Square from the shade of an aromatic coffee shop? Or should I head for the mountains, spend a year in Turkey, or maybe in Umbria, high up in the sweet-scented hills or down by the tumbling dark rollers on the coast, walking barefoot over miles

231

of demerera-sugar sands? I feel a flicker of bitter-sweet excitement at the memory.

'I did dream of living abroad in the days when I was still at university.' I smile sadly at her. When all the cogs and wheels of an ordered life at home still turned beautifully and smoothly, oiled by the careful ministrations of capable Auntie Flo . . .

Before the rest of my life happened and I forgot how to dream.

'You could resurrect that dream.' Chrissie leans in towards me earnestly. 'You couldn't live it then, but you don't have to stay here holding the fort, keeping the home fires burning or whatever it is you think you should be doing. Scarlett's gone, a grown woman now and a very capable one. You have the undying love of a good man instead. Richard adores you, Hollie. He won't do anything to hurt you. But consider – no matter what you promised Flo, I'm sure she'd release you from it if she knew what a shackle this place had come to be for you now.'

I look up at the clock, my heart constricting painfully because it is half past two and there is still no sign of my husband. Or of my sister who is, as Chrissie just pointed out, a grown woman and a very capable one. Capable of keeping my husband by her side far longer than she needed to, if they were simply carrying out the one act?

'It is too late for all that now, Chrissie,' I tell her in a cracked voice.

'Why, Hollie?' she begs. 'Don't throw it all away, love. You've got your whole life before you yet.'

She's right, she should be right. But there is Bluebell Hill and there is Scarlett and Richard.

My eye falls on the disconcerting picture of Rochester Bridge again: . . . *the bridge thrusts forward past the viewer; the rippling light on the water snakes towards the foreground; the platform juts out from the left* . . .

'Too much water under the bridge,' I murmur softly. I have

sacrificed too much and the hour is so much later than she knows. And after today, I have my doubts about whether my darling Richard will still adore me as much as she thinks he does, or whether he will hate me.

Scarlett

'Scarlett.' Richard takes in a deep breath, turning now to look at me and choosing his words very carefully. 'You love me. Of course you do. But not that way. You think that because I've been such a fixture in your life since a young age – I've been married to Hol for ten years, haven't I? And no matter what you *think* you might feel for me now, I belong to her. And a woman like you . . .' his eyes flicker involuntarily downwards for a fraction of a second, taking in my breasts '. . . someone as smart, beautiful and compassionate as you are, you'll have no trouble finding a man of your own, believe me. You have a boyfriend out there in Brazil, don't you? Hollie said that she thought you might do . . .'

Why does he bring that up now, pushing me away with it? And why does he have to bring my sister's name into every sentence he speaks? Hollie said that she thought . . . Who gives a bloody damn what Hollie said or thought anyway?

'Yes, there is someone,' I say slowly. 'I could have him if I wanted to. His name is Guillermo. He's the one person in all this time I've thought that maybe – just maybe – I might be able to make a go of it with. He says he loves me.' I lower my eyes. 'I think maybe he does too. He's not just one of those guys who wants to get your knickers off, anyway.'

'And do you love him?' Richard asks softly.

I clench my fists under the bed covers. Right now I only want *you*.

'Christ, I even went to the Amazon because of you . . .' I get out.

'You worked so hard to get that job, Lettie. I haven't forgotten how desperately you wanted it. And we were so proud when you got it. That was something you really wanted,' he reminds me. 'You didn't go there because of me.'

'I went there because of you,' I repeat through gritted teeth. 'I wanted that job so badly because it was the furthest place I could think of to take myself away from you. Because . . . every day I had to stay living under this roof, watching the cosy little unit that is you and Hollie . . . it was driving me insane. Because I thought, if I don't get away from here, I'm scared I might end up trying to seduce you . . .' I stop, registering the shock that's sinking into his face at my words now.

'Don't say such things, Scarlett. None of that can be true . . .'

'It *is* true though. I've loved you for years. Why do you think I've never found any other man? Why d'you think I haven't taken things any further with Gui? He even asked me to marry him. But you know what's held me back? You. The thought of you.'

'Me?' His voice changes now. Am I imagining it or has his face grown darker? 'You've really wanted me for all these years?'

'You're the only one who's ever chased the loneliness away,' I tell him simply. 'You know that loneliness you feel when you wake up in the middle of the night and it's all dark and quiet and it feels like there's nobody else left in the world? All I ever have to do is think of you and that feeling goes away. Because I know that you're there. You exist. It's what's kept me going all this time, Rich. And having to hide it from you has been the worst hell imaginable . . .'

His brows are furrowed, his lips parting as if . . . as if he's angry?

'So you say you love me? And your sister – she knows this?'

'Of course not!' My voice is hoarse. 'She'd never have

suggested we two should be together like this if she had even the first idea . . .'

'So you had your own reasons for agreeing with her suggestion, did you, Scarlett? You wanted to use me – just like your sister does, in point of fact. Only you want me for sex, and she wants me for a baby?'

I shake my head in horror. It isn't like that. It's never been like that.

'I could have had *sex* with pretty much any man I've ever met, that isn't the reason why I wanted to be with you, Rich. And don't look at me like that. Just because I'm not the sweet and innocent young woman you've always thought me to be. I'm a grown woman for heaven's sake!'

Why is he looking at me like this? As if he wants to slap me.

'What is the reason, then?' He turns round and climbs back into the bed with me, his breath coming hard and short. 'Is it because you're a woman as heartless and single-minded as your sister? Is that why? Is it because when you set your mind on something you want then you have to have it, no matter who else will get hurt by that, and no matter what it costs?' He's straddling me now and I can feel him, pressing up close against me, challenging me to deny it. I look up at him in shock. 'Is that the reason, Scarlett?'

'Hollie isn't heartless, Richard. She loves you,' I defend her, despite myself. 'That's why she's doing this, because she loves you. More than all the world.'

He gives me a long hard look before he answers. 'Not more than all the world, Scarlett. There's something else she wants more, isn't there? And you? What about you?'

I cannot answer him. My throat has closed up and my voice has deserted me entirely.

'Well?' he demands. 'Are you sure you want this? Just say the word. Say the word and I'll go.'

I've wanted this, haven't I? I've wanted it for such a very long time. I close my eyes, nodding my answer because I am here and he is here with me and I know if I don't take my chance now it will never come again . . .

'Well, then,' he says, and his voice is hurt, distant, and he does not sound like the Richard I know at all. 'One chance to make Hollie's baby and one chance for you. I hope you both get what you want.'

I close my eyes, a sob catching in my throat because he sounds so cold and his hands are so quickly cupping my breasts, no sweet words to precede the act, his knees pushing aside my legs far too roughly. I thought he would be gentle. I always imagined he would be sweet and slow and deliberate just like he is in every other area of life.

'Richard, you can't . . . just . . .' I gasp, raising my head from the pillow as his mouth comes down on mine, full of desire, full of need, just like I always wanted him to be – except there is no love. How could he be like this, Richard, who was always so gentle and loving? I turn my face away from his at last, and it's wet with tears as he makes to enter me because there is no victory in this. Roughly, too roughly and in too much of a hurry, he is taking his pleasure. Is this what he thought I was urging him to do? Treat me like a whore with no consideration for my feelings at all? I hear the deep animal cries coming from his throat as he thrusts, but his eyes are closed, he does not see me.

I need him to see me.

But he does not. He doesn't care who it is. At this moment it's just an act of sex for him and that is not what I wanted, it's never what I wanted from him and I can't make it be something that it is not. So I just lie there and let him do it because maybe it's my sister and me who have turned him into this – her with her desperate need and me with mine. Maybe this is what we have done between us. *Heartless and single-minded*, he called us. The words keep echoing in my head like some terrible mantra that won't go away but . . .

He is right, I know it.

Immediately afterwards he gets up and goes to the bathroom. I hear the tap running for a while and the splashing of water as if he wants to make sure he has washed every bit of me off him.

'Rich?' Oh, God, what have I said, what have I done? This feels so wrong. I can feel my heart thudding wildly. All of a sudden I feel scared and guilty. As if I have just taken everything that is good and centered and steady at the core of my life and smashed it to smithereens . . .

Eventually he comes and sits back down on the bed again to get dressed. 'Richard?' I say softly, stroking his back gently. I want him to say that it's all right. That he forgives me. I can't bear for him to be so angry with me. I'm not letting myself even think about what I've just done to my sister . . .

'Will you stay? Please stay.' I pat the duvet but he shakes his head.

'I won't stay, Scarlett. And you shouldn't either. Go back to Brazil, back to Guillermo.'

Go back to Brazil? I prop myself up onto my elbows, staring at him wordlessly. Now we've done it he can't wait to get rid of me quickly enough. Is it because of what we've just done or because of what I confessed to him – that I love him, that I've always loved him? The momentary triumph I felt was short-lived, tinged already with so much regret because he was right. Everything's changed. Now he will never love me or even see me the same way again.

'What about the baby?' I whisper.

'This was never about the baby for you, was it, Scarlett? Why ask me now?' He picks up his shoes and heads for the door. 'I've done my bit. Whatever happens next, you sort it out with your sister. I'm leaving now. Do you want me to call you a cab back to the house? Don't worry, I won't be going back there till you've left. You needn't worry about me being there.'

'You want me to go back to Brazil?' I call out to him. 'Do you?'

'You should go back to Guillermo.' Rich's voice breaks now, the hard glint of anger that has sustained him through the act is subsiding and I catch a glimpse of something – I do not know if it is regret, sadness, or compassion – in his eyes. 'By the sounds of it he loves you. And that means he can offer you something that I never can.'

Hollie

I see I owe you an apology after all.

I run my finger along the top of the picture of Helen beside my own wedding photo on the wall and my pinkie gathers up the line of dust. For what? For ever imagining it might be easy for you to not follow your heart. For wanting you to stay here with us, no matter what it cost you.

Oh, I know I've always toed the line; I've said I understood why it was you felt so compelled to go off travelling, leaving us with Flo. But I didn't, not really. Richard saw that. I've never understood it deep inside. How could you just leave us? How could you have let something be so important in your life that it mattered more than us, your own children, your two little girls?

I vowed I'd be different to you. I'd be the loyal one, the one who cared enough to stay behind to sacrifice it all for love and now . . . Oh, but now, I trace the face which looks so much like that of an old-fashioned movie star, so very like my sister's – now I see I've not turned out so different from you after all . . .

The legacy you left has caught up with me. Who and what I am. Where I come from. Because I too have followed my dream – my desire – so obsessively that I've blocked out all the people in my life who truly love me. I've alienated Richard, who's driven back up to Lincolnshire with Chrissie this morning and who's warned me not to expect him back here for a while. It's work, he says, but I know it's more than that.

I've alienated my sister; for all her follies and her faults she loves me too, I know that, but she's hardly been able to make eye contact with me ever since . . . since I drove them to be together.

So you see – even without your presence, the guiding hand of your influence has extended to both your girls. We've turned out to be true daughters of your blood after all.

And too late, I know that if the chance came round again to do the same again, I would not take it . . .

Scarlett

Fuck it, I hate this. I'm stuck here now till God knows when and I feel as if I can't breathe.

I hate this place. I wish I had never come back. Ruffles ambles in and lies disconsolately down on top of a pile of clothes. He knows that something's up.

How did we ever come to this?

When I pull down the map of the five continents that has spanned my bedroom wall for the best part of a decade, the water-stains and the thin ragged crack that it covered are still there. In one movement I squash the whole world up in my arms. The ubiquitous photos in their frames on the wall beside my dressing table already came down last night. All those pictures of us: of Flo in her pinny, who died so selfishly just when I needed her the most; of my mum, Helen – the intrepid explorer. I drop her photo into the black bin liner along with the others. As for that picture of me and Rich, well, I don't even want to *see* him any more, ever again. I don't want to see him and I don't want to have his baby.

Enough damage has been done. When I stand up on the bed, a feeling of pure nausea shoots through my belly, reminding me that my hormones are already going haywire. There are things I want to get on with but I'm as giddy as a ship that's set out on a stormy sea and it's as much as I can do to stay afloat just now – never mind steer course. Still, I can do this if I take it slowly.

I am going to take every thing and every reminder and every part of me away from this place. Because once I make it out of here this time, I'm leaving for good.

One by one, I pull off all the little curtain hooks that connect the chintzy curtains to the pole and I throw both of the drapes onto the floor. I open up the dusty window and let the cheerless morning light into the room. It is cold and grey; I long for the endless blue skies at Manaus, the warm rain bucketing through the trees, the sweet scent of the white moonflowers outside the mission buildings, the never-ceasing racket of a thousand birds. It is too quiet here.

I can hear my sister creeping about like a mouse, moving from room to room outside, dusting and gathering up bits and pieces as she goes. She's been like this for the past two weeks, ever since Bluebell Hill. She told me last night that she'd be in with a test kit this morning and I played along with her. I'm not supposed to know officially, am I? But it all feels so very wearying and meaningless now. Everything here does. Be careful what you wish for, Duncan was always fond of saying when we went out together. I thought he was just being cautionary and boring, just because he never wanted to do anything exciting at all. But maybe he was right. All the magic has gone, somehow. I got what I wanted and it turns out it wasn't what I wanted at all.

I jump down off the bed and stuff the curtains into the black bin bag. The whole room is now varying shades of faded cream and dirty white and used-up beige. Was it really me that brought all the colour to this place?

Once the sickness passes I could fly back to Brazil on a tourist pass, I suppose. Once Tunga sorts me out, I could hang around the edges of everybody else's work while that new woman decides if she wants me to stay. Except – I can barely walk two paces at the moment without wanting to throw up. And who knows how long this is going to go on for? I tie up the edges of the bin bag, pulling the knot as tightly as possible. The way things are, I'm

243

stuck here with Hollie, a prisoner of my own body. What if this sickness lasts the whole nine months, dear God, and I never get to escape at all? How will I bear it? How did I ever imagine I'd be able to?

What if I miss the boat with my Brazil job and they take on somebody else? I don't even know what's happening with José and his family at the moment. Nobody is telling me anything. I haven't had a text or a call from Eve in weeks. And even Gui's texts are drying up . . .

The quiet knock on the door interrupts the maelstrom of thoughts.

'In here, Hol.'

She's not looking too good either. Her face is all pinched and white like she's sickening for something. Maybe she's just missing Richard? She's got the test kit in her hand, I see. Any moment now she's going to find out for certain that I'm pregnant. Which is going to make it all the more difficult for her when I have to leave her. Her eyes take in the stripped bare walls, the curtainless windows and the bed in one fell swoop. Then they're back on my face.

Does she know about me and Rich? Did he tell her, before he left on his latest trip out to Trieste with his dad, what I said to him that day in his flat at Bluebell Hill? These past two weeks, stuck here in the cottage with my sister, both of us so subdued and awkward, I have been utterly unable to tell. She hasn't said anything to me, but then that's just her way, isn't it? She could still *know*. I blush to think of it now, how I opened myself up to him and how he . . . he spurned me.

'Is it too much?' she says now, sitting down at the little dressing-table stool, the test kit in her lap. 'Am I asking too much of you?'

My eyes flick up to her. I wish more than anything that she would just go away.

'Perhaps you are.' My throat is dry, my voice rasping. Too late now, though. It's done. And I had my own reasons for complying too.

244

'It's going to be positive, isn't it?' She glances at the unopened test kit and we both know I'm not going to actually need to use it.

I pull a face at her.

'How long have you known?' Her voice is high-pitched, strained.

'You don't sound very pleased,' I accuse. 'I thought this was what you wanted. I'm pretty sure I'm pregnant, yes. All the signs are there, aren't they? Tender boobs, fatigue to the point of exhaustion, nausea . . . I can use that kit to confirm it if you like?'

'If you don't mind.' She lets out a long, slow breath as if she's just gone into shock. What's wrong with her? She should be hollering and jumping up and down for joy, just like Lucy and Roma and . . . and everybody else when they find out. She should be *happy*.

I get up and go and take the kit off her lap but she doesn't move. She's still looking around the room as if she hasn't seen it properly in ages.

'I hadn't realised how jaded this room had become. I'm sorry. I'll redecorate the whole thing for you now of course.'

'No need.' I bite back the comment that's ready on the tip of my tongue – wait and do it up for the baby. 'I'm not planning on staying here the entire pregnancy, Hol. I don't think that would be such a good idea, do you?'

Her eyes widen and I see she knows what I'm talking about.

'Did Richard . . . did he . . . ever say anything to you about what we did two weeks ago? About how it was?'

'No, Lettie!' She turns to me, distressed. 'And I don't want to know. Better we never speak about it again.'

'He was right about one thing though.' I'm turning the little cardboard box round and round in my hand. 'It *has* changed things between us. He doesn't feel comfortable being here any more, does he? He's not away just because of his dad and the business, is he, let's be honest. He can't bear to be in the same house as me any more . . .' I get up and walk out into the corridor and she follows me.

'It isn't that, Lettie. He's had so much to do . . .' she begins but I shrug her off.

'*Don't*, Hollie. Just don't. Let's be real with each other. Just for once.'

She folds her arms, inclines her head a fraction.

'You know, for the longest time I've been – well – I've been envious of you.' She takes in a breath when I say it but she doesn't interrupt. 'For having what I thought you had but I never could.'

Hollie shakes her head, frowning, but I carry on regardless.

'Everything has always been so *perfect* between the two of you, hasn't it? You actually do love each other. You have something special. Whatever it is, I think that I will never have that.' I had meant to go to the bathroom but a thin line of sunshine draws me over towards the French doors now, burning through the mist.

'What on earth are you talking about?' Hollie grabs hold of my shoulders, stops me twisting the box round and round in my hands.

'It's a myth, isn't it? Love. For most people, it's just a myth. And I can't stay here.' I put the test kit down on the coffee table and open the French doors wide. A small chill breeze enters the room.

'You're planning on leaving. Now? Why?' She drops my shoulders and takes a step back. For the first time I see an energy in her, alarm bells going off at the thought that I'm not going to stay here under her wing. 'And why do you think you will never have your own man to love?'

'Why?' I give a little laugh, walking through the French doors and out onto the dew-spattered lawn. This is the only time I ever feel . . . truly at peace, I realise. When I'm out in the open, among the grasses and the plants, the living things of the land. 'Because love is a four-letter word, Hollie. It's just a dolled-up word for lust, isn't it? Or dependency. People say it to each other all the time but what do they really mean by it?' I turn to catch sight of her uncomprehending eyes. 'I don't think I know, really.'

'Scarlett, you *know* what love is. There are so many kinds. And so many people have loved you in your life. Flo loved you. And me. And . . . and . . .' She can't quite bring herself to say Richard.

'Yes, yes, I know you have. But have I loved you back? Sometimes I think I've got a cold splinter in my heart, where the love-chip should go. I don't think I have ever *loved* you, Hollie. I thought,' I choke, 'that I might have been in love with . . . oh, look, never mind. The thing is, I wanted to have this baby partly to show you that I could do something for you too. I know how much you've done for me throughout my life. I don't always show it but I do know what you sacrificed for me. I wanted . . .' I touch her arm, willing her to understand. 'I thought maybe I'd changed and I wasn't selfish any more and I could really do it. But I'll be honest now, before this goes any further. I don't know if I *can* go through with this.'

Her eyes narrow, becoming so hard that I'm forced to look away. 'Are you saying that you might – you just might – change your mind. You'd abort my baby?'

I'm trying to be honest with her. She has to know . . .

'And you think I would just stand there and let you do that. Do you?' She grabs hold of my shoulders again now and this time she shakes me, her eyes shot through with a darkness I don't remember ever seeing before. 'I . . . I even let you sleep with my husband. I risked my marriage! And you imagine I would just let you get rid of it, now? You aren't going to do this to me, Scarlett, so you can stop thinking this way. Not even for one minute. I won't let you.'

I look at my sister archly, folding my arms now because she forgets whose body it is we're talking about here. Whose life. She forgets how much I will stand to lose now.

'Don't you understand what I just told you, Hol? This isn't how I want it to be – this is just how I am. This is how it is.'

Heartless and single-minded, he said.

'I wanted to do this for you, I'm trying, God knows. I'm fighting myself on this, you must try to understand that.'

'You'll keep my baby.' It's a statement not a question. And in this moment, standing right here in front of her, seeing everything that I see swimming in the depths of her eyes, how could I doubt it? I draw back, clenching my fists, not wanting to get swallowed up whole by her desperation.

'Fine. I'll keep the baby. I'll try. But on my terms, not yours. First of all, understand that I *will* go back to Brazil, just as soon as the nausea lets up. Agreed?'

She squirms uncomfortably, but she has no option but to concede. She nods at me tersely. 'And second?'

'Secondly, you'll have to decide if you're prepared to give up what's most precious to you as well. I want you to sell Florence Cottage. If I can't work I'm going to need money and this is the only way left to me to get hold of it, OK? We've reached that bridge we talked about all those weeks ago, Hollie. Now it's up to you whether or not whether you're prepared to cross it.'

Hollie

Rich hasn't called.

I stare at the phone, willing it to ring, but it doesn't. *Come on!* I know Chrissie was expecting you and your dad back in Lincolnshire some time this morning, so why haven't you been in contact?

All along, I've thought that by the time spring starts showing through, the worst of it will be over. Scarlett will be expecting and my baby will be on its way and now – it's actually happened. Through the pattering of a sudden shower on my windowpane I can spy a bright, cold, blue-skied morning in March. The crocuses are all shivering like brave little gold and purple flags.

I pull the little wand out of my pocket and stare at it again. 'Pregnant', it says, in incontrovertible black and white. It's true. It's really true. I'm waiting for the floodgates of joy to open and fill up my heart; I'm waiting for the euphoria to descend but it hasn't yet. Maybe it's because I haven't been able to share it with Rich yet. Should I ring him?

Ordinarily, I wouldn't think twice about it, but something is stopping me. He's been in Trieste ten days and in all that time he's rung home only once. And when we did speak, he was just as distant and cold with me as he was before he left.

I pick up the three heavy bin bags Scarlett just gave me to add to the rubbish I put out for today's collection. Outside, it's still raining and I hesitate by the front door. When I asked them to sleep together – is it possible that I was being far more incredibly naïve than I knew? Scarlett implied as much this morning. We've not spoken of it till now but then this morning she asked if he'd ever said anything about 'how it was' between them.

Rich would never bring that up. It isn't like him not to phone, either, or to stay away for so long. I hate to think that Scarlett might be right and he might actually be avoiding us.

Oh, when is it going to stop raining? I'm going to get soaked taking these out. I should have cleared out that room a long time ago, I just never wanted to touch it. It's been in limbo all this time – neither properly Scarlett's nor decorated for anyone else. I always thought it would be the baby's room.

Damn it. I drop the bin bags outside the front door just in time to see the refuse men already working their way back down the other side of the road. Oh, why does everything always have to be so complicated? Why can't I just have what I want for once, and let it all be the way I thought it would be without all the thorns in my side? And why is it, after all this time and all I have sacrificed and everything I have gone through, I still just don't feel . . . *happy*?

I want Richard back. I miss him. Oh, have I made the hugest mistake of my life? If he feels this bad about what he had to do to get this child, will he even be able to love it once it's born? Or will it always remind him of what they did? I close the front door, my heart thudding in my chest. I can't keep thinking like this. I've got to stop torturing myself, I'm becoming so maudlin.

I wander back into the kitchen, and when the phone rings it nearly makes me jump out of my skin. I run to it, nudging it off its hook so quickly that I nearly manage to disconnect us.

'Richard?'

'Hello, darling.' He sounds tired but also so – my hand goes to my heart – so much more like himself again.

'Rich, I've missed you so much! Where are you? Are you back at your mum and dad's?'

'The flights have been delayed. We're still at Trieste, Hollie.'

'Oh. I've hardly heard a thing from you this trip – have you been terribly busy?' I don't quite succeed in keeping the reproach out of my voice. He goes quiet. 'Will you come here straight after you've dropped your dad off?'

He clears his throat. 'I can't.'

Damn, damn it!

'Because Scarlett's still here, you mean?'

'That's right. I got the impression she mightn't stay around for too long though?'

'You did?'

'She seemed keen to get back to Brazil,' he says tersely.

'Oh, she is, believe you me. Except she can't because she keeps throwing up every two minutes . . .' He goes silent at the other end now. It's a thick, palpable silence which is very different from the joyous reaction I'd been hoping for.

'Ah, right,' he says at last.

'Yes, Rich! We're pregnant. Look, we have to talk,' I plead now. 'Come home. Please?'

'No,' he says. 'But I have missed you too. Come to me?'

'Up to Lincolnshire, you mean?'

'Why not?'

I let out a groan. 'I can't leave her, Rich. She's got terrible morning sickness. She can barely do a thing for herself at the moment, and given that that's all our doing I can hardly leave her to it, can I? Aren't you even a little bit pleased?' I accuse after a while. 'I've just told you we're expecting. We're going to have our baby at last. Aren't you happy?'

'I'm happy if you're happy. It's the single reason I agreed to go along with it in the first place. You know I never wanted to . . . to be with her. I can't be around her, Hollie. And I'm pretty sure she feels the same way about me.'

'What *went on* between you?' I get out. 'Whatever happened that day up on Bluebell Hill?'

'Can't you imagine, Hol? You're getting what you wanted at long last, love.' His voice takes on the slightest edge. 'We'd best drop it, OK?'

A shiver goes through me then. By the gently burning fireplace I glance up at the one and only wedding photo ever taken with the three of us in it. I move closer to it now, peering up at it. *You're getting what you wanted at last.* That's what she said to me too, isn't it, the day I married him. My fourteen-year-old sister had refused to be in any other picture and I'd been so radiantly happy, so filled with my own good fortune and joy that I hadn't properly noticed her absence till the end. Oh, she'd been moody and sullen and just generally difficult the whole year prior to the wedding. Ever since Flo had died in fact . . .

'OK,' I say softly. 'But will you please, *please* just come home?' Scarlett might have morning sickness for ages yet – she mightn't be able to escape this place as she intends to, for quite a while. 'You can't stay away from here indefinitely. And I can't leave her.'

'Hang on a minute, love. They're posting some new flight info up on the departure board . . .'

He falls silent for a while and I take down the photo and stare at it more closely. I always thought of this as the time when I was at my happiest. Newly married to the man I adored and not yet aware that our union would be blighted by my infertility. I always thought Scarlett looked so sweet in this picture, too – her hair full of tiny yellow roses that match her pale primrose dress. It was only in the months after this was taken that she really changed, became so rebellious and angry and aloof. I thought maybe it was just her hormones kicking in, combined with all the upheaval – Flo's passing away and the change at home because now we were three. I never for one moment thought it might be because I got married. To Richard.

252

I frown, my fingers gliding over the glass of the frame. I remember asking her – begging her, in fact – to smile just for one photo, just one.

'It's all right for you,' she'd said. 'You've got what you wanted now, haven't you?'

To be married to him, she meant. I remember how, even at the time her words had jarred. The way she had spoken them, they'd fallen about my senses like the heavy, sickly-sweet scent of the coriander I'd brushed up against one time in Flo's herb garden, all out of sync with the freshness of the lavender and thyme. Back then I'd thought – maybe she's cross because she's lost Flo and now she thinks she's going to lose me too? But what if it was the other way around? What if it was really *Rich* she was frightened of losing and not me at all? They'd been friends all that summer long. They'd been dancing together in that barn for weeks before I even met Rich. Was she in fact angry at me for taking Rich away from her?

Is she still angry?

My legs give way and I sit down on the edge of the couch. 'Rich?'

'I can't come home while she's still there. I won't.' And you – I think miserably now – what are you so scared of, why won't you come back? You don't fear you might have feelings for her too, do you? 'I don't want to be around her.'

Why? I feel my voice catching in my throat because I cannot ask him. He is so far away from me at this moment – not just in miles, but in his heart, too. Now I think I know, I have caught a glimpse, of the reason why. Could it be because of something that I have not dared to let myself see, so blinded by the thing that I longed for and wished for all these years?

'I've got to go now, darling. I'll ring you when we land at Gatwick. We'll sort something out, OK?'

'OK.'

The rain splashes down outside, the water running in a column just outside the window where the guttering has broken again, a torrent beats down right onto the plastic bags I left outside the front door. I'll have to bring them in again, I suppose. All Scarlett's discarded rubbish that I didn't get out to the refuse men in time. I wanted her back, didn't I? I wished for that. And I wanted her to stay but now, as long as she's here, Richard won't come home.

I put the phone back in its cradle and go back to the door, reaching it just as the doorbell goes three times in quick succession. My heart sinks. If that's Beatrice I'm going to have to let her in – I've put her off twice this week. But it isn't.

'Right, Ms Hollie.' Duncan's standing there with his hands in his pockets, pale face set and determined-looking as I open the door. 'She's in today, I know, because I've been watching the house – so don't bother denying it. She's in. You're in. And Richard's not. Today you're going to let me in, aren't you?'

Hollie

'This is a nice place you've got here. A very nice place.'

Duncan is leaning back comfortably on the largest sofa, the china teacup I've just handed him perched precariously on his knees. I invited him in. What else could I do?

'I remember your sister brought me back here once or twice when . . .' He pauses, obviously thinking better of whatever he was going to say, then abruptly changes course.

'So is she coming down to see me or isn't she?'

'She isn't.' I sit down on the armchair opposite him. 'She's been throwing up all morning and she's lying down right now.'

'A bug?' he raises one eyebrow sarcastically. 'What a coincidence. Just as l'il ol Duncan comes along. But she's not going to get out of it so easily this time, I'm afraid.' He jumps up now as the sound of a car draws up outside, tweaks back the curtains a little. 'Who's that?' He indicates outside with his head.

'That'll be Jane, the midwife. She's due in to visit Scarlett today. My sister hasn't got a bug. It's morning sickness. She's pregnant, Duncan.' I look directly at him, expecting him to laugh that one off as well, but he doesn't.

He turns from the curtains, stares down into his teacup.

'Well, I'll be blowed. Then it's true,' he breathes. 'And . . . do we know whose it is?' His eyes meet mine suddenly. I catch a glimpse of something that looks remarkably like pity.

255

'We do know.'

'It's your husband's, isn't it?' he says softly and I feel my face go red. How does he know that? Scarlett had to be such a blabbermouth, didn't she? She told Beatrice, I'm pretty sure. She probably will have told Lucy Lundy and all her mates, too. Word gets round quickly . . .

'Poor Hollie.' Duncan lies back on the sofa again, draining his cup. 'You poor woman. She took him from you after all.'

'She most certainly did not!' I glower at him. What does he mean, *after all*? 'My sister offered to become a surrogate for me so it has all been done with my blessing.'

'Really?' He looks dubious.

'Look – what is it you actually want from us, anyway? I've let you in. I'm talking to you but she won't, so say your piece and just leave . . .' We both look towards the hallway as the front doorbell goes. I hear Scarlett trundling along in her slippers to answer it and I know he hears her too.

'What do I want?' He moves to stand a little back from the lounge door, peering into the darkness in the corridor, hoping to catch a glimpse of her. 'I want her. I've loved her for such a long time, you know.' I hear his voice catch in his throat. 'But what you've just told me confirms some suspicions I've had. It certainly puts a different complexion on things.'

The front door closes and we can hear the two women chatting on their way to Scarlett's bedroom. He's silent for a time, listening to the low murmur of voices. His eyes follow the line of sound though he can no longer see them. I don't like him being here. I don't feel comfortable with it. But is he dangerous? Should I be inching away from him, making for the phone? But what would I say? There's an irate ex-boyfriend of my sister's in the house and he's threatening . . . he's threatening what? I have no idea what he's planning – or even what he's capable of. I've always thought him creepy and sleazy but would he really do us any physical damage, especially now he knows she's expecting?

I doubt it. He believes in retributive karma so I don't reckon he'll try anything funny. He's spiteful, though. Last time, on the phone, he spoke before of pulling her job out from under her, didn't he? Would he do that? Could he do worse?

I look at him uncomfortably now. Scarlett knows him better than I do. I warned her just now when I went to make the tea for him that he was here – I had to, I didn't want her wandering in – and she went as white as a sheet.

'Get rid of him,' was all she said. She's scared of him. My unflappable, devil-may-care sister was truly spooked at the thought that he was in the house. But why?

'She's betrayed us both, hasn't she, in the end?' He's sat back down again now, almost sagging, leaning his chin against his open palm, propped up on the armrest.

'I'm sorry? Look, what's your grievance, Duncan? Spit it out, why don't you? What did she do to you?'

'All right, I'll tell you, fine.' His eyes take on a malevolent glint 'Seeing as you ask. She did a very naughty thing. You know that marvellous assignment she wrote that landed her the PlanetLove job? She faked it. And I helped her, God help me.'

'You helped her?' I say faintly.

He shrugs. 'She'd spent three months that summer trying to get it right and she couldn't. We'd been working on a similar project at uni after all, and my results were heaps better than hers. I knew I was onto something that could land her the job she was after and she knew it too. So we struck up a deal . . .'

'A deal that entailed her passing off your work as her own?' I say slowly. I remember her now, staying up till all hours towards the end of that summer, in tears a lot of the time, re-drawing diagrams from a folder, sketching out plants . . . 'She had to hand-draw some of the pieces so they'd be her own work, right? But those were just the sketches. You're saying now the experimental results were your own?'

'Something like that,' he affirms. 'I helped her enormously.

She's not the most academic of people at the end of the day, is she?' He smirks. 'We faked a load of results that we couldn't get right – I mean, that we couldn't get to prove the premise she was after demonstrating.'

'How very scientific of you.'

He shrugs again. 'Not ethical maybe, but in the long run we figured it'd be for the greater good, you see. Because of what she'd bring to that job that other, more academic applicants wouldn't. Her humanitarianism, for one.'

'And your end of the deal was . . . ?'

'She promised to become my wife, Hollie. To have and to hold till death do us part. That's what she said.'

She promised to *marry* him? God, even for Scarlett that's . . . that's too much. I try not to let him see how taken aback I am because I can sense he's telling the truth.

'How very ironic, don't you think? You helped her to cheat – but you never imagined that she'd be capable of turning that cheating streak on you.'

His eyes take on a haunted look. 'Why would I think that? I trusted her. I loved her, Hollie, and no, I didn't think she'd do that to me, betray me. Would you?'

I shake my head, an involuntary shudder going through me when he says that.

'The deal was, after she'd been there for a while she'd recommend me for a post within the camp and I'd join her. We both knew I had a year to run on my course before that'd be even possible so I didn't begin to worry till last autumn.'

'And has she been in contact with you all this time?' I look at him disbelievingly.

'On Facebook, yes. We kept in touch. She was happy to send lots of chatty messages until – well, until last August when I reminded her of our deal. Then she seemed to think she was going to be able to back out of it! She claimed she didn't realise I still had any expectations. Can you imagine that? I've been in love with her all this time and she's betrayed me. You love her too,' his eyes narrow now, 'and she's done the same to you.'

'No, she hasn't, Duncan. Scarlett hasn't done anything I didn't ask her to do . . .'

'I'm afraid she has. You may have asked her to be your surrogate but you didn't ask her to have an affair with him, I'm sure? Look, I *saw* them together, up at your husband's flat, a few weeks back. They'd been – you know – going at it, or so I reckoned. Your old man left first. When your sister came out she was all red-cheeked and puffy-eyed like she'd been crying.'

I gasp. He knows!

'I think I need to stop you there . . .'

'No, Hollie. Don't stop me. Listen to me.' He comes over and puts a commanding hand on my arm. 'I saw them, OK? I saw them kissing. They'd left the curtains slightly open . . .' His eyes glaze over suddenly, he looks – strangely enough – as if he is savouring the memory, but I can't bear it. I can't sit here listening to this and at the same time I find myself unable to move, unable to stop his words.

'She was wearing some very pretty underwear.' Duncan breathes in now, remembering. 'Pink, it was, with flowers on it, but she'd already taken off her bra. She's shapely, your sister, you can't deny it . . .'

'You . . . you're lying.' My hand is trembling so hard I nearly break the china cup when I put it down on its saucer. *Fuck!* What am I doing using a china tea-set anyway, nobody cares about such niceties any more, maybe not even Richard, who's always said he loves the way I'm the only person of my generation who doesn't use mugs. Maybe he doesn't love it? Maybe he'd rather I cared more about other things, like . . . like sallying around in Agent Provocateur underwear like Scarlett does.

'I'm not lying and you know it. I told you, they were standing by the curtains. If it's any consolation to you it looked like he took some persuading – a man with a conscience, your Richard – but she can be pretty persuasive, your little sister,' Duncan tells me solicitously. 'Obviously once they moved away from the window I couldn't see any more. But I don't suppose it takes too much imagination to fill in the blanks. She slept with him, OK? Now you tell me she's expecting . . .'

'What on earth would you have been doing up there watching them anyway?' I feel my face flame red with embarrassment. I don't just hate Scarlett at this moment, I hate Duncan too, for bringing all the intimate details right to my attention. 'You *have* been stalking her, haven't you?' I turn on Duncan defensively. 'First you phone me saying you've been watching her in the garden, and now you know where she's been with Richard.'

'I wasn't stalking her.' He looks hurt. 'I knew it was one of the properties you owned. It was empty. If she wasn't with you – as you'd claimed – she might have been staying up there. That's the only reason I went.'

Now Duncan knows. But he can't prove anything, can he? Nobody can really say that's what they did.

'I'm surprised at your reaction, Hollie.' He seems genuinely taken aback for a minute. 'I've just told you I saw your sister with your husband and all you can worry about is what was *I* doing up there. What about what *they* were doing together up there? Doesn't that trouble you at all? I'm telling you the truth, I swear it. Don't you believe me?'

'I . . .' I think fast, pushing down my mortification that other people too might be speculating about what went on. 'I don't know what to think. You say she betrayed me with him?'

'I'm certain of it. If she wanted to get pregnant for you there are more civilised ways of going about it,' he says knowingly. 'Which wouldn't have needed any contact between them.'

'How,' I say carefully, 'are you so certain? She could have been taking a shower and not realised he was in that bedroom and . . .'

'No!' He looks affronted. 'I'm not that stupid. She had her

arms round him, Hollie. I saw them at the window together. And – I'm sorry to say so – but she had that look on her face when they eventually came out that said it all for me. She had the look on her of a woman who's just got what she wanted, if you see what I mean. The cat that got the cream.'

I wince. That might be just a little too near to the truth for my liking. 'You just said she'd been crying?' I protest.

'That too. It was odd. Maybe she felt guilty after all? Either way, Hollie, putting together what I saw and what you've just confirmed to me, she's betrayed you, face it. Just like she did to me.'

'If what you're telling me is true, Duncan . . .'

'I swear on my life that it is.'

'Then we are both injured parties,' I say slowly, turning my face to him so he can clearly see my eyes. I'm not faking the pain, either. If Scarlett really is a traitor that's something I'm going to have to deal with later. For now, I'm just holding onto the thought that – that maybe Duncan's exaggerating everything out of all proportion. Making out he saw and knows more than he really does, just to get me on his side so he can get his revenge. Let's face it, if I can't even trust my own sister, why should I trust him either?

'What are you suggesting we do about it?'

'I want you to back me up,' he says eagerly. 'Do you remember anything about her behaviour that summer before she sent the papers off to be assessed?'

'I remember that she was desperate to get the job, to go to Brazil. I remember that she was convinced she hadn't done anywhere near enough the amount of work she needed to do to get it.'

'She'd done the work all right,' he comments. 'But experiments don't always run smoothly. Things didn't go according to plan. The key thing is,' his eyes narrow, 'I recall her telling me that she'd asked you to post off the assignment in the end because she ran out of time, is that true?'

I nod. He pauses and pulls a scruffy-looking manuscript out of his bag, and hands it to me. 'Did you ever look at it? Could you say if this is what she asked you to post in the end?'

'Why do you ask?'

'Because,' he squirms impatiently, 'the ungrateful little minx – after all the work and effort I put in to help her out – rang me up and told me that the assignment she'd put in, in the end, was her own. She'd felt guilty, she said. She'd not been able to go ahead with our plan. I think it was her way of jettisoning me from her life, now I look at it. She didn't want to keep up her end of the bargain, so she pretended that my end never happened. I don't believe her for one minute though – do you?'

'What do you want from me?' I ask now. I glance at the document he's just planted in my hands.

'Is this the document she asked you post off for her, Hollie? Do you recognise it?'

'"Medicinal uses of Orchidacea throughout South East Asia",' I read out, feeling my face grow hot. 'Yes.' I say at last, faintly. 'This is the one she gave me to post. I recognise the title, yes.'

'Bingo!' He punches his fist in the air, making me wince. 'Then we've got her. If you're prepared to testify to that, and that she spent a load of time redrawing the graphics in her own hand from my originals, I think we've got a pretty solid case. She'll lose her job, which is no less than she deserves, agreed?'

I hand the document back to him, and my hands feel greasy just from having touched it. He wants me to help him cast the net around Scarlett that will bring her to the justice he feels she deserves. He thinks I have every reason to do that; that I'm on his side.

'I thought you were going to let the universe do the work?' I remind him. 'Let karma work its way back to her all by itself? Why have we got to do anything about it?'

He laughs. 'I talk like that sometimes, Hollie. When I've taken

262

a little – you know, *something,* to help with the pain of life. Forget I said it. Hey, it's laudable that you hesitate before jumping in to get your own back – especially after what I've just told you. But I'm not asking you to do anything that'll bring bad karma down on yourself, you understand. If that's what you're worried about?' he says solicitously. 'No – you'll be exposing a wrong-doing, that's all . . .'

'Why don't *you* expose it?'

He pulls a pained expression. 'Because I – to my eternal shame, and blinded by my love for her – was involved myself, wasn't I? I can't afford to be implicated, Hollie. I need you to do it.'

Perhaps if he thinks I'm going to be the one to expose her, then he'll back off? Leave me to it. Better if he thinks that.

'You told me last time we spoke, that you'd written my sister a note – five little words – in that envelope you sent out to her in November. The red balloon, remember?' I look at him curiously now. 'What were they?'

'I wrote: "I know what you did". Hey,' he shifts gear suddenly, 'I just said I was probably tripping out when I told you all that, OK? Forget about that. She's never going to get that message now, anyway, is she?'

'You're not stoned *now,* though, are you? But you came here hoping you'd still get something out of that bargain you two struck up. You knew she'd been seeing Richard, yet you still hoped she'd be true to her word to you . . .' I remind him.

'I'm a fool, aren't I?' He looks directly into my eyes. 'And you've been a fool too. Perhaps we can both stop being her fools now. Do I have your agreement?'

'Fine.' I stand up, affecting an aggrieved air. 'You want me to contact PlanetLove, saying I've been asked to send them evidence, testify that the document she asked me to send them wasn't one she in fact produced herself? She'll lose her job, Duncan.'

'Which is no more than she deserves, I'm sure you'll agree?'

He follows me to the front door. 'I'll leave you to it, then?' He turns at last and shakes my hand. 'I'll await the outcome with interest.'

Yeah. I shut the door on him at last, and my legs are shaking, my palms all sweaty. You await it.

Scarlett

Tried to ring u last nite, I text Gui, *but no ansr*. He isn't answering now, either. I click off the phone in disgust. One minute he's all over me like a rash and the next thing he goes quiet for days. Why? He doesn't know what I got up to with Rich on Bluebell Hill so there's no reason for him to go silent on me. I even rang up his PA at Chiquitin-Almeira last night, I was that desperate. She sounded rather surprised. I felt a bit stupid, saying, 'It's his girlfriend ringing.' Is that even what I am any more? Maybe I've left it all too late.

I push down the waistband of my jeans, feeling irritable, rubbing at the red weal where they've been digging into my flesh. I keep telling myself it's all Hollie's home-cooking. I'm not wearing those elasticated-waist ones Hollie wanted to buy me. Not yet. It's too soon to be getting fat. I don't even want to be pregnant.

My phone rings now. I look at it and see that Emoto's sent me a sweet pic of him and José in the forest. They've found another orchid-rich zone, apparently. The photo's pretty dark so I can't make out what species there are surrounding them but he's written a message: *Me and José in Aladdin's cave. Wish you were here to see it.*

You don't know how much I wish it, too, Emoto. Only last week he rung me saying he'd heard rumours flying around that PlanetLove were investigating me for something. How in the world *that's* got out when they won't even tell me what I'm supposed to have done . . .

Anyway, he said he heard someone had put in fraud allegations against me. He sounded worried. He hinted that I really could do with being back there to defend myself, look into it all properly. I feel so . . . completely helpless here, that's the problem. I can't get hold of anyone at PlanetLove head office at Berkeley Square, no matter what I do.

I can't get hold of anyone that I really want to, can I? Rich has been away for – what, four, five weeks now? They're still keeping up the pretence that his absence is work-related but if Hollie really believes that then she's even more naïve than I've taken her to be. She surely must see that everything has changed? This place drives me potty. *She* drives me potty. I tried to do what I could to help others and what have I ended up with? Richard's ignoring me, Gui's ignoring me, my whole career is about to go down the pan due to some mysterious allegations that I'm not in Brazil to defend myself against . . . Oh, it's enough to make me see why our mum would have wanted to run away from everything. *I* want to run away.

If Rich doesn't come back sometime soon, maybe I will, too.

Hollie

I turn back to the house, my arms laden with bathroom towels I've just rescued from the sudden April squall. The deep purple tulips Christine brought me back from Holland last year stand in a line like bare green spikes, all their petals blown to the ground too soon. This isn't the spring I was dreaming of.

Maybe this time next year my washing line will be full of Babygros? It's what I wanted but everything feels so wrong, so out-of-place. The cottage feels so empty and lonely, even though Scarlett's here. But Richard still isn't.

The bottom gate's been left off the latch. That won't be my sister's doing, she's always particular about closing the gate behind her. Besides, she's not exactly out and about much at the moment. But that gate has certainly been left open, which means somebody's come in ahead of me.

Could it be Rich? My heart soars with hope for a moment. He's been in Lincolnshire for weeks now, and – true to his word – he has not come back down to our cottage. With Scarlett as sick as a dog I've not been able to get up to him either and I've been desperate to see him. Heaven knows what he's told his parents, they'll be wondering why on earth he's stayed away for so long.

Unless he's told them the truth.

I run back up the garden path, the cold breeze fluttering a shower of cherry blossom at my back like confetti at a wet wedding.

If it is Richard, he never called to say he was coming. Could it be a spur-of-the-moment thing? Perhaps he's realised how much he's missed me?

Just inside the hallway I spy Scarlett's bedroom door ajar at the top of the stairs and I stop. Maybe the visitor is for her, and not for me? Whoever it is, she's sounding rather pleased with herself, I can hear her throaty chuckle from here.

'About time you turned up again,' she's saying, 'seeing as I've been so sick and all. I was beginning to think you didn't care. Do you want to see my tummy?'

I freeze. Who the heck has she got in there with her?

'Your hands are cold!' she shrieks after a while. 'You need to warm them up a bit . . . Hey, that tickles!'

'Sorry, my love.'

I drop the towels in the hallway and creep up the stairs, trying to spread my weight evenly so as not to make them creak.

'So, have you been a good girl? Like we discussed on the phone?'

'Oh, yes.' Scarlett sounds uninterested suddenly. 'Vitamins. Water. Fresh vegetables – those I can keep down – and gentle exercise.' I wanted to do all that, I think, suddenly disconsolate. I wanted to do all those things to grow a healthy baby, I was looking forward to it, but for her it's just a huge inconvenience . . .

'Excellent. Roll up your sleeve for me, there's a poppet. I want to check your blood pressure.'

Oh. The midwife. I skip the last few steps and pop my head round her door.

'Hi, Jane.' I give them both a cheesy smile. 'Didn't know we were expecting you today.'

'Thought I'd pop in, seeing as she wasn't too bright last week, were you, my love?' Jane straightens, then pumps up the blood pressure band around Scarlett's arm. 'That's all excellent. Now. D'you want to pop up onto these scales for me, please?'

Scarlett climbs onto them obediently and the midwife gives a small tut-tut sound. 'Not keeping enough down, are you, really?

Still, the baby'll take what it needs – it's you that's going to go downhill if you can't manage food. I'm going to ask you to wee in a bottle for me in a minute. Do you think you can manage that?'

'Anything for you.'

'You're lucky to have such good support, here.' Jane cocks her head, indicating me. 'My next lady has two kids under two, she's every bit as sick as you but she doesn't get to lounge around all day.' She's teasing gently, making a sweeping gesture that takes in the numerous drinks bottles, banana peels and magazines surrounding the bed. 'And here's you, being waited upon hand and foot like a princess. But this is one thing you're going to have to do for yourself though, lovey.'

Scarlett smiles, takes the little plastic bottle proffered her and stalks off to the bathroom.

'I hope the dad's helping out too and not just leaving it all to auntie?' Jane glances up at me enquiringly once my sister's gone. I watch her rolling up the blood-pressure machine, winding up the wires and folding them all neatly back into her bag. I want to ask her so many questions but it doesn't feel like my place to do so.

'Yes,' I say faintly. I fold my arms, turning my head at the sound of the back door shutting. Is that the wind? My arms were full of towels, I can't remember – did I leave it open?

'She's quite young, isn't she? I take it this one *was* a planned pregnancy?' Jane turns to me now, curious rather than judgemental.

'She's not as young as she looks. She's twenty-four.'

'Still. . . .' she flicks through her notes '. . . twenty-four is still young to be going it alone, isn't it? At the end of the day, it always helps a first-time mummy if the dad's on board with it, that's all.' She looks up as Scarlett reappears with her sample bottle.

'Wee's fine,' she confirms after a few moments. 'Now, would you two ladies like to hear the baby's heartbeat?' The midwife puts some Vaseline on my sister's tummy and then suddenly there's this *whoosh-whoosh-whoosh* sound, loud as a waterfall beating in my ears. 'Lovely and strong, isn't it?' Jane smiles.

'That's . . . that's *him*?' I can hardly get the words out. I go and sit down on the little chair by Scarlett's bed, my hand on her arm. Is that my baby? He's real. He's here. I stare at my sister's flat stomach and the whole thing seems unfathomable, would be totally unbelievable if it weren't for that *whoosh-whoosh-whoosh* that's filling up the whole room and filling up my heart. I feel my own stomach contract involuntarily. What wouldn't I give to be her right now, lying on that couch? I want to be the one waking up every morning complaining of sickness. I wouldn't mind. I would be *happy*, if it were me.

'Him *or* her,' Jane reminds me. 'That's a good strong heartbeat your infant's got there. Very strong, in fact.' She frowns slightly for a moment, as if something's perplexing her. 'Have you had your scan yet, lovey?'

Scarlett shakes her head. 'You booked me in but the letter that came through said it would take a few weeks . . .'

'You'll be looking forward to that, won't you?' The midwife's eyes light on hers softly and for a moment Scarlett looks as pleased and happy as any newly expectant mum. 'Will the dad be accompanying you?'

'He . . . he might. My sister will come, though, won't you?' She looks at me for confirmation. 'In any event, this baby's going to have the best daddy in the world,' she puts in unexpectedly now.

'Sure,' I say.

He'll make the best daddy in the world if he ever comes back home again. I shift from one foot to the other uncomfortably. I want to hear my baby's heartbeat again. What does that feel like? I glance at my sister enviously. What does it feel like to have someone growing inside you?

'And at least once the scan's done we'll be a bit clearer about your dates . . .' the midwife's saying now.

'My dates?'

270

'Date of your last period, darling.'

'Oh.' I watch as Scarlett's tongue goes to the side of her cheek. 'I told you what the date was.'

'Indeed you did,' Jane glances at her notes. 'Call it intuition – or maybe fifteen years' experience on this job – but I've a feeling you're a bit further ahead with this pregnancy than you think . . .'

My sister pulls an uncomfortable face.

'We're a hundred per cent certain about the dates, Jane,' I say as I watch her putting the heartbeat monitor away in her bag. 'Scarlett's been trying to get pregnant since January, so it might have been possible, except all the other pregnancy tests were negative, weren't they, Scarlett?'

My sister nods, inexplicably tongue-tied all of a sudden, and Jane laughs. I look from one to the other, perplexed.

'These things are often far more hit-and-miss than you think. Your sister might have *thought* she'd had a period, but not done so in actuality. If there wasn't enough pregnancy hormones around at the time she used the test kit then it wouldn't have picked it up. Still . . .' Jane zips up her bag with a flourish. 'All's well that ends well, eh? And I bet you had fun trying.' She winks at Scarlett.

'Trying what?' I snap before I can stop myself.

'To get pregnant,' Jane says baldly.

'She didn't,' I assure her, my face growing hot. 'She's acting as my surrogate. She's having the baby for me and my husband so she didn't . . .' I look at Scarlett and my throat just closes up in the strangest way.

'No, I didn't,' Scarlett confirms hurriedly. 'It wasn't like that.' But her face has gone as pink as a stick of seaside rock right now. She can't imagine I would spill the beans to this lady about how we actually went about it? Her tongue is planted firmly in her cheek and she's staring at the floor. Her hands have dug deep into her dressing gown pockets as we speak and she reminds me so much of her seven-year-old self for a moment it's almost comical; she looks exactly like she used to look whenever she'd been caught out at something.

I push away the image that Duncan planted in my head a week ago of Scarlett and Richard kissing at the window. And her *topless*. I frown, scrutinising her a little closer and my sister offers up a wan smile.

'I really don't think there's any mistake about my due dates either, Jane.' Her chin juts out and she stares at a spot on the wall in front of her while Jane finishes up her notes.

'I've been wrong before,' Jane admits, 'though not often.' She snaps her file shut but I can't tear myself away from my sister's face because I've got the strangest sensation that Scarlett's just lied to us both.

Scarlett

'Hey, that's really terrific.' I put down my magazine as Christine holds up the newly-framed picture of Rochester Bridge.

'You'll have to apologise to Beatrice Highland for me, Hollie.' Richard's mum props the picture up on the table so we can get a better look. 'I don't suppose they'll be using *my* framing services again in a hurry.' She laughs disparagingly and we both look towards Hol, who seems to be more preoccupied with her own thoughts this morning. Three guesses why.

I glance up the stairs but there's no sign of Richard coming down. He and his mum arrived in the early hours of last night; I was in bed by then, it must have been two a.m. when I was woken up by the sound of them all talking on the stairs. I have no idea where he's got to now.

'Beatrice knows we've all had a lot on recently.' Hollie barely glances at the drawing. 'She understands. Still, hopefully things are all returning to normal now. Slowly but surely.'

I watch her curiously as she arranges a vase full of red and yellow tulips on the dining table. Are things really 'returning to normal' for her? I wonder how they could be. Richard's stayed away for weeks now – it's all to do with work, the official story goes – but we all know it's much more than that. She won't be drawn on it. Still, I'll see him today. He won't be able to avoid me forever. It's ridiculous he should try to, anyway.

'Slowly but surely,' Chrissie echoes. 'I can see you're feeling a

273

'lot better too, aren't you, Lettie?' She keeps trying to include the two of us in the conversation. The strain between us must be palpable, especially now Rich is back in the house.

'Not so nauseous.' I throw Chrissie a small smile, because she is kind and she drove all the way down here this weekend not just to deliver the picture but to see me, too. She wanted to thank me personally for the favour I'm doing for her 'two favourite people'.

'In fact, I've been thinking I might soon be well enough to make the trip back to Manaus, as it happens.'

'Oh.' My sister frowns, letting the tulips slide from her hands, and the whole bunch sag out to the side of the vase immediately. 'Have you had word from Eve then? Or that new lot who are taking over who contacted you?'

'No,' I allow. 'But no news is good news, isn't it?'

Hollie looks perturbed. 'I just meant – perhaps you should make sure it's still all OK. Before you book the tickets. There was that letter saying they were looking into those allegations, don't forget . . .'

Chrissie looks at us both quizzically and I shoot my sister a furious glance. What on earth did she have to bring that up in front of Chrissie for?

'All nonsense.' I wave my hand dismissively at her. 'I've done nothing wrong, I told you that.'

'You miss your work in Brazil desperately, don't you?' Christine leans forward and touches my arm gently. 'I'm really impressed with how you've coped these past few weeks. It can't have been easy for you.'

'It hasn't been.' That momentary touch on my arm, the kindness in her eyes, it drags something out of me that I didn't even know was there.

'Oh, my dear. What's brought all this on? Don't cry.' Chrissie wraps her arms around me in a warm hug and over the top of her shoulders I spy my sister scrambling around for a tissue.

'I'm not sad, Chrissie, honest. I'm just . . .' I gulp. I'm just what? Empty. Lonely. I miss him, that's all. His friendship at least.

'What you're feeling right now – it's just natural, darling. It's the hormones. They do that to you, make you sick and make you weepy and all sorts . . .'

'I miss all my friends back in Brazil,' I tell her staunchly. I do miss them. I miss Gui because everything was all so uncomplicated with him. I miss the tribe. I miss my PlanetLove colleagues. I miss Rich, too.

Christine smiles softly. When she does that thing, wrinkling up the sides of her eyes, she reminds me of Rich and I have to look away from her.

'I know, darling. But when you leave here and go back there you'll miss *us* too, won't you?' She glances up at my sister and I get the impression she's doing her best to re-establish some of the rapport that's been lost between us.

Does Christine even *know*? Richard's been staying at his parents' place since he got back from Italy last month. He must have spoken to her about what went on, surely? I can't believe he wouldn't have said something . . .

'Look, where's Richard this morning?' I blurt out at last. 'I haven't seen him since – well, since I got pregnant. Is he planning on staying away from me forever?'

'Away from *you*, Scarlett?' Christine looks at me in surprise. 'Well – you were asleep when he and I arrived last night of course, but I thought you might have seen him this morning?' She looks from Hollie to me questioningly, then runs on. 'This whole restructuring of the business thing – it's been a complete and utter nightmare, of course. And with you being so unwell, he thought he'd best stay up with us and sort out work and leave you two girls to it. I'm sure Hollie's told you that?'

'Is that the reason he's given for staying away?' I feel my mouth drop open slightly. I want to tell Chrissie the truth, I really, really do because if we've got to keep up this whole pretence for very much longer I think I am going to explode.

'He had to go out to his local office first thing,' Hollie puts in hurriedly.

'He'll be . . . he'll be home tonight then?' I breathe.

'No, Lettie, he won't be here tonight. He only came down to bring his mum and then he's off again. He and I have a lot to catch up on.'

'You'll have had plenty of time to talk. I need to see him too, you know. He hasn't yet thanked me personally for that the fact I'm carrying his child. He hasn't even had the decency to . . .'

'Scarlett!' Christine's eyes have widened in horror. 'I think you can understand why Richard and Hollie would need to have time to reconnect with each other. They are married after all.'

Hollie gets up slowly and walks out of the room. I'd go after her if Christine didn't have her hand on my knee, preventing me.

'It's been really hard for them, darling. You must try and understand that. What you're doing for them is truly wonderful, but it doesn't mean you've . . . how can I put it . . . earned the right to any place within their marriage. I haven't known how much you've been aware of – it's delicate, isn't it – one never knows how much one should say. But I suspect there's been some unhappiness brewing between Hollie and my son and the Italy business is only part of it. I do think it's odd he hasn't wanted to come back home sooner than this. And I know she's been really unhappy at the prospect of him having to look so far afield for work. Quite apart from the fact that he's wanted to give you both your space . . .' She touches my shoulder gently. 'Well, you know how it is.'

I fold my arms. 'You think they've been at loggerheads then? About what? Is it the baby?' I look at her through lowered lids.

'I suspect that may be part of it. He's not told me the whole story of course. I thought maybe Hollie might have filled you in on more details?'

I shake my head. 'I just can't believe he'd come home and not even say hello to me,' I mutter out loud, because that's the thing that's really hurting. 'And then to sneak off in the morning without even . . .'

'Well, it was very late last night . . . Look, this isn't about *you*, darling. Please don't take it personally. There's stuff going on between them. That's why I came down really. I've offered to look after you for tonight while they go out and enjoy themselves somewhere. They both need the break, don't you agree?'

Hah! Is that why Hollie had her little travel case out on the bed this morning? They're going away for a minibreak so everything can be all lovey-dovey between the two of them again.

'I don't need anyone to look after me now, Christine,' I say stiffly. 'I'm feeling much better. I just said so. I'll be going back to Brazil very soon.'

'That's hardly wise now, is it?' she says gently. 'You're bound to be feeling fragile for a while yet. Why risk any harm to yourself or the baby when you're so well looked after here?'

'Because it's stifling me!' I tell her candidly. 'I have a life outside of Rochester. At least I had one. I have to get it back before it all slips away from me for good. What Hollie said about PlanetLove looking into allegations about me – that's bugging me too. I really need to get back to find out what all that's about – somebody must have made a mistake somewhere – but it's one that might prejudice my job.' I'm hoping that all this talk of mundane matters will put her off the scent of what's really on my mind.

I've been feeling gradually better over the last few weeks, it's true. I've only hung on in the hope that I could come to some sort of truce here – with Rich and with my sister too. I didn't want to leave with this horrid atmosphere still hanging over us, but it doesn't look as if it's going to go away that easily.

I stand up, my legs shaking, and go over to the table, my eyes lighting on the drawing of the bridge that Christine propped up there earlier.

'My sister doesn't get this picture at all, does she?' My fingers run over the smooth edge of the dark silver frame as I take it in again. 'You know why? It's because she doesn't like to see the darker side of things. She once told me that the chapels they built on either side of medieval bridges weren't put there just for grateful travellers to give thanks for their safe passage over. They were there so that outbound travellers could pray they wouldn't get mugged or murdered while going across, either.'

'A dangerous occupation crossing these medieval bridges . . .' Christine joins me at the table. 'But without them, I guess the "other side of the river" must have seemed as far away to your average peasant as the moon is to us.'

'I think it's what Hollie's scared of, you know: the possibility that if she reaches out far enough and long enough to get the thing she wants, that there might be some very unlovely things waiting there for her, too,' I hint.

'Aren't *you* scared of that?' Christine looks at me curiously now. I shake my head slowly.

'I've been right to the other side of the world, Chrissie. And I've come to the conclusion that the most scary things are often the ones we leave back home.'

Well. Maybe it's about time my sister stopped going around as if everything in life came straight out of a Disney movie. Maybe it's time she woke up to how things really are, to how I'm really feeling about this whole rotten set-up – to what *really* went on between me and her husband that day up on Bluebell Hill.

Before they have their sweet little reconciliation tonight, I think she really needs to know.

Hollie

'All ready for your date?' Scarlett peers at me from her favourite position up on the coal bunker. She's almost hidden behind the wisteria right now; it's climbed so high this year up the old pear tree it's made a whole curtain but I can just about make her out there behind it. I knew I'd find her down here. It's where she always comes to lick her wounds.

'Lettie . . .' How to put this? 'I'm really sorry . . .'

Sorry that Richard won't see you any more because of what I asked you both to do; sorry I ruined the familiar and comfortable relationship you two had with each other; sorry I've caused you to stay away from the work you love; and sorry that you can't come with us tonight.

'. . . For everything,' I add, because there is such a long list of things to be sorry for. 'I feel I haven't treated you right.'

'Ha!' Her eyes range darkly over mine. 'Never mind, Hollie.' She swallows, as if making an effort to gain control of herself. 'Look, just go now please, go and have your dinner with Richard. I want you to go away before I say anything I'm going to regret, all right? Go away and have a nice evening and . . . talk to Richard.'

'Why don't you invite some of your mates over to . . . ?'

She shakes her head fiercely.

'I'm not in that kind of mood. Look, stop worrying about me. I'll be fine here with Chrissie.' She turns away to look back over the fence. I pick my way delicately over the grass towards her, my heels sinking into the long grass as I go. I'm meeting Rich at the gastropub in Rochester High Street in half an hour, then we're planning to spend the weekend on the coast.

'I just wish that . . . that things were different at the moment, and I could invite you out with us tonight and we could all celebrate the pregnancy like you said – but I can't.'

Scarlett doesn't turn round. She's staring at the static barge the engineers have set up on the river; there's a guy manning a small crane that's busy manoeuvring sediment into place even at this hour.

'They've been there for weeks now, haven't they?' She deliberately doesn't answer me. 'Makes you wonder how bad the problem under the bridge could have been, really.'

'They've got to shore up the abutments,' I tell her distractedly. 'With the weight of all that water that's flowing by all the time, it's a delicate operation . . .'

'Just think. It might just have collapsed one day when all the traffic was on it. Imagine the mayhem that would have caused. Might have brought on a few headaches back at the office, don't you think?'

'It's already been the cause of a few headaches, Lettie. Many of them mine. Look, we need to talk, don't we?' I put in suddenly. 'I know you're mad at me because Richard's cut you out of his life. He's pretty much cut me out too, can't you see that? It isn't just you. If I don't do something about the state of our marriage . . .'

'They've torn down most of the old buildings that were part of that business complex along Strood Esplanade – have you seen that?' Maddeningly, she's still batting away my every attempt to have a proper conversation. She lifts the pendulous lilac blooms of the wisteria so I can see the river better and she points towards the opposite bank.

'I'm not interested in the buildings, Scarlett.' I want to make our peace, but she keeps bringing in red herrings. Reluctantly, I

280

rise up on my tiptoes and pretend to peer out over the wall. I'm not going to look where she wants me to. I can't. 'OK,' I breathe.

'How does that feel?' she says after a while. Then, when I don't answer her: 'Like an old wound you never wanted to look at, eh?'

'Look, let's not go there, shall we?' I look at her entreatingly. I've got twenty minutes before I meet up with Rich. I need to concentrate on the here and now, put right the things that have gone wrong again. That's the most important thing just at the moment.

'Lettie. I want things to be OK between us. I want a truce. The atmosphere in the cottage this last month has been pretty unbearable. It must have been for you, too?' I take a step nearer to my sister but she crosses her arms and legs, keeps her distance.

'It's always been like this though, hasn't it?' she observes.

'What d'you mean, always? It hasn't *always* been like this.'

'It has for me,' she says shortly. 'I feel stifled here. I've always known I wouldn't stay.'

'You've always had ants in your pants,' I agree. I lean my elbows up on the coal bunker and point at the line of ants making their way along the wall. She doesn't smile back. 'Do you remember that time at Flo's birthday party . . . ? It must have been her fiftieth. A whole group of us went down to that hall at Aylesford. It was such a beautiful evening. The river was so calm and flat and . . .'

She frowns at me now. Maybe she doesn't recall? She couldn't have been much more than four at the time.

'When the sun went down,' Scarlett continues, 'each of Flo's guests wrote a special wish on a piece of paper for her.'

'Ah, so you do remember . . .'

'Then we made little paper boats out of them and put a candle inside each one and set them off down the river.' My sister's eyes narrow. 'I ran along the riverbank after the boats. I ran and I ran, trying to keep up with them and then I got to

281

that bend in the river where there was a fallen tree trunk and you wouldn't let me follow them any more.'

I take in a breath, because she still remembers how I held her back. She doesn't remember – even now – the reason why.

'I'm not like you, Hollie,' she says softly now. 'I never will be.'

'I understand that. Really I do. I know how hard it's been, remaining cooped up here for all these weeks. And even though I'd do anything in the world to make you stay here – at least until you give birth – I know I can't make you. And maybe it would be unfair of me to try.' I hesitate, glancing at my watch. 'I've got to go to Rich now. I know things have been . . . hard . . . recently, but all that's going to change, I promise you. Things are going to be all right.'

My sister gives a pained laugh then. She shakes her head disparagingly. 'Things are not going to be all right, Hollie. It's gone too far for that. Don't you know that? Can't you see *anything*?'

'What is it?' I hesitate, torn between needing to make a move and not wanting to leave her like this, feeling sad, words left unspoken.

'Do you honestly want us to be real with one another? I don't know that you could take that, Hollie. I mean, properly real – instead of just glossing over what's actually going on?'

'Go on, then.'

'Well for one thing.' She looks at me painfully. 'I'm not going to give birth in December. I'm expecting for November. That midwife was on the money about my dates being wrong.'

'She was?' I look at her, startled. 'So – you're further ahead than we thought? That's . . . that's wonderful,' I say resolutely. 'It means we get our baby all the sooner.'

My sister shakes her head at me in disbelief. 'Is that all you can say about it? Hollie, why won't Richard see me?' She's watching me closely.

'He feels awkward and uncomfortable, I guess. Oh, we've been over all this, Lettie. You know how shy he is. When I asked him to be with you,' I swallow, 'it must have been unbearable for him.'

'He won't see me because – that day up on Bluebell Hill – I told him that I was in love with him.'

Hollie

I can barely breathe. It feels like the whole world comes to a stop for a moment.

'Well – why on earth did you go and say a stupid thing like that?' I stutter. 'No wonder he's feeling so bad about being around you. Hell, Scarlett . . . !'

'Why did I say it?' Scarlett's face has gone white, her fists clenched into a ball just like when she was a kid. 'I told you to just bloody go away and have your dinner, didn't I? All this . . . this pretend intimacy between us sisters, all this gratuitous honesty and you're so . . . so bloody stupid you wouldn't see the truth if it were emblazoned on the front of a high-speed train that was about to hit you.'

'Scarlett, I have no idea what you're on about.'

'No, you don't. Because you don't want to know. Go away, all right? Just go!'

'No, I won't. I can't, not after what you've just said to me.' I step closer to my sister, put my hand on her arm and she flinches away as if she's just been bitten. 'Why did you feel the need to say to Richard that you were in love with him? I can understand – under the circumstances – if you might have needed to get some sort of role play going on in your head, but you didn't need to say it out loud to him.'

'I said it,' she puts in through gritted teeth, 'because it is true.'

I swallow. 'You do not love my husband, Scarlett. Please – just stop and consider what you're saying for a moment because words . . . they last a lifetime. You can't take them back afterwards. Oh God, Lettie – what did you say to him?'

'I told Richard that I loved him,' she says, high-pitched now. 'That I have always loved him.'

'My Richard?' I feel the blood drain from my face now. Why did she – oh, God, she's just told me she's expecting in November, not December. Does that mean she was already pregnant in February when the two of them slept together? I'm shaking, unable to think straight. It's too much. Too much to take in, all at once.

'Mine first,' she says, almost inaudibly. 'I met him first.'

'I beg your pardon?'

'I met him. That day out along Rochester Esplanade when Ruffles got run over, have you forgotten? He came over to me. He wrapped Ruffles up in his jacket and he walked with me down to the vet's. He didn't take his car because he said I should never get into a car with a stranger. He made me call you,' she gulps, 'to say where we were.'

'So – he took you to the vet's? What's that got to do with anything?' My voice is rising though I'm trying hard to keep it level. Scarlett is . . . she's obviously fraught and upset and hormonal and conflicted and saying lots of things that she doesn't really mean. She *can't* mean them. She's talking rubbish. She's got to be.

'You can't know how I felt about him all that summer. When we were teaching each other to dance . . .'

'In the vet's old cow shed you mean? Oh, Scarlett! Are you talking about the time I came in and found you two dancing together?' I search my memory and all I can come up with is that I thought she looked so sweet. And . . . so happy and I was glad she'd found a hobby that would take her mind off all the bad things that had happened that year.

'But there was never anything between you. You were thirteen, for pity's sake.' Her face looks like thunder but I continue on regardless. 'So you had a crush on him? Maybe you did. I'm sorry I didn't notice. I had plenty enough on my own plate if you recall – I was only twenty-one myself, and I'd had to take on the house, looking after you, everything.' I had to leave my creative arts university degree at Canterbury unfinished so I could look after her – has she forgotten? I lost it all! Not just Flo – the only person who'd ever been a parent to me, but the education that would give me a shot at the fashion career I'd always dreamed of.

'I was due to have gone away to do my year abroad.' I stutter now at her white face. Does she remember any of that? If she was ever even aware of it she doesn't care.

'I wanted you to go abroad, don't you know that?' she shoots back. 'I was looking forward to your going. I never wanted you to stay behind and ruin everything for me, make the sacrifice, be such a bloody *martyr* . . .'

I stop. She is distraught, my sister. She is hysterical. Is this what the pregnancy is doing to her? Filling her so full of hormones that she can't think straight anymore? I have to be the one who stays calm here. I *have* to.

'I'm sorry if . . . if I didn't notice how you felt about him, but let's face it, that was over ten years ago, Scarlett. You're a grown woman now . . .'

'You didn't notice because . . . everything I ever did back in those days was always put down to me "going through some teenage phase". You and Beatrice used to sit in the kitchen for hours on end discussing me, don't think I didn't used to hear you. You were both very fond of droning on about how I was "going off the rails".'

'I had to talk to *someone* about you,' I defend. 'I didn't have anyone else. And you *did* go off the rails! You were totally out of control and you gave me hell so don't deny it.'

Scarlett laughs hysterically.

'I only went out with Aaron and all that crowd at the Blue Jazz café because I wanted some friends of my own. People that had nothing to do with you! I never wanted you to get involved, Hollie. I never asked you to intervene between me and Aaron.'

'Don't even *talk* to me about Aaron, OK? Don't ever mention his name again.'

'No,' she says bitterly. 'We can't mention it. We can't talk about anything that went on that night, can we? Even though I know you blame me for what happened. Even though I never wanted . . .'

'You put yourself in danger, Scarlett. I *had* to come out and get you—'

'I didn't want *you* to come, you fool! I wanted . . . I hoped Rich would come. Not you. After you two started dating I never had another moment with him alone. You stole him away from me. I wanted him back, that's all.'

'I didn't steal him away from you, because Richard has never loved you, has he? Not that way.'

'He didn't have much trouble getting it up for me when we were together, that's for sure!' she shoots back.

I stare at my sister in horror. It feels as if she's scooping out my entire innards with the cruel pick and shovel of her words.

'Maybe that's why he doesn't want to see me again. I'm not a thirteen-year-old any more am I, Hollie? Maybe he's scared he's fallen for me, too? Has *that* ever occurred to you?'

What is she trying to do to me?

'Just tell me one thing,' I get my voice back at last. 'Because I know I have played my part in this. I asked you two to be together. You both . . .' I stumble over the words '. . . begged me not to ask it of you, but I insisted and I know that is my doing and I'm paying for that now, aren't I? Just tell me. In March, when you were both together, *did you know*?'

'About the pregnancy?' My sister lets out a strangled cry. She puts her hands to her face, shaking her head. Then she looks up at me piteously, her tongue planted firmly into her cheek once more and her face glowing pink.

'God, you're lying, aren't you! You *did* know you were pregnant, Scarlett.' I grab hold of both of her shoulders. I want to shake her till her teeth rattle. I want to shake her till they all drop out. 'Admit to me that you knew it!'

'Let go of me!' She looks up at me at last, eyes blazing. 'I'll come clean,' she throws back. 'I did know it. But I only lied to spare you, Hollie, because now you know that I betrayed you, I can never take it back again, can I?'

'You . . . you're telling me that you slept with him even though you didn't need to? You knew you were already pregnant? *Why?*'

'Why?' Her face is swimming before my eyes, I can barely see her any more and there's a rushing sound in my ears like all my blood is flowing out of me and my heart is giving up because she has broken it but beyond all that there is something else – something small and spindly and weedy like a forgotten shrub at the bottom of a neglected garden that has just woken up and realised it's still there, it's still alive . . .

She shakes her head now, because there is no satisfactory why. She did it because she could, that is all.

'And – and Richard,' I whisper in trepidation, 'did he know too?'

'Of course he didn't know! He loves you, doesn't he? He never wanted to do it. He only did it because he loves you.' She's telling the truth now, the complete and utter truth, I see it. She flinches her shoulders back and I let her go.

'What do you want to do now, Hollie?'

'I want . . . for you to go away from here now and I don't want to see you again as long as I live.' I walk over to the blue and yellow estate agent's 'For Sale' sign that I finally agreed she could have put up last week and grab hold of it with both hands, wrenching it out of the ground. All the wet turf comes up with it when I hurl it to the floor. 'And I am not selling Florence Cottage. I am not letting you chuck me out of the only home I have ever known. I am not looking after you any more, either.'

288

'Where will I go?' she begins. She has her head so deeply buried in her hands that I can't see her face and I don't know if she's crying. It sounds as if she is but I don't care.

This girl is carrying my precious baby. All my hopes and dreams are still inside of her but I see now I have made the biggest mistake of my life.

And what can I do about it? Nothing, that's what. Nothing ever comes back to haunt Scarlett, does it? It's always the people around her, the people who love her who lose out and Scarlett seems to sail on through.

Well. If I have to lose the one thing that gave my life meaning then I'll let it go now.

I want her out of my life for good.

Red Balloon

'Hey, man. How'd you get on?'

Jamie Liddell turns at the sound of the voice echoing down the school hall, experiencing the same cringing feeling in his belly he's had every day since retaking his exams. He shakes his head once, briefly.

'If you mean my A2s I think I pretty much ballsed them up,' he mutters softly. The college student who's come out to meet him pulls a disappointed face at that. Liddell won't want to buy his laptop, then? No A levels, no uni – probably no need for a laptop, he reckons silently.

'It mightn't be all that bad, mate,' he consoles. 'And,' he hesitates, 'everything happens for a reason.'

'I'm thinking of taking some time out, anyway.' Jamie sticks his hands in his pockets, his fingers brushing against the ten crisp ten-pound notes he's got in there. He's already accepted that he's never going to be any good at exams. That dream of uni he had – *was it ever even his dream?* – is fading fast. He'd come here this morning to check out the notice board, see if there's any student work going. You're not going to need any computers now, are you, his mum had reminded him on his way out. He hadn't intended to buy it. He was going to say he'd changed his mind, but . . . his eyes glitter covetously as the student unzips the bag. It's a top-of-the-range model. At a knock-down price.

'I still want the laptop,' he assures the guy. 'It works OK, right?'

'It works.' The student pulls it out of its smart black case. A couple of worksheets flutter down to the ground as he does so. 'Didn't get to sort all this stuff out,' he grins half-heartedly. 'I can do it now . . .' he half-looks over his shoulder, 'or you can just chuck anything you find in there in the bin. If you need me to show you how anything works on it I can stay but my girlfriend's waiting in town and you know how it is . . .' His eyes light up involuntarily as Jamie produces the hundred quid.

'Nah. These things are a piece of cake. I'll take it from here.' Rush back to your girlfriend, he thinks enviously. I've never had one so, no, I don't know 'how it is'.

'Good luck with it. Hope your plans work out, dude.' The guy's backing out towards the door already, waving a cheery goodbye.

Plans, Jamie thinks, his brain a fumbling mass of half-baked ideas, unexplored possibilities fanning out in all directions. What plans? He hasn't got any now he's flunked the exams – he's not holding out any hope for miracles when the results come out. Now there's just this messy void in which all the structure of the known world has been left behind – school, childhood – and there's no handy platform in sight to lift him up onto the next phase . . .

Man, that guy wasn't kidding about leaving his trash in here. When Jamie unzippers the side compartment, two one pound coins come rolling out. And some empty chocolate wrappers, one condom packet (empty, he notes enviously), a wad of crushed worksheets and – what's this? Jamie tugs at the piece of string and there appears to be a whole deflated red metallic balloon tethered to the end of it. It's even got a letter attached. He glances up through the glass doors just in time to see the student sailing off on his bike, oblivious. Damn.

Who's the letter for? Jamie turns it round. Scarlett L. Hudson. He does a double take. Hasn't he already seen that name once this morning? He has, he furrows his brow, trying to recall where. It was up on the student notice board, that's where it was. She was one of the contact names on the bottom of that 'Amazon volunteering' card. She was a looker too, there was a little picture of her stuck onto the bottom of it. Oh, yes, he'd like to meet *her*. He'd thought about taking the number down. He'd imagined himself turning up back at his house announcing he was off to the rainforest for the summer – how envious his younger siblings would be.

Everything happens for a reason.

Well, now he's got this letter . . . maybe he *has* got a reason to go out to Brazil. He can deliver it to that girl Scarlett Hudson himself, can't he, and won't she be blown away?

Hollie

I cannot believe I am sitting here at this table in this restaurant, pretending to be *normal*. But I don't know what else to do. I have told her to go. And she has done so. My sister crawled down off the coal bunker and she scuttled off. I didn't call her back and I didn't feel any remorse for all the things I'd said to her, I just wanted her gone. And right now maybe I should be feeling a great big gaping hole in my life, torn out of the centre of me because she – and the baby she's carrying – are gone, but I feel nothing. Just numb.

And the funny thing is, from my little table in the corner of the restaurant, I can see the rest of the world carrying on as normal all around me, as if nothing has changed. The waitresses here are still bustling up and down, still taking the drinks orders, still delivering food in their brisk, efficient way; the proprietor – a paunchy Italian in his mid-fifties – is still standing at the doorway, greeting the early evening customers. The couple who came in before me are still minutely examining their menu as if their whole lives depended on the choices they make tonight and I want to stand up and scream: 'No, no, it doesn't matter what you decide on. It's me who's made the most momentous decision of my life tonight, not you. I just told my sister to get out of my life forever.'

And still I feel nothing.

Richard is late. I pour a glass of water from the jug, glance at my watch. Twenty minutes late. Could he have changed his mind and gone back home after his meeting instead? I half get up out of my seat at the thought – could he have come across a distraught Scarlett, running away from Florence Cottage barefoot, tears streaming down her shameless face, and stopped to deal with her? But I can't go and check that possibility out because he might still turn up here any minute. I sit back down and pick up my glass. After a while I gulp the water down thirstily, stemming the rising flow of panic I feel at the thought that he might not come after all. His mobile phone is switched off.

He could have changed his mind about me and our marriage and our future. He could have. I lick my lips nervously, picking at the olives in the little dish as the proprietor turns and looks at me curiously. He knows how long I've been sitting here on my tod without ordering so much as a side salad. He smiles sympathetically.

Things were not good between me and Rich last night. He felt like a stranger even though we were both trying really hard to be normal with each other. I guess I don't know what normal is any more. He's had reasons enough – excuse after excuse – to spend time away from here, and we've both known that all of them originated from his discomfort at the thought of spending any time in Scarlett's company. He asked for us to meet up tonight out here, away from the cottage and his mum and my sister, so we could have some time alone together and 'clear the air'. But my God, how is he going to take this latest development?

I feel the weight of my head sink into my hands and my gaze is glued to the chequered tablecloth beneath me. I don't even want to think about what Scarlett's just confessed to me tonight. It's too terrible. I told her to be careful about what she said. I *warned* her, that some words can never be taken back.

But I *also* said that I'd like her and I to be open and honest with each other, didn't I? I wish I hadn't now. She could have had my baby and taken her secret back to Brazil with her, buried it deep in the foliage and humus littering the forest floor and we needed never to have spoken of it, ever.

I look up as Rich sits down opposite me. Thank God! His face looks dark and pinched though his eyes are bright with an intensity that I have not seen before.

'Sorry, traffic on the bridge held me up.' He sounds strained. 'Have you ordered for us?' he asks after a while. An ordinary question for an ordinary day. I shake my head dumbly and the waiter sidles over as if summoned by magic. It's just starting to hit me how shell-shocked I'm feeling. I didn't hear him say anything to the man but the waiter's definitely gone off on a mission.

'So . . . did it all go well? In Trieste, I mean?' My voice is strangled with the effort of normality.

'You should know; my weeks away from home have not all been spent idly.' He gives me a significant look. 'Signor Bonomi has offered our firm the contract in Trieste.'

I look at him, startled. 'He has?'

'In fact, he's gone one better than that. He's offered us permanent employment out there at a rate that seems, frankly, beyond competitive. We wouldn't have the stress of constantly chasing contracts, and he's agreed that my dad can work at a pace that'd suit him best. It's an offer that would take away all the strain of running the business and allow Dad and me to just get on with doing the surveying and assessing of buildings that we love and do best.'

'Out there?' I get out at last. 'We'd have to move out there to – to Italy? What about Florence Cottage? What about my job?'

'It's all still at the consideration stage, Hol. You know I wouldn't make any major decisions without taking your wishes into account.' He doesn't add – but look what I have sacrificed for you, because of the child that you wanted so badly, you needed

295

so desperately. 'You OK?' Rich leans forward suddenly and grabs hold of both my hands. I shake my head again, unable to speak.

I am not feeling *nothing* after all, I realise. I am feeling – I'm feeling riddled with remorse and guilt and confusion and above and beyond all that I have the strangest sensation of this thin black line of rage beginning to trickle out of me and I can't stop it no matter what I try to do with it.

I want to *kill* her!

'Rich, I have just told Scarlett to leave,' I begin thickly. 'I told her to get out of the house and that I . . .' I lower my voice as the old couple opposite smile at us holding hands, 'I just told her I never want to see her again as long as I live!'

I see Rich's head lower a fraction, his whole being suddenly silent and still.

'She betrayed me with you, didn't she?' I challenge.

He frowns, sucks in his lips as if weighing up how much I know. But how much does *he* know?

'She – you asked her to do it, Hol. I'm not sure what you're . . .'

'No. I never asked her,' I gasp. 'Not to do that. Did you know,' my fingers tighten on his across the table, 'she was *already pregnant* when she slept with you that day up at the flat?'

His eyes widen momentarily and then close in shock. I hear him draw in a heavy breath and he removes one hand from mine, puts it across his heart.

'She confessed to you that she was in love with you, didn't she, Rich?' I battle to keep my voice low, not to sob, but several heads turn to look in our direction nonetheless.

'Christ, what has she said to you?'

'She . . . she told me tonight but you've known it for weeks. You never said. You kept it from me, Rich!'

'I swear I didn't know she was already pregnant. That's – unbelievable! And what was I meant to do, when she suddenly turned around and professed her love for me?' He leans in suddenly, the intensity on his face almost frightening. 'I never had the first

296

idea she felt that way. And you'd asked me to sleep with her for Christ's sake . . . you'd already made it clear where your priorities lay. You wanted the baby. You were prepared to risk the emotional fallout you said. *What else did you want me to do?*'

We both fall silent for a moment. Out of the corner of my eye I can see the waiter approaching with intent but then, thinking the better of it no doubt, he turns away to give us our space.

'I was really angry with you,' he adds quietly after a bit. 'I was angry that you were prepared to put me through all that. But I didn't want to repeat her words to you. I knew how much they'd hurt. I couldn't come home with *her* still there. And she couldn't leave while she was so sick with the pregnancy – I haven't known what to do for the best. And now she's told you . . .'

'You were *angry*? At me?'

'In fact, Hol, I'll be honest with you. I've had moments over the past few weeks when I've wondered if I could really come back to you at all.'

I look at him in horror. 'What did *I* do?' I whisper. 'What did I ever do, other than try and make us a family?'

'What *did* you do, Hol?' he asks remorsefully.

'I never knew she felt like that, Richard! You can't imagine for one moment I ever had the first idea . . .' I judder to a halt, because maybe I should have known, I think now. Maybe the only reason I had no idea how my sister really felt was because I didn't want to see it.

Of course he must have been angry! If I'm honest I saw it that frozen day along the Esplanade when I first broached the subject. I just didn't want to let it stop me. I've been ruthless, I realise now.

'I *was* angry, Hol. That's why I've stayed away. But I've realised that I love you more. I didn't want us to be apart any more so I've come home to sort it out with you if we can. And I'm partly to blame too. I could always have refused your request.'

I swallow nervously. 'I have to ask you this, Rich, forgive me, but I have to. Did you feel anything for her? Anything at all?'

He looks up sharply. 'Good God, Hollie!'

'Just – tell me, OK? I'd rather you did. I'd rather know.' Even though the truth is, I don't. The razor-sharp silence hangs like an axe-blade in the air between us, then:

'No.'

One word. Stark. The waiter swoops in, sensing his moment, lands our drinks deftly on the table and is quickly off again.

'No,' Rich repeats when I don't answer him. 'OK?'

I swallow down some of my wine. More than half the glass, in fact, without realising it. I look at my husband through pained eyes.

'The trouble is . . .' Richard leans in a little closer, his eyes boring into mine '. . . you will never be sure now, will you? No matter what I say. No matter what I do. You'll never be sure whether or not you can really trust me because I've slept with another woman – your sister! God, if only you knew!' He lets out a half-laugh but there is not the slightest trace of humour in it.

'If only I knew what . . . ?' I whisper.

'If only you knew how much time I have had to regret going along with your plans, Hollie. Time enough all these past few weeks when I've been away, to reconsider a lot of things. And I've *hated* being apart from you. I missed you.'

'You have?'

He nods. 'More than you know. But I've also realised that I was wrong to work so hard to try and please you. I needed to trust my own judgement on this one. I didn't. I let my desire to please you rule my thinking, and that was clearly a mistake.' There's a pause as we both reflect for a bit. 'But dear God,' his voice catches suddenly as another thought occurs to him, 'if your sister was *already* expecting then why in God's name did she go through with it?'

'I think we both now know the answer to that.' I drain the rest of my wine glass with unaccustomed ease and he takes the bottle from its chiller bucket and refills it for me.

'So you've told her you don't want to see her again?' He looks at me sharply now. 'And the baby?'

Ah, the baby. I have been feeling all sorts of conflicting emotions rising to the surface but suddenly I'm back to numbness again.

'Have you thought about that?' he persists.

'I haven't . . . I didn't think about anything earlier on beyond getting that girl out of my sight.'

'Don't you think,' he adds softly after a while, 'that you'd better go after her now?'

I look at him uncomprehendingly. What does he mean? I make to raise my wine glass to my lips again but he stays my hand.

'Hollie, you need to go after her,' he repeats. 'Before it's too late.'

Scarlett

Oh fuckety, fuckety, fucking hell, what have I just done?

I didn't want to say all those things to her. So many horrid words. I wanted to tell her how I felt but I didn't mean it to come out like that with such spitefulness, so many little nasty thorns of truth like arrows aimed with hatred right at her heart. I hurt her more than I ever imagined I could. Get out of my life forever, she said, and she meant it.

Thank God there is no one in the bathroom right now because I need to throw up. Shit. I'm not going to make it in time. No time to bolt the door, no time to tie my hair back. I barely make it to the loo before I begin to heave. It isn't the baby making me throw up this time either, it's just me.

I thought I'd feel better if I told her. It's been niggling away at me for so long I couldn't stand it any more. All the pretence, it was killing me. All her unending gratitude towards me when I've been such a bitch and she's been so . . . so . . . good but also so stupidly and obstinately blind to everything I've really been feeling. Couldn't she see I loved him? Wouldn't a blind person have seen it? I couldn't help loving him. I felt bad and I wanted her to know. Surely – surely she needed to know?

But not like this.

I clutch at my lower abdomen with all the pain of retching when there is nothing in your stomach to bring up. What have

300

I just done? I can still see her face turning grey when I said those poisonous things.

What is this disgusting feeling? I feel so uncomfortable and . . . bad, deep in my stomach. Is this what Auntie Flo always meant when she'd say to me: 'You should be ashamed of yourself'? Is this it . . . shame? I always laughed at Flo when she told me that because I never did feel what she'd thought I should. An elemental, she called me, a law unto myself. But I do feel it now, so maybe she was wrong and I had it in me after all, this capacity to feel so totally out of place, so unsure. So in the wrong.

I try and lift my eyes to the bathroom mirror to look at my face but I can hardly look at myself. Who is that girl in the mirror? I hate her. She's not me. When I look at her I see someone so much younger and more vulnerable than the person I am. My hair all stuck to my face like that with the water I've just splashed over it – it makes me look like the teenager I must have been, once before: raw with bereavement, scared to the core, angry, so angry at having been abandoned.

I never cried for Flo.

I put my hands up to my white face now, pressing my taut skin, feeling all the muscles and bones underneath it, peering into the hollow raging eyes in the mirror now, the eyes that no longer look like mine. No, I don't remember ever crying for Flo when she died. All I can remember is feeling mad at her for leaving me, for dying so selfishly and unexpectedly and ruining my life. And I never wanted for Hollie to step into the breach. I never asked her to.

I lean against the little washstand now, gazing closer into the bathroom cabinet mirror. I didn't want her to give up her dreams of a career after university. I never expected that she should sacrifice her life to stay and look after me. All this time, here was I thinking she'd changed her plans about the year abroad so she could carry on hanging out with Richard, and now she tells me it wasn't like that at all. She tells me she wanted to go! Can I believe that? That my scaredy-cat, stick-in-the-mud sister actually once had some dreams of her own that would have taken her far away from the tiny little world she now inhabits? I do believe it, though. The minute she said it, I knew it was true.

My stomach feels raw and tense now that I'm leaning so close up against the washstand. That isn't just because I've been retching. It's because of the baby, I know. The gift I promised her so glibly last Christmas. The gift I thought it would be so easy to give to her. It needed to be done as an act of love, just like Richard said, but this baby was never that, was it? Never made by an act of love – only by the insertion of a cold plastic tube inside me – and I had no love from Richard either, even when, so desperately needing him, wanting him, I tried to steal it. I offered this gift because I wanted to get my hands on the money from this house, too, in itself a charitable desire, but not the kind of charity that begins at home. Not the kind of charity that comes from people who love one another, who do little acts of kindness for each other because of love and nothing else, with no hope of gaining anything else.

Fingers shaking, I turn on the taps again, let the clean, purifying water rush through the sink, swirling away the remains of the mess I've just made; but the odour remains. The empty, hollow pain in my gut remains. Hollie wants me out of here, and with good reason. There's no going back from this, I'm on my own now. Like I would have been if Hollie had just upped and left me all those years ago after Flo died. And the loneliness at that thought is greater than the unending Amazon I travelled to come back home again; it's more impenetrable than the densest green part of the rainforest. When I look into this stranger's eyes in the mirror I know she's going to have to travel to some pretty scary places.

In my heart, I always knew that. That the scariest challenges I'd face would be the ones I left back home. Oh, Hollie! What did I just do to you? The sounds of grief coming out of my throat don't sound like my own, they're somebody else's. Someone I left behind such a long time ago. I don't know her, though I recognise her. She isn't pretty and she isn't me, though she may be who I was. But the one undeniable thing I know about her is this: she is honest, she is real.

I don't stop for anything but my handbag, not even a change of clothes because I need to be out of here before Hollie comes back again. I can't face her. I slip out of the back door quietly so as not to alert Chrissie who's still sitting in the living room, and my heart gives a lurch. I won't see her again either, will I? I'm leaving them all behind. Halfway to the garden gate, looking back over my shoulder for the last time at the cottage I once couldn't wait to get away from, my prison, when I was younger, I see it all now in such a different light.

Auntie Flo's garden still has so many of my childhood memories tucked in among every clump of violets and peeping out from behind all the garden gnomes and ceramic fairies she planted in each shady corner. There's the yellow witches' broom Flo and I grew from cuttings taken on a holiday in Devon when I was eight. There's the wooden pergola – heavy now with early wisteria – that Hollie and I clubbed together to put up for Flo's sixtieth birthday. God, I love this place. I love it more than any other place in the world. Why has it taken me coming to the brink of losing it all before I could see that?

At the carp pond, the sweet sharp fragrance of Daphne still lingers, though the pink and white confections at the end of each branch have long disappeared. They always made me think of wedding cakes. I thought I'd left all this behind, I thought none of it mattered to me any more. When my fingertips brush against the leaves of the Daphne bush, the golden edge of their dark leaves takes me back to the sunlight spinning down through the dark green canopy of the Yanomami forest and I try with all my might to feel gladness, because I have a second place I can call home. I have a second family I can run back to. I'm not going to be alone.

But just at that moment, Ruffles pushes his nose into my hand, a low keening noise resonating deep in his throat because even though I'm carrying no suitcase he *knows* that I'm going. He knows that I can't come back, and all fantasies of Brazil vanish into the dust. Oh God, they can't matter as much as my real home, my real family.

I stand up straight and just run for it, the dog too slow to keep up with me now, the old wooden gate slamming shut behind me, before anybody can come along and see I'm still here where I'm not welcome any more. I've got to let her get on with her own life in peace, just like she would've done if she'd left me all those years ago. It's better this way.

Hollie

'Before it's too late,' Richard repeats. 'You know how impetuous she is. If you girls have had a big bust-up there's no telling what she'll do next . . .'

But it *is* too late. Doesn't he see that?

'She betrayed me,' I choke. The proprietor gives me an anxious look as I cover my mouth with a napkin.

'Hollie. *You* are the one who gave her the opportunity to do so, don't forget. You are the one who brought this poison into our marriage . . .' I flinch, but he continues regardless. 'You knew and I knew it, what repercussions it might have, but we went ahead regardless. And you remember the reason why? This was always all about the baby, wasn't it, Hol?'

I turn away from him, pushing my chair to the side so as to escape him but he won't let me, he takes hold of my wrist, forcing me around to look at him and face him.

'Now she's pregnant. There's a real baby involved. It's still got to be about the baby, hasn't it, Hol? Now you go back out there after her and get our baby back.'

'No!' I flare at him. I can't. I won't. I don't want her near me. I don't want her around me, ever again. 'She betrayed me, Richard. That's the worst thing she could possibly have done.'

'So you keep saying. You could still have our baby, though.'

'Could I?' I yell, and then, lowering my voice for his ears only, 'Do you know she even hinted she'd abort the child?' I see him shudder. 'She said it, Rich. The day after she came back from Lucy Lundy's party.' I recall her words now, spoken at a time when I'd had no idea what she'd really meant by them. 'She must have known already that she was expecting. She said, she didn't know if she was up for it, if it became a reality, if she could really go through with it . . .' I choke. 'I should never have trusted her, Rich. You said it yourself, she's like a weathercock, always changing and swinging round to another point of view depending on what suits at the moment. I wish I'd never trusted her . . .' Even that doolally Duncan guy, he was right about her all along, I realise suddenly. He knew her better than I did, my own sister. He warned me that she'd use me and then change her mind as it pleased her and I ignored him, but God knows he was so right . . .

'She has done you wrong, I know. But don't forget what we've sacrificed to get this far.'

I stare at my husband now, perplexed, because he doesn't seem to understand there can be no going back from this, there is nothing to retrieve, not even my baby.

'I have sacrificed my marriage vows,' he reminds me. 'I sacrificed the peace and the love that was between us. And yes – seeing as you seem so determined to know how I'm really feeling about all this – I miss her too. Not the way I miss you. I miss the gentle and innocent relationship I used to have with my sister-in-law. That's gone now. I accept that. I accepted it the day I agreed to go along with your plans even against my better judgement. So you don't need to worry that I'm hankering after Scarlett. I'm not. I never was. This mess we all find ourselves in now, it was always for you, it was always because I loved you that I went along with it, don't you see? For your baby. Are you prepared to have made the sacrifice for nothing?'

I shake my head even though deep inside there is some growing urge that wants to say 'Yes, OK, I will do it.' I will swallow my pride as he says, I will trust his judgement on this.

'I want to,' I shake my head again, slowly. 'But this is all so much bigger than that.'

I see his body language change. He drops my wrist and sits back, his arms folded across his chest now, and observes me through half-closed lids.

'I have always thought it must be, Hol. Why else would you have been prepared to go so far, to risk so much? It had to be *her*, didn't it? There's been a reason all along why you wanted her to be your surrogate and no one else . . .'

'I never wanted to blame her.' I look at him, desperately.

'Blame her for *what*, darling?' He takes my wrist again, stroking it gently.

For everything, *for everything*, I think. And yet – was it really all her fault that I lost my chance of ever having my own baby? Because none of it would ever have happened if only I had learned how to swim.

'Richard, I'll go back and look for her, even though I don't want to. There are some things I've never told you,' I confess. 'But . . . this isn't the best time to go into any of that because, like you say, once she's gone we'll never get hold of her again.' I swallow down my feelings about what she's done and stand up unsteadily while Rich settles the bill, wondering how soon we can get back to the cottage, wondering how I am going to cope with seeing him and her together now that I know all those things I was never meant to know . . .

But when we get back, before we even open the bottom gate, I know, I can tell from the sorrowful noise that Ruffles is making, that she's gone. Her clothes are all still there, her toiletries, her jacket, all her things, everything except her shoes and her handbag but I know, deep in the surest part of me, that she's already gone and this time my sister won't be coming back.

Scarlett

I tighten my hold on my canvas handbag as a group of young South Americans surge past and through the airport doors, jostling me. Crap. One of them bumped into my bag on purpose there. I'm sure he did. I frown at his retreating back. Did he take anything?

I've got to calm down. I've got all my money and papers and stuff here in my bag in front of me, where I can see it. Everything at Caracas International seems so frenetic today. It feels so much busier than I remember it. All the hustle and bustle that seemed so exciting the first time I got here – it just feels like too much today. I must be tired, that's why. I'm worn out. I didn't get much sleep on the flight over. There was a woman with her toddler who cried the entire time, I remember. Its high-pitched whine sawed into my nerves like an electric drill; I wondered why she didn't throttle it.

Then I looked at the woman and saw her dark hair falling forward over her face that was full of love and concern and she reminded me so much of Hollie I wanted to cry.

I take a sip of water from my plastic bottle and immediately the unbearable pressure on my bladder reminds me that I need to visit the bathroom again. I'm turning into an incontinent old woman, I swear, and all for what?

I didn't want things to turn out this way. I'd do anything to take those words back. He's hers, just like he was always meant

308

to be and the funny thing is . . . I don't even think I'm in love with him any more. I can't explain it, but it's as if the scales have dropped from my eyes. Like I was living some kind of illusion, only imagining that I wanted and desired him when all along I didn't. Because now I'm away from Florence Cottage and the spell that place always casts over me, I can see I don't really miss Rich. Not in that way.

I've never understood Hollie, not really. Maybe that's the problem. I've never felt that she understood me either.

I rummage inside my canvas bag again to check everything's still there – my money, my passport, my camera, my printout of the email from Eve that I received the day I left England. My fingers close over it, protectively. I already know what it says off by heart.

Such excellent news! she'd written. Can't wait to have you back here. Your pregnancy has cast a whole different light on so many things, as I'm sure you can imagine.
Have so much to fill you in on, but will just leave you with the wonderful news that you've made the short list for the Klausmann Award. Congratulations!

The news that Eve wasn't upset about me coming back to Brazil unexpectedly pregnant has come as a huge relief. It'll cast a whole different light, she says – but she doesn't imply that it'll make things impossible. We can work around it, maybe? I was worried she might say it would be a complete no-go. Because of the nature of the job, the dangers involved. I didn't think about it when I was in England but ever since I knew I was returning, the possibility of that has been on my mind.

But to hear that I've been shortlisted for the Klausmann Award after all that's happened is nothing short of a bolt out of the blue.

I'm thirsty again. Despite the fact that it'll mean another trip to the loo, I've got to have a drink. The water in this bottle is warm already. Well, it would be. I've been standing out here for over an hour already. Eve's late, she said she'd pick me up. Did she get the time wrong? I haven't been able to call anyone. My mobile is still searching for a connection.

Eve's been fantastic though, I remind myself. Without her, at this moment I really don't know what I'd be doing. She's rallied round me and I mustn't complain.

'Get yourself on the next flight out of here,' she said the minute I told her about my dilemma. That is, I told her about the pregnancy. I told her that Hollie had chucked me out. It didn't seem appropriate to go into any more detail than that. 'That's . . . that's wonderful news! And don't you worry about a thing,' she'd reassured me. 'We'll get it sorted.' I'd been so *relieved*. Just knowing that I still had people who were prepared to stand by me meant the world just at that moment, more than she'll ever know.

Still, won't be long now. Things are working out, that's what matters. Eve has even sorted out the problem with the mysterious 'allegations', I know that much. She'd heard about them, she told me. But she doesn't seem worried in the slightest. 'You leave it all to me,' she'd said, when I rang her last week. 'I'll speak to Gillian Defoe and let's see if I can't persuade her that this is all a storm in a teacup.'

After all that time I spent worrying about it all, too! I should have just gotten in touch with Eve in the first place and explained it all. She's a miracle worker, Eve. There's nothing she can't do.

'Ha-*lloooo*!'

I turn, hearing her voice at last.

'Oh my goodness!' I'm dragged into an eau-de-cologne-drenched embrace. 'No baby bump, yet?' She pats my tummy fondly and looks me up and down as if I were a brood mare.

'Not yet.' She can't imagine I'm actually pleased about this, can she? 'It's so good to be back,' I breathe. 'I've missed South America more than I ever missed England, that's for sure.

And there's been so much going on here while I've been away . . .' I watch her snatch up my luggage as if it held nothing more than tissue paper and manoeuvre both it and me towards the taxi stand.

'It was really kind of you to come out to fetch me, Eve,' I begin.

'Coach isn't till two p.m., lovey, so we've time for a drink and freshen-up first. *Of course* I came out to get you. I could hardly let you make the trek out to us all by yourself, could I? Especially now you're carrying your little bundle of joy.'

'I never had you down as someone who'd go dotty about kids,' I smile.

'Oh, not generally,' she assures me. 'But this kid is somewhat different, you'll agree?'

Because it's mine? I smile at her, fondly. That's the best thing about having great friends. They love everything you do and everything about you, just because you're you. She's probably thinking I'll ask her to be godmother or something. Bugger it. Perhaps I should have explained a bit more over the phone?

'So – how's the new boss?' I venture once we're ensconced in the taxi. Eve knows a little place ten minutes' drive away from here where the atmosphere will be quieter and calmer and she promises they'll have something I can eat.

'Ah.' Eve pulls a face that leaves very little to my imagination. 'Let's just say she's more of a tough cookie than I first took her to be. She's made a lot more fuss over protocols and procedures than anyone I've known before. She's a penpusher, frankly. I don't believe she has a clue what she's doing. But she wields a lot of power over our little outfit so at the moment we have to kowtow.'

'I spoke to her,' I remember now. 'She rang me up a few weeks back. She told me not to come back till I could be certain that the job was secure and that she was looking into the allegations against me. Eve, what the hell was all that about, anyway?

311

Who'd put in a complaint?' I turn to look at my friend and colleague and she sobers up a bit.

'Oh yes,' she frowns slightly. 'Gillian Defoe looked into that. Apparently there were some allegations of cheating put in against you by a fellow called Duncan . . .' She searches for his second name and I feel myself tense. I already know full well who he is. '. . . Bright,' she finishes. 'Duncan Bright. But he never provided any proof. He emailed Gillian recently to say that someone else – close to you, but unnamed – would be providing the evidence to support his allegation, as he hadn't been directly involved himself. That's all I know.'

So it's not finished yet. Maybe he wasn't just making idle threats to Lucy when he said he'd get his own back on me, after all . . .

But only Duncan and I ever knew about our plan to help me cheat and I pulled out of it before we ever went through with it. I asked Hol to send off *my* thesis. Not the one Duncan and I cooked up.

I freeze, a horrid thought immobilising me for a moment. She didn't send off Duncan's by mistake, did she? If she did, that could come back to haunt me. Then an even worse thought occurs; the two of them couldn't be colluding with each other to get their revenge on me? They'd both have reason to. I wipe my forehead with the back of my hand, recalling that day he turned up at Florence Cottage and Hollie had to get rid of him. She'd been really weird after he left, I remember now. They couldn't have been plotting to . . . ?

No, no . . . I rack my brains but the answer, like a guardian angel to the rescue, is at hand – she handed me Duncan's thesis back. I binned it. So she must have sent off *my* one. Besides, when Duncan came to the cottage, she didn't know at that point that I'd betrayed her. It's all such a tangle. I cheated on Hollie, yes, but I never did cheat with the thesis . . .

'Don't look so put out, m'dear. It'll all be sorted, I'm sure.

You're in the ascendant at the moment anyway – the Klausmann, remember?'

'I know,' I breathe. Eve is right. It isn't like me to get so het up. I'll sail through it like I always do. 'It's amazing. I feel very chuffed about that. You know, when I first applied for this job, I'll be open with you, I didn't think I stood the first chance of getting it – not on the basis of the thesis I'd submitted.'

'Didn't you?' Eve smiles. 'You're too modest. It was judged to be an exceptional and original piece of work by the PlanetLove board, backed up by my testimony of your abilities and work here of course. Anyway, as for those mysterious "allegations", Gillian is sure to pursue the matter till the bitter end.' I flinch, but Eve continues brightly, 'That's good, don't you see? Once you're vindicated it will never be brought up again.'

'I guess,' I sigh half-heartedly.

'Between you and me, she's got one of her own people up for the award, and having your piece out of the running would have made things easier for them, no doubt,' she mutters darkly. 'D'you know, it wouldn't surprise me one bit if she cooked the whole thing up herself.'

'Oh, no, Eve. Surely not?' I demur.

'Well, never mind, she'll have to drop it in the end. I won't deny it will help us having a little bit of leverage over the situation.' Eve leans forward and pats my stomach encouragingly.

What's the baby got to do with this?

'I told her about your pregnancy, I hope that was OK?'

Since when has Eve been so deferential to me? I restrain a frown. 'She's had to back-pedal a little since she learned about that. She was all for getting rid of you, that's the truth. Frankly I suspect she's got a few of her own people lined up to take over the PlanetLove jobs. She told me I could keep only one of mine – she's made me sack Emoto, the bitch.'

'So you kept me on instead of Emoto?' That's what I wanted, wasn't it? But I wanted to earn that place on merit, not because

313

I'm expecting this baby – is this something to do with equal opportunities or somesuch? Is that what all this is about? I liked Emoto. In all fairness, he should be the one up for the Klausmann Award, not me.

'You shouldn't be forced to let him go,' I say softly.

'You bet I shouldn't,' she comes back fiercely. 'Gillian liked him, too. She tried to insist I choose him and not you but I wouldn't be moved. Still, it'll all be worth it in the long run. If we can get rid of Ms Defoe and her lot, get our operation back under our own jurisdiction, I'll get Emoto back onboard once we're running our own show again.'

'So . . . how're you planning on going about that?' I give her a look of frank admiration. I'm feeling pretty gratified by her show of loyalty to me, too. I think if I were in her shoes I'd have kept on Emoto instead of me. And especially when you consider the fact she knows I'm pregnant! It's pretty amazing, really. On the other hand, Eve's always been one to back a winner and I did miraculously get on that short list when Emoto didn't.

'How indeed?' Eve laughs. 'Until you came out and announced you were expecting the other day I had absolutely no idea. Now, of course, we'll have the Chiquitin-Almeira board eating out of our hand – well, your hand – but I like to think you'll be guided somewhat by me . . .'

'Why on earth would they give two hoots?' I blurt out.

'My dear.' Eve gives me an astonished smile, 'These South Americans are mad about family, don't you know that? Now you're *enceinte*, you'll be – well, in the inner circle, so to speak. Guillermo will no doubt insist on you two getting hitched and – if it isn't out of order for me to say so – I'd love to be matron of honour. Just imagine the power and influence that's going to result from this! Here, let me get the door for you.' She jumps out as the taxi slides to a halt and rushes round to my side to open the door. 'We don't want you straining yourself, risking any damage to your precious cargo . . .'

314

My precious . . . ? I just look at her, open-mouthed.

'Don't look so astonished, my dear. You falling pregnant with Guillermo's child is really the most extraordinary stroke of luck for us all. You'll be able to work on him so eventually they take up our cause again, won't you? We can give the Europeans the old heave-ho . . .' She pays the taxi driver and pushes me towards the doors of a plush and expensive-looking hotel where she's going to stand me lunch. She probably imagines it's going to be a worthwhile investment for her. She thinks I'm the cavalry, arrived with all the backup that's going to save PlanetLove and our patch of forest because of course, if Guillermo were on board with it we wouldn't have to worry about a paltry half a million quid to buy our patch of forest.

I see now why she's been so excited and delighted about the pregnancy. Why I'm suddenly the golden girl; why the 'allegations' that someone's cooked up against me aren't troubling her over much. Could this even be – my heart sinks – why I've suddenly been shortlisted for the Klausmann Award, over other contenders like Emoto who I know deserved it more?

When she finds out this isn't Guillermo's baby she isn't going to be so pleased though, is she?

'Are you all right, my dear, is everything all right?'

'No.' I put my hand to my mouth as a rush of acid vomit rushes into my throat.

I am going to be sick.

Hollie

Forgive her, Richard says. Again – I already forgave her once before. But what good does forgiveness ever do? 'Are you okay, Scarlett?' Eve's eyes narrow and I can feel her impatience. The sick feeling has passed but I am far from being okay.

I straighten my back and lean the spade up against the trellis that supports Flo's favourite old yellow dog-roses. There's scarcely a bud on them this year and I have a sneaking suspicion I know the reason why. I pull off my gardening gloves and examine the fibrous stem that has patiently wound itself up the lattice work over the years, but the leaves seem somehow tired, sapped of energy. Then I look a little closer and I see that I'm right. The thin and persistent tendrils of bindweed are everywhere. The Choker, auntie Flo used to call it. The tubulous white bells it produces later in the years are pretty but deceptive. I spent ages last summer trying to get rid of this stuff.

I drag at the intricately-entwined bindweed and follow the tortuous path back to its roots. The damn thing is everywhere. It's invidious. It's . . . it's deep in the system of this garden. Way past the yellow dog-roses it's in amongst the peony bushes too. It's snarled up amongst the sweetpeas and the lupins and the jasmine. It's bedded down in the woody stems of the Forsythia and in and out amongst the azaleas and no matter how much I pull it out I can't seem to get to the bottom of it.

The worst of it is, I have a growing sense that I may not

even need to. Will we even still be here, next year? If Rich has his way, we won't. He has come back from Italy subdued, willing to forgive, but also with more of a sense of his own purpose. As if he's fully realised the implications of following my dream so closely that he's had no time to nurture his own. For the first time I've come to see that he really does want to move to Italy.

It's as if . . . my dream of having a family has been the only thing that's bound him to this place – maybe I've been The Choker for everything he wanted to establish for himself? That isn't a pretty thought.

I wipe a trickle of sweat off my face. I've managed to pull out half the established garden along with the bindweed, I realise now. Still, no matter. The important shrubs and perennials will grow back. This thing needs to be dealt with.

I hurl a huge bundle of etiolated weed stems through the air and into the pile that's destined for the compost. I haven't got the time for this gardening lark. Scarlett could have done it when she was here seeing as she supposedly loves it so much but I scarcely saw her lift a finger . . .

I wish . . . I wish I could find some way to forgive her. Not for her sake, but for my own. To find some peace. If only there were some way, like the weeds – to dig out your bad feelings and put them into the bin for recycling . . .

God, there are nettles in here too. I put my gardening gloves back on to protect my fingers. Forgiveness. I frown. You put all your resentment and your bitterness, like choking weeds, to one side. No matter what was done to you. No matter how bad it hurt. Or still hurts. You let it all go.

But how? And how am I ever going to get to the end of this blasted bindweed? Shall I go to the end of my days dragging it out and untwisting it and fighting it just because I can't figure where it all comes from? Damn it I'll dig up the whole garden if I have to!

317

'Is everything quite all right down there, m'dear?' Beatrice's face appears from her spare bedroom window next door. She's opened it up wide and she can see clearly the trail of destruction I've just wreaked.

'Quite all right,' I tell her firmly.

'We're going to have quite a few bald patches around for the garden party,' she presses hesitantly.

'No worries. Um. The thing is – there isn't going to be a garden party now.' I look up at her impatiently. Damn it I never told her I. 'We're cancelling.'

'Just you hang on a second.'

When Beatrice reappears, this time through my side gate, she's holding two large glasses of transparent liquid that I suspect holds something a little stronger than just water.

'Just you sit yourself down and explain, young lady.' My neighbour clears my gardening tools off the plastic 'patio set' chair and places it by me. She's looking worried. But she needn't be.

'I was just trying to get rid of the Bindweed,' I tell Beatrice calmly. 'It looks pretty, but in the end it chokes up everything.'

'What's happened to Scarlett?' Beatrice looks at me closely and I can see she isn't fooled by my calm act for one minute.

'She's gone.' I take a swig from the glass she's just handed me and I was right. G and T. A stiff one. 'I told her to go, mind,' I add after a bit. 'And she's . . .' I hiccup, 'she's taken my baby, Bea.' I sit down on the chair at last and she takes a pew beside me.

'She's taken your baby' she says gently. It is neither a question nor a statement, just an echo of my own words. 'Do you know where she's gone?'

I shake my head briefly.

'To hell, I hope.' I can't forgive her. I can't. 'She wanted us to sell off this place,' I gesture towards the cottage, 'did you know? She was so desperate to get her hands on the money I believe she'd have done anything to get her hands on it. But in the end she wanted something else even more than she wanted that.' I smile at Beattrice wanly, aware that I'm probably not making any sense to her but Bea doesn't smile back.

'I knew there was trouble brewing,' she murmurs now. 'And I knew I should have spoken up before this . . .'

Oh no. First Duncan. Now Bea. Don't tell me Bea's another person who knew what we were up to all along?

'About what, Bea?' I swirl the G and T around in my hand recklessly. If she does know, the realisation dawns on me – I'm past caring . . .

'She told me about the promise that Flo extracted from you, never to sell up, my dear. Flo loved this old place. It's been in the family for generations. She was named for it, you know. And I respect your reasons for honouring her wishes it's just that . . .'

'Just that Scarlett's been round yours moaning that she was left out of the inheritance or some such? Oh, Bea, she'd have frittered it all away on . . . on a wing and a prayer. She never stops to think, that's the trouble.'

'Maybe so. But did you realise it was never really Flo's to bequeath to anyone in the first place?'

'Of course it was Flo's. Don't be absurd,' I don't care about any of that right now; the cottage, the inheritance, all those things . . .

'It belonged to her brother and . . . my dear, this is the bit I've been meaning to tell you because I'm pretty certain Flo never did . . .'

'What?' I stare at her askance. If Flo had a brother she certainly never spoke of him to us. Bea just looks at me over the top of her spectacles and I can feel my own face reddening because it's suddenly become obvious what she's going to say next. No!

'Flo's brother – he . . . he wasn't our dad was he?'

Scarlett

'Eve, look, you've got to understand something.' I leave my hand on her arm as she helps me out of the taxi. The cool interior of the Montana Hotel beckons enticingly and she turns her head, wondering why I'm not as keen as she is to go straight in. The midday sun is blazing down on our heads right now, I can feel the heat dancing on my scalp, but still I hold her back. After what I'm about to tell her she might not be so keen to buy me lunch.

'Are you OK, Scarlett?' Eve's eyes narrow and I can feel her impatience. The sick feeling has passed but I am far from being OK.

'I need to tell you something before this goes any further.' I take in a deep breath and then I sock it to her all at once. 'This isn't Guillermo's baby.'

The shocked look on her face says it all. 'How could it not be?' she gets out after a few moments. She sounds angry. Very angry. 'You were going steady with him – that was my understanding? He's as much as asked you to marry him. You told me that the day he brought you back on his boat . . .'

'Yes. Yes, he did. Nonetheless, this isn't his baby I'm carrying.'

'You . . . you stupid, *stupid* girl!' Her face seems to be getting redder by the minute.

'Steady on, Eve! This isn't what you think it is,' I stammer.

She's frowning and I can almost hear the cogs whirring round in her brain. 'I can't believe this is happening. No, I can't believe it. You're seriously telling me this is not Almeira's child? *Are you sure?*'

'I'm . . . absolutely sure.'

'Look.' She pulls me in a little closer as our raised voices draw the attention of curious passersby. 'Gillian Defoe backed down over my insistence that we keep you on instead of Emoto only because of the Almeira connection,' my boss growls at me now.

'I don't understand.' Maybe it's the heat, stewing my brain, but I can't fathom what she's talking about.

'Your connection,' Eve spells out, 'through pregnancy, to the Almeira family. In the long run, the European Alliance people are relying on Chiquitin-Almeira backing just as much as we are.'

'What do we need them for then? If they have no money to run the outfit . . .'

'Because they're bringing in *some* money, obviously!' she rants. 'Enough to keep us afloat till some bigger fish come in. For God's sake, Scarlett Hudson, I thought when I sent you off first at Christmas you understood I was hoping you'd be able to pull together the funds for us?'

I stare at her, stunned. 'Well – that's exactly what I was trying to do by having this baby, Eve! I'm acting as a surrogate for my sister, you see. I thought if I had her baby, then she'd be prepared to sell Florence Cottage for me and with the proceeds I'd be able to help save our patch of forest.'

Now it's Eve's turn to stare. 'And what about Guillermo Almeira? Did you not once think about him?' she says faintly.

'About how he'd take it, you mean? I thought about it a lot. That's why I didn't tell him, in fact.' I try to swallow but I've got a lump in my throat. Maybe I didn't think this through enough? 'I was hoping in the end he'd understand why I needed to do this. I wanted to help my sister and I wanted to help PlanetLove. I thought it was for the best.'

'No, you didn't, Scarlett, that's the trouble. You didn't *think* at all. You're still not thinking. What I meant just now was – didn't you ever consider just asking him for the money? Using

321

your influence with him to get Chiquitin-Almeira back on board?'

'Why ever would I?'

'Because you *could*.' She pulls me into the shaded area of the pavement and we both cower under a shopfront awning for a bit. 'He's mad about you,' she continues now. 'He's made no bones about that. He'd give you anything you wanted. The moon, the stars. £400,000 . . .'

'I didn't think about asking him,' I tell her miserably. 'I thought you said Chiquitin-Almeira had already pledged £250,000?'

'Of course they have, but that's from company funds. He could have pledged a lot more from his own pocket if he'd a mind to. Why didn't you just ask him, you silly little cow?'

I blink back the angry tears that spring to my eyes now. I open my mouth but no words come out.

'What did you *think* I was expecting you to do?' snaps Eve. 'I mean, how else could you have had a hope of getting the amount I'd asked you to raise? You agreed to do it. I thought it was understood that you'd have to ask him for the cash . . . oh, for Pete's sake!'

The ramifications of Eve's words are finally filtering down into my over-heated brain. 'So that's why you chose me over Emoto?' I manage. 'Because of my potentially useful connections with Almeira's son?'

'Precisely. Got it in one. I mean, let's face it, you aren't the brightest bunny in the basket when it comes to academic stuff, are you?'

'I'm up for the Klausmann,' I remind her. But she ignores that.

'Look.' She scrapes her hair back and I suddenly remember how much I've always been repulsed by her high forehead with its crisscross of tramlines etched into it. 'Does Guillermo even know about this? You being up the duff, I mean?'

I shake my head slowly. Up the duff, she says. What happened to my 'precious cargo'? This can't be happening to me. A car horn blares out suddenly, the driver cursing a reckless pedestrian who's just ran in front of him, and it nearly makes me jump out of my skin. I feel dizzy; I must still be on that plane and dreaming all this. Eve turning against me like this – it's just unthinkable! I'm starting to think maybe I was just being used all along.

'I haven't told him yet,' I tell her numbly.

'And you don't think you could get away with passing it off as his? Don't be selfish here, Scarlett. I'm looking at the bigger picture – the future of the Amazon, not just one more spoiled brat.'

I just stare at her, aghast.

'Well, OK, OK,' she concedes, seeing my expression and misinterpreting it. 'He'd want DNA-testing no doubt, seeing as he's worth a bob or two. Unless we just strung him along for a bit – keep him sweet and then you "lose" it? Oh, but then the timing would be out though, wouldn't it?'

'How can you be so *callous*?' I breathe, horrified. I put aside for the minute that I've harboured thoughts of termination myself.

'Of course, I forgot.' Eve puts her hand to her chin thoughtfully. 'It's your sister's child, isn't it? She'll be expecting it back. But hang on a minute – didn't you tell me your sister chucked you out of the house?'

I nod dejectedly.

'Bit ungrateful, wouldn't you say?'

'I slept with her husband,' I put in miserably.

'Ouch!' Eve laughs out loud. I shoot her a killer stare from behind my sunglasses. For all her high ethical principles about saving the planet, it appears this kind of immorality doesn't rank too highly in her list of cardinal sins.

'It was the biggest mistake of my life,' I say through gritted teeth.

'Well, does she want the child or doesn't she?' Eve's suddenly become very businesslike. 'If she's chucked you out . . .' And then,

323

before I can answer, she continues: 'We need to retrieve the situation here, Scarlett. If you're only twelve weeks gone, then termination is still an option, isn't it? It might be the best option, under the circumstances. I'll tell Defoe that you miscarried. She need never know it wasn't Guillermo's child – and you can carry on going out with him and still be the golden girl, can't you?'

I remain silent for a few minutes while she thinks this all through.

'Don't you see – it's the Yanomami I'm thinking about here, Scarlett?' Her attitude changes, becoming suddenly solicitous. 'You do realise what a dire situation they're in at the moment, don't you?'

I feel a trickle of sweat run down from my scalp and across my cheek. I wipe it away with the back of my hand.

'Maybe it was a mistake to keep the worst of it from you,' she muses now. 'Let me just say there's a certain amount of division in the tribe at the moment. Yes, *your* tribe . . .' she says deliberately, seeing my frown. 'The elders know they're being threatened with obliteration. Some want to leave the forest, to go and work in the shanty-towns . . . They'll lose all their heritage, all their plant lore will disappear . . .'

'No!' The plastic water bottle I've just put to my lips slips in my sweaty hand and a trickle of warm water dribbles down my chin. I feel limp, helpless.

'I see you get the picture. That isn't all. There's been a bout of measles within the tribe, Scarlett. Many of them have perished.'

'How many? Not . . . José?'

She shakes her head. 'Seventeen, last count. José wasn't affected. They've no natural defences, have they? Look, I know you think I'm being callous but the truth is I'm trying to save these people, that's all. I thought that's what you were committed to doing too?'

'I am,' I say faintly. 'They're my friends.'

'Then,' she takes hold of my arm firmly, 'you're going to have to make some difficult choices here, Scarlett. You have to look at the bigger picture in all this. We could still save this patch of ours – I'm certain of it. With the right backing, we could even save a larger area. It's got to be purely a matter of time before the world wakes up and sees that we can't afford to hang about any more, don't you know that? But if we don't all do what we can it'll be too late. Let me take you down to our old base camp and show you the damage that's already been done . . .'

'You don't have to, Eve,' I shake my head. 'I get the picture.'

'Look, I know I've come across as harsh today. You've had a shock today, right? Well, I'll be honest, so have I. We need political muscle and leverage now more than ever and I honestly thought you might be pivotal in helping us attain that. I suggest we go in and have a drink and wait for Guillermo in the cool of the hotel – what d'you think?'

'He's coming here?' I say in surprise.

'I thought you'd be pleased so I told him you were arriving. I couldn't think why you hadn't rung him to say so yourself. Listen, when you arrived to take up your post with us nearly two years ago now, I sensed from the start you were something special, you'd *bring* something special to your work here. And you have. You've done some great work here, you know I think that. More than that, you've opened up great possibilities with the Almeira connection. We can't afford to lose that, Scarlett.'

'I'm aware—' I begin.

'Sometimes, things are just meant to be,' she says grandly. 'They work out just how they're supposed to. You have a mission to accomplish which only you can.'

What if she's right? I stare into her serious face while I digest the import of her words. It's true that Hollie doesn't want me in her life any more. Maybe if I stay here and build on what I've got I could still make a go of it here. All the bad things I've done will just go away – be forgotten about.

Eventually.

Hollie

'Beatrice Highland, will you please just answer my question?'

Bea takes a large swig of G and T, for fortification. Then she nods slowly.

'Flo's brother was your dad, my dear. It's true. Though never acknowledged, you understand. He was already married to someone else at the time . . .'

I stare at Beatrice for a few moments, getting my voice back.

'She only ever held this house in trust for you two. I'm not sure quite how Heinrich her laywer would have explained the position to you but . . .'

'Heinrich . . . read out a letter with a lot of legal terms in it and asked me if I knew what it meant, if anyone had explained it to me. I told him Flo had . . .'

'Perhaps she hadn't explained it adequately then?'

'Bea,' I lean forward, stopping her. 'This is all besides the point. I can't believe you knew all along – you both knew – who my father was and nobody ever said . . .'

'I was never comfortable about the secrecy, dear, but it wasn't my place to say. And Flo had her reasons. Her brother was a well-respected barrister. He had a wife and two sons, and he stood to lose more than Helen if the truth ever came out,' Bea runs on. 'Helen loved him desperately, you know. He was part of the reason she carried on working in South America.He had a lot of business over there . . .'

'So you're saying Flo really WAS our aunt after all?' I have to concentrate on that. Her having a brother - the father that I never knew, who nobody ever even spoke about seems too much to take on board right now.

'Does Scarlett know?'

'Not from me, if she does. Hollie, dear . . .' Bea puts her hand over mine.

'And does he have a name?'

'Geoffrey,' she says baldly, as if hanging on to the last vestiges of his anonymity. As if it matters anymore.'Perhaps I should have told you sooner. It's just that I saw his obiturary in the Times recently. I thought maybe, now would be a good time to say . . .'

So he's dead? Here and gone in the space of a few seconds.

'Flo's brother was our dad?' My mind is spinning. 'And now he's gone. Just more water under the bridge.' He fathered us and he left us the house but he managed to get away without being our dad, I think, a sudden storm of fury in my head. Just like Scarlett thought she would get away with everything . . .

'You dad's gone, Hollie. But your baby has yet to be born, remember, and if you can't find a way to re-establish contact with your sister – no matter how badly you feel about her just now – then you lose the child as well.'

I blink and the chaos I've just wreaked in Florence cottages garden comes suddenly into sharp focus. Good God, what have I done? I blink back a tear.

'I've made a mess, here, haven't I?' Huge swathes of broken foliage are piled high at various points along the flower beds. I've cut off heaven knows how many branches in full bloom and many more with their ripening buds just about to open, like some kind of maniac with shears.

'This will recover,' Beatrice pats my knee encouragingly. 'You've given it a drastic haircut, that's all. Plants grow back though. They're forgiving.'

Just like I'm going to need to be.

Scarlett

'Choose what you like,' Eve's saying. We're sitting in the palm-decorated bar area at the Montana and she's persuaded me to change out of my jeans into the pretty white dress she's brought along just for the purpose. She's trying to be nice to me, to retrieve the situation, just as she said. I can entirely understand her reasons for everything and yet I know I'm never going to feel the same way about her again. She apologised, as we sat down, for her earlier 'over-zealousness'. She said that's just how you get after so many years of being 'committed to the cause'. And it's a good cause. I know this. I believe this. I believe in the same cause.

She said she'd thought I understood what my part in her grand rescue plan for PlanetLove was. She hadn't realised, she said, quite how naïve I still am. That was her error, she admitted. She should have made things all a bit more overt, but she assured me that we could still rescue this.

I'm not saying much. She seems to think that ridding yourself of the encumbrance of an unwanted pregnancy will be no more difficult than taking an aspirin to cure yourself of a headache. I never thought too much about it before, but when I hear her talk about it in this dispassionate and unconnected way I realise that it's not going to be so easy for me after all.

I'm feeling really weirded out now. I tell her it's the long-haul flight but it's not that. She's just messed with my head, that's all.

I thought I knew where I was within the PlanetLove structure; the lie of the land, the terrain beneath my feet all seemed comfortable and familiar and welcoming, but now it feels as if all along this woman, who I took to be my friend, was simply using me as a pawn in a bigger game. I was never really that valuable to her after all, not as me, not Scarlett, *myself*. It was only what I represented that meant something to her. At the end of the day, the cause is more important.

And can I really blame her for that? I've backed the cause to the hilt myself. I've been prepared to throw my sister out of her home for it. I've been prepared to carry another person's baby for nine months. Will I now have to terminate it, in the name of the same cause?

Then I ask her the one burning question that's still left in my mind.

'What about the Klausmann?' I get out at last. 'Are you going to tell me now that Guillermo Almeira was the reason I was shortlisted for that as well?'

'Oh, no,' Eve attests. 'The Klausmann nominations have nothing to do with us. They're judged at King's College, as you know. The outcome is entirely out of our hands.'

That's one good thing, then. The relief I feel at this last piece of news is for some reason enormous. Because – almost miraculously – the thesis I sent to PlanetLove has earned me the respect of some of the most prestigious workers in the field today. And that recognition is really worth something to me, despite Eve's observation that I'm not the most academic bunny in the warren . . .

'It's a highly prestigious award,' Eve admits. 'And if you get it, that'll work to your advantage too. The Almeiras are a highly status-conscious clan, as you know. Winning the Klausmann will be a feather in your cap that Gui can show off to his family – she's not just a pretty face, sort of thing. He was very proud when I told him, you know.'

He was proud. Despite everything else I feel so shit about right now, that makes me feel good. If Mum were around today, I feel sure she'd be proud of it, too. She'd be proud of the work I'm doing here, too. She wouldn't have wanted me to give it all up, I know. Not now.

'Here he comes, honey. Be sweet to him. You know what he means to us so don't cock it up again . . .'

And when I turn round to look behind me, there he is.

Red Balloon

Where is Andreis? Jamie rolls the cold beer bottle over his hot forehead, vaguely aware through the haze and the drumbeat of Rio Carnavale that his whole body is covered in sweat. But where is the laughing, thong-clad, feather-adorned girl he met up with at four p.m. yesterday, who has scarcely left his side since? His new . . . girlfriend. He tilts back the bottle and lets the icy beer trickle over his face. Now he will stink of beer, too.

But it hardly matters here, does it? There must be – he ranges his inexperienced eye over the heaving crowd of Carnavale-goers – what, maybe twenty thousand people here this afternoon and he's spotted only two Portaloos so far. The roads are already steeped in urine – and worse. The barefooted, light-hearted Andreis hardly seemed to care either, he recalls, as she samba'd the last four hours away with him, their bodies heaving and contorting to the rhythmic drumbeats of the Bloco del Paradaiso.

Jamie laughs deep in his throat at the absurdity of it all. He's got a girlfriend! He's barely settled himself into his hotel yet, and already he's slept with a woman there. When he booked those two nights at the Hotel Village Novo he had no idea that it backed out onto the starting point for the Barra to Ondina Carnavale circuit, or that there'd be so many bodacious babes just crying out for a bit of fun . . .

'Bugger off!' he snarls as a ten-year-old steals her hand into his pockets, hoping to snatch his change. This'd be the best party on earth if it weren't for those thieving fuckers. They nearly had his mobile yesterday. Now he's learned to come out with his money in his shoes and to carry nothing on him worth nicking. The only thing he's got in his pocket is the change from the beer he bought earlier and that red metallic balloon with the letter for that girl on it. He brought that out to show Andreis because she said she'd like to see it. She'd been enchanted by the idea of a balloon travelling so far.

And now Andreis is back, snaking her hips through the sunlit crowd as she moves over to meet him, mesmerising him. She's just met her uncle, she tells him, who wants Jamie to come and sell beer to the tourists with his nice English accent and he'll give them some dinner. Maybe her beautiful white boy can work there all summer, she suggests, and stay near her? And why not? he thinks. Forget PlanetLove. There seems to be plenty of rainforest left from what he can judge. And he's never had a girlfriend before. Andreis smiles at him and her pearly teeth are as white and straight a model's.

When she puts her arms around his neck, this time Jamie barely feels the tug of the urchin's hands in his pocket while his girlfriend's lips work so expertly on his. The urchin gets his small change and then she tugs and pulls at the string attached to the red balloon, hopeful of unearthing some greater treasure. But the envelope turns out to contain no money when she peers inside it. She hurls it into the gutter behind her where it narrowly misses falling into a puddle – whether of urine or rainwater, it is too crowded to tell – and it is kicked about for a while as the Bloco del Paradaiso start up their *batucada*, the *timbaladas* and the *maracutu* rhythms again.

Scarlett

'So, my dearest heart, you have come back to Brazil. But why is it that I learn this from your boss and not from you?' Gui's reproach is restrained, but he's disappointed, I can feel it.

I pull myself back from him, my fingers lingering over his crisp, expensively-laundered white shirt, and I let him see my eyes filling up with tears. Eve has already silently slipped away.

I know that when I explain how terrible the last couple of weeks have been for me – how Hollie threw me out of the house after I got pregnant for her, and I had nowhere to go – then he will understand. I had nowhere to go. I even had to book into a B&B till I could get a flight out. The humiliating memory rushes back – I couldn't even go home and get my clothes, I just sneaked in one day when she was out and grabbed what I could, my passport and my laptop and . . . and it's been *terrible*. I feel his fingers softly massaging the back of my neck now, and he ushers me into a more secluded corner of the lobby, his eyes creased with concern.

'Tell me everything.' His voice is full of compassion. 'My darling, what has happened to you?'

'I'm sorry.' I can't meet his gaze and my eyes drop to the floor. I want to tell him. I'm burning to tell him everything and yet . . . what if Eve is right about how he might take it?

Damn it to hell, because now I really don't know what I should do. If only I had called Gui first and not Eve, I'd never have been put off my original plan which was to be open and honest with him. Without mentioning Richard of course – even *I* realise that might be going a bit too far. But Gui would have understood about the surrogacy thing; if Eve hadn't put her oar in I would have just told him like I always meant to. But now I feel conflicted.

'I meant to tell you I was arriving today,' I get out. I try to say more but my throat keeps closing up treacherously. And my face – I can see from his reaction that I must look so odd right at this moment.

Bloody stupid Eve! Why did she have to go and tell him I was arriving today? I haven't had a chance to get my bearings yet. I feel ill. I feel – cut up, disappointed. She should have never said anything to him at all. And yet, I remember, she thought it was his baby I was carrying . . . I put my face in my hands.

'Are you not well, my darling?' The genuine concern in his voice only makes me feel worse.

'It was a long flight,' I croak. 'I just need a little . . .' I indicate my throat and he calls for some water.

'Something has upset you? *Someone* has? What has happened?' he insists. Am I imagining it, or is there a glint in his eye when he says this? I gulp down the water that the waiter brings and take heart from the thought.

'Nothing's happened to me today, Gui. And I've been longing to see you, truly I have. I just wasn't sure if I'd make it out on the standby flight. I didn't want to waste your time.' He gives a little impatient gesture, as if standby flights are beneath his consideration, but my excuse seems to have appeased him. 'But you're right that I'm upset. Something *has* happened that I need to speak to you about . . . Gui, I haven't told you the whole reason why I stayed away for so long. And I know that while I've been away I haven't paid you half enough attention, but I've *thought* about you. A lot.'

The number of phone calls and texts coming in from him have slowed down a lot in the last few weeks too, I remember. He shifts in his chair – is he waiting for me to cut to the chase?

'The truth is . . . some very . . . difficult . . . things have happened to me while I've been back home in England with my family.
I didn't know who to turn to . . .'

'My darling.' He looks shocked, his face darkening with sudden
anger. 'Has someone *hurt* you?'

Gui will support me. I know he will. He loves me. I throw my
arms about his neck suddenly, desperately, and I feel the protect-
iveness in his arms as he pulls me in close. If there's one person
I can rely on to support me after all the shit that's happened,
it's him.

'Is that it? Has somebody hurt you? Some *man*?'

I swallow back my tears. Something about the way he just
said 'some man' is ringing very loud warning bells in my head.
It has never occurred to me before and I thought Eve was totally
wrong when she warned me that Gui would be the jealous type
– but I see now she might very well be right.

'No.' I shake my head rapidly, deflecting his anger. 'It's my
sister.'

'Your sister?'

'Yes, my sister. She . . .' My thoughts are spinning out of control
suddenly, jumping like bubbles in a steaming pot. If I confess that
Hollie threw me out of her house then I'll have to give Gui a very
plausible reason why. If I tell him just *part* of the truth then he'll
know straightaway that it doesn't add up. He's looking at me intently
now, his instincts alert and sharpened down to a fine razor point.

I am never going to be able to blag this. But I have got to.
'You've got to turn this around', Eve's words return to haunt me.
This isn't just my future and wellbeing at stake here. I wipe my
sweltering brow with the back of my hand.

'It's not been an easy time for me,' I mutter brokenly. 'My
sister's been very upset and – unwell,' I invent. 'And unhappy,
because she and her husband can't have babies. And I felt . . .' I
stutter '. . . I felt so sorry for them and I wanted to do what I
could to help.'

'What could you do, my beautiful girl?' Gui's hands are around my shoulders now, rubbing them comfortingly. He cares. He really cares.

'What could I do?' I hesitate. Has he ever even heard about surrogacy? He *must* have. 'Sometimes, when you love somebody, you feel you would do anything in the world to help them, do you understand that?'

'That's natural,' he murmurs approvingly. 'She's your family, after all. And you told me your sister has been almost like a mother to you in many ways. Family is the most important thing we have. What else matters, in the end?'

'I promised her I'd help her out,' I say brokenly. 'But I betrayed that promise.'

'Ah,' he says at last. 'I see now why you have flown back from Europe so sad. But come, it distresses me to see you so upset. Your heart is too large, Scarlett.' He smiles ruefully. 'Sometimes I think that you want to heal the whole world.'

As we have been speaking he has ushered me into the marble-floored dining room. The opulence inside is at once dazzling and shocking.

'What? It is beautiful, no?' he smiles softly. 'You would like us to eat here?'

'This place is such a bubble, isn't it?' I turn to him once I can manage to drag my eyes away from the gleaming chandeliers that hang from the ceiling, the immaculately turned out women with their smart-suited husbands, the cut-crystal glasses on every table. Even wearing Eve's pretty white halterneck frock, I look distinctly underdressed in this place.

'And I know I can't heal the whole world,' I tell him uneasily. 'I'm too selfish and unworthy and . . .'

'You are none of those things.' He frowns, shaking his head dismissively. You think that only because you don't know the real me, my heart is crying out. If only I could be real with you, Guillermo! If I could tell you everything . . . but I can't. I let my

336

head sag as we're led to our table. I sit down and immediately a soft damask white napkin lands in my lap.

'You could help heal some people in the world, my darling. You could heal *me*.'

I manage a smile. I could, perhaps, and he could do the same for me. I want to tell him the whole truth. It would be such a sweet release to be open and honest with him; to find that he would support me and love me and care for me, even after . . . after *that*.

Because *that* – what I did with Rich – was the straw that broke the camel's back for Hol. My sister never wants to see me again. Even Lucy thinks I'm a bitch. If I could tell Gui – confess to him – and he still loved me, then *that* would be true love, I decide. That would be worth giving up everything for.

One thing at a time, though. I need to get him on board again with the cause. I don't want to give him any excuse to back away from me right now.

'I missed you,' I confess. 'More than I ever thought I would.'

He smiles. 'Did you? Is that why you came back?'

'Of course. I want to make my home here. I've decided I want to stay.'

'With me?'

'Definitely. If you'll have me.' And it is true. Why have I never seen it before? Gui is the man for me. He is handsome, generous, kind and he loves me. 'And that means he can offer you something that I never can' – isn't that what Richard said? At the time that he said them, the words felt like a knife to my heart. I didn't appreciate the truth of it.

'I am so glad, Scarlett.'

The feeling of relief flooding through me at this moment is nothing short of overwhelming.

'You don't know how many prayers have been said that you might come back,' he continues. 'Tonight, you will drink champagne. You will sleep in a bed strewn with rose petals . . . if you can stand to live in this *bubble*.' He laughs disparagingly.

'Gui, I can't,' I put in. 'I'm planning on travelling back to base camp with Eve later on tonight. I can't abandon all my friends right now. You have been in touch with Eve so you'll be aware of all the things that've been happening to PlanetLove since I left?'

'Ah, yes.' An impatient look crosses his face for an instant before he throws his napkin onto the table and leans forward to look at me earnestly. 'PlanetLove. I've heard. Your loyalty to your friends commends you. You are a good and beautiful woman, and of course you care deeply,' he says soothingly. 'What is happening out there – it's a shame.'

No, it's more than a *shame*, I want to shout. He's an educated native of this country. Doesn't he know, can he really not see that what's happening here is going to affect the whole world, and sooner than everyone thinks, too . . . ?

I bite back my words. 'Will you help?' I ask him tentatively instead.

He draws back a little now, chooses his words carefully. 'Perhaps this is a discussion for another time, my darling. I haven't seen you for so long. I want us to be together as a man and a woman tonight. Not as – how shall I say it? – an employee and her boss. We don't have to talk about work matters.'

No, I frown, but we do. And what does he mean, employee and boss anyway?

'I'm not your employee, Guillermo. Chiquitin-Almeira have all but pulled out. We've got that European Alliance Group running the show now, and a pretty poor show it is too . . .' I stop, seeing his face, feeling his hand encircle my wrist.

'Please,' he says. 'You are a compassionate woman, a loyal ally to your friends, and I appreciate that. But you aren't going to be able to help them any more. Not in the way you wanted to. We will speak more of this, I promise you. But for tonight, let me just enjoy being once more in your company. Let us not talk of hardship and despair . . .'

338

'Only rose petals?' I offer, pulling my hand away from his, even though I'm tempted to do exactly as he says – to leave, to forget that other, harsh mosquito-infested world – for now and just enjoy the luxury and opulence of his.

'That *is* my world, my love. It is full of beautiful things, and luxury and privilege, I grant you that. But never think for one moment that it is not real. It is every bit as real as yours, don't doubt it. You are one of the lucky ones though – you get to take your pick, which of them would you rather inhabit?'

'Either one of them, if I could be with you,' I say without thinking and, to my surprise, I really mean it.

'Then you need to know something. You need to understand this. I cannot help your friends to save their natural home. I will help to re-house and to educate and employ any of them who come to me through you for assistance. But I can't stop the tide of what's happening in your part of the forest.'

'But the tide must be stopped,' I urge. I have to make him see. '*It must!* Can't you – influence the police or the government or . . . or somebody? You told me that influence and power were everything. The tribe has been infected with an outbreak of measles now, did you know that? You told me . . .'

'I *told* you I didn't want to discuss these matters today. And we shall not; that is an end to it, Scarlett.' He snaps his fingers and a waiter appears in an instant, ready to take our order.

'I don't *care* how much money and influence you have.' I stand unsteadily, ignoring the waiter and pushing the chair out behind me with my knees. 'You're not going to gag me, Guillermo. I'm sorry if you don't think there is anything that can be done to save the forest or my people but it isn't a view I share with you. And it *is* important to me. I can't sit here sipping champagne and pretending it all away. Even for you.'

Don't do this, don't do this . . . Eve's earlier words about how much we need this man are buzzing about my reddening face like flies and yet as I run to the door, I can't seem to turn back.

I need him too. I scrunch up my fists and bash the beautiful glass door of the lobby open so I can make my way out. For the very first time, it seems, I have realised how much I need him.

'Then stay with me for one week.' He's manoeuvred himself in front of me so I can't go through the door without barging past him. 'Just one week, Scarlett. I will take you to meet my family, show you my home. Then you can decide how you'd rather spend the rest of your life . . . Please?'

Hollie

'I have tried to get hold of her, Mr Huang. I've tried every route I can think of but unless she wants to contact me . . .'

He hands me a tissue and I blow my nose miserably.

'It is good that you forgive her though,' he says quietly and I look askance at him.

'I want to get hold of her because she's carrying my baby. I didn't say that I *forgave* her.'

'Ah,' is all he says. As if the two things – forgiveness and the baby – were somehow interlinked, and they are not – how can they be? He needs to understand how it is.

'All along, she's been jealous of me, Mr Huang. All this time, my sister was jealous of me for being with Richard, and I never knew it. How could I have been so *stupid*?'

'Sometimes not so easy to see these things, huh?' He bows his head sympathetically and I marvel at how easily the whole sorry tale spilled out the minute he asked me how my sister was doing.

'She told me the other night how *angry* she was when I first started going out with Rich. It turns out now that she's been holding a candle for my husband all these years. The fact is, she's allowed her fantasies to grow instead of stifling them. I could have forgiven her for having those thoughts as a teenager. I can't forgive her for still harbouring them as a grown woman.'

'Situation most difficult,' he agrees. I watch as he carefully places a teacup on a saucer down in front of me. I didn't mean to say so much. I only came in here because I saw the 'relocating' sign and I wandered in to find out what was happening. I don't suppose he and his wife ever had any similar problems after they tried the 'natural' route? I scan his face for clues but his expression is inscrutable.

'What I've found the most difficult thing of all to stomach is how easily she was prepared to betray me,' I run on. Now that I've started to spill my feelings out, I find myself quite unable to stop. 'She slept with him when she knew she was already pregnant, Mr Huang. She used my desperation to achieve her own ends. I guess what I'm trying to say is – how do you ever get over that kind of betrayal?'

Mr Huang considers for a bit. 'Difficult, huh? But sometimes . . . we can hurt ourselves more with our own thoughts than anyone else can ever hurt us.'

He's right. I've been tormenting myself with my imaginings of what really went on between them ever since that day I told her to leave . . .

'Resentment and anger,' he says softly, 'Stored in the liver, causes bad flow of *chi*, yes?'

Ah, we're back to *chi* again. That's what got me into this mess in the first place, I think grimly.

'But . . . she still wants Richard,' I stutter, 'after all this time. Do you think I *shouldn't* be angry? She's taken my baby. She's . . . she . . .' I shake my head, frustrated that he doesn't seem to understand me. 'Look, how do you suggest that I stop feeling so resentful and angry, then? Acupuncture isn't going to do it, is it?'

He smiles, then. 'You work for the Bridge Trust,' he reminds me softly now. 'This you tell me is the largest charity in Britain, yes?'

I nod.

'There is a saying I have heard in this country. You say charity begins at home, huh? What does this mean?'

Oh, OK. I get it.

'You're telling me that I need to forgive her. Get over it, right? She may still be expecting my child, don't forget,' I get out. 'There is a large part of me that wants to do just that, believe me. I just don't know how. I don't know if I can.'

'Child more important than grudge,' he reminds me. 'Child more important than anything . . .'

'I know. I know! It's just . . . hard to forgive someone who makes a habit of betraying those who love her. She did the same thing to an ex-boyfriend of hers. She promised him she'd marry him then dropped him when he wasn't useful to her any more, she just used him . . .' I pick up the Chinese tea and finish off the cup in one go. 'I'm sorry, Mr Huang, I've taken up enough of your time already and I can see you're packing . . .'

I pause, realising I haven't asked him a single thing about his own progress.

'Will you be sorry to go?' I ask.

'Very sorry. I will miss many things here, Miss Hollie. The birds. The river. My friends . . .'

I'm going to miss you too, I think.

'I think – maybe you come back here, Miss Hollie, and you learn to lose fear of water, yes? Before Mrs Huang and I must leave?' He stands up and bows reverently to me just like he always does. 'Come soon, please?'

'I will come,' I promise him. Because part of me knows that that's important too, maybe more important than I let myself know. I *am* going to learn how to swim. I want to, I realise. 'It's something I want to do for me.'

But now that Duncan's in my mind again, I'm also thinking about what he said to me. Perhaps I need to ring that number again, the one I've been ringing to make contact with PlanetLove in Manaus. They told me she wasn't there, nobody knew anything. But if I could speak to someone in charge and say it was about Duncan's allegations, then maybe they'd sit up and take notice,

343

because if I know Scarlett she will certainly be making her way back there sooner or later.

If it ever did come to light that the thesis Scarlett submitted wasn't her own, she'd be well and truly scuppered. She'd lose her job for sure. Her friends wouldn't think so highly of her either. Worse than that, she'd have to say goodbye to any hope of winning the Klausmann, which is no more than she deserves.

But maybe, even more importantly, she'd have to come home and face the music.

Red Balloon

A scrap of paper. Just a little scrap of paper, where is one when you want it? Mairie switches off her engine and rubs her face with her hands, feeling hot and flustered. By the mother of God, she doesn't need this right now. Already the traffic on the road from Rio de Janeiro to the city of Santos, São Paulo, is starting to move again, snaking its way past the hold-up, several drivers pausing long enough to beep their horns as they pass by and get a good look. The joker in the BMW – unscathed as far as she can tell – has already got his BlackBerry out, he's taking down notes.

He's taking notes! What's his problem? Mairie's the one with a complaint to make. It's her little car that's had its rear fender all dented just because the *hijo de puta* wasn't looking where he was going, too busy talking on his mobile phone, making all the time business like they do . . .

Mairie delves a little deeper into her handbag. So much make-up but where is a paper to write down his name and his registration? The police will deal with him. She's got Luciendo's party to organise for next week, his tenth birthday celebration, and he's waiting for her. She promised him Mama wouldn't be too long and now she's got involved with this joker. American, by the sounds of him.

She throws her handbag down, gets out of the car. Near here they had the Bloco party last week and there is so much rubbish

345

littering the streets, beer bottles and greasy fast food wrappers and all sorts. She's not touching *them*. The rubbish men have been on strike and it's all been piling up for a while. It smells! Mairie bends, her thick waist groaning, and picks up the little envelope she's just spotted attached to a deflated red balloon.

That reminds her – Luciendo asked for some balloons like these for his party. She'll pass the shop on the way home and she'll pick some up then. With an eyebrow pencil, she takes down the other driver's name and number on the corner of the envelope. She squints at the strange name on the front of it – *Hudson* – mildly curious but more agitated than anything else because – is she hearing right? *This American is threatening to sue her?* Huh! Wait till her sister – who spends most Saturday afternoons in bed with the local chief-of-police – hears about this.

Mairie slumps back into the driver's seat, the red balloon and its letter thrown onto the seat beside her. Too many things on her mind. One thing at a time, Mairie. She checks her aggrieved reflection in the mirror, treating the American to a death-stare as she reverses out onto the road. She'll deal with him later. Right now she's got Luciendo's party to organise. And she needs to remember to get some more of those balloons.

Scarlett

'I didn't know if we should expect you back here, Scarlett.' Emoto pulls the 4x4 into a surprisingly large gap in the trees. The ground beneath our vehicle is thickly muddy and wet; I can feel the wheels straining to pull straight. 'After a whole week at Almeira's luxury pad?' He turns and looks at me frankly. 'What would make the girl who now has everything come back to this, the mud and mosquito capital of Brazil? What is the *one thing* that could have enticed you to come back, I wonder?' His voice is thick with sarcasm because he thinks he knows the answer – my hopes of winning the Klausmann – but he is so wrong . . .

I've come back here because after a week under Guillermo's family roof one thing has become clear above all else. I can't keep this baby for Hol. Gui and his family would never understand or approve. I *had* to come back here to get the herbs I need from Tunga, if I wanted any hope of remaining with Gui's family. Because without Gui's connections, it's pretty clear, I have no hope of helping the tribe.

Just wait till he learns I've got barely a week here before Gui insists I go back. It was all he would agree to, to let me 'say my goodbyes' – after that he wants me at his side again. I thought I was going to find that a wrench, but we've only just arrived back at base camp and I can already see that it won't be.

Everything has completely changed. Not just the location. This place is a dump. It feels too open, too exposed. And it *smells*.

347

I don't know of what, but it makes my nose wrinkle up it's so strong.

When I jump out of the jeep all I can spot are a few tents dotted here and there and some people who I don't recognise going about their work, their heads down.

'Defoe's lot.' Emoto indicates with his head in their direction and the immediate impression is one of division between the camps. 'We're over here. This one's Eve's tent. She and Gillian are both at the Forestry Conference in Manaus so you can kip here till morning. I put the ground sheet down for you but I warn you we do have to take them up during the day due to the risk of flooding.'

I nod, shielding my eyes. The minute we're out of the protective canopy cover the sun is baking hot. 'So hot, and yet still so muddy,' I murmur.

'There's been some unseasonal flooding in this area. When the site was picked, it wasn't anticipated that it'd be so damp. You do have your mosquito net, spray, tablets, yes?'

I nod, looking at him blankly. Where are the tribe, though? He hasn't mentioned them yet and I need to see Tunga . . .

'You'll definitely need the nets. Defoe deliberately chose this site so we can evacuate with the jeep or by boat if we should need to – European Alliance have a "minimalisation of risk" policy,' he continues drily. 'That didn't include the mozzies, of course.'

'It doesn't sound as if you'll be all that sorry to go,' I put in tentatively. He's already mentioned what I already knew – that he's barely got any time left here. He's flying out virtually as I fly in. I wish he wasn't. I'll miss Emoto, I realise suddenly. He may have been a rival for the Klausmann but he's also been a good friend.

'I *will* be sorry to go,' he corrects. 'If I'm honest, I was praying . . .' he smiles crookedly now, 'I was hoping that your boyfriend would woo you into staying with him. Then you wouldn't come

348

back to gather the species samples you still need to be eligible for the Klausmann and that way I'd still be in with a chance.'

'Well, you still *are* in with a chance, aren't you?' I frown. 'It's not in the bag yet.' And it's not as if I'm getting out of this mess as lightly as he thinks I am. I'm pregnant for God's sake! I'm going to have to take some herbs to terminate this child and . . . I didn't want to have to do that. I wanted to keep it for Hollie. I know she's mad at me and she hates me and she'll never forgive what I did, but I didn't want to have to do this to her.

'It's not as if you *need* to work any more is it?' Emoto puts in unexpectedly. 'You're going to be pretty much set up for life with that boyfriend of yours . . .'

'Emoto.' I straighten up now and put a hand on his arm. I wish Emoto would stop being so mean to me. God, how I wish I could just *tell* him. But I can't. There's been this reserve between us from the beginning, because we've always been rivals as well as co-workers, all because of this bloody award. 'You've been sulking ever since you picked me up from the coach station. I'm sorry if you didn't want me back, but I'm here because I still care about helping the tribe, even if you don't believe that.'

He falls silent now, and I know there's still something eating away at him, my old friend and rival. Of course there is. Eve told me when she first picked me up, didn't she? They'd all have preferred to keep *him* on – I was only chosen because of my links with Guillermo and it's hardly any wonder if Emoto's feeling hard done by.

'It's my intention to help you too, you know. I want to help. If I have any influence on the way things work out here I'll use it for everyone's good . . .'

'I know.' He hangs his head. 'I apologise for sounding bitter. I shouldn't. It's partly my fault. I just thought all along . . .' He holds up the tent flap and looks at me frankly. 'I always took you to be just a pretty face. I thought you were like so many of the other UK students that have come and gone, here just to

349

have a bit of fun. Then I was here in Eve's tent the other day, collecting my things and I saw your paper, Scarlett. The one that's up for the Klausmann.' He gestures into the little white tent and I see a pile of my things on the metal table now. I duck inside to take a better look and he follows me.

'These are all the things we saved for you from the fire.' He pushes his smooth hands through his short black hair, looking uncomfortable as he remembers, no doubt, that I lost all my seeds . . . 'And some of the things that Eve had in her keeping – like this.' He picks up a folder of papers and places it into my hands. I've never seen it before. 'I read your work, Scarlett, and it's damn good.'

'Oh.' I feel a glow of pleasure at his words. 'Everyone keeps telling me so and yet I never thought . . .'

'No, seriously, you shouldn't have talked yourself down like that. I thought I was in with a chance of winning until I saw yours. As it is . . .'

I don't ask him, because I can see he's still upset. I sit down on the chair and open up the folder, leafing through it while, unbidden, Emoto goes to fetch the rest of my stuff from the car. There must be two theses in here – maybe Emoto's is in here too – because this is much thicker than the one I submitted and . . . anyway, it's all about Mycorrhizal fungi. No wonder everyone keeps getting my work mixed up with this one if they're both in the same folder.

What the . . . ?

I turn the folder round, my breath suddenly coming in short gasps as a thought occurs to me. I read the name on the front: 'Scarlett L. Hudson'. It doesn't say anybody else's name, just mine. I turn to the title page: 'Observations on Myccorhizal Biodiversity by Scarlett Hudson.' And the date, two summers ago. But I never typed that page. It isn't mine. *I never typed that!*

What the fuck?

I glance up at the tent flaps but Emoto is still out at the car.

Just as well because I know my face has just gone the colour of beetroot. If he saw me right now, looking like this, he'd guess the truth! This isn't my thesis. This isn't the thesis I gave to Hollie to post off for me two summers ago.

I know whose it is, though.

How the hell could Hol have got the two of them mixed up? How *could* she? She'd never have done it on purpose, surely? She wouldn't have understood what she was doing – Hollie couldn't tell fungus from fudge, she wouldn't have had a clue. Oh, how could she have made such a stupid mistake? And – if it *is* a mistake – then who typed up the front page with my name on it? Crap. First of all I had the 'allegations' that miserable git Duncan tried to pin on me and now this. Does Hollie even know what she's done?

If anyone ever found out, does she realise the deep shit I'd be in? My name would be mud in ethno-botany circles. I'd be finished. I push the thesis back into the folder and shove it out of sight so I don't have to think about it any more. There's too much at stake for me to go back on this now.

I am in real trouble now. I didn't cheat, but this sure makes it look as if I did, and if Gui finds that out then I'm done for. He can't abide liars, he's always saying. That's part of the reason he loves me so much. Because he thinks I can't tell a lie!

I am royally screwed. Unless of course there is some way to keep it quiet. Nobody has realised the mistake up till now, have they? All I have to do is make sure that nobody ever finds out what Hollie has done.

Never, ever.

Hollie

How am I going to start this letter?

I stand up on Scarlett's little bed in the bare-walled beige room that she left in such a hurry and I reach up for the last time to close the darned window. There's a stiff breeze blowing off the Medway today. I can see the sun sparkling on it in little silver patches here and there and the sight makes me pause in mid-reach. It's not such a bad view, really. We've had some good times here by this river. We've never sailed on one of those real sailing boats but we sent plenty of paper boats spinning down the river in our time.

Funny how Scarlett only remembered how I'd stopped her from chasing after them that night after Flo's birthday party. She didn't recall I was holding her back for her own safety, she was only a diddy thing. If she'd have jumped in and tried to swim after them she'd have got swept away, no question about it. So I'd pinioned her arms to her sides and held onto her for dear life so she couldn't jump in.

I thought her heart would break. I remember us standing there for the best part of half an hour while I tried to drum it into her head that the little paper boats were gone. For good. And I have never forgotten the look on her determined little face when she turned to me and declared, 'I will get them back, Hollie. When I'm bigger I'll get on a boat myself and follow them all the way out to sea and I'll search and search till I find them and you won't be able to stop me, no one will.'

I feel a lump in my throat now. Maybe that was the first time I realised that one day the tide would come that would take my Lettie away from me.

My eyes flicker over the static barge and its crane and the bags of sand it's still off-loading to shore up the piers. They'll be done in a few weeks, they tell me. After all my worrying and fretting, it's all going to be sorted and the bridge isn't going to fall down after all. What doesn't kill me makes me stronger, as Flo used to say – and I must be a hell of a lot stronger than I used to be, I reckon.

Strong enough maybe to look towards the site of the Blue Jazz café, the spot where I fell into the water all those years ago? All these years we've lived right opposite it, and in all this time I've never once looked at it. That's why I like the window closed. I raise my eyes very slowly, very tentatively, to the place where my downfall took place. And then I do a double take.

It's gone!

The Blue Jazz café has been pulled down and in its place is nothing but a small empty field. Is *this* what Scarlett was trying to get me to look at, that evening when I sent her packing? This place that has haunted my nightmares for so many years till eventually I blocked out my dreams altogether . . . It's gone. All gone.

I watch as some strange-looking birds circle round and round before landing on the fence by the water. Some very rare Chatham albatrosses maybe? I manage a small smile, feeling a strange sense of relief flooding through me. Dear old Mr Huang would know. He lives on the other side of the river. His house would be that one with the blue door. And then I remember the sign– 'Closing down sale, returning to China for family reasons'. He's leaving and I still have so much unfinished business – will I ever get to learn to swim after all?

Anyway. I shake my head to get rid of these thoughts, trying to focus on what I came in here to do. I come down off the bed and pick up the writing pad again. How *am* I going to start this? What shall I say to the PlanetLove people when I write the letter that Duncan was so keen for me to write? It won't be easy. I flick open the folder which I've kept stashed away on top of Scarlett's wardrobe for the past two years. Inside is the envelope which she asked me to post for her; her thesis on Orchidacea. She was honest enough to decide against using Duncan's work and instead submit her own. I'm no botanist but I've learned a fair bit just from reading Mum's old papers when I was a kid. And Scarlett was being foolhardy if she thought her own work would cut it. Even I could see that it wouldn't. So I sent off our mother's thesis in its place.

Mum's magnum opus on Mycorrhizal biodiversity that she slaved away so many years for – devoted her life to and, partly, stayed away from us, for. It never got published or ever saw the light of day because she died before she could do anything with it. I don't regret what I did – and why would I? Why waste it? Her work got to be of some earthly use in the end. Scarlett got accepted for the Amazon job that she so desperately wanted and Mum actually got to be useful to one of her girls.

Well, now she's going to be useful to me too. I need to just get on and write this letter.

Scarlett

I crawl out of the tent and straighten my aching back. I am frozen to the bone and every part of me hurts. It's been raining for days now, pelting down steadily on the canvas outside but this morning at last – at last! – the downpour has stopped. High up above the canopy there are patches of bright blue sky visible from the ground. The day is going to be hot. I've been confined to base camp since I got back but I'm finally going to be able to get moving.

'Hey.' I look up blearily as Emoto comes off the jeep radio and joins me outside Eve's tent. 'Looks like today we'll finally be able to make a move out of here, get on with some work.'

'I'm afraid not, Scarlett.' I watch as he pulls off his thigh-length wellies. They're covered to mid-calf in mud. 'The forest floor isn't just muddy and mired – it's impassable. For the time being, people like you and me have to stay put.'

'*For Pete's sake!*' I groan. 'I need to find the tribe . . .'

I stand outside the tent for a while and squint up at the sky. If it could get hot quick enough, maybe everything would dry out and then we could make a move? That noise I've been hearing in the distance is louder now that I'm standing outside. It sounds like . . . like the noise I've heard the loggers make with their electric saws. I frown at Emoto, indicating with my head towards the direction it's coming from and he stops in the middle of pulling off his boots. Are the loggers here? Even in all this mud?

'Get back inside,' he says thickly.

'Emoto, I've been stuck in there for three whole days. I'm not going to miss out on the chance to get on with what I must do just because those bastards are logging illegally. If they can move about in this mire then so can we. They have no business being here, anyway. We have to do something to stop them . . .' Strange, but the noise is already twice as loud as it sounded a moment ago. And it seems to be coming from everywhere all at once.

'There is nothing we're going to be able to do that'll stop this lot. And you can't go out looking for the tribe in *your* condition.'

He knows? I look at him, shocked. 'When did you find out?' I ask faintly.

'I overheard Eve tell Defoe all about it. You're expecting Almeira's baby, aren't you? Oh, don't worry,' he adds as my face colours. 'I didn't spread it about. I imagined you might prefer to keep it quiet for now . . .'

'Thank you,' I manage.

'But the truth is, you don't *need* to do any of this any more. You don't need to put yourself through these harsh conditions. If this is all about finding some seed samples to replace what you lost, I'll give you some of mine.'

'What makes you think I *want* yours?' I challenge. 'Even in my condition. I don't. I don't need your pity, Emoto. I'll find my own samples. Don't think you can prevent me.'

'Not right now you won't. *In,*' he growls, advancing as if he's about to push me into the tent.

I turn to him and stand my ground. 'You've been surly and sulking ever since I got here, Emoto, and I've just about had enough of it. You aren't going to tell me what to do any more so you'd better . . . Ow!' I yelp as he pushes me forcibly back into the tent. The ground is so uneven I miss my footing and it's only because he reaches out to catch me that I don't hit the floor.

'What the . . . ?' Alarmed, I back off, while he fumbles with the tent zips, sealing us in hermetically. I look at Emoto shakily, rubbing my sore wrists where he grabbed hold of me to stop my fall. The noise outside has grown exponentially louder in a matter of seconds. The bright white light that was hitting the tent's exterior has gone, the sky has clouded over again, and now the tent canvas is being battered again but this time by – by *hailstones*? Huge hailstones by the sounds of it.

'Mosquitos,' he informs me.

'They . . . it *can't* be.' They couldn't be so big, there couldn't be so many of them. The black bodies continue to pelt thickly against the outside of Eve's tent for a few minutes. Oh God, now I feel sick. I sidle up to Emoto and push my fingers into his, my anger melting away into fear.

'If there's one thing I hate about this country it's the insects,' I say in answer to his surprised look at this sudden gesture of intimacy. 'I love everything else but the huge-winged, creeping, crawling, sticky, black, segmented . . . I can't stand them. They won't be able to get in here, will they?'

'They shouldn't be able to,' he assures me, but I can see the sweat forming on his brow. 'Let's sit down, it's going to be a while before this passes. You know, the insects were the one thing that nearly put me off coming on this whole trip.' He smiles shakily.

'You hate them too?' I never knew. 'Sorry about before, I just . . .'

'Don't worry about it, Scarlett. The minute after I heard them I knew what was coming. We've had several of these swarms since you've been away. If you're out in it when they arrive . . .'

'Yeah. I can imagine. At least there won't be any of these waiting for you when you go back to Tokyo, eh? That's one advantage to leaving Brazil.' Despite steeling myself to try and stop, I'm trembling pretty hard. I just can't help it and he must think I'm such a wuss. The swarm is still passing overhead. The noise coming from outside is almost deafening. Somehow we're now both sitting bunched up together on the groundsheet and he's got his arm comfortably around my shoulders . . .

'You'll have that job at Tokyo Uni to go back to, I guess?' I say to distract us, shouting above the sound of millions of insect wings. He always seemed dead keen on the lectureship idea but now he shakes his head despondently.

'I won't . . . I won't be getting an offer for that job, Scarlett. It was always contingent on my doing well in this post. I think they expected me to get the award. That's why they were mooting it, but . . . look, forget it.' He taps my arm consolingly. 'Just before that mozzie storm arrived I heard some good news over the car radio . . .'

'What d'you mean you won't be getting that job?' I question. 'I thought you'd already been offered it? What'll you do if you don't teach?'

He shrugs, trying to brush off how much it matters to him but I can see how very much it does. He looks at me silently. The electric drill noise outside is beginning to fade as rapidly as it came.

'I am not going to win the Klausmann, so I will not be offered the post,' he says simply. 'Perhaps I can work in my brother's electrical shop till I sort out something else.'

'In an electrical shop?' My eyes widen at the thought. 'That would be a complete waste of everything you know. Besides, you're the cleverer of the two of us. We both know that. You might still win it.'

'Perhaps it was you who was the cleverer one, though?' He looks at me sidelong and unlinks our arms. He reaches for a towel to wipe his face with.

'How so?'

'Getting in with Almeira. That was your smartest move, no?'

'I never . . . I never wanted to go with Gui for that reason, Emoto. I was cool towards him for ages precisely because I didn't want to use him.'

358

'It's all worked out in your favour though, hasn't it? Every-thing. Even though you didn't plan it this way. There is no move that you can make that will mean you lose.'

'That's what you think.'

'Ha! Scarlett, I bow to my superior opponent. You. You will get the man and you will command his riches and you will have his baby and you will win the award. Simple as that.'

I look askance at him. One minute ago we were hanging onto each other for dear life and now he sounds so . . . so bitter and envious and . . . jealous?

'You think . . . you think my life's like a candy-coated version of some movie-star's, don't you? You think I don't have to make diffi-cult decisions ever? You think I don't suffer at all? That I never do anything out of truly charitable reasons and not self-interest?' I let out a long breath and he remains silent. 'This isn't Gui's baby, Emoto.'

He looks at me disbelievingly.

'It isn't. It's my brother-in-law's child. It isn't what you think.' I say quickly in answer to his shocked look. 'My sister asked me to be her surrogate. But things turned ugly. She chucked me out of the house.'

'It really isn't his?'

'No. And now I have to . . . terminate this pregnancy before Gui ever finds out or else he won't want to help us out here at all, will he? I need to find the tribe, Emoto. I need Tunga to give me some herbs to end this pregnancy.'

'*Shit.*' He turns the towel round to find a clean spot and uses it now to gingerly wipe away the sweat that's formed on my fore-head. I'd take the towel from him myself but my limbs are still like lead, immobilised with fear. Those horrible insects, are they gone yet? I get a quick flash of Hol, awoken by me in the early hours one winter night to remove a huge spider from my bedroom, and doing so kindly and without making a fuss because she knew how terrified I'd been. I haven't always been so compassionate about her fears, have I?

And Emoto probably thinks I'm a heartless, grabbing bitch. Now I've told him about the child too, and what I have to do with it. I put my face down, covering it with my hands, because it is all too much.

'I'm so sorry. It looks as if I've misjudged you, after all.' Emoto has put his hand back on my shoulder. 'And if you really need to see Tunga that badly, then you'll be even more pleased to hear what I just learned on the radio a few minutes ago. Barry's found Tunga. They're making their way back. *They* can do it.' He shakes his head as I raise my eyes to his, answering my unspoken question. 'We couldn't. The river's about to break its banks. I was out looking at the bridge this morning. It's on its last legs. Without the right kind of vehicle, there's no way we can go anywhere. They should be with us sometime in the next twenty-four hours, however.'

I stare at him. Tunga is coming here? He's coming here and that'll mean I'll get the herbs to make my way clear with Gui again. It's what I wanted . . . no, it's what I *needed* to happen.

But why do I feel so strange now? I glance at Emoto.

I've got the feeling very deep inside that something has changed and I don't know what.

Hollie

I don't stand there this time as I have done so many times before, looking at the light shimmering off the surface, bouncing off the ceiling in its eerie way. Rich squeezes my hand – I am so glad he offered to come with me – and I go straight to the metal steps that lead down into the shallow end. I can do this. I am going to do this.

As the water hits my ankles, then my calves, then my thighs, I draw in a shocked breath, but this time it is not fear causing the trembling in my limbs, it is only the cold. I brace myself. I look up at Mr Huang who is waiting patiently by the poolside. Rich is beside him, holding the towel. The rest of the pool is silent and empty, just as they'd said it would be at this time of day; the sole lifeguard sitting at the other end has her head down, probably texting.

I'm feeling strangely calm after my acupuncture session. Mr Huang told me: 'It will help steady your nerves, Miss Hollie, but the rest is up to you.' Rich nods encouragingly in my direction and I take the next step down the rung and into the pool. The water snakes around my hips but it feels strangely peaceful. There are little blue underwater lights making the whole place brighter and I do not feel in the slightest bit afraid. I'm not sure why or how this can be, unless it's the acupuncture, but it feels like a marvellous release to be here in the pool, and to not be afraid.

I take a few steps further in and the water comes up to my

chest. The weight of it feels quite heavy against me now. I'm not sure I'm entirely comfortable with it. No, if truth be told, I don't like the feel of it at all, but I've come this far.

'We're right here with you, Hol.' Rich calls to me from the side. He wanted to come in too but I preferred to do it this way. It's enough for me that he's here. He feels a long way behind me now. I'm still striding out, my legs moving in big slow water-retarded arcs, like an astronaut making strides on the moon, and the water has risen above my chest and up to my shoulders and my arms are moving out to the sides now, steadying and balancing. I close my mouth so as to not accidentally gulp down any pool water. I close my eyes and pretend I'm just like any kid who's plunged headlong into the pool for the very first time. I've seen them all do it, and they don't feel any fear, they just *go for it*.

Like Scarlett. Just like Scarlett's always done everything she ever wanted to do. How strangely heavy this water feels, dragging against my back and chest now, swaying me first one way and then the other so that I feel the need to constantly readjust my position. Behind my closed lids I can see my sister clear as daylight in her little pink costume. I'm sitting on the side and watching her with Tim, and he's cupping his hands to his mouth and is yelling, 'You can do it, Scarlett, go for it, girl!' and her, simpering and preening and pretend-swimming and not imagining for one minute that she'd go down, laughing and splashing and somehow unimaginably buoyant, floating. How little must she have been then. Maybe five?

'You OK, Hol?' That's Rich again, I can hear him but he's so far away now on the other side of the great watery expanse. All that pool water lapping against the sides dissolves his words away into echoes and the lights above us suddenly dim right down.

'Just ten more minutes till closing time,' the girl from her high chair at the deep end warns us.

Ten minutes to face a lifetime's worth of resistance. I turn to

362

look back at Rich and my old Chinese friend. I wave at them both and Rich shoots me a little smile. Mr Huang looks confident. 'Stay here where feet can touch bottom, please,' he reminds me. He goes and sits back down again but his face remains watchful.

Ten minutes.

I know full well why Scarlett wanted me to do this. God, how might her life have turned out differently if I *had* drowned that day outside the Blue Jazz café? She might have ended up with Richard after all. Except . . . if he were not mine, would she ever have even wanted him? I feel a surge of anger flash through my chest now, firing up my intent. I can still stand where I am here. My feet are firm against the smooth pool bottom. I pull in a breath and then, for one long cold and unimaginably dark moment, I plunge my whole head beneath the water.

Oh, but I didn't know the panic was still there, waiting so quietly beneath the surface to erupt. My carefully saved breath comes spluttering out all at once, leaving my lungs empty, filled immediately with pain instead of air. Suddenly my feet, scrabbling and slipping against the pool bottom which is as greased glass, can find no safe place on which to stand. I can't get my head back up. I can't breathe.

A pain shoots through my pelvis now, an old, familiar pain. That blade running through my innards again. I imagine the pool growing dark with freshly-spurting blood from my sides where that boy Aaron plunged the knife in. The wounds he inflicted were the cause of multiple infections. That I am unable to have children of my own has come about directly of a result of my being at the Blue Jazz café that night.

And I was there because of her.

There is no air, there is no air. My lungs will explode any moment now with the weight. Where is Rich who was watching me so closely? Where is Mr Huang? Where is the girl who warned us about 'ten minutes till closing'?

Ten minutes is long enough for someone to rob you of every chance of the life you've always dreamed of. It was long enough, all those years ago, for me to get between my tearful, drunken fourteen-year-old sister and her out-of-his-head boyfriend when I found them fighting that night. They were arguing outside the nightclub along Strood Esplanade, him brandishing that knife that he 'never meant to use'. He backed us both right to the edge of the water, slicing the air with that blade. He backed us up so tight against the wall that in the end there was nothing for it but for me to turn to her and scream at her to make her own escape . . .

And now – did I just pass out? I'm lying here on the wet poolside leaning over onto one side coughing up pool water and Rich is sitting there dripping beside me, rubbing my hands. Did he just pull me out of that pool? I have no recollection of that.

'How could I sink in this amount of water?' I cough. 'I could reach the bottom with my feet for God's sake! What am I made of, lead?'

'Your heart is heavy,' Mr Huang murmurs.

'She jumped, Mr Huang.' I look at him intently, wanting him to understand. 'My sister jumped down into the river and she swam away. Because she could, don't you see?' I was the one who stayed behind to deal with the blows dealt out in frustration and anger that had been meant for her.

'Her boyfriend stabbed me instead of her. I stood between them and let her get away and that's when he stabbed me – here . . .' I point to all the old wounds that Mr Huang once spent months trying to help me heal.

'Are you saying that lad who attacked you soon after we started going out – that was Scarlett's *boyfriend*?' Understanding is dawning slowly on Richard's pale face. 'You were out picking her up?'

I've never told him. We'd only just started dating when it happened. He became a regular visitor at the hospital when I was first admitted, it made us all the closer, but I hadn't wanted to tell him the full story.

'I never told you at the time because . . . how would it have looked, what kind of family would you have thought you were getting involved with?' I put in now. 'Then afterwards, there never seemed any point in dragging it all up again.'

'So that's why it had to be her,' he marvels now. 'Did *he* know who you were when he attacked you?'

'Aaron only knew I was getting in his way. Who I was didn't matter at that moment.'

'You sacrificed yourself,' Mr Huang puts in now. 'Because you love her.'

Rich and Mr Huang help me to my feet now.

'I *loved* her,' I correct him. Past tense. 'More than all the world, I did. That's why I went out looking for her that night when she didn't come home. There wasn't anyone else to do it, was there?'

'So long?' Mr Huang looks sad. 'A heavy burden to carry, yes? This is why you sink. It is clear now, ha. And sister?' He shuffles alongside me, looking perplexed. 'Same sister she carry your baby for you, yes?'

He understands now, I can see it in his eyes: why I needed her to be the one who would put it all right for me. He glances at Rich and I know he's remembering what I told him.

'She has betrayed me, Mr Huang. In the worst possible way that she could. All I feel for her now is . . .' I'm suddenly shivering, but whether through shock or cold or anger I cannot tell. 'Hatred, to tell you the truth. I hate her, Mr Huang. I hate her because she made me lose my fertility. I hate her because she tried to steal away my husband.' I glance at Rich and I can't help but see he looks remorseful. 'And I hate her because for all I know she's still carrying our child and I will never, ever get to see it. Are those good enough reasons for a person to feel that way?' I catch the sudden look that passes between him and Rich.

The lifeguard has long since departed to gather a load of forms that she feels I need to fill in.

'That is another heavy burden, hatred,' Mr Huang observes. 'Difficult to swim in pool with so much weight about your shoulders.'

I lift my hands to my face because now the memory of Aaron's eyes, boring into mine, won't go away.

'All these years,' I stutter, 'ten years – I haven't been able to recall what he looked like.' Aaron's been a dark shadow that destroyed my life. Something I locked away. Now here he is, his face as fresh and living in my memory as if it happened moments ago. 'I thought he was really going to hurt her! I thought, when I saw him waving that knife about . . . and I couldn't let him do that. I wanted to keep her safe, that's why I stepped in front of her . . .' For such a very long time it has all been a blur, the sequence of events, who moved first, who said what. There was shouting and she was crying and then he pulled his knife out. 'We were backed up against the wall, you see. I told her to jump, to get away. That's all I could think of, that I had to help her to get away.' She was just a child after all. My little sister.

I gulp, because it's all coming back. Aaron's eyes; a kaleidoscope of emotions unfolds before me – frustration, scorn, anger. 'Get out of here, you stupid bitch, this is nothing to do with you.'

'He didn't want to hurt you perhaps?' Mr Huang suggests. I didn't realise I had spoken the words out loud, but I must have. 'You weren't involved.'

'My God, I thought I would lose her! I thought Aaron was going to kill her. How could I let that happen? If I lost her, how could I ever live with myself again?'

She was my beautiful Lettie, turning into an adolescent pain in the neck, maybe, but still my Lettie. For a moment that night, I got a flash of what my life might have been like if I had to live the rest of it without her. It hadn't been something I'd been prepared to risk.

'I knew in that moment, it was either her or me,' I tell them both now. 'I couldn't stand by and do nothing.'

Scarlett hesitated so long on the wall, she hadn't wanted to leave me. In the end I threatened to push her over. I knew she'd be OK. She'd be able to get away.

'You chose her safety over your own,' he affirms.

'I am not a violent person, Mr Huang, but in that moment – if I'd had to turn that knife back on him in order to save her, I would have done.' Rich places the soft white towel he's been holding around my shoulders now. I pull up the end of it to dry my face, to dab at the chlorine that's stinging my eyes.

He never meant to do it, Aaron said afterwards, he was stoned, didn't know what he was doing.

'He did time in prison for it, I know.' I look up at my two supporters now, my throat aching. 'But I have done so much more time than he has, haven't I? The legacy of what he did that night is going to last me a lifetime. He's still here, still in my head, in the wounds he inflicted; he's never going to go away.' Rich puts his arms around my shoulders. For a split second I see Aaron's face in the darkness again, shocked and stunned at his own actions before I fell back, into the water.

'But maybe,' Mr Huang says softly, 'this man remind you of how much you love sister too?'

I stare at my old friend, open-mouthed. 'That . . . that's not true! Nothing he did has had any good come out of it, Mr Huang. I don't accept that, not at all. I don't know why he's come back into my head right now, but I'm going to push him out again, that's for sure.'

Then it hits me.

The energy blocks, is this what he has been on about all this time? I'd blocked out Aaron. Now he is back.

'But surely – he remind you of how much it hurts to lose her,'

Mr Huang points out and I frown furiously at him for doing so. I look down at the puddle of cold water at my feet and I'm still shivering but I can't help the feeling that maybe he's right? Aaron *has* reminded me of how desperate I was not to lose her. And now I've gone and sent her away forever, all by myself.

It's strange, but for some reason I just don't feel so angry any more. I want to. I feel I ought to, but I can't. The fury that I've felt towards her for so many days now has just gone. I still feel sad at the way things have turned out between us but I can't feel *angry* any longer.

I wonder if . . . if I will be able to go in, now. If I will be able to start to learn to swim? Because the blackness that was the memory of Aaron isn't waiting in the water any more. I can feel it.

The girl who's gone off to find the 'incident forms' hasn't come back yet. Rich is still here though, his eyes looking sadder but calmer than I've seen them for a long while. At least now he understands.

And the pool is open, calm as a pond on a summer's morning, still waiting for me.

Scarlett

'So you got the herbs?' Emoto's voice is rendered both muffled and echoey by the heavy mist lying over the swollen riverbank this morning. He's come up behind me and is looking over my shoulder at the little herb pouches I've been contemplating for the last two hours.

'Yep. These are the herbs Tunga gave me last night,' I confirm. The powders that are going to make me a free woman again; free to do what I can to help what remains of Tunga's people. The powders – I shiver – that are going to put an end to Hollie's baby.

But I have a commitment to others here too. Tunga only came back because Barry told him I had returned. The rest of the tribe were due to follow, arriving here by dawn. They've come because they still believe I can help save their land.

'I've got to mix these powders together and take them all in one go dissolved in water.' We both glance at my little tin cup which I've perched on the rock beside me. It's got about two inches of rainwater in it at the moment and more is collecting every second.

'Just waiting for the cup to fill up, eh?' Emoto smiles kindly.

'Waiting till my cup runneth over . . .' I can't quite bring my eyes to smile back at him. He knows what's at stake here.

I don't want to do this.

'Barry has warned he expects the river to burst its banks some time today.' Emoto stands up suddenly. Shielding his eyes from the rain, he uses the vantage point of the rock to peer a little further down the river to the ramshackle bridge. 'I don't want to rush you, but . . . he reckons there's a high chance the bridge is going to be swept away too. We have to get the jeep over before it won't take the weight any more. He sent me to tell you.'

'We're leaving?' I look up at him, feeling a stab of desperation. I've been sitting on this rock for so long waiting to . . . just bring myself to the point where I was ready to do it. I thought I'd made my decision. Why can't I just *do* it?

'Yes, we're leaving.'

'I can't . . . I can't go yet, Emoto. I'm not ready.'

'Scarlett.' He sits down beside me on the rock. His Kangol anorak is pouring with water, his face is dripping wet. 'Look.' He takes my chin and guides my gaze back in the direction of the hissing and bubbling river, swollen to enormous and angry proportions by the rain. Barry is right. It is going to break its banks. A few metres down we can hear the creak and distress of the wooden bridge, groaning with the weight of water rushing past it.

'It reminds me of home,' I say softly.

'Was it ever as bad as this?'

'No,' I laugh, despite myself. 'But it reminds me of when I used to sit on the coal bunker and watch the river for hours as it hurtled by.' Something . . . wild would get into me then. The feeling that I was like the water, that I owed my allegiance to no one and no place. 'I'd get a feeling of such power, watching it. The feeling that I could never be tied down to anything, that nobody could ever hold me back. Have you ever felt like that?' I glance up at him, but his face is inscrutable.

'This child could hold you back,' he reminds me and I catch my breath at his words.

'I've got to . . .' I open up the palm-leaf pouches slowly, 'mix these two up together.' Emoto makes no move to help me.

370

The rain runs down his flat forehead, drips off the bridge of his nose. He just sits there in silence, watching me.

'Do you think I'm doing the right thing, Emoto?' I shoot him a sidelong glance as I tip the first pouch of herbs into the cup. 'Or do you think that it's wrong to take a life? I used to think so. The funny thing is – this baby I'm carrying – it would inconvenience my life in every way imaginable; it would ruin any hope of help from Gui, any chance of a life with him. And yet, deep in my heart, I still don't want to do this . . .'

Emoto doesn't say a word.

'She hates me, you know. My sister. She hates me with a vengeance, now. She should, too. I've ruined her life, really. I dangled all her hopes in front of her like carrots and then threw them away. I've betrayed her at every turn. Even now, doing this. It's all for a good cause, but it's the greatest betrayal of all . . .'

I pick up the little tin cup and swirl it around, waiting for the powders to dissolve. I've hardly got enough water in the cup. It's ridiculous; the sky is full of water; the river is full of water; my heart is full of tears; and yet there is hardly any water in this cup!

'What do *you* want, Scarlett?'

What do I want?

What does it matter any more, what I want? I can have it all anyway, now, can't I? I will. Any dress. Any car. Any home. The love and devotion of a good man. The protection of a powerful family. What else is there? I look at him dully.

'What do you *want*?' Emoto repeats. He kneels down beside me and takes the cup from me, placing it back on the rock. He takes my hands. 'Is it the Klausmann? What you offered me? The validation of your peers and profession?'

I shake my head. 'No. Not any more. I did want that. But not any more.' What *do* I want? 'There's something I thought – I almost had, once. But it slipped through my fingers.' I turn my face skywards and let the cool rain patter down onto my skin.

371

It runs into my eyes and down my neck and trickles down under my T-shirt . . .

I remember how it rained around four o'clock every day that August. The weather had got into a funny kind of loop, doing the same thing over and over. Like me; I'd stand by the cracked window in the disused cow shed beside the vet's office and live for the moment when I'd spy Richard hurrying up the road, his collar upturned, rain pouring down his cheeks. If he missed a day I'd be gutted. It felt like a whole day wasted.

Ruffles rallied; the vet told me my dog wouldn't have to be put down but we still didn't know if they'd manage to save both his legs. I hung about a lot. It was only the thought of Richard's visits that made my life bearable at that point.

And he was so shy! I never understood how someone so handsome could be so shy around women. He'd create a real flurry of interest around the nurses every time he came in, I knew 'cos I could hear them wittering away from my hide-out in the shed next door. But he never stayed talking to them. He came to check out how me and Ruff were doing, that was all. And he knew exactly where he'd find me.

'*Love*, Emoto. Once, I thought I knew what it was to truly, deeply, love someone. Have you ever been in love?'

Emoto smiles but does not reply.

'That feeling that – you're so filled up with the other person that at that moment you'd do anything, *give* anything, to be with them?'

'Do you feel that way about Guillermo Almeira?' He shoots me a sideways look.

I pause. I thought I might love Gui; that maybe I could come to love Gui. This past week we've spent together has been so good in many ways and yet . . . The truth is, if I live the rest of my life out with him it would be a compromise, nothing else.

I shake my head. 'Even if I don't really know what love is, Emoto, I know what it's not.' The realisation of that fills me with a sadness so huge I can't even look at my friend any more.

And then – out of the blue, something extraordinary happens.

'Oh!' Even through the tears that are streaming down my face, I laugh, I can't help myself, I look up at Emoto, beaming.

That can't be what I just thought it was, can it?

Emoto is leaning over me suddenly, his hand on my shoulder in concern. 'I'm OK, honest, I'm OK!' How can I tell him? How can I actually *say* this?

'I *think* I just felt the baby move.' Is this what it feels like? 'It feels like a little butterfly fluttering. Like someone's suddenly arrived.' The one I've been waiting for all my life.

'You felt it?'

'Yes!' I take his hand and shamelessly place it low down on my belly. He looks surprised, but I can't help myself.

'Here. That's it. I'm sure it is! Oh, blimey – there it goes again, OMG!'

'I feel it, Scarlett,' he laughs. 'You're looking a bit shell-shocked though. It must be a very strange sensation. What does it feel like?'

'It feels – just like that feeling I just told you about a moment ago,' I tell him thickly.

'Like *love*?' His eyebrows go up in surprise. 'Is that what you're saying?'

'Like love, yes, but love *isn't* what I thought it was, Emoto! It's something else,' I gush. I never knew it till this moment. 'It *isn't* the feeling that you'd do anything to have that person, or to be with that person . . .'

'No?'

'No. It isn't about possession at all. It's about what you'd be prepared to sacrifice for them. It's about what you'd be prepared to give. That's what love is.'

'And – what are you prepared to give?'

I watch as he picks up my little tin cup with Tunga's herbs in it and offers it to me. I shake my head a fraction and he turns and throws the whole contents out into the sizzling river. And then, just to make sure, he sweeps the palm leaves off the rock too. We both watch, laughing as the leaves bob and sway for a few moments before hurtling out of sight beneath the creaking bridge.

I didn't anticipate this. I didn't know it could ever be as wonderful as this.

'Hey, look . . .' Emoto's voice darkens suddenly. He turns his head from the river to look at me and I can see the disappointment in his eyes. 'Your boyfriend's here. He's come for you early, Scarlett. He must have heard about the danger from the floods . . .'

'Gui?' I look at Emoto, startled.

'He might just understand, Scarlett.' Emoto's hand touches mine for a split second, reassuring. 'Don't be afraid. You've made your decision now. Just tell him the truth. Come on,' Emoto pulls me to my feet. 'That bridge may not even last another two hours. You've got to get your shit together. We may not be back this way again.'

I have a feeling he is right. I didn't even have to make the decision in the end. Somehow, it was already made for me.

And after today there will be no turning back.

Hollie

I don't know why I imagined they might have laid him to rest beside you, Mum. I slide my bunch of freesias into the little glass vase I've brought and place it apologetically on top of Helen's grave. Geoffrey Wincanton. Your Geoffrey. Our dad. He's not here. He'll have been buried with his own people of course and you still can't be together. Just like when you were both alive.

It explains a lot. Why you wanted to go away so much, why you didn't choose to stay with us. It wasn't just the work. It was him, the father I never knew but from whom I apparently inherited my dark hair, the shape of my eyebrows; maybe my seriousness too?.

He's not here. I plump up the freesias which are all sagging to one side, falling over like exhausted soldiers on parade drill, and I catch sight of the old familiar words etched over the grave: intrepid explorer, mother and friend.

I used to think, that isn't enough, it's not enough to fill in a lifetime, is that all? But I understand now that your life did mean more than that. Because you loved someone. Because you were loved. Flo left all that bit out, didn't she? Well, she shouldn't have.

As for me, I have loved and been loved, too. Now it's my turn to become an intrepid explorer. I feel an old tug of excitement in my belly at the prospect. I never thought I'd feel this way again but I do. Rich took me out to visit the old farmhouse where we'd be living and I fell in love with the place, Mum. I couldn't help it.

There's a cool stone outbuilding with high windows where the sunlight pours in for most of the day, lighting up every surface. Perfect for a place to sit and be creative. I might take up knitting designer garments again. Signor Bonomi's wife owns a little boutique in the town . . . oh, it's exciting in a way I never imagined it could be. A whole new dream.

I won't tell you that I don't still think about Scarlett every single day because that would be a lie. I won't tell you I don't ever wonder if she's still carrying my baby or not, of course I do. And it's true that my insides are aching with tears every time I think about what she did – and what I did, too.

But I've got to carry on because . . . maybe it *isn't* the most important thing in the world any more if I don't get to be a mother. If I'm lucky and it comes to me then I'll embrace the chance with all my heart. If it doesn't, I'll embrace all the rest of my life just as gladly.

I stand now, the wind parting a ragged cloud so that a swathe of sunshine falls into the cemetery, picking out the one word with the chip in the stone beside it that always used to perplex us so much every time we came up here, years ago.

Friend?

Yes, Helen. Friend. I give a small smile. I'm sad that I won't be coming back here very often any more because soon I'm going to be far away. But I'm glad because at last I've found some measure of peace.

I hope you have, too.

Scarlett

Tell him the truth, Emoto says. What truth is that, though? The one about how this baby was conceived with honourable intentions – or the one about why my own sister never wants to see me again? Maybe Emoto means tell him the truth about how I don't love him, I was hoping that those feelings might come but I think now that they never will. But if I tell him the truth I'm going to hurt him – another person I'm doing that to – and it also means that my tribe will suffer.

And now we're almost at the bridge. Gui has come nearly the whole way over to greet us, beckoning us to him; he's having to shout over the deafening roar of the water. 'Come on, come now. This bridge isn't going to hold out much longer.'

'I've got to go back for the others.' Emoto cups his hands to his mouth. 'Got to get the jeep.'

'No time,' Gui yells back. 'This thing won't hold the weight of a vehicle; get the people, nothing else. And you, my darling,' he hugs me briefly, gratefully, 'you come with me.'

'I've got to get my . . .' I begin, but he shakes his head fiercely.

'In times like this, Scarlett, you must choose life over possessions. Don't fight me on this.'

We both look down then as one of the vertical wooden struts on the other side of the bridge suddenly cracks and breaks away entirely with the force of the water on it. In an instant, it spins off downstream and disappears. My boyfriend looks at me, as much to say – if the bridge goes down when we're on it, that could be us.

When I turn to see if Emoto also witnessed it, it's too late; he's already gone back.

'I've got my jeep on the other side. As long as we can get everyone safely to the main road I can call for backup. We can get everyone out. Right now it's you that's my priority.'

I smile at him gratefully. But for once, I am not my own priority. Hollie's baby is. Just at this moment, nothing matters more. I take his hand and he doesn't let me hesitate, he virtually pulls me across the bridge. The structure seems to be splintering up underneath us even as we run, the force of the water tearing it apart piece by piece.

Oh, where are the others? How long have they got? I do a quick calculation in my head. Without me to encumber him, Emoto would have made it back to base camp in under five minutes; say another two minutes for him to get everyone out, and another five to get them back here – we could still all make it out, if they hurry. Barry seriously underestimated the amount of time they had left. And Gui's right, there is no way anyone's driving a jeep across this thing today.

'You get in.' We've reached the main road and Gui is holding open the door of the jeep for me. 'I have to go back and help the others . . .'

'Don't go!' I put a hand on his arm to stay his departure and a warm smile spreads over his face at my touch. It's a beautiful smile. Why did I never see it before? A smile filled with such love. How come I never noticed before how attractive that is, how attractive *he* is, because he loves me?

'I'll be safe,' he promises me. 'I'll be back soon.'

'Gui, I need to talk to you.' I keep hold of his arm. 'Before the others get back here. It won't take a moment. *Please* . . .'

'To tell me that you realise now you made a mistake coming back here? You wish that you had listened to me?' His voice is warm, teasing, not triumphant. 'Or do you want to tell me that you're ready to accept my proposal of marriage?'

I blink as the water from my soaked hair runs down my face, into my eyes. What if he gets on that bridge and he goes down and he never comes back? What a time to ask me that question. I squeeze his fingers in reply. Through the gap in the trees I can just make out the edge of the bridge from here. The others aren't there yet. Surely they must arrive soon?

The tribe were due to rejoin Tunga this morning too, I remember suddenly! Which direction will they be coming from? And what will they do if they arrive to find the only crossing for miles is down?

'So troubled, by so many thoughts.' Gui is still looking at me intently. 'But you missed me, yes?'

Somehow, without me noticing it, he has drawn me close to him. But I have to be honest, now. I really need to tell him the truth.

'Don't go, Gui. I have to tell you something. I should have told you when we had that week together but I didn't. I didn't say anything because I didn't know how you'd take it. I was scared of . . .'

'Scared of *me*?' he pulls a puzzled face. 'Surely not?'

Oh, God. I swallow, because suddenly I feel very sad. I am going to lose him, it dawns on me, and I never realised how much that would hurt.

'Scared of losing you.'

He gestures me inside the jeep and slides into the seat beside me, closes the door. Even in here, the air is misty and dank as if the low-lying cloud outside has seeped its way into our space. I feel a shudder go right through me, but whether it is of cold or fear, I cannot tell.

'And why are you going to lose me?' He's suddenly very still and intent.

'Because I don't think you're going to understand – what I've done. You won't accept it, I know.' He raises his eyebrows questioningly and I clear my throat.

'I am expecting a baby, Guillermo. A baby that I offered to have for my sister,' I gabble. 'As a surrogate. I did it because she can't have any of her own and it's the only thing that she feels will give her life any meaning. I offered it because I love her and I wanted her to be happy, but . . .' I hesitate, trying to gauge his response '. . . I also did it because I thought it'd mean she'd have to sell up the family home if she had a child and that way *I'd* get enough funds to help my friends out here . . .'

'*Funds?*' His face has suddenly paled in disbelief. 'Scarlett, Scarlett . . .' his voice is pained. 'What have you done? *Why didn't you just ask me?* The money would have been yours. If you had asked me, we could have also found a woman to help your poor sister.'

'No,' I choke. 'It had to be me who did it for her. For so many reasons that I can't tell you. But it had to be me.'

'Why didn't you just tell me all this?' he says sorrowfully. 'Why keep it from me? You must see it comes as more of a shock now . . .'

'I was going to tell you, as soon as I got back. And then Eve said . . . she said . . .' I look at him hesitantly, because here we're getting into muddy waters. 'She thought you'd be mad at me. She thought maybe you wouldn't believe me.'

'Why shouldn't I believe you?'

I shrug, not trusting myself to speak.

'I understand your motivation well enough – even if I don't know quite why it had to be you and no one else who helped your sister. I'm sure you had your reasons. As for not believing you . . . I'm a businessman, Scarlett. I have a businessman's fine instincts for detecting treachery and lies. Of course I believe you!'

'Can you forgive me, though?' I look at him hopefully. He's upset, of course he is, but he's taking this so much better than I'd expected . . .

'For not trusting me enough to tell me, you mean?' He considers this for a bit. 'I could forgive you anything, my love. Anything at all, except one thing.'

I turn my head suddenly as the sound of shouting from the other side of the bridge draws our attention.

'What is that, Gui?' I turn to him hopefully. 'What couldn't you forgive?'

'Betrayal,' he says without missing a beat. 'You would never betray me with another man, would you, Scarlett?'

'Oh, look, it's them!' My face colours as I can still feel his eyes searching mine intently. He doesn't look away. 'It's the others.' I tap his hand, trying to get a response.

'Gui, shall we go to them?'

There's just a fraction of a second's hesitation before he assents and we both jump out of the jeep. He's quickly ahead of me as we race towards the bridge, though. Through the driving rain I can just make out Emoto and Eve and Barry and at least four European Alliance people, though not Gillian Defoe because apparently she stayed behind at the Forestry Conference, networking. A couple of her people are carrying heavy rucksacks, which Emoto is trying to persuade them to leave behind.

The bridge is creaking ominously. I can't see Tunga. There's a lot of commotion going on. One of the women is crying, saying she won't cross. The next minute, Gui is striding over the bridge. I stand on the far side and watch him, heart in my mouth. He doesn't need to do this. He could have just stood here with me and helped beckon them over. If he falls in the water now – my heart skips a beat – he'll drown, no matter how much of a good swimmer he is. Anyone would. They'd be swept away in an instant and go down.

And I don't want that to happen to him. Even though I know that what I feel for him is not – can never be – love. I wanted to love him, for so many reasons. For his smooth brown hands and his deep, dark honest eyes with their curly eyelashes. Even now,

I love that he cares so much about people that he'd risk his own life to save them.

As for me, I've done the right thing this morning, saving Hol's baby. But maybe that baby has saved me, too? Once I felt it move I think it must have opened the floodgates of my heart.

And now the people, one by one, are travelling tentatively over the bridge. Like a beast of burden, sagging and broken-spirited, the bridge sighs and shudders under their weight but somehow, after the longest fifteen minutes of my life, everyone makes it safely over to our side. Their faces all look pale, hollow-eyed, shocked as molluscs scraped by a fisherman's knife off their rock.

'Where's Tunga?' I turn to Barry, missing him suddenly. 'Did he not come back with you?'

Barry frowns. The thin cotton vest he always wears looks grey and worn today. I can see the hairs on his forearms standing out proud, his muscles shivering in the sickly cold that the rain has brought with it.

'I didn't see him go.'

'He turned back,' Eve pipes up in her nasal voice now. 'I saw him turn back.'

'Why would he have turned back?' I turn to Barry in distress. 'The bridge is going to fall . . .'

'This is his land,' Barry puts in. 'He knows what he's doing. The tribe are joining him this morning, don't forget – perhaps that's why he didn't come.'

A sudden and almighty sound of splitting wood drowns him out now as the last two remaining struts holding up the bridge cave in and splinter like matchsticks. The whole structure collapses in on itself and tumbles into the water, becoming driftwood in seconds. Only the jagged ends where it was connected to the banks, remain.

'Jeez, Gillian is going to be devastated when she gets back.' Barry turns and takes everyone in, his eyes lighting at last on Gui. '*Thank you*,' he says gravely. Gui spreads his hands dismissively, but his face looks – it looks dark. Is he upset, shocked even, at how quickly the whole thing collapsed? Strangely – perhaps because they too, are still in shock – no one seems to be in a hurry to move away from the riverbank. They're all just standing around and staring. I suppose someone should marshal them into some sort of action, get them back onto the main road?

'Gui?' I go up and thread my arm through his. 'We didn't finish our conversation properly, did we?' I whisper into his ear. 'Thank you for being so understanding. About the surrogacy. I just want to be sure if you're really OK with it?'

'I'm OK with it.' But his body feels stiff and unyielding under my touch. He feels cold, prickly all of a sudden. Maybe he's more hurt about the whole thing than he's letting on? I look at him anxiously.

'We did use a syringe, you know. To get pregnant, I mean.' I peer at him, feeling the worry mounting in my chest because something's bugging him, I know it.

'So I imagined.' He turns to me suddenly, pulls me out of earshot of the little group. 'I understand what you did. I don't like it, to be frank, but I won't judge you for it because you did it out of love. Under the circumstances, I can even forgive you for not telling me sooner. There's just something . . .' he looks directly at me suddenly '. . . something not quite right.'

Why is he looking at me so strangely? I've never seen that expression on his face before.

'Just tell me that you never slept with another man while you were away from me. Tell me that and I will have the peace of mind I need.'

I hesitate as I feel my face growing instantly hot.

The truth. He's asking me to simply tell the truth, but how do I dare? My throat feels like it's swelling up to twice its normal size, closing up because of the lie I'm going to have to tell now. I *have* to say it because if I don't, then I lose everything, the Yanomami will lose everything.

I lift my face skywards, eyes closed, feeling the dank, humid raindrops splashing on my skin. For a second, my mother's grave flashes before my memory. Her little, unobtrusive, barely-marked spot that hardly anybody knows is even there or cares about. *I wanted to make a difference!* Not like her. But still, in part, I wanted to do it *for* her. And I wanted – I grasp Gui's hand desperately – I wanted someone to love me as much as this man loves me, as much as that man who forgave his wife and built her a monument with that fabulous marble angel. All these things flicker through my mind in an instant.

Oh Gui, I want you to tell me that it doesn't matter, what I did. I want you to tell me that you love me enough to forgive me and maybe . . . maybe I can come to make you feel the way I do about things. Maybe you will still help my people?

I gulp.

'I never slept with anyone, Gui.' I say it. I say it looking him straight in the eye, but something fails me, something fails me and he knows it. He sees it.

'It is a virtue, Scarlett, to be an honest woman. But it is one that betrays you now, do you know that?'

Red Balloon

Luciendo is insisting that she send this one off too, Mairie explains to her son's bemused guests. The ten-year-old's party has gone well. Her husband Alto has just spent the last half-hour filling an assortment of animal-shaped balloons with helium gas from a canister and the kids are about to let them all off into the air. Including the one on which she took that careless driver's number down because Luciendo wanted that one to go off, too.

The American's already been pulled in by the police, so Mairie doesn't need his numbers any more. That envelope brought them good luck, she reflects with some satisfaction. The man's been thrown in jail for a couple of days and he's been ordered to pay for the repair of her car too. Maybe it's only fitting and fair that she should send this balloon message off again, she tells the curious parents of her party guests – who knows, with a strange name like that on it, maybe someone will actually know the girl it was intended for and she'll get it one day? She's a romantic at heart, she tells them, she likes to believe in such things.

Alto has already cut away the old balloon and attached a new one, bright red, just the same so it's good as new. He's pumped up about twenty animal balloons for the kids and now they all go out to the balcony to let them off. The wind conditions are perfect today, Alto declares. There's a steady high breeze and the afternoon sun is as warm as an oven on everyone's backs as they lean out over the balcony, watching their animals take flight.

Whoever's balloon climbs the highest or travels the furthest before disappearing has been promised a special prize.

Birthday boy Luciendo claims it in the end, though there are some suggestions that Alto may have pumped up the giraffe a little more full of helium than the other animals. Others claim that the red helium balloon went the furthest before dropping out of sight, but while Mairie doesn't refute that, Luciendo still gets the prize because, as she says, the red helium balloon doesn't actually *belong* to anyone, does it?

Scarlett

I watch Gui as he turns on his heel, head down, and makes straight back for his jeep.

'I'll send some people out to fetch you,' is all he mutters to Barry on the way back to the road. After a moment of shock, I make to go after him but Barry steps in front of me before I get the chance.

'Let him go.' His voice is regretful; he shakes his head. 'I don't know what's just happened between you two but I've only ever seen him look like that once before – when someone reneged on a business deal. I think you've lost him, Scarlett.'

'No, I . . . I *can't* have.' I could have told him the truth, oh, if only I'd just told him, like he asked me to . . . I could still come clean, I could still make it all right.

'I know him.' Barry is saying quietly. 'He won't change his mind.'

'Scarlett.' Emoto is back at my elbow now, hissing into my ear.

'What?' I scowl at him. Why can't they all just leave me alone?

'It's the Yanomami. I've just spotted them on the opposite bank. I think they're waiting for you to say goodbye . . .'

I rush to the water's edge again. On the other side, the mist has come down even lower, shrouding the trees in a nebulous glow. The bridge is gone. There is no way I will get to say goodbye to *any* of them, now. The mist is so low, I can't see anything!

I stand as close as I dare to the water's edge, looking out over the river, but it's as if everything that was on the other side has just gone, disappeared into the fog – the little gap between the trees which leads back to all our tents and all the things we left behind; the rock on the riverbank where I mixed up those powders just this morning – it's all invisible now.

'They're over there, look.' Emoto takes my hand and gently guides my line of sight to a group of what looks like faint shadows in the mist. 'There's José, look, he's waving at you – see?'

I stare for a few moments, my eyes watering with the effort, till at last I can make out his shape. I can make out half a dozen outlines, but they seem to be moving on now. Only the little one is still there, hesitating, as if he's looking out for someone. I lift both my arms up and wave them up and down frenetically. The sound of a macaw echoes through the trees and I imagine its flash of bright feathers, gold and green and blue. I cannot see it. It's all fading now, like a dream fading from my sight when I wake up of a morning to the real world.

'Over here, here!' I like to think my young friend sees me. I don't know. 'Emoto –' a sudden thought hits me – 'did you get the chance to bring anything of mine away from the camp? Anything at all?' He looks blank. 'Did you get my monkey paw?'

He shakes his head, smiling sadly. 'Scarlett, I don't think even *that* would have the power to reunite you with them now . . .'

'But I haven't even had the chance to say goodbye! This can't be it, the end. There's got to be *some* way I can get back to them . . .'

'I don't think there will be, Scarlett,' Barry is saying, beside me. 'The flooding goes on for miles around here, there's no other way to cross. And it looks like PlanetLove are pulling out of here for now. Even the weather has worked against us. Sometimes you've just got to accept when a thing is over . . .'

But I haven't got anything to show for it! And these people were my friends.

'José!' I screech, lowering myself perilously close to the water's edge. He sees me now, he does, I know it. And I think that, through the mist, I can just about make out his wave. After a while, he lowers his arms and melts away into the forest along with the rest of his people.

That's it then.

'I'm not going to see them any more, am I?'

Emoto looks at the ground. 'It's worse than that, Scarlett. I have a feeling you may not be seeing Guillermo Almeira any more, either. Are you sure you still want to pass up my offer of getting some seeds for you to put in for the Klausmann? You'd still be eligible.'

'What are you on about, Emoto?' I look at my Japanese friend uncomprehendingly.

'The Klausmann.' He indicates my former boyfriend's jeep retreating into the distance now. 'By the looks of it maybe you *are* still going to need it, after this.'

Hollie

I turn at the bottom of the garden, allowing myself one final glance at the newly planted chaenomeles under which we placed Ruffles' ashes yesterday. It's near enough to the coal bunker where he spent so many happy days with his mistress when they were both younger. He didn't go back down there after she left this time; I think he knew that she wasn't coming home.

I wipe my eyes with the back of my hand and try and pull myself together.

'OK. All ready?' Rich has appeared looking all dapper and suited up for the big celebratory event tonight. I don't think either of us feel much like celebrating but it's the big re-opening of Rochester Bridge celebration down at the Bridge Warden's chambers and there's no way we can't not go.

'Did you post off that letter you wrote to PlanetLove, in the end?' Rich takes my hand as he walks alongside me. He knows now, all about how I helped Scarlett get the Amazon job. We've come clean with each other on a lot of things over the past few weeks. I confessed to how the horrible jealousy I've felt towards Scarlett over him has been eating me up. He opened up and was able to say how he regretted ever going along with me on it. But he'd never choose her over me, that much is clear.

It's not been the easiest time in the world but it has been healing, being able to strip everything back to its bare bones – a bit like Scarlett's room.

'It wouldn't have brought her back, you know,' I say at last. 'Even if I had posted it. I thought long and hard about what ruining her reputation might do – about whether she really deserved that. She didn't, because it was me who switched the papers, not her. I'd have had my revenge, but in the end, I couldn't go through with it. What would have been the point?'

'You don't think if she lost her job she might have been forced back – to the UK at least?' The slightest tension in his voice betrays his feelings. It's his child too, I remember with a pang. He must want to know, at the very least, if it still exists.

'I don't imagine anything on this earth would entice her to return, now. She's stubborn as a mule, you know that. She's guilty and ashamed and if she did come back here and I found out that she terminated the pregnancy – which she may well have – I'd . . . I'd just start feeling bad about her all over again. Maybe I'd rather not know.'

He puts his hand into mine and gives my fingers a tight squeeze. 'It's your call. Perhaps one day we'll know the truth. Put a brave face on now, love. We're nearly there and I see they've got the paparazzi out in force too.' We can see a photographer from the *Kent Messenger* and a van marked 'BBC South East' out front. I need to get my head back in gear. We're here on a PR exercise tonight: Rochester Bridge is back in action, they've got the new bridge picture hanging up in the entrance hall and it's all systems go. I plaster on a smile, gripping Rich's hand a little more tightly . . .

'How about you? Did you manage to get hold of that woman from the National Trust?'

He inclines his head a fraction. 'She was very interested in coming back to see us in the morning. I explained we'd be likely to give them a leasehold for three years only in the first instance, just in case things didn't work out and we needed to return, but . . .'

But we won't return, once we leave here. I don't believe that either of us will want to. I have had to accept that I may never

391

know what has happened to my sister and the baby she was carrying for me. So, we're gearing up to leave this place instead. I've been dreaming of a house in the mountains in Trieste where the air is sweet and still; of waking up in the mornings to the faraway blue of the sparkling Adriatic, ripe olives and sunshine-bright lemons for a salad picked from my own tree ... a whole new dream.

Richard drops my hand and turns to me to smile. 'Your arm, my lady.' He offers me his and we leave the garden, the rusty latch dropping into place behind us as we start making our way up the Esplanade. It's early evening, still sunny and bright. The sounds of music and merrymakers coming from the castle grounds beyond remind me of happier days; fair-time again.

A solitary red balloon drifts off into the blue evening sky. Has anyone made a wish on that one, I wonder? And do wishes *ever* come true?

Scarlett

'Did you ever try and get hold of Gui in the end?' Emoto hands his last wine gum to the toddler gawping at us over the top of the coach seat in front. The child snatches it and sits down. 'Make that call you've been putting off for the last three weeks?'

'Nope.'

'Nope?' His dark eyes are looking at me intently. 'So it wasn't just the cramped conditions and lack of privacy at Eve's flat in the city centre that stopped you from making the telephone call there?'

'I changed my mind about him, Emoto, that's all. I had to. I realised that maybe there are some things we can't go back on. Me lying to him was one of them. But we wouldn't have made such a fab couple in the long run, would we?'

Emoto shrugs. 'Everyone else seemed to think you two were pretty cool together.'

'We were using each other, that was all. Every time I tried to imagine what I'd say to him if I called, I could see that more and more. Besides, he hasn't tried to contact me, has he? And he's the one who walked away.'

My Japanese friend shifts his body round so he's facing me. 'Does that mean you're a free woman now, Scarlett?'

I manage a laugh, looking pointedly down at my swollen belly. Hardly free. 'You offering to take me out on a date?'

Emoto smiles disarmingly. Bloody hell. He's actually shy, not aloof as I've always thought. Why did I never see that before?

'You'll be getting on a plane to Tokyo after London,' I remind him, 'and I'll be entering a contract into slave labour for the next three months . . .'

'Barry set up that temporary au pair's job at his brother-in-law's hotel for you then?'

I nod unenthusiastically.

'Why don't you just go home, Scarlett?' he says feelingly.

I turn my head as the loud hiss of the coach signals that, at last, we are on our way out of Manaus.

'I can't go home,' I tell him thickly. 'I wish I could, but I can't.'

I can feel him looking at me curiously for a few moments, his eyes darting over my face till eventually he lowers his gaze.

'Perhaps for the best, eh? If you're still here then some other environmental group are bound to pick you up. Would have been better if you could have stayed on with Eve maybe but with the way things were . . .'

'Yeah,' I offer up a wan smile. 'I wasn't exactly flavour of the month by the end, was I?'

'It did get a bit . . . cramped,' he admits. That's one way of putting it. 'Hardly surprising,' he runs on, 'five of us cooped up in a two-bed flat while we were trying to regroup and figure out our next move.'

'Yeah. I thought Barry's offer was the better one, which is why I'm on this coach with you now. And I'm glad, you know, Emoto. This is the first time we've been properly able to get to know each other, isn't it?'

'I'm glad, too,' he says. 'And once you get the award, you just wait, they'll be queuing in the aisles to offer you another job . . .'

Ah yes. The award.

The two-year-old in front is staring at us again. He's just

thrown his dummy at Emoto's head and Emoto grins, bending to retrieve it for him.

'You're going to make someone a fantastic daddy one of these days,' I say before I can stop myself. 'And you're going to get the Klausmann,' I add to cover up the confusion the last statement has thrown us both into. 'I won't be submitting any seed samples so that means I'll be no longer eligible. Don't try and dissuade me either. I've had the last three weeks to think long and hard about this.'

It wasn't just the thought of Duncan, waiting in the wings to expose me as a wrongdoer, that swung it in the end. It was discovering that Emoto really was the one who deserved it. It was never *my* thesis that impressed them all so much. It was my mother's. Her work did do some good in the end, though. It brought me to this place. It gave me this opportunity. I won't use it to steal away Emoto's big chance now.

Emoto pushes his short dark hair up into spikes on his head and rests his trainers up on the seat in front of him. The toddler lets off a high-pitched scream and he promptly removes them, grinning guiltily.

'You don't have to do this, Scarlett.'

'I do, though, Emoto.'

'Come on! You don't want to spend the rest of your life pulling hair out of plug-holes and straightening people's beds, do you . . . ?'

'Not the rest of my life, you wally. Just till I've got myself sorted, that's all.'

'And have you figured out yet how you're going to do that?' He arches his brows and looks pointedly towards my belly.

'Yes,' I tell him assuredly. 'I've got it all planned out. How I'm going to manage . . . things and stuff.'

He snorts, because he knows me better than that. I lean my head back against the seat now, feeling my lids starting to droop. If only I could let my sister know how very sorry I am for all the pain I caused her. What wouldn't I do, what wouldn't I give, to take it all back? But she wouldn't want to know. She wouldn't believe me, anyway.

And who can blame her?

Hollie

'So, the Italy move is going ahead?' Bea's face falls, a picture of disappointment. 'So soon? What about the cottage? *Please* don't tell me the developers bought it?' Our neighbour is looking very alarmed.

'Now we wouldn't do that to you, would we, Beatrice?' Rich grabs a couple of glasses of champagne from a passing waiter's tray for us ladies. Nobody can say the Bridge Wardens don't know how to put on a party.

'It's going to the National Trust. They're mooting plans for opening up the garden and serving cream teas and such to the coachloads that come to see the castle.'

'And you two are *definitely* headed out to Italy?'

The bubbles in my champagne glass rise and pop like new ideas, so many new possibilities coming to the surface.

'Hard though it is to believe, I'm really looking forward to it, Bea,' I nod. 'There's nothing keeping us here any more – even Ruff has passed away. I have to . . . dream a new dream, I guess.'

'Smile!' The photographer from the *Kent Messenger* demands. We're all gathered outside the little entrance area at Number Five the Esplanade, all the Bridge Wardens and the mayor and various local dignitaries – and then Bea and me and Rich squeezed in at the edge. It's a relief when a few minutes later the photographer calls for a thinning out of the crowd and some of us troop inside.

'All's well that ends well.' Ben Spenlow's glass chinks amicably against mine. 'Bridge never did fall down, eh? You were convinced that's what was going to happen, weren't you?'

I don't answer him, just smile into my drink. Maybe I should never have told him I used to dream about that happening, a long time ago before I blocked it all out. I used to dream about a deep brown river, much wider and faster than our one, hurtling past an old wooden bridge, straining and pulling at it till eventually the weight of water collapsed it all. And I'd go down with it, every time.

'This looks jolly good too, don't you think?' Beatrice intervenes. I stop. There, just inside Number Five, in the coolness of the spacious hallway, they've put up the new Rochester Bridge picture.

'It looks *different* somehow . . .' I stare at it for a good few minutes, trying to fathom out what's changed. I've already seen it with the frame on. Could it really just be the setting?

'You were never really taken with it, were you?' Bea's at my elbow. 'I think it's marvellous, myself.'

'Actually, I think I see it all in a different light now, Bea.'

'It's a masterful amalgamation of the old and the new, don't you see? The tragic past fades into soft and nostalgic tones behind us, the future veers up sharply, almost *dangerously*, in front of us . . .'

Does the past always fade into nostalgic tones behind us? Only if we can let it, perhaps.

'I don't know why I couldn't see it before. It's a really arresting picture. Stunning, even. I can see it now. Maybe it's because I'm not frightened of the water any more?'

Bea looks at me, suddenly interested. 'You *did* it?'

'I've started classes at the local pool. I managed a whole width yesterday. Before you know it I'll be doing lengths just like everyone else . . .'

'Bravo!' Bea suddenly goes quiet as a new thought crosses her mind, I can almost see it. 'Is it true you've had no news at all from Scarlett?'

'None.' I shake my head thoughtfully. 'But if she ever does get in touch, I have forgiven her, Bea.'

'For everything?' A look of relief crosses Beatrice Highland's face. I'm not even going to dwell on how much of *everything* she might know.

'I've had to,' I shrug. 'I realised I couldn't . . . I couldn't spend the rest of my life carrying that much weight of resentment around with me.' I turn away from her and close my eyes for a moment. Behind my closed lids, I relive the sheer and utter bliss I felt the first time I spread out my arms in the water, pushed my legs backwards off the pool bottom and just *swam*.

And didn't sink. The sense of freedom I felt was indescribable. Bea gives me a small, self-conscious hug.

'I am so very glad, my dear.' She's silent for a bit. She knows that even though there are so many things turning round in my life right now, there's still one thing I have no control over.

'Shall we go up? There are canapés upstairs, very good ones, you'll miss those when you leave here, I promise you . . .'

She's right. The hallway is getting very crowded, and as we start making our way up the stairs I let myself acknowledge all the things I am preparing to leave behind.

I am going to miss my beautiful Florence Cottage with its glorious Olde Worlde garden. I am going to miss the view from my kitchen of the river through all its seasons: from the soft and lazy rolling water of high summer to the headstrong hurtling of waves swollen by the winter months. I am going to miss the way the soft light shines through these stained-glass windows here at the bend of the stairwell in the Bridge Warden's chambers.

But life is always full of so many possibilities, isn't it?

I *have* started dreaming again, just like Mr Huang promised me I would, little snapshots and cameos of things, that's all: like walking down a long narrow shaded street, tall buildings rising to either side of me, or another time, climbing up a grassy slope somewhere, where it's hot and the breeze is blowing my hair back. Somewhere that's not here. Italy maybe? I smile at Rich, who's been hijacked by a redhead with a martini and a notepad. He's always there in my dreams with me, so I don't need to worry that *she* will get him. Someone else is there with us too. I've not got to look at him properly yet, but I think it is someone little. Someone lovely.

Who knows?

'I shall enjoy the Mediterranean cuisine though, and you'll have to come out and spend part of next summer with us . . .' I turn to her as we reach the table groaning with canapés at the top. 'Wow. Such a crowd . . .' I mutter as we go and stand by the windows overlooking the Esplanade. 'All here for the bridge re-opening?'

'Medway council has put on a celebratory free concert in the castle gardens.' Ben has joined us, his plate piled high with goodies. 'They've got a fair on – all the usual attractions. Another red balloon stand.' He raises his eyebrows at me. 'I keep seeing them go up. D'you remember the autumn when they let them all fly off together? I've never seen anything quite like it. You wished for the bridge to be fixed, didn't you?' He smiles one of his rare smiles at me. 'Well, you got your wish.'

I didn't wish for that, though.

I turn away from the table, watching the crowds all congregating towards the castle grounds now. Lots of families with young kids. Lots of babies in their prams.

'I've been wishing for pretty much the same thing all my life,' I mutter under my breath.

So many people . . . I look out over the multitude of bobbing heads and then I realise after a while that I'm not the only one doing the scrutinising. There's a young couple with a pram just opposite standing by the stone railings looking up at me. Who are they? I peer a little closer. And why are they both looking at me so intently?

Maybe they aren't looking at *me?* I glance behind me. Nobody else is standing by the window. Maybe it's just the party scene which the couple are fascinated by? But it isn't. When I look again, the young man has crossed the road and now he's standing right beneath my window. He's pulled his hood off so I can get a better look at his face and now I see, my heart thudding in my mouth, that I *do* know who he is.

The shock of recognition goes through me like so many volts of electricity. But for the fact that his face returned to me so clearly in the pool a few weeks back, I'd never have known him. It's that boy Aaron. Except he isn't a boy any more, he's a man and with a young child of his own by the looks of it.

I feel my fists clench, leaning against the wide stone window frames. It's *him*. It was him in the archway that night by the Cathedral. It was him that frozen day when I met Rich up on Jackson's field and I had to stop myself from running away from the park. I've been running away from him for such a long time now, haven't I, and here he is, with a child of his own – has he come to gloat?

I want to look away but I can't because he's mouthing something up at me. I can't quite make out what it is. Oh, he'll be like Duncan, after Scarlett no doubt – they always are! You've got a child of your own now, I think furiously. Now you'll know what it feels like to feel vulnerable because that's what love does to you . . .

I screw up my face, turning away, but now the bugger has thrown a small pebble up to the window to catch my attention again. Does he know what these windows cost?

'What do you want?' I sign at him. 'Go away!'

'I'm sorry,' he mouths back.

'*What do you want?*'

'I . . . AM . . . SORRY!' he mouths again.

He's *sorry*?

He turns and waits for the traffic to clear before he can cross

401

safely back over to his family again. When he gets to the pram I see him bend over, tuck in the little one gently. I lean so far forward then that my head is resting against the glass pane, my fingers smudging on the edges of the glass. He's sorry. That's what he wanted to tell me. I've been avoiding him all this time and that's all he ever wanted to say? I feel a bubble of laughter rising up in my stomach.

'Oooh, look, they're off again!' Everyone is crowding round the window suddenly, to see the flight of the released red balloons as they soar up and quickly spread like a splodge of red paint against the canvas of the early summer sky.

'Did you make a wish?' Richard is suddenly beside me, his breath warm in my ear. He knows I always do.

'Not this time,' I turn towards him, leaning in close to his chest. 'Maybe for the first time I can see that I've already got everything I need.'

Scarlett

'Hey, Scarlett.' I wake up as a dark-eyed Emoto is patting my wrist gently. The coach has stopped. We've arrived at Caracas International.

'This is where we say goodbye, I think.'

But I don't want to say goodbye to him, though. We've got to know each other better over the last few days and weeks than we did in the entire year before it. Emoto is far more like me than I could have imagined. He's totally into the rainforest and travelling, he loves conjuring tricks and he has a truly wicked sense of humour . . .

'I'm going to be in London for a whole month,' he told me late last night. 'If you change your mind, you've got my mobile number, right? In fact, ring me anyway when you're settled. Promise?' He'd been fussing over me like a mother hen. The memory of that unlikely scenario makes me smile, even now.

Gingerly, he pulls up the blinds by our window and the bright morning sun streams in. 'Have you got very far to go from here?'

I rub my eyes blearily. I've got to get on another bus, but I'm not sure which one. I need to find that scrap of paper Barry wrote down all the details on.

Man, I'm tired. I barely slept a wink, it was so hot, even with the air conditioning and that child in front was whinging all night. He's snoring softly now, but everyone's making a move and his mama's going to have to as well, in a minute. I shoot her a sympathetic glance which Emoto intercepts.

'Want some help bringing your bags down?' he offers kindly. I've got up to let him by, but now I'm just standing in the aisle like a dummy. In a minute, Emoto is going to leave and I'll be left here all on my own. Who would have thought I'd be feeling as devastated as I do about that?

'Come on, girl. It won't be as bad as all that.' Emoto helps me with bringing all my luggage down. Then he helps the mum in front of us with her toddler. She thanks him profusely but I can see he's already glancing at his watch. Is he going to be late for his flight?

'Scarlett, I feel really unhappy leaving you like this.' He hesitates.

'Have you even sorted out where you're going next?'

'I'm sorry?' I look at him blankly.

'The address you're going to next. Look, why don't I call you a cab . . . ?'

'Too expensive.' In a daze, I follow him down the coach steps and out into the heat of the day.

It is so bright standing out here. The air is so hot you can smell it. Was it really only one month ago I stood here waiting for Eve to arrive, imagining that somehow returning to South America was going to be the solution to all my problems back home?

'But are you going to be OK?' Emoto is still hovering, unsure of what to do next. 'You look like you could do with some help, only I'm supposed to be booking in for that flight to London some time soon . . .'

I turn away from him deliberately so he can't see my face. Man, I wish I was the one getting on that flight. There was a time when I couldn't get away from England quickly enough. There *was* no place on earth that could have been too far away from home for me. Yet now . . .

The hazy afternoon air shimmers off the pavement and my memories flicker like a colourful kaleidoscope of images before my eyes; the stone lions on the bridge at Rochester, Michaelmas daisies in the garden at Florence Cottage, Ruffles with his tail wagging, deliriously happy to see me, *Richard* . . .

I have forfeited all that, I recall, for the thing I thought I wanted more than anything. But it wasn't worth sacrificing my sister's peace of mind for. It wasn't worth losing her and Richard's love and goodwill over. Nothing could ever be worth that.

'What'll you do now?' Emoto still seems reluctant to leave this damsel in distress.

'Scrub toilets, pull the hair out of plug-holes like you said, help peel potatoes in the kitchen . . .' I run through the list of duties Barry warned me would be on the rota if I accepted the au pair's job.

'No, I mean, *right* now. How are you going to cope? The whole band has scattered. You're going to be so alone, aren't you?' He knows, that's the thing. He can see right past my 'I'm up for it' act.

'Alone?' I force a laugh, indicating the pied-piper throngs surging out of the airport and all around us. 'It is difficult to see how when there are so many people in the world.' A food vendor smiles, waving the greasy smell of arepas under our noses, a parrot on a chain stretches his wings out, balancing on a man's shoulder, a flower seller places a single orange bloom in my hand.

'You won't be lonely, Scarlett. Remember you're the one who told me that the Yanomami say: "Whatever you need, do not look too far. It'll be right there in front of you",' Emoto says feelingly.

'I know.' It was always true, too, when I was out there with them in the forest. Will it still be true now?

'Oh, crap!' Emoto dives out suddenly as the toddler who was our companion and tormentor on the bus wanders happily right into the middle of the road. His mum took his eyes off him for a second and he must have caught sight of that sinking red metallic balloon . . .

My hero scoops up the toddler and balloon seconds before he's crushed by the bus that's just pulled out into the street. I give him a round of applause, laughing as he crosses back over the road to me.

'That was a close call,' I grin. 'Hey, little fella.' I smile at the toddler, who seems oblivious to all the drama. I watch as Emoto pulls off a little envelope before handing the shining balloon over to the child, passes the boy back to his mother.

'Bloody **hell,** Scarlett.'

I give him a clap, laughing as he crosses back over the road to me.

'That was a close call,' I agree.

'Yes, it was. But look at this . . .' The way he's waving that little envelope in his hand, you'd think it was some kind of precious document.

'You're going to miss your flight,' I remind him. I don't like balloon messages. Not since Lucy Lundy warned me Duncan had sent one off with a nasty message about me inside it. Bastard. 'Chuck it in the bin,' I advise him.

'*You* chuck it.' Emoto hands me the envelope, his eyes shining in wonder and anticipation of my response. 'After all, it is addressed to you.'

Scarlett

No!

I shiver as he hands it over. It can't be. Who the hell would be sending me messages like this?

Gui? Duncan?

I pull the thin card out of its envelope, my fingers trembling. There is one little sentence on it on it. That's all. My eyes have misted over . . .

This isn't Duncan's handwriting, though. I'd recognise this neat script anywhere.

Darling Lettie,

I feel a lump in my throat at her use of my old pet name. God. I miss you, Hol. I miss you so much . . .

All is forgiven. Come home.
Hol x

How in God's name did this get here?

And could she really have forgiven me? For *everything*?

I turn the card quickly over, looking at the date. There's a lot of other stuff written on the envelope too – this card has been doing the rounds – but it looks like this was originally sent last autumn. So maybe she's talking about Aaron, here?

In the autumn I was still out in the rainforest gathering seeds, dating Gui at the weekends, enjoying my time with the tribe. In the autumn, Hollie must have had her letter through from that doctor in India. She'd have realised that I was the best chance she still had left. She'd have realised that all these years of holding onto resentment at what I'd brought her to, was never going to help. When she asked me to have this baby for her, I see now what that must have cost her. She swallowed her pride.

That's what I'm going to have to do, now. Could it be possible that, somewhere deep in her heart, she still wants me back? I'm not after her Richard any more. I know now what a deep mistake that was. It was what we two sisters did to him that brought out that other side of him that I discovered that day up on Bluebell Hill. He is still a deeply loving and loveable man. But he's *her* man.

And this baby I'm carrying – it's their baby, and I know I could still get it back to them. There's a flight out of here this afternoon, if I spent every last penny I have, I could be on it. The sudden realisations tumbling through my mind feel . . . they feel like the release of white doves at a wedding. If Hol forgave me for Aaron, she might forgive me for everything else as well. I could be on that flight. Oh, I don't know how this baby's parents will receive me if I go back, whether they'd be more angry than pleased, or whether they'd welcome me with open arms . . .

'Is this the bus that you need, señorita?' The South American lady is bustling around, picking up her bags and her son now.

The bus. Oh, God! Should I get on that bus? I have a job waiting for me. I have a chance to stay here a bit longer, see what comes up, see how it all pans out. For a split second I'm my four-year-old self at the bend of the river once more, stamping my feet and crying after the little boats Hollie said I would never get back again, because I still believed in the possibility of things and she did not. Have I given up on that now? Do I really believe that it will never be possible to retrieve what we have lost?

The bus screeches to a halt on the other side of the road. The little lad waves goodbye. I can just about see him still, his fists flailing a wave over his mum's shoulder, still holding tight onto that crumpling red balloon, the one that has travelled so incredibly and inexplicably far to get to me today. I take in Emoto's puzzled face, realising that I've still got some explaining to do.

Whatever you need, don't look too far for it, because it'll be right there in front of you . . .

I glance back towards the airport doors. The weltering throng heaves and settles like an Amazon Blue parrot shaking out its feathers on some branch high up in the mist-topped canopy.

I don't know where that bus is going. I shake my head at the lady from the coach because, wherever it's headed, I'm not getting on it. Instead, I turn to cross back over the road with Emoto, back towards Caracas International.

I am going home.

Points for discussion on *A Sister's Gift*

1. Sisterhood is shown as conveying a great responsibility in *A Sister's Gift*. How does it affect Scarlett's decision to become a surrogate? Is Hollie wrong to place such a large demand on her sister?

2. Examine Scarlett's role as a botanist. In what way does this highlight the differences between her and her sister?

3. In what ways are the themes of fertility and infertility explored in the book?

4. What is the significance of the balloon imagery and the Old Rochester Bridge throughout?

5. Consider the sisters' relationship. In what ways are the two similar/different? How does Hollie's role as the older sibling affect her outlook on life?

6. Compare and contrast the different male figures within *A Sister's Gift* – Richard, Duncan, and Guillermo. What are their values, concerns and priorities?

7. How much of Scarlett and Hollie's behaviour can be attributed to the fact that they were deserted by their mother at a young age?

8. Every character has something to hide. What and why? What are the repercussions of their respective secrets?

9. 'Single-Minded and Heartless'. Despite Richard's love, Hollie feels that she is not complete without a child. Are her actions in trying to get 'the miracle she so desperately craves' selfish?

10. What is Scarlett's attraction to Richard? What does he represent to her? How much sympathy do we feel for her when Richard denies her his love?